UPCOUNTRY

A NOVEL

R.M. DOYON

Open Kimono Books
www.openkimonobooks.com

This is a work of fiction. Names, characters, places and incidents are the product of the author's imagination. Any resemblance to actual persons, living or dead, business establishments, events or locales is entirely coincidental.

ISBN: 1452898014
ISBN-13: 9781452898018

To Shelley, for your creativity,
encouragement and patience.

This story is as much yours as mine.

RAVE REVIEWS OF UPCOUNTRY

FROM READERS LIKE YOU!

"Upcountry is an ambitious story about the complicated bonds of family...with its strong, creative characters, you'll want to know what's coming on the next page!"
--Diana Buckingham, Cockeysville, Maryland

"A rocking tale of revenge, faith and redemption!
--Corien Kershey, Ottawa, Ontario

"Doyon's Upcountry is a deft and confident first novel. The plot is fast-paced, the characters are believable and the issues are important. Political maneuverings and family tensions play out in a wonderfully described small-town, rural world. Difficult to put down, this book seems designed for the big screen and begs a sequel."
--John-Peter Bradford, Ottawa, Ontario

"A suspense-filled romp through the Adirondacks! Read it!"
--Diane Smith, Cicero, New York

"A dark, intriguing storyline right from the first page! Chapter after chapter, the writer brings the story alive...and hard to put down! A great read!
--Ruth Brown, Sudbury, Ontario

"This book should carry a warning label! That by the end of it you will be tired. I was up all night reading it!"
--Shelley Taubman, Ottawa, Ontario

"A non-stop page turner that tells a riveting story of heartache, retribution and forgiveness..."
--Vicki Lambert-Hood, Sudbury, Ontario

"Doyon's Upcountry steers us down a gripping road to loss, redemption, and new beginnings..."
--Angela Swann, Ottawa, Ontario

ONE

At daybreak, Jane Schumacher awoke to discover that she had spent the night on the couch. She was still dressed in the same white silk blouse and navy-blue, pleated skirt she had worn the day before. Good God, she moaned, as she raised herself up and surveyed the situation. It wasn't pretty.

After a moment, she found the strength to walk towards her living room window and peered out. The freezing rain that had threatened to paralyze the city the night before had finally ended, and in its place a steadily rising sun had turned the dominant sugar maples, now barren of their leaves, into sparkling prisms of light. She squinted. It was almost too much for her hangover to handle.

Well, no worry. This sunshine won't last, she concluded. It never lasts.

It was November, after all…in *fucking* upstate New York.

She let out another big sigh. Over the rooftops across the street, Jane could see the southwest corner of the capitol building where she and the governor had met the media yesterday. Soon, she thought, the day's activities would pick up. Soon public employees would be scurrying to their cubicles as taxis, limos and buses jostled through traffic. Through the plaza, the practitioners of *real* politics—the lobbyists and influence-peddlers—would be racing to yet another meeting on their mission to stop progress in its tracks. Later, perhaps, a few tourists, mindless of the late season, would stroll over the stately grounds. Maybe they figured they'd get lucky and catch a glimpse of someone famous.

Whatever.

It was just another sunrise in the most dysfunctional state capital in the nation, she thought. Nothing changes.

But today, Jane now noticed, was different. Why the hell was it so quiet? Normally at this time of the morning she expected to hear the detonations of the city. Where were the honking horns? Or those annoying garbage trucks? With their gears in reverse, emitting their familiar beeping sounds as they approached restaurants and stores?

Then she remembered. Oh, shit, that's right. It was Thanksgiving, and the streets were nearly abandoned. All commerce came to a halt on this most overrated holiday of holidays.

Jane let her eyes wander across her penthouse apartment, and it was not an appealing sight. From the evidence on display, she slowly recalled what had happened the night before, and she groaned again. She could see her briefcase. It was on the floor near the condo's entrance, open and askew, its contents spread haphazardly down the hall. Her mail, too, had been strewn across the carpet of the living room. On the counter separating the kitchen from the dining room sat a half-empty bottle of Scotch. Next to it was an abandoned bag of microwave popcorn.

"Jesus, I guess that was dinner," she muttered to herself. "Keep me away from a mirror."

She moved slowly to the kitchen and towards her coffee maker. Opening the lid, she looked in and saw the grounds. A layer of white, fuzzy mold had formed, the sight of which started to turn her stomach. Jesus, I might be growing my own antibiotics here, she thought. When was the last time I was home? I can't remember. So much for my so-called life.

Jane was standing at her sink when her fragile lungs released another violent and painful cough that seemed to originate from her toenails.

Man, now *that* one hurt!

Slowly, she recovered but the pain lingered on. After a few minutes, a new brewing process commenced and she waited impatiently for the first full cup to materialize. From above the stove, she reached for her favorite mug, the one with a photo of the White House. She remembered its origin; it was a gift from a friend at *Meet the Press,* a producer who attached a card saying, "Jane, consider this your first bribe!" It was then that she remembered a bottle of Baileys in the refrigerator.

Oh, why the hell not?

Jane glanced back at the mess she had created the night before. Screw the briefcase, she thought, but maybe I should check my mail. She walked back to the living room and gathered the pieces that she had cast aside in anger the night before.

It was all coming back now. Her memory was returning. Upon entering her apartment, she had tossed her briefcase into the air with such velocity that she now spotted a deep gouge in the entrance wall. Moments earlier, she'd struggled with the lock so long—the damn key wouldn't fit!—that she had nearly given up, pounding on the door as if brute force would solve her dilemma.

Her spectacle caused such a commotion that she had aroused the concern of her elderly neighbor in the next condo. Well, I must have been pretty loud and profane, Jane now conceded. That old bat is nearly deaf. The widowed woman—she couldn't remember her name—had peered out and had enquired, innocently, if Jane was all right. No, I'm *not* all right, she now remembered declaring, so why don't you mind your own goddamn business! Or something even ruder than that.

Whatever.

Jane promised herself she'd apologize later to her lovely, caring neighbor. I'm not that much of a bitch, am I? Well, maybe.

Fortified coffee in one hand and her mail in the other, her next destination was a return to the couch. Almost in a trance, she plunked herself down and discovered the television remote under a cushion. She flicked the set on. A local morning channel popped up and a blonde anchor, a bit too chirpy for this time of the morning, was suddenly head-and-shoulders on screen. Immediately, one of her favorite Don Henley songs came to mind.

How did it go?

'We got the bubble-headed bleach-blonde who comes on at five.'

She glanced at the clock in her kitchen.

Well, make that more like seven-fifteen.

The governor's face came into focus, and Jane turned up the volume.

"Now to the capital," Her Chirpiness announced, "where Governor Foley delivered a take-it-or-leave-it ultimatum to legislators yesterday. His message? Either cut spending or face his veto."

The next verse.

'She can tell you 'bout the plane crash with a gleam in her eye....'

The news program cut to a shot of the governor in front of a phalanx of microphones. As his press secretary, Jane was standing by his side. Jesus, I could stand to lose five pounds, she thought. Well, my *weight* won't be a problem now. Especially after yesterday.

The song in her head continued.

'It's interesting when people die.'

Now there was a clip from the boss.

"New Yorkers are pretty fed up with the partisan games being played by the other side. They know I'm serious about this out-of-control spending, and we need it to stop. Don't they realize what the rest of the nation thinks about this state? We're a laughing stock."

She recognized some microphone holder from Westchester County interjecting. "Or what, Governor? Are you going to veto this bill?"

Jane forced a smile. Even that hurt.

Then she remembered the last line of the title song.

'Give us dirrrty laaaun-dry.'

Indeed, she thought.

Before flying back to Albany yesterday, Jane had spent a few days in the city shepherding her boss around Manhattan. Their tour of the media included a couple of playful interviews on the morning shows before he attended several editorial boards at the *Times* and *Daily News.* Then it was off to *NBC* to tape an interview with its shrewd and popular anchor. It went well, the boss was on track, and that clip would provide an excellent prelude to what she expected would be a gushing, almost embarrassing, profile this Sunday night on *60 Minutes.* That is if the venerable program wasn't preempted by goddamn football.

The purpose of the Manhattan media blitz was simple: the governor of New York was—and, under her watch, would remain—the most popular politician in the country and Americans needed to be reminded of that. That was why these interviews were important. Granted, most of the questions he faced were softball in nature. That was not the point; he still had to hammer them out of the park or, at minimum, slam a few ground-rule doubles. And he did.

It would not always be this easy, she had thought. The time would come when the front-runner would be tested. Perhaps as early as next week, after Thanksgiving, when she had confirmed appearances on a couple of late-night comedy shows. Though the comedians slanted left-of-center, theirs were tough interviews; they loved to skewer hypocrites from both sides of the polar landscape.

But her candidate—no phony—liked the pointed, intellectual debate offered by the late-night shows. He knew voters loved politicians who could laugh at themselves. The benefits were many; as Jane surmised, one or two cool appearances on the late channels would deliver his message to millions of the under-twenty-four crowd. Unlike other demographics, youngsters are engaged; they vote in real numbers now.

Over the past year, Jane had thought a great deal about the media and how she would play it. The mainstreamers—the old papers, the big networks—were still players. Fading from relevance, yes, but players nonetheless. They were the Picassos of politics, painting a picture that most could admire, if not remember. They still remained the thought leaders. They still cared about serious issues. But, sadly, Americans now received their news in snippets and bytes. Fewer and fewer voters—even if they bothered trudging to the polls—subscribed to a daily newspaper or tuned in at six-thirty. Cable and the blogosphere were nipping at their heels.

Jane snapped back from her daydream. That was *so* yesterday, she swore. Today's another story. So, screw the media, and the creeps who populate it! And for that matter, screw politics too!

Hell, why put *limits* on it?
Screw everyone!

She continued to glare at the television screen. The news clip ended and little Miss Chirp-a-tude burst back on to the screen, joined by an older white-haired dude. A feeling of resignation came over her. How original, Jane thought. Every newscast in the country held fast to this format: a dazzling blonde or brunette teamed with a geezer only months away from shuffleboard.

God forbid if the reverse was ever attempted. How about a young stud with a sage, older woman? Now that would be interesting. Would their ratings go up? Maybe. There are more women in this country than men. But would that happen? Not in a million years; the local news was vacuous, formulaic and carved in stone. If people tuned in, it was probably just to check the weather forecast.

Jane glanced once again at the sunshine streaming through her living room window, and inhaled deeply. Her pain returned.

When did she become so *fucking* cynical?

What has happened to me?

Slowly she turned her attention again to the television.

Her Chirp-a-liciousness continued.

"Well, John, Governor Foley seems to be using his popularity to push his way around the capital. He seems to mean business. Will he be successful?"

Okay, let's hear it, Jane told herself.

"Well, Meghan, I don't know if they will be influenced by Foley's threats," the older anchor intoned. "The legislature marches to its own peculiar drum. But this governor doesn't care. It's no secret he wants to launch his presidential bid in a couple of weeks and his people are hoping that a good dust-up with state lawmakers might help him nationally."

Jane took a moment to be pleased with herself.

She was "his people."

Point made. Checkmate.

As the newscast switched to another item, Jane took a quick look at her mail. Nothing of consequence, she determined. A letter from the condo association. A couple of bills; one from the phone company, the other from American Express. Jesus, I don't want to open either one, she thought. She continued rifling through the envelopes. Another flyer or two from real estate brokers. A menu from the shwarma joint around the corner. Not much.

Then from the clutter appeared a letter with a postmark that read Morgantown, New York. The return address was simply a post office box. She ripped open the envelope and read the card inside.

In simple script, it said, *"Wishing you a Happy Thanksgiving."*

It was yet another card from her father. No message. No, "how are you?" No "hope you're doing well."

Nothing. Just a simple signature.

Dad, was all it said.

For a long, meandering moment, Jane sat there and stared at the card.

He *never* forgets a holiday, does he?

Jane was about to turn the television off when her Black-Berry began ringing loudly. She looked at the screen and it was Roberto.

Oh, shit, I'm not sure I want to answer this one, she thought. Jane knew his plans were to escape the city after work and drive the hundred-plus miles to his managing partner's cabin in the Catskills. Like her, he was an early riser and knew that chances were good she'd answer her phone.

Her two days in the New York media meat market were exhilarating, but what she did at *night* was another thing altogether, and that brought a brief expression of satisfaction to her face. Stealing a night here and there, she was able to make some time for a personal life—at least for now, before the real work began. Especially if an excursion to the city included her handsome Argentinean immigrant and lover.

Ah, yes, Alvarez…Roberto Alvarez. She was fond of that man. A lean, muscle-ripped man in his early forties, Roberto was a Wall Street attorney with a Columbia pedigree. They had met in Negril a year ago, at one of those resorts that bragged of fine snorkeling, hundred-and-fifty-one proof rums and limitless opportunities to prove your heterosexuality. A week-long romp in the sand ensued. That was followed by a steamy reunion in the city only days later, made more convenient now that her boss preferred Manhattan over the capital as his principal place of work.

Roberto was also hot—for a Republican.

That stimulated her too, because Jane knew she could impress him with her intellect, her knowledge of American history and her grasp of how politics really operated. She was a political missionary whose duty it was to convert non-believers. Of course, if wit and intelligence didn't work, then her glistening, auburn hair that tumbled gracefully just beyond her shoulder blades *always* did the trick.

So far, at least one of those tactics was working.

After making the media rounds and bidding adieu to the governor at their midtown offices, she and Roberto had had a lively dinner at a normally serene restaurant in the east seventies. They argued politics so noisily that the nearby patrons were getting pissed off.

"You're missing the point, Rob," she had said, her exasperation increasing with her alcohol consumption. "Everyone knows the governor of this state isn't the one with the magic wand. The real power lies in the legislature and the dictators who run it. Most New York governors don't even *want* to be governors! Go back in history. Most have just used Albany for their own purposes, and Foley's no different. He wants to move south, and I don't mean Newark."

"You really think your guy could be the next FDR?" he had asked, incredulously.

"Or his distant cousin," she replied. "Foley's good in the bully pulpit."

Alvarez rolled his eyes at the comparisons.

"You've had one too many Rodney Strongs, babe. Not only is Foley *not* FDR, or any Roosevelt by any stretch of your overactive imagination, I'm telling you, this country will never elect another New Yorker president! Will never happen. So why don't you just admit it, ditch the politics and move to Manhattan? We could do this more often."

Jane had ignored his suggestions and remained on track.

"Never say never, my Latin lover. He may not be FDR— hell, he may not even be Grover Cleveland—but mark my words, the party will nominate Foley and the country will elect him. With my help, of course."

Rob smiled.

"I think that's one of the reasons why I admire you so much," he replied. "Your hopeless, delusional confidence is very appealing."

"Is that all you can say? That you *admire* me?"

Roberto had looked into her mischief-laden hazel eyes with affection. She was thirty-nine but could pass for a woman much younger. Her attractiveness, he felt, emanated from her independence and spirit, and probably a few superior genes, too. Not runway-beautiful, mind you, but close. Certainly not like some of the leggy, fleshless women he had dated after his divorce.

No, Jane was different. At nearly five-eight, she reminded Roberto of his many travels past, to places like Oslo and Copenhagen, Munich and Prague. Especially Prague. Maybe throw in a few women from Stockholm and perhaps Johannesburg too. Her cheekbones, truly Nordic in nature, were high and proud and dominant. Her demeanor told everyone she was a woman of elegance and poise—maybe even trouble. Don't mess with her.

If she had any singing talent—and she didn't, since Jane couldn't carry a tune in a laundry basket—she could easily be mistaken for one of the current beauties on the country music circuit. Not that he listened to such stuff but he knew who they were. Personally, his musical tastes tended towards reggae, progressive jazz and the blues. Or *Rock en Español* from his native continent.

But to him, it was clear; Jane was the type of woman who would get better looking as she got older. His kind of woman.

Moments later, he signaled for the waiter and they were soon taxiing to his condo on the Upper East Side.

For another post-Negril romp.

Still in her stupor, Jane thought about that lovely night with Roberto as she let her BlackBerry ring five or six times. She was still debating whether to answer the call.

Finally, she picked it up.

"The sun is shining," he announced, his voice sounding chipper. "I'm preparing a holiday feast and the champagne is chilling and there's another log on the fire. And, most importantly, the sheets are fresh. Why aren't you on the road by now?"

Jane sighed.

This was the call she was dreading, even before she opened the letter from her dad in Morgantown. She glanced at his card again.

Right then and there, she decided her weekend plans would be changed.

"Uh, Rob, um, I have some, uh, bad news for you. I can't make it to the cabin this weekend."

"What the hell?" Roberto's disappointment was apparent.

"I'm sorry," Jane replied.

"What are you talking about?"

"I have to go to Morgantown today instead."

"What? Why? You haven't set foot in that town for, how long? Years? Jane, I can't remember you ever speaking about your family."

Jane was in no mood to debate the decision with Roberto, but she knew she had to nuance this conversation.

"I know, I know, Rob," she said, sullenly. "But it's my dad. He's sick and I have to go see him before the campaign starts...before it's too late."

Roberto lowered his voice, too. He was concerned.

"What's wrong with him?"

Jane was clearly getting more and more uncomfortable with her escalating lie and wanted this phone call to end.

"My sister called—"

"—your sister?"

"Yeah, my sister said my dad had a stroke and that I should get up there," she replied. "I really should go."

Roberto was perplexed.

"I don't remember you ever really mentioning her either, Jane."

"Well, we haven't spoken in a while," she conceded. "But she called me this morning to say that my father is really sick."

Roberto's enthusiasm was now clearly deflated. He wanted to be with Jane this weekend.

"I could go with you," he suggested.

"No!" Jane immediately replied. "I...uh...mean, this is something that I have to do by myself. Okay?"

He was taken aback by the bluntness of her reply. She was almost *too* quick to reject his offer.

"Okay, babe," he said after a long moment, a pregnant pause if there ever was one. The doubts he'd had before returned. Theirs was a tempestuous relationship. Why do I bother, he asked himself.

But, recovering, he offered his support.

"Go to Morgantown and see your family. I'll be here if you change your mind."

"Thanks, Rob," she said. "Anyway, gotta run. I'll call you later."

Before he could say another word, Jane hung up the phone.

TWO

J oanne Lowry glanced at her watch as she bounded down her wobbly, back stairs towards her truck, a rusty maroon Ford Explorer. That the old junker started every day despite the fact its odometer read two hundred and seventy thousand miles was a minor miracle, she thought. The screen door banged loudly behind her. Shit, she cursed to herself. I have to get started on my meal soon and I've got so much to do.

Her house was a two-storey wooden dwelling that looked every one of its sixty-five years and perhaps older. Its small back stoop, tilting badly and rotting in places, had been ignored for years. More than a few of the gray, weathered cedar shakes meant to protect the house from the long, vicious upstate winters were missing and presumed dead. The paint around her windows and doors was peeling after many years of neglect. Not all homes looked like Joanne's in northern New York, but hers was not uncommon either. For this was Morgantown, one of many, mostly forgotten hamlets nestled in the foothills of the Adirondacks.

At one time, Morgantown was the destination for hordes of men riding the railroads, descending on the iron mines nearby desperate for a day's wage. Or at the lumber mills along the Oswegatchie, a narrow, winding river that flowed darkly, almost sadly, through town before its trek inevitably ended at the mightier St. Lawrence. The area's best mining and forestry days were long gone, however, and so were the fortunes of many small manufacturers that once thrived in the region. To prop up the dying town, the state did what it could; it built a medium-security prison to house criminals that "down-staters" didn't want in their midst. But the facility was welcomed; it had created hundreds of jobs.

At thirty-nine and standing five feet seven with long sinewy bottle-blonde hair, Joanne looked like she could be pretty if she tried. After all, her slim yet curvaceous build portrayed a sense of optimism—a hint of conviction perhaps—that life could begin at forty. Joanne wasn't in bad shape. But her mirrors had begun to betray her. First a few wrinkles appeared. And then she noticed crow's feet beginning to branch out like cedar roots, nearly eclipsing the power of her gray-blue eyes. She knew the source of her premature aging, or at least one of them. She smoked too much, and couldn't recall how many times she had tried—or pledged—to quit. But like most smokers, she enjoyed it. It was one of her life's few pleasures. But pretty? Maybe ten or fifteen years ago, but not now. Besides, pretty was way too much work, and there was no one around to appreciate it. Her appearance, like her life, had become increasingly irrelevant.

Normally, at this time of day, a large, yellow tanker truck would sit idly in her long driveway in front of an equally dilapidated garage. On its oval-shaped tank, in large black lettering, the truck's identification simply read DENNY'S SEPTIC SERVICE. It was owned by her husband of two decades. He told anyone who'd listen that his service was one that was always in demand—or words to that effect. Joanne was simply glad he paid the bills. She would *never* quote him verbatim.

But today the large tanker was missing and the path to her Explorer was easy. She secured her keys from the bottom of her purse and was walking toward her SUV when she recognized a familiar face across the yard.

"Hi Dad, how ya doing today?" she yelled.

Joanne's dad was Hubie Schumacher. At sixty-six, Hubie was a tall, broad-shouldered man, perhaps still over six feet if he could resist the urge to stoop and sag as he went about his work. Like many men his age, he was thick at the waist, the result of a forty-year penchant for beer and beefsteak. But he still had his hair, which had turned a wavy, cotton-ball white.

The hood of his one-ton was raised and his ample frame was draped over an engine that refused to idle properly. Beside his double garage, the blade of a snowplow waited patiently for the inevitable change in seasons. It had rested there since spring, and weeds—now foot-tall, yellow and wilted—had flourished around it. Sitting lazily next to his truck, his ears attentive to the sound of Joanne's voice from across the yard, sat a large chocolate brown Labrador retriever.

"Another day closer to winter, Jo," he replied, pointing to the plow. "Gotta get that blade on this clunker soon."

Joanne took it in stride. The dog was now standing, his tail wagging. It started walking toward her.

"Dad, you're supposed to be retired and, besides, it's Thanksgiving."

"Not a corpse yet, Jo. Besides, my post office pension doesn't buy me a helluva lot of beer," he replied.

"Well, Hubert Schumacher, you're the only one I know who can't wait for snow. As if we don't see enough of that stuff around here."

"Keeps me off the couch," he said.

The dog arrived at Joanne's house. She bent over to greet him.

"Hi Griz," she said. "How are ya boy?" The dog beat the air with his tail.

Father and daughter continued their conversation across the yard.

"Where's Denny?" he asked.

"Out doing calls."

"Doing calls? And you yell at me for working on Thanksgiving? I never see that guy."

Joanne was growing mildly impatient and was anxious to hit the road.

"I don't see him much either, Dad," she said, a tone of resignation evident in her voice. "It's his busy season, you know? If he's not out putting in leach systems or new tanks, it's pumping them out. I don't follow him around."

Hubie wasn't buying it. Maybe she should, he thought.

"Right. Well, all I know is that damn truck of his is gone most of the time."

"Dad, I haven't got time to get all worked up. I have to get to the grocery store and then get the turkey in the oven. But listen, when are you and Delores coming over?"

"What time do you want us?" he asked.

"Well, anytime after three works for us. Denny should be home by then and cleaned up."

Hubie nodded while Joanne proceeded to open the door to her SUV. Griz was still hanging around.

"You'd better go back to Dad now, Griz. I gotta run."

Hubie whistled for his dog, and the retriever responded, galloping happily back to his master.

"We'll be there. By any chance, you didn't hear from your sister, did you?"

She stood there, staring at her father.

"Dad, you ask that question around every holiday. What've you been smoking?" Under her breath, she also mumbled something about planets and stars.

"I quit, remember? Unlike you."

"I don't mean that, Dad. And you know what I'm saying. Jane? What would bring her here?"

Hubie responded.

"I wish I knew, but I don't."

Joanne continued.

"Whatever, Dad. You know that Jane doesn't have time for us. She's a big shot now. Wouldn't show up in MoTown unless her press bus blew a tire!"

She waved to her dad.

"Anyway, I've got to go. See you later."

Joanne jumped into her truck and pulled away. Minutes later, she was cruising slowly through the center of the town of several thousand souls. Sadly she shook her head as she surveyed the state of the only town she'd ever known. It's going downhill fast, she thought. Many of its brown-bricked storefronts—once considered stately and elegant—were now boarded up, or left to decay on their own. In its hey-day, Morgantown's business district was a lively, bustling center of commerce. It had boasted dress shops and haberdashers, a couple of cafés and several competing five-and-dimes. Even a bookstore. Across opposite corners, a couple of banks had once faced off in friendly competition.

These days, its decrepit thoroughfare displayed little signs of life. There was a large dollar store with a home-painted sign, a law office or two, and insurance agencies. At the corner, where one of the banks once called home, a pizza and video parlor now occupied the site. It was still a thriving entity since MoTowners, as they called themselves, could still afford take-out and a movie once in a while. Next to it was the Salvation Army store. She knew that place well, Joanne found herself thinking.

On the opposite side of the street, there were even fewer businesses, since the buildings no longer existed. A series of early morning fires over the past thirty-five years had created vacant spaces, prompting Hubie to quip that the volunteers "hadn't lost a *lot* yet." Of course, the fires destroyed not only the town's lone movie theater, the *Strand*, but a couple of vintage, 1920s-era hotels as well—the same rooming houses that once bedded and fed the itinerant miners and loggers. Only their concrete foundations survived, if that was the way they could be described. The locals suspected the once-handsome structures had been torched for cash, but inspectors never found proof of arson.

The fire department, itself located at the end of the business section, was quiet today. There were no emergencies to address. However, Joanne remembered it became a hubbub of activity, at least once a year, when the farmers descended on the fire hall each April. That was when the firefighters held their annual bullhead supper, named after the bony, tasteless fish from the nearby lakes. She didn't care for bullheads but the rhubarb pies were good.

Once, not too long ago, there was a rumor—not so silly that people *wanted* to believe it—that the famous retailer from Arkansas might locate here, threatening to smother everything commercial in its wake. Whatever business that was left, of course. But that rumor was a cruel hoax. With a population about half it was during the Depression, Morgantown was now just too small, too impoverished, for a store like that to locate here.

With the holiday, the town was nearly deserted. But Joanne wasn't surprised; she'd lived here all her life and had watched it fester over the years. Her SUV continued its way through town and came to a yield in the road. Not even a stop sign now, simply an excuse to slow down. She remembered when this intersection once hosted the town's lone traffic light, but the mayor decided it wasn't required any more. He removed it nearly six years ago—literally, since his full-time job was as a lineman for Niagara Mohawk where he got to operate one of those hydraulic bucket trucks.

She glanced over at her father's post office. It, of course, remained a popular venue with the locals but today Joanne knew the place was closed. Normally, a steady stream of people would be seen entering and leaving, hoping to strike up a conversation with a neighbor or kibitz with Hubie's attractive replacement. It was the highlight of their day. Next door, at the Wishbone Café, one of only two restaurants remaining downtown and one which she also knew well, Joanne could see some action at the breakfast counter. Its "kitchen sink" omelet was the most popular item on the menu.

Soon she arrived at her destination—the town's lone grocery store—and drove across a parking lot nearly packed with last-minute Thanksgiving shoppers. Unlike other stores in town, it had to remain open—until at least noon.

Joanne found a parking spot and put her Explorer in park. She reached up and turned her rearview mirror towards her. She would make a last-minute check on her hair. As her reflection appeared, she could see the sign for TURN-BULL'S SUPPLY, the town's hardware store, behind her. It was located on the opposite end of the parking lot from the grocery outlet, and had been her place of work for nearly fifteen years. Thankfully it was closed for the day.

The store was named after an enterprising man from Liverpool who immigrated to the area in the late nineteenth century. His ambition was to sell apparel and other dry goods to woodsmen and prospectors who arrived to harvest the timber and mine the minerals. His stores soon sprouted everywhere and now Turnbull's sold everything from drain cleaners to baby clothes—even televisions. So far, it had enjoyed a monopoly but there was another rumor, probably started by the mayor, that another national chain had set its beady eyes on Morgantown. Again, that too was a joke. Joanne knew her little store would survive. There was nowhere else to shop.

Peering into her mirror, Joanne stared at herself for a moment, and didn't like what she saw. I'm running pretty rough, she thought. And this hair, well, there's not much I can do with it unless I just cut it *all* off. That would make my life a little easier, she thought, but Denny would just go ballistic. Then she pushed the collar of her blouse down towards her shoulder and glanced at the left side of her neck. Not getting much better, she concluded.

She glanced again at Turnbull's and, as her eyes lingered, Joanne recalled an awkward and embarrassing moment she'd had with her boss the day before. She had just donned her uniform, a dark-blue, faux silk vest with a name tag pinned to her lapel when he had approached her. His name was Darryl, a puffy-faced, rotund man of about fifty who always seemed to carry a smile on his face that told people that life was what you made of it.

"Morning Jo," he had said, cheerfully.

"Hi Darryl. How are you today?"

"Can't complain."

"Well, you never do, Darryl, and that's why everyone loves ya."

He smiled warmly.

"I'm hopin' that it'll be a busy day today. Good thing, too, because…well, you know…business hasn't been that great lately."

Darryl was a divorced father of two, and was attracted to Joanne, but he knew that nothing would happen. She was married and he honored that. But that didn't discourage his fascination for Joanne, the popular, hard-working cashier he'd had for years. This appeal was not lost on his friends;

not even the slow-witted ones on his bowling team. They suspected he had a hankerin' for Joanne Lowry.

"Ya know her situation, Dar," they'd say. "Ya know who she's married to? So what's stoppin' ya from dippin' your pen in some hardware store ink?" Then of course they'd snicker with delight. But he had always dismissed his pals, village idiots all, and their lewd remarks. He was a gentleman.

Darryl had watched as Joanne placed her cash drawer in the register and punched a few buttons. She'd been working at the hardware store for so long that her routine was second nature to her. The job didn't pay much, but it had given her the medical insurance she needed. Besides, she liked to meet and talk with people.

Then he had noticed an olive-green bruise on her neck peering out from under the collar of her open-necked blouse. It seemed to extend beyond the base of her neck, but Darryl couldn't be certain.

"What happened here?" he had asked, pointing.

Taken aback by the discovery, Joanne had become flustered.

"Oh…*nothing*, Darryl. Just some sort of rash that came on the other day. These things come and go."

Her boss, however, clearly had not accepted her explanation.

"Don't look like a rash to me," he had replied. She had remembered the look of deep concern in his eyes.

"I'm okay," she had tried to reassure him. "Really."

"You sure?"

"Yes," Joanne had replied, turning toward her purse for distraction. She had wanted to make sure she hadn't forgotten her latest *Sudoku* book. Joanne loved the numbers game, especially the diabolical ones. The game challenged her, and so did the *New York Times* cross-words. Often, when the store went quiet, she would pull one or the other out.

For a few moments, they had both stood there in stony silence and she knew his eyes had been glued to her. Then, mercifully, he had changed the subject.

"Got a gang coming tomorrow?" he had asked.

"No, just my dad and his girlfriend. Maybe my cousins."

"Brent got too much homework?"

Darryl had been referring to Joanne's son, a senior at Syracuse University.

"No, he's in his last year now and has it all figured out. Straight A's, or close to it. More like a girlfriend who's keeping him away. And you know he and his father don't see eye to eye anymore. If they ever did."

"Well, I'm sorry to hear that," he had replied. "My kids and I have gotten along okay since my divorce. I'm a lucky man."

"Yes, you are, boss," she had replied, not knowing whether she was commenting favorably on his marital status or his relationship with his children—or both.

Darryl then returned to the business at hand.

"I have to head out to the Gouverneur store for the day, so just lock up when you leave, okay? And have a good Thanksgiving. See you Friday."

"It would be even nicer if we had Friday off as well, Darryl. Hint…hint."

"Well, Joanne, you know these guys," her boss had said, pointing to an aisle where a familiar customer had been approaching, his large cart loaded with sheetrock and several large plastic pails that contained drywall compound.

"If we close up for more than a day or so," Darryl had continued, switching to an exaggerated hillbilly accent just out of earshot of the shopper. "They'd say, 'DaaaRuuul…open uuup. We need more muuud. Open uuup!'"

She remembered Darryl's loud laugh. She recalled her sense of relief when he had turned and walked back to his office.

Tightening her collar, Joanne returned the rearview mirror to its rightful place, exited her Explorer and walked towards the grocery store. She was retrieving a shopping cart from the outside patio when she heard a gravelly-sounding voice behind her.

"Just can't stay away from this parking lot, eh, Jo?" the voice asked.

The sound was familiar. She turned and recognized its source; it was Bernie White, and he was pushing a cart filled with several plastic bags of groceries. He was the drywaller who Darryl had mildly disparaged yesterday. A scruffy, unshaven man about her age, perhaps a few years older, Whitey—nobody called him by his first name—was dressed in the same farmer-styled denim overalls that he had been wearing the day before at Turnbull's. They were torn at the pockets and grease-covered as if he had been working under the chassis of his tractor.

"Morning, Whitey," she said. "Guess we just keep running into each other, huh?"

"Oh, this here town's pretty tiny, Joanne," he had replied, with a guttural drawl that seemed to have worsened over the years. Town came out sounding like "towwwn." Whitey's like me, she concluded. Too many smokes.

"Did you get started on your sheetrockin' job, Whitey?" she asked.

"Yeah, got 'er goin'," he replied. "You know, if I don't get that goddamn job done, my old lady's gonna *stroke* out on me!"

Joanne smiled.

"Even though it's Thanksgiving?" she asked.

"Have to, Jo. It's the only time I got. You know I spend most of my nights in the shed out back, carvin' deer. That's where I make my dough these days."

"Well, we all gotta do what we gotta do, Whitey," she said.

Joanne had known Whitey since he dropped out of high school. But when the slaughterhouse over on County Route 6 shut its doors a couple of years back, he was forced to set up shop in his garage, charging hunters sixty-five dollars under the table to butcher every brown-eyed buck they carried in. Of course, some of those animals were the unfortunate victims of his customers' pick-up trucks as its owners made their way back from a night out at some bar. It was no secret that road kill occasionally found its way to Whitey's shop in the middle of the night. The troopers didn't care, and neither did the road maintenance crews. One less carcass to haul away.

But most of his customers were legitimate hunters and sometimes lucky ones too. Joanne had heard stories—who knows if they were true?—that some of Whitey's patrons simply opened the screen doors of their double-wide trailers at dawn, taking aim at deer munching in their gardens. Couldn't get easier than that to fill a freezer for winter.

"So now you're doing the grocery shopping too?" Joanne asked.

"Yeah, the old lady works just as hard as I do, Jo and she sent me over here. Course, she didn't ask me…just *sent* me," Whitey replied with a smile. "But I don't mind. Deb's

a good ole' broad!"   Broad was pronounced "brawwwd."
Another smile. He somehow knew she wouldn't be offended.

"Well, a happy, sheetrockin' Thanksgiving to you,
Whitey," she said as she bid him good-bye and entered the
store.

She rolled her eyes heavenward.

Home, she thought.

THREE

An hour later, Jane emerged from her building's underground garage and pointed her gunmetal gray Mercedes away from the capital towards Morgantown. Instead of taking the Thruway west towards Utica and then turning north—the easiest choice—Jane opted for a more scenic route past Lake George. The roads were winding and slippery in the wake of yesterday's ice rain, but the road crews had been out salting and sanding, allowing her to drive at the maniacal speeds she liked to drive.

Maybe the route through the foothills would be a distraction, she thought. Right now, *any* distraction would be welcome.

Though she detested her childhood upbringing in rural upstate New York, she had always reveled in its landscape, even in late fall as winter approached. The Adirondacks had a unique ability to produce rugged, astonishing vistas. For miles, she watched as the towering, untouched stands of maple, birch and ash competed with their coniferous cousins, the black spruce, hemlock and pine. It was pastoral.

Jane wished she had been here a month earlier, when the mountainous foliage was at its best. But wasn't she in California, Oregon and Colorado a month ago? Doing town-hall meetings, attending fund-raisers, meeting the media? Or were we in Minnesota and Wisconsin? She couldn't remember.

It was all a *fucking* blur.

Well, maybe next year, she found herself thinking. Maybe next fall she'd return to the Adirondacks and enjoy the colors. Maybe bring Roberto, if he was still in the picture.

Right, she concluded. As if *that* would happen.

Jane's mind wandered. Her thoughts returned to the day before. Only twenty-four hours earlier, as she raced through LaGuardia to catch her shuttle to Albany, her BlackBerry rang so loudly that it had jolted her from her political daydreams.

It had been Marcia on the phone, her executive assistant back in the governor's office. An extremely-fit woman in her late twenties, Marcia Bell's most distinguishing features were her short, raging-red hair and a sea of freckles that seemed to engulf her entire body. Though she was not unattractive, a few journalists—male, of course—had characterized Marcia as "Jane's plain Jane." This had angered Jane, since Marcia was a young woman of substance. She had graduated from the University of New Hampshire *magna cum laude* but could only land a job paying about eighteen grand a year as a girl Friday at a small public relations firm in Burlington.

Marcia had figured she was happy in Vermont; after all, her life's mission was to be an over-educated ski bum at Stowe or Killington. It was a vocation at which she was having considerable success. But after meeting Jane on a chairlift one winter day two years ago, Marcia wisely accepted an offer to join Foley's office.

"When are you boarding?" her assistant had demanded. Jane admired Marcia's spunk and played along.

"In a few minutes, mother Marcia," Jane had replied. "I'll be there in about an hour and a half. What's up?"

"Well, we're nearly set for the news conference. The governor is ready. Got here yesterday, while his talented press secretary chose to stay behind in New York and play."

Jane had laughed. She loved sarcastic people. It took one to know one.

"It wasn't all play, I can assure you, Marcia," she had said. "You should know by now how hard it is to stage-manage the media, especially as well as I—"

Jane had been interrupted again. A persistent cough that she'd had for weeks had returned. This had alarmed Marcia.

"You're not canceling your doctor's appointment *again* today, are you?"

"No, going this afternoon. I promise."

"Well, if you don't, I'll have her come to the office! You've had that cough for weeks."

"I know," Jane had replied "But Schaefer's done all her x-rays. Taken all her swabs. Completed all her tests. If she had a *cat*, it would be out for the night."

Jane had known, however, that Marcia was skeptical. Her assistant believed her duty, among a hundred others, was to keep her boss on schedule. To do that, Marcia felt, Jane had to remain healthy.

"Listen, Jane, you know I'm going to personally shove you out the door later today," Marcia had vowed.

"It's just friggin' bronchitis, I'm sure, Marcia. I've had it before and it returns from time to time." Jane appreciated her young assistant's devotion. Marcia had signaled that she wanted a real education in politics, and who better to provide that than Jane Schumacher?

That was when Jane had decided to change the subject.

"Are the budget statements and releases ready?"

"Yes, madam press secretary. Everything's in order. We're just waiting for you."

Bidding her assistant a good-bye, Jane had glanced around the crowded New York airport terminal and allowed her mind to return to her favorite topic—politics, and the presidential race. It was now game on, and even though Foley was still an undeclared candidate, it was clear to everyone in the political universe that he was not only in the race, but in it to win.

His interviews had been superb. He had skated around the ultimate question—"are you, or are you *not* going to run?"—like a sleek Russian ice-dancer who knew the gold medal was his if he just got through the long program. Man, he was good, Jane had thought.

But it also made her ponder just how Foley might have fared a couple of generations ago. She knew her history. It was a bitch to run for the top office today. Just think, JFK was a scalawag, a rascal—even a slut—and got away with it. Of course, every second president since Jefferson was rumored to have had a concubine on the side. But today's level of political correctness had gone too far. It pushed good people out. If you have the slightest skeleton in your closet, forget it. Never mind that a candidate might have an original thought occasionally—a good idea or two—that could pull this country out of its quagmire. No, it was more about whether the handsome dude can keep his pecker in his pants.

Foley was clean and bright, maybe even visionary, and certainly someone who "got it." A couple of weeks back, some pundit from the Clinton era figured the New York governor had all the "fixins" for a successful run. The political authority—self-proclaimed, of course—described Foley as a potent political beer, a unique fermentation of confidence bordering on cockiness. In some hands, this concoction was often poisonous. In others, it was political dynamite and, for Foley, the latter was the case.

But Jane, no fan of beer, told a more upscale story. Over a glass of red, not surprisingly, she compared Foley to an exciting new wine, an engaging and different varietal, one that brave, New World vintners were attempting to discover every day. She too was a vintner. Her job was to create a new varietal for Americans to sip and savor.

She knew, however, that her guy was not the second coming of the savior. No mortal was. Yet, it was clear; deep down, as voters professed their desire for something new—a fresh face, a creative force—they were simply yearning for the politics of old. They harkened nostalgically for the days of Roosevelt, both Teddy and Franklin, of Truman and Kennedy—even Reagan. They felt the country was better then and they wanted it back.

Jane had arrived back in the capital on time, and the governor's budget scrum had been successful. Well, mostly successful.

Minutes after the news conference had ended, she had been cornered by a twenty-seven-year-old snot from some right-wing yet impossible-to-ignore blog that was gaining fifty-thousand new followers a month. Some guy named Jason or Jayden, or something like that and a guy who professed little interest in Foley's stewardship of the Empire State. He cared only about the governor's presidential ambitions.

"I don't know why you're getting so impatient with me, Jane," he had said. "I'm covering Foley's presidential run, and I'll be writing about him—with or without talking to you. And you know what Mark Twain said."

"Yes, Jayden, every j-schooler wet behind the ears knows what Twain said about the press a gazillion years ago. Never get into an argument with a man who buys ink by the barrel!"

The blogger had just chuckled.

"Only we don't use ink any more—who the hell does?" he had replied with more than a hint of smugness.

"The *New York Times* and a slew of good papers would beg to differ," she had retorted, but decided quickly that that line of thinking would go nowhere with this guy. The blogosphere was contemptuous—dismissive even—of the mainstream media, and Jane knew it wasn't worth the battle.

Jane had realized, however, the young reporter was right. Presidential contenders, especially Democrats, had to master the Web. They had to raise gobs of money electronically, in increments of five, ten or fifty dollars, or forget about keeping up with the opposition.

The Internet, of course, could also be a mine-field, she remembered. Yes, it could propel an unknown aspirant to the top. But a single event taped by some zit-faced teenager shadowing a rising candidate can capture a mistake in seconds, and before you can say the words 'oh, fuck', you're on YouTube. God, don't get caught like that dumb shit southern senator did a few months back and utter a racial slur, thinking that nobody was watching. Well, *everyone* is watching! And before you know it, you're done.

"All right," she had said and proceeded to tell the arrogant little bastard what she had professed to Roberto the night before. That Foley would use his political clout to cajole, threaten or embarrass the local yokels into doing what they should have been doing. That's what real leaders *do*, she said.

But she *was* impatient. She couldn't wait to leave Planet Albany—as some scribes called it, for its chaos and dysfunction—and move on to the *real* game.

Jane had become so wrapped up in work that she almost forgot about her doctor's appointment late in the day. As promised, Marcia literally pushed her out the door and Jane had made the two-mile drive through rush-hour traffic to her doctor's office. A light, misting rain throughout the day had begun to freeze on contact, and the drive was both slippery and perilous.

She was her doctor's last patient of the day and was alone in the waiting room. Fidgeting, she had picked up magazines and dropped them. She had paced back and forth, thumbing away on her BlackBerry. Finally, the nurse had called her into an inner office, a large stylishly-set room with a panoramic view of the city below. On the wall were the doctor's Vassar and Yale degrees.

After a minute or two, Dr. Schaefer had made her entrance. This was only the second time Jane had met with her—since her late teens, Jane had always shunned doctors—but she had noticed that Clare was different. Here was an intelligent, smartly-dressed divorcée who might have been close to fifty but didn't look it. She wore fine Italian jewelry, including a pair of thin, black glasses that made her look like the chief librarian from *Maxim* magazine.

Of course, Jane had figured that most of Clare's female patients, jealous to the bone, had probably wanted to claw the bitch's eyes out. But not Jane. This woman's comfortable in her own skin, and she had admired that. God knows, this friggin' world needs more women like Clare Schaefer.

But there were few smiles yesterday. Shaking hands with Jane, the doctor had directed her to a couple of retro, JFK-era wingbacks facing each other in the corner of the office. This furniture was making a comeback, Jane had remembered thinking. That was a good omen.

Never mind FDR, she had thought. A return to Camelot would be more relevant.

The doctor had looked into Jane's eyes.

"Let's sit down, okay?"

FOUR

The big tanker truck roared to life as Denny Lowry flicked the starter switch, and the product—as he called it for customers, but shit to everyone else—began its sixty-foot final journey up the manicured property to the road. It was approaching noon on Thanksgiving but he didn't give a damn. If the owners of these homes—the snazzy ones along the river—didn't want their bowls to back up when all their hoity-toity friends and family were visiting, then they'd have to put up with him and his truck. What choice did they have? A holiday service call from the sewage man, or an over-flowin' toilet with fifteen or twenty people wolfin' down turkey? He smirked once again.

As usual, he was alone on his calls. It suited him just fine. This particular job would take him longer than the usual twenty minutes or so that it normally took to purge a fifteen-hundred-gallon tank of shit. Dickie Owen, one of the county's hotshot car dealers, owned the nicest shack on the river. He and his old lady could afford it since he made his dough by sellin' all that Jap and Korean junk for years. What's up with people today, he wondered. What the hell was wrong with Chevys and Fords?

Denny gazed over at the sprawling, chalet-styled home. Dickie's place had to have been at least five thousand square feet with a tank to match. Hell, he thought. That tank's big enough to hold at least three hill country women, he snickered, since most of those beasts probably outweighed me. They pushed *two-fifty* if they were an ounce! The only *thin* ones that ever ventured into the Paddle Inn, his favorite saloon, were probably not from Morgantown because... well...they had *all* their teeth. Denny chuckled to himself once again. He was one funny man. Too bad the old lady doesn't share my sense of humor. Or anything else, for that matter.

His pumper made a loud whining sound. The product was moving. Who says shit only runs downhill? That calls for another Old Milwaukee, he figured, and he reached into a cooler behind the cab. Popping the lid on the can, he drained the beer in two or three gulps. Then he threw the empty through the truck's window to a space behind the passenger's seat, where it joined ten or twelve of its fellow travelers.

Denny was forty now, and it showed. When people guessed, that is if they cared, they aged him by as many as five years. That he walked with a slight but noticeable limp in his right leg didn't help either. More like a *gimp* walk, as he called it, a condition Denny blamed on the Syracuse doctors who botched his surgery when he was in his senior year at high school, leaving one leg slightly shorter than the other. Fuckers, he'd often rant. They weren't there because they finished first in their class.

Denny was a monster of a man. His face, after many years of abuse, had sprouted reddish veins across cheekbones that connected to a bulbous, rouge-colored nose. A three-pack-a-day habit of Mohawk Reds from the reservation didn't help matters either. He used to roll his own. But a couple of years ago, when his old lady took a second job, he said fuck that. Too much work. He was a mess, but then again he didn't care. They can all kiss my ass, he muttered to himself often, especially if he caught a frown on someone's face or a judgmental glance when he'd say something stupid.

Just then, he let out a loud sustained hack that shook his lungs. Inhaling deeply, almost gargling, he gathered a pearly gob of saliva and spat. It was a windy day; the wad carried more than fifteen feet into the air, coming to a rest only inches from his truck. Jesus Christ, that hurt! If I didn't have smoker's cough, he thought, I wouldn't get any exercise at all!

Denny knew he could do another four or five calls today if he wanted to. It was a busy time of the year and he hadn't had much sleep. He always felt he could do this job *in* his sleep, which may as well have been the case given the copious quantities of beer he consumed daily. He had been a sewage man for so long he couldn't remember when he started. A crappy job because, well, people shit a lot. He'd never be out of customers. And the money was good.

Opening yet another beer, Denny reached into his pocket and retrieved his cell phone. He decided he would give his uppity kid a call. Maybe wish him a happy Thanksgivin', he thought. Joanne had hounded him—well, she never shut up about anything—about his drinking and dialing. But he ignored her most of the time. That fuckin' kid of mine has no respect for his pop, he thought, and it was time he reminded his twenty-year-old college son of that.

Denny remembered the last time he saw Brent; it was in August, just before he left Morgantown to begin his final year at Syracuse. They'd nearly come to fisticuffs after Brent told him he wasn't gonna help him dig leach lines and install septic tanks again next summer. Instead, he accepted some la-di-da job from his girlfriend's rich old man who owned a string of hotels in the Finger Lakes.

Brent was makin' noises about stayin' in college even longer. Somethin' about goin' to Cornell. Now that's an even more snooty college than Syracuse. Studyin', of all things, *hotel* management. Who the fuck goes to college to learn how to *run* a hotel? Just get a job in one, for Christ's sake. They'll teach you everything you need to know about changin' sheets, cleanin' toilets and how to keep your mouth shut when travelin' salesmen were drillin' the local ladies.

Jesus! Never could understand that kid of mine.

Now he remembered their last battle.

"What the fuck do you mean you won't be workin' with me this year," Denny had demanded. "You know it's my busiest time…and you know that I have to make my dough when the goddamn ground isn't frozen cock stiff!"

Brent stuck to his guns and faced his father down. Like his dad, well over six feet, he was solidly built. But unlike Denny, he didn't carry an extra thirty or forty pounds and, through daily workouts and varsity lacrosse, was determined never to be like his father. Winning an academic scholarship to SU three years earlier meant the brainy and brawny twenty-year-old could eventually leave Morgantown behind. And that was going to start next summer by staying in Geneva.

Brent's cell phone rang off the hook before his voicemail kicked in. Denny finally said screw it and hung up. He wasn't gonna leave a message, he thought. Brent probably saw his number and ignored it anyway, the little prick. Well, he didn't have anything new to say to *Mr. College* anyway.

Noticing the pumper had finished its job, Denny decided to call it a day and forget his last remaining calls. He could get to those people tomorrow.

He was about to disconnect the long black suction pipe from Dickie's tank and return to the tanker when he heard a child's voice behind him. A boy of about eight or nine was sitting on a motorized three-wheeler. It looked a like a miniature all-terrain vehicle. Goddamn, these kids have everything these days, the septic man thought.

"Hi mister," the boy said. "What're you doing?"

Denny looked down at the kid and wondered who owned him.

"What's it look like, kid? I'm pumpin' sh——." He quickly caught himself before he swore in front of the youngster. "I'm cleanin' out a septic tank at this house."

"What's a *skepptic* tank?"

"I said *septic* tank, kid. Never heard of one before?"

The kid shook his head. "Nope. What's it do?"

Denny frowned. "Ah, kid, why're you askin' me? Why don't you ask your old man? That's his job to answer all your friggin' questions. Where's he?"

The kid pointed to a house a couple of doors down the lane.

"He's over there," the kid said. "He's not working today. School's closed."

Denny grimaced. "He's a schoolteacher?"

The little boy nodded. Denny shook his head.

"Gets every friggin' holiday off, and more, huh?"

He watched as the youngster gave him a puzzled look. But then he noticed the kid couldn't take his eyes off the pumper truck.

"I just came over to see your neat truck here," the boy said.

Denny suddenly took a liking to the kid. Any kid his age who liked his truck was all right in his book, he thought. He wished Brent was like him when he was eight or nine. Or even now.

"Wanna help me, runt?" Denny asked.

"Sure!"

"Well, get around here and you can operate the switch," he said, pointing to the control panel on the side of the truck.

The kid stepped off his three-wheeler and ran over to the side of the truck. Denny pointed to the switch.

"Okay, now…when I yell over to you, just flick that lever right there. And don't fu—." Again, he stopped short of swearing. "—screw it up!"

The kid beamed.

"What's your name?" Denny asked.

"Gunnar," he replied.

"Gunner? That's a strange name for a kid," Denny said. "Like you're shooting off guns?"

The kid shot Denny another curious look. He had no idea what the older man had said. Denny noticed Gunnar's puzzled reaction.

"Oh, I get it now. Your parents must be krauts…er…I mean German, right?"

"I don't think so," Gunnar replied. "I think we're American."

Denny shrugged. "Whatever."

Then he walked over to the opposite side of the truck where the suction pipe remained connected to the home's septic system.

"Okay, Gunnar, flick that lever."

Gunnar did as he was told and quickly moved from the side of the truck to see if Denny approved. It was then he noticed the man's distinct limp.

"What happened to your leg, mister?"

A bit of a nosy little shit, Denny thought.

"I hurt it a long time ago and when they operated on me, they screwed it up," he replied. "That's why I have a limp now."

"They screwed it up?" Gunnar asked.

"Yeah, long story kid…well, now, you'd better get outta here. I don't want you and that three-wheeler of yours in my goddamn way when I back up."

"Okay, mister. Nobody comes down this lane much. I really like that truck of yours. Never saw one that big."

Denny grinned.

"Thanks, runt. Now get goin'!"

"Okay," Gunnar said. "Bye."

With a dismissive wave, Denny watched the boy motor down the road. Not a bad kid, but with a name like that, he'll get beat up a lot in high school. Still, he wished his own kid would have taken some interest in the old man's work.

After Gunnar disappeared, Denny looked around to see if anyone else was watching. Good Christ the kid's gone, he was thinking. I have to piss like a bull moose! He proceeded to take a leak beside his truck.

He then reached for another hose, one connected to fresh water, and began to wash the long suction pipe. Grayish, foul-smelling water ran down the customer's driveway and into the yard. No big deal, he thought. It'll probably rain or snow tonight, anyway. Then he climbed into his cab and fired up the big rig's engine. He was about to put the gears in reverse when he reached for another brew from the cooler behind the passenger's seat.

He made his decision. He'd stop at the Paddle for a couple of cold ones before going home to the ball and chain, and her turkey. Maybe that new bartender—what's her name—Mandy? The one with legs so long they made a pretty nice ass of themselves?

He smiled again.

FIVE

The holiday traffic was thin and Jane's Mercedes was rolling through the northern landscape at a good clip. The cool, crisp skies she'd experienced out of Albany had begun to cloud over and there was a threat of rain, or perhaps snow. Another few minutes or so over these narrow, twisting roads and she'd be home. *Home?* Is that what she just called it? That was odd; she hadn't put the words "Morgantown" and "home" in the same sentence since she was a teenager.

She had thought her life, though hectic and wild, had been on track. Sure, there were times when she could barely keep her head above water as she dealt with the turmoil around her. But she knew she'd chosen a frenzied existence; a world where hundred-hour work weeks were not uncommon. She had become a politico and a player. Someone who stood off to the side as a serious candidate was making his move.

Off to the side, but not that not far off.

But that was until yesterday. Now, she didn't know what lay in store. Now the only real change happening was the life of Jane Schumacher.

Her life was in limbo.

At last, she saw a sign indicating that Morgantown was less than ten miles ahead, and it caused her to shudder. She inhaled deeply, and again her chest began to ache. It was the same painful feeling she had felt yesterday. Soon she would be back in the town that she had abandoned years ago—Joanne's words at her mother's funeral, not hers—but an accurate description of events.

Still, there was no remorse; it *was* what it was, and she couldn't change history. But maybe she could do something about the present.

As she crossed the bridge and continued towards the center of town, her memories of her mother resurfaced. Suddenly, Jane was eighteen again. She heard a loud bang and it was the unmistakable sound of a screen door slamming behind her. She had been to this theater before; she'd had a front-row seat in fact. The same supporting actors, a familiar script. In it, she was running down the rickety stairs of her adolescent home on a quiet village street, her mother and sister in quick pursuit.

"And where the hell do you think you're going?" her mother demanded.

"I don't know, Mother, but what I do know is this: I'm getting the hell outta here once and for all," Jane replied, as she threw a bag into the back seat of her old Datsun, the rocker panels on its white exterior heavily corroded with rust.

Standing idly near the garage, Jane could see her father witnessing the heated exchange. He was wiping his oily hands with a cloth. Working on his precious snowmobiles, as usual, she thought. And as usual, saying nothing. Contributing nothing. Doing nothing. Joanne had followed her mother into the driveway and was in near hysterics as well.

"Let her go, Mom!" Joanne screamed. "Jane doesn't give a shit about any of us, so just let her go!"

Leaning on her car door, Jane recovered her composure slightly.

"You know something, Jo?" she said. "You're right. I'm not going to stay here one more goddamn minute. And *become* you."

"Up yours, Jane!"

Shaking her head in disgust, Jane continued her tirade.

"You can keep Morgantown and that dipshit of a boy-friend of yours in—"

Joanne clenched her lips in abject hatred for her twin sister and flashed her middle finger. But Jane was not finished.

"—in this shithole of a town!"

"Jane!" her mother screamed.

"That's what it is, Mother. You knew it twenty years ago, and you know it today. So, I'm getting out. I know what you think of me. But I don't care. It's my life and I'm not gonna let you control every move I make."

"That's rich Jane!" her mother replied. "You're the one who's made one lousy decision after another and I'm the one who's at fault? Maybe it's time you took some responsibility for yourself."

"I didn't say that, Mother," Jane replied, defensively. She always did that to me, she thought. Whatever I said she'd turn it around.

"Oh yeah? Then what are you saying, Jane? That it's *my* fault that you can't keep your legs closed?"

She remembered standing by the driver's side of her car—stunned. She couldn't believe what her mother had just said. How could a mother say such a thing to her daughter?

Donna Schumacher was never a happy woman, and Jane knew why. As a teenager growing up in Watertown in the mid-sixties, her mother had been determined to break with family tradition and get an education. Be somebody, even. None of her siblings had ever displayed more than a passing interest in going to college, and their parents never encouraged it either.

But Donna was different. She would make it on her own. Her passport to independence was an education. She had always excelled at math and science, and her plan was not only to get a science degree from Cortland State but then apply to Upstate Medical School.

"You want to be a doctor?" her friend Joyce had asked incredulously, making it sound as if she wanted to be a god-damn astronaut or the first woman president, or something even more exotic.

"Don't be ridiculous, Donna," Joyce had said. "Women don't get to be doctors! We become nurses! Remember? Nurses *marry* doctors. Then we're expected to spit out a lit-ter. And then you and doctor hubby will buy that bigger second or third house on the hill. "

Donna interrupted her.

"Oh, is that right?"

"Yup," Joyce replied. "But let me continue to paint you a picture. Now, where was I? Oh, yeah, then you'll organize a weekly bridge game, too, before mixing martinis for the old man before dinner. That's if he makes it home for dinner after screwing his secretary on his desk. Of course, then you'll have *your* affair—with the tennis pro or pool boy. Nothing dangerous, mind you; hubby's income is too important. But, I tell you, Donna, that's what *we* do. With your looks, it's preordained. It's the natural order of things."

Donna laughed, telling Joyce she was painting an amus-ing but inaccurate portrait of her and the life she was bound to lead. She simply disagreed with her caustic friend's pathetic domestic scenario. After all, she was going places and it all started with school. She was going to graduate from Cort-land State come hell or high water. She wasn't going to find herself dependent on anyone, especially a man.

She didn't even like kids.

Well, the high water didn't materialize, but her own ver-sion of hell did. That spring of 1966, after her first year at college, she met a soldier stationed up the road at Camp

Drum. A career Army sergeant, he had survived his first tour of Vietnam and was likely returning for a second when he met Donna. The next thing they knew, Donna was pregnant with twins, he had retired from active service and they were headed to some God-forsaken village near the Adirondacks called Morgantown for a post office job.

The post office!

If that wasn't hell, she didn't know what was.

Jane reflected on her mother's decisions as she continued her drive through Morgantown. What was that expression? That life was what "got in the way" when you were making other plans? Or whatever the friggin' saying was. She let out another gut-wrenching cough, and it hurt. Once again, Donna spoke to her.

It's my fault Jane that you can't close your legs?

Goddamn it, that woman could say some mean shit some-times, Jane thought. After that fight, she and her mother didn't see or speak to each other for more than a dozen years. But a week before Donna died of ovarian cancer, just short of her fifty-first birthday, mother and daughter had a reunion of sorts.

It might have lasted an hour, but it felt much longer to Jane.

That was eight years ago.

SIX

Joanne was standing at the sink and was washing yet another round of dishes when Denny entered the kitchen. It was mid afternoon and she had been working feverishly to get her meal prepared. As she told Darryl the day before, her Thanksgiving gathering was a small one, but a turkey dinner was always a major undertaking.

She was saddened when Brent announced last week that he was spending the weekend with Tracy and her parents downstate. Saddened, but not surprised—for a number of reasons. She had met Tracy about a year ago when both business majors arrived in Morgantown for Christmas. A nice girl, Joanne thought. And smart. If Brent decided she was the "one," it would be okay with her. They seemed good together.

Brent hadn't had many girlfriends in high school. But by the start of his sophomore year at Syracuse, he began to shed his sullen teenaged personality. Of course, Brent would never discuss his love life with his mother. Maybe that was a topic between fathers and sons, but not in Brent's case. She could never imagine Brent and Denny discussing anything personal. Theirs was a gasoline-on-the-inferno type of relationship and had been since Brent entered puberty.

Christmas had been a disaster. Joanne recalled how she had pleaded with Brent to come home and introduce them to Tracy. She got the sense from her son that he had met someone special, and although Brent wasn't one to call her much—probably because his old man might answer the phone—they did like to text each other on their cells. A rare day went by without a message or two. Even if it was just to talk about the weather or how one of his courses was going. That was fine, she thought. It didn't matter how they communicated.

They arrived on Christmas Eve just after lunch, armed with presents that Tracy had picked out and wrapped, only to discover Denny at his argumentative worst. The kids had barely removed their coats when her husband launched an attack, a sarcastic tirade about how Brent never called him. You know, I have a freakin' cell too, hotshot, Denny had bellowed. Only he didn't use the word 'freakin.' Joanne had always hated the F-word and wouldn't even repeat it to herself. But Denny was awful. I know you and your mother spend all your wakin' hours talkin' to each other. But do I get the *same* courtesy? No freakin' way. Again, he didn't say *that* word.

Brent had warned Tracy about what might happen. He told her what she could expect. You never know how goddamn drunk my dad will get, he'd said. I'm only asking you to do this because of my mother. Perhaps he was hoping against hope that Denny would curb his behavior for a lousy twenty-four hours. For Christmas, at least.

Tracy, to her credit, agreed to the trip and tried to assure Brent that it would be okay. Perfect families only existed on the Disney Channel, she had told him. So against his better judgment, Brent had agreed to the visit, telling Tracy they were doing this for his mother—and only her. But even he was shocked at the greeting they had received.

With Brent seething with anger and Tracy in a state of utter disbelief, the two marched the fifty yards across the snow to his grandfather's house and stayed there. Denny, triumphant in his victory, grabbed the keys to Joanne's Explorer and drove to the Paddle Inn. He knew the beer joint would be open, even on Christmas Eve.

All of these memories came back to Joanne when Denny entered the house as she was cleaning her kitchen.

"You done for the day?" she asked

"Yeah," he muttered, almost under his breath.

"You came home pretty late last night," she said without turning to address him.

"Well, you know I had calls to make," he said, removing a dirty overcoat and hanging it on a hook behind the kitchen door.

She wasn't buying it.

"How many calls can you do till midnight? That's when I finally fell asleep," Joanne replied. "And you'd better watch the beer too. If you get a DUI, that truck of yours'll be gone."

Denny decided to ignore her comments about his drinking.

"Jo, you know goddamn well that I put that spotlight on the truck for a reason. So I could get more calls in. So, get off my fuckin' back."

Wiping her hands with a towel, she turned. She was almost at the point of no return. There was little fight left in her.

"You were out the door pretty early today too."

Denny's temper was rising as Joanne continued her inquisition.

"Jesus Christ! A guy spends all fuckin' morning pumpin' shit, on Thanksgiving Day no less, and this is what I get?"

Joanne looked briefly at her husband before turning her attention to the task at hand. But Denny persisted.

"What's for lunch?"

"This counter's closed," she said quietly but firmly.

"Jesus, you're a piece of work, aren't you Jo?"

She shot him a look of exasperation. It bordered on contempt, and it didn't go unnoticed.

"Don't give me that look, Jo."

Joanne decided to lower the temperature by continuing her work. There was no point in angering him once again and especially on Thanksgiving.

"Denny, can't you make yourself something? I've got to get a sixteen-pounder in the oven."

"Sixteen pounds? Why do we need such a big, fuckin' bird? There's only gonna be four of us!"

"Well, Dan and Marjory told me yesterday that they can make it too."

"Oh, fuck me gently," he cried. "Just what I need. Your asshole cousins too."

Joanne finished wiping the sink and counters and was folding the cloth. She once again turned in his direction.

"Denny, they're the only family I have left. Brent's not here and we were only planning on my dad and Delores. So, I thought—"

Denny became enraged and moved within a foot or two of his wife. He made a handgun in the shape of his fore finger and thumb, pressed her nose firmly and pulled the imaginary trigger. Joanne, her eyes locked on her husband's, stepped back.

"Oh, you *thought*, did you? Well, do me a fuckin' favor, Jo, and just don't fuckin' think!" he said. Opening the refrigerator, he grabbed a beer and stormed off in the direction of the living room.

SEVEN

"Hey, anyone alive in here?"

Dressed in denim jeans and a sweatshirt, Hubie was sitting in an antique rocker at the back of his garage when he heard a familiar voice. Griz was dozing beside him but perked up at the sounds coming from the front. It was Brian Boychuk arriving to deliver a deer license, a habit that dated back for as long as they could recall.

Hubie knew Boychuk was nearing his lunch break and was planning to stop over. The imposing, uniformed man, sporting a brimmed police hat, entered the garage and made his way through the cluttered building. He was the sheriff of Morgan County, a cop's cop and a commanding figure.

"I'm back here, Brian," Hubie replied.

After weaving past a couple of snowmobiles, an all-terrain vehicle and assorted metal shelves overflowing with tools and other junk, Boychuk spotted his friend cleaning one of his shotguns.

"There you are old man," he said, smiling. Boychuk bent over and patted Griz. The dog responded to the affection by licking the cop's hand.

"Watch it kid," Hubie said, lifting a cocked, double-barreled twelve gauge. "I know how to use this thing!"

"Ah, you wouldn't shoot me, Hubie," he replied. "Then you'd just have to explain to everyone how you made such a mess in this *spotless* garage of yours."

Hubie registered the sheriff's sarcasm but chose to ignore it. He raised an eyebrow briefly with the policeman and then returned to the business of cleaning his shotgun.

"As promised, our deer licenses," Boychuk said. "Who else but me would make deliveries on Thanksgiving?"

"Thanks, as always, Brian," Hubie replied.

"We'd better get out soon, Mr. Schumacher. We only have a few weeks left."

Hubie shrugged.

"I've been waiting on you, Brian. I'm retired remember?"

"I know, Hubie, but I've been busy with a couple of chiefs' conferences and recruiting and all. I got Denny's license too."

"Well, I'm not sure if he'll be able to get out with us anytime soon," Hubie said. "Haven't seen much of him lately. His truck seems to be gone most of the time. But I'll be joinin' him for supper later today and I'll give it to him."

Hubie had known Brian Boychuk since the sheriff was a teenager and always liked him. Maybe it was because the kid knew exactly what he wanted to do since he was sixteen, and that was police work. And becoming a cop was the next best thing to serving in the military. Boychuk originally wanted to join the FBI but he quickly found out a college education was required and probably a letter from his congressman, whoever the hell that was. Not that he wasn't smart—far from it. He probably would have succeeded in college but Boychuk, a young man in a hurry, simply had wanted to get his police career going. And so at eighteen, when he heard that the Morgan County Sheriff's office was recruiting, he signed up.

But to Hubie, it was more than that. He had liked Boychuk from the day Jane brought him home to introduce the young man to her parents. Unlike the other boys whom the twins had dated, Boychuk had shown a special respect for his elders. Always called him "sir" or "Mr. Schumacher," and the former Army man in Hubie liked that. That Brian now called him "old man" was more a sign of friendly fun than disrespect. Throughout their senior year in high school, Hubie had wished he and Jane could have hooked up for good. Brian was a fine man.

But that was not to be. Not with his daughter.

"Guess who I saw on TV the other day?" Boychuk asked.

"Lemme guess. Joanne's older sister."

"Yeah," the sheriff said, smiling. The girls were born a month premature, but Jane had arrived about five minutes ahead of Joanne.

"Well, that's about the only time I see her too. She's usually with her socialist boss who wants to be king," Hubie sighed. "Have no time for Foley."

"Jane always was full of piss and vinegar, Hubie. You know she always had other designs. Hell, I knew *that* twenty years ago."

Hubie nodded.

"You're right," he said, returning his attention to the shotgun on his lap. Brian watched as the older man held a cloth in his hand and dipped it in linseed oil. Hubie noticed.

"Gives the gunstock a longer life," he said.

Despite their differences in age, Boychuk enjoyed spending time with the retired postmaster, and not just because he had dated his daughter twenty years before. He liked their quiet camaraderie. In spring and summer, they'd enter fishing contests; by fall, they hunted the deer that roamed upcountry. Once or twice, they had travelled to Québec or Newfoundland to pursue larger game, usually moose and bear.

When Boychuk turned twenty, his rancher father, mentor and hero, died of a heart attack within weeks of the young man's swearing in as a deputy sheriff. The young cop was devastated by the loss. Hubie was there for him, took him under his wing and consoled him. Boychuk never forgot that act of kindness and generosity.

"Well, I gotta run, Hubie."

"Okay, Brian. Unless it snows, let's get out there."

"Sounds good. I have two days off next week. Now, don't go pointing that gun at anything other than a duck or two, okay?"

"Well, maybe I'll get lucky and a Democrat will show up," he said. He was only half-kidding. "What're you doing today?"

"Heading over to Susan's sister's place," the cop replied. "Her boys are at the age where we like to horse around a bit."

The older man smiled at the thought of Brian and his wife. Susan was a nice girl, he thought, but he had wished the sheriff had ended up with Jane. He would have made a fine son-in-law. Or a fine son, for that matter.

"Well, happy Thanksgiving, Brian."

"You too, and give my best to Joanne," the Morgan County Sheriff said as he exited the garage. He didn't include Denny.

As he emerged from the garage, Jane's Mercedes pulled into the driveway. She opened the door, and climbed out. She stood for a moment, not sure what to think of the scene. A police vehicle? What was going on? Then as Boychuk raised his head and the former sweethearts recognized each other, Jane's worries were assuaged.

Boychuk spoke first.

"Well, speak of the devil!" A smile came over his face.

"Chucky!" Jane said, looking him up and down, as he did the same. They couldn't decide whether to shake hands or hug. Finally...a hug.

"It's really good to see you again," she said. "For a moment there, I thought there was something wrong. Or that my dad was being arrested. But when you came through that door, everything made sense."

Boychuk took a long look at Jane and smiled. In his eyes, she was still the beautiful girl he fell for when they were seniors in high school. But today there was something different, and not just because it was twenty years later, he thought. No, she looked tired and drawn, not quite the image he had seen often on TV. Still, he offered her a compliment.

"You're looking good, Shoes," he said. "All those years in the corridors of power have been good to you."

"Thanks, Chuck, but you always were a terrible liar," she said with a grin. "You're not so bad yourself. But I can't say I'm surprised to see you here or that you're the first person I've seen in Morgantown in years. How long has it been? Or do we want to answer that question?"

Boychuk shook his head.

"Maybe we shouldn't go there, Jane," he said, removing his sheriff's hat to reveal a receding forehead and thinning hair the color of beach sand.

"Not as much of a mop as the old days," he laughed. "I guess I'm looking more and more like my old man every day."

Jane smiled warmly.

"Still a cop, I see."

"Actually, head cop now, Jane. Elected sheriff two years ago. It's a small department, but I like it."

"Congratulations, Brian. You've done well for yourself."

He appreciated the praise; she seemed genuine. A painful memory returned and he knew the exact moment. It was prom night, a cool spring evening of their senior year around the time that the black flies arrived. He had appeared at her house with more than a corsage. He surprised her—shocked would have been the better word—by wearing his new deputy sheriff's uniform. He wouldn't leave for the academy for several months, but the uniform was issued nonetheless.

She wasn't pleased, and for years he wondered why. Mistakenly, he had thought she'd be proud of him. But he was wrong. Then it dawned on him; it wasn't because he wanted to be a cop. After all, he felt she might have supported an appointment to the FBI, or another federal agency. No, it was more like he had no plans to leave town and that was a deal breaker for Jane. She would have no part of Morgantown.

Then Jane noticed the wedding band on his finger.

"Got hitched too, I see," she said, tapping her left ring finger, though hers held no jewelry. Aside from hooped earrings and a necklace consisting of a simple gold chain supporting a single pearl, Jane had shunned most ornamental trappings.

Boychuk felt his face redden. Her question, though logical, was unexpected.

"Yeah, almost seven years now, Jane," he replied. "Susan's a very successful school administrator." There was no hint of affection in his voice. There were no details about how they met. Just a reference to her curriculum vitae.

Jane nodded. "Any kids?"

She was a former journalist, and wasn't afraid to ask a question. If she wanted to know something, she'd ask.

"Not yet…well, probably not ever," Boychuk replied. "We've just been too busy, I guess…"

He decided to return the subject to her.

"You're doing pretty well yourself too, Jane," he said. "Working for the man, now. The *boss* man. And he seems to have bigger plans."

Jane smiled, but didn't know where Brian leaned politically. Foley wasn't as popular upstate as he was in New York

City or in so many other places. Most of these northern counties were as rabidly conservative as the Deep South, having voted that way since Edison invented the light bulb. Regimes, both state and federal, had injected huge sums of cash into these desolate, economically forgotten backwaters, yet railing against government had almost become a spectator sport. Jane couldn't decide whether it was hypocrisy or ignorance—or both.

"Been with the governor for a couple of years now," she replied, but decided not to debate Foley's presidential aspirations. It wasn't worth it, she thought.

"I'm busy, but I thought it was a good time to see my family. It's been a while."

Boychuk nodded.

"That it has, Shoes…that it has," he said. "It's great to see you again."

"Same here, Brian." She gestured in the direction of the garage.

"My dad around?"

"Back there, cleaning his guns. I have a feeling he's gonna be surprised. I sure as hell am."

Jane and the sheriff made eye contact for another moment. Clearly, there was some residual attraction. Then she started walking towards the garage's side-door entrance. There would be no second hug.

"Watch your step out there, Chuck," she said. "You're a politician now…and a politician's *first* job is to get re-elected."

EIGHT

Jane entered the garage, and without making a sound, made her way to the rear of the building. Hubie was standing below his prized gun rack. He didn't hear her approach. Griz looked up at the sound of yet another arrival but didn't flinch. He was a retriever, not a watch dog.

Hubie had finished cleaning his shotgun and had turned his attention to a short-barreled Winchester 30-30. He had always liked this weapon. Its lever action allowed him to get shots off fast, and it didn't kick like a mule. With a twelve-power scope, he'd relate to his hunter friends, this sucker was ideal for kills under a hundred yards. Which was a good thing too, he thought; he couldn't see that far anyway. If his hands didn't twitch, this weapon could drop a deer in its tracks.

"Hi Dad," she said, finally.

He jerked his large and aging frame around to see who it was. Jane was immediately sorry for sneaking up on him.

"Dad…Dad, I didn't mean to scare you," she said, apologetically.

Recovering from the shock, Hubie stared with his mouth agape. He couldn't believe his eyes. There before him was a daughter he had not seen in…how many years?

"Jane….what're you doing here?"

Jane peered wistfully at her father but didn't know what her senses were telling her. Had she missed him? She wasn't sure. What about him? Was there any affection for her?

That their relationship could be described as indifferent didn't do justice to the word.

His nine-to-five position at the post office meant he was usually home every night. Not to mention for lunch too. As the village's sole postmaster, mail sorter, stamp seller and story teller, he could lock the door at noon every day and return by one fifteen. Every day. How many people can walk two blocks to their jobs? And maybe sneak in a twenty minute nap in their La-Z-Boys?

When Roberto would ask Jane about her father and what he was like, her answer was simple and direct: she really didn't know. The impression she had of him was that he had made *no* impression, or at least that was what she believed when she was a teenager. Hubie was the type of father who was always around but was never really there.

Maybe it was because she sensed her father never stood up for himself, at least with her mother. But perhaps that too was unfair. Hubie was a hardened Army veteran and had seen horrible combat. So, why was he so weak-kneed around his wife? Was it because he detested confrontation and preferred silence over battle? Play along to get along? What Jane did know was that her father couldn't get a word in edgewise with Donna around. So much so that he told his VFW pals he once didn't speak to Donna for almost ten hours. When surprised friends would ask why, he'd deadpan, saying, "I didn't want to interrupt her."

Jane could count on one hand how many times Hubie had watched her or her sister play sports. When he did attend, he'd arrive late and leave early, especially in the dead of winter when he'd run off to his night job plowing snow. In summer, instead of pulling up a lawn chair at the softball or soccer field as other parents did, he'd escape at dawn with his bass boat in tow. Or he'd simply stroll over to the banks of the nearby Oswegatchie, always alone and loaded with fishing tackle. Never mind hunting season. It was the same then too. Hubie had been a loner, and Jane guessed it was his way of grabbing an hour or two away from Donna. But was that any excuse for not being a father?

Her dad rarely, if ever, spoke of his Vietnam years. As a teenager—her curiosity started early—Jane had read stories in *Newsweek* and *Time* about combat veterans whose hearts and minds were as black as the river ice. They were thrill seekers, perverted by the power of a uniform and a carbine. Of course, most of the GIs transported unwillingly to Southeast Asia simply did their conscripted duty and just wanted to stay alive. She respected that. But there was a mercenary element as well, and Jane had hoped her father wasn't one of those guys.

The central question of her father's military career remained unanswered. Did he kill anyone? Well, she didn't know, because he never spoke of the war. However, that didn't stop Jane from trying to pry out a few nuggets of information. Vietnam had been over for a decade, but Jane— ever demanding, always skeptical—wanted details. Often, this meant jousting verbally about his military combat. She would set the bait.

"I know you were there, Dad," she would say, "but don't you agree now that Vietnam was a total disaster? Over fifty thousand Americans died in that friggin' war, and for what? So LBJ could say that he would not be the first American president to lose a war? And Nixon wasn't much better. They both lied to us!"

That did it. Hubie would rise to the challenge. He would respond with a tirade that bordered on bigotry, railing about the "goddamn red Chinese" and how they stirred up all kinds of crap. He would compare their atrocities to those of Hitler, and how "our friends…all those European pansies" would be goose-stepping today if America hadn't stepped in. Once he ended their conversation by saying he knew they called her Jane for a reason; there was more *Fonda* in her than Schumacher.

Why these memories returned as she greeted her father in his dimly lit garage for the first time in years was a mystery. But Morgantown had always had that effect on her. It was one of the reasons she had to escape.

"Is that all I get, Dad?" she asked. "No, 'Hi Jane, glad to see ya'?"

Hubie laid his rifle down on his work bench and clumsily moved to give his daughter a hug. "Of course, I'm…I'm glad to see you," he said as he stepped back to survey his offspring once again.

"I got your card, Dad," she said.

"Oh, good. I was hoping you would."

She nodded.

"So, I thought maybe I should drive up and see you…and surprise you."

"Well, that you did, Jane. It's been a long time. I was beginning to think that that governor of yours would never let you out of his sight, especially now that he doesn't want to be governor much longer."

Jane shrugged off his comments. Griz approached, asking this stranger for some affection.

"Who's this?" she asked.

"That's Griz," he replied. "Best damn huntin' hound I've ever had."

"Hi Griz," she said, bending down to stroke the fur under the dog's neck. She resumed her awkward conversation with her father.

"Guess now that Donna's not around anymore, you can have another dog?" she asked. She watched for a reaction from her father, and she got one.

"Now, why would you bring up something like that?"

Jane decided to tone it down. She'd made her point.

"The governor sends his regards," she said. "Only yesterday he asked me why I haven't been back in Morgantown for so long." It was a small white lie. The governor hadn't the vaguest idea of where Jane was from.

"I've been wondering that, too, daughter," Hubie said.

"Well, as I said, when I got your card, I thought I'd come and crash your Thanksgiving dinner…assuming there is one."

"Yeah, of course. We'll be going to Jo and Denny's. They'll be glad to see you too."

Jane rolled her eyes, and her father noticed it.

"Ah, yes, my sister and her loving and devoted husband. How are they?" Jane felt she needed to enquire. But her sarcasm was not entirely lost on Hubie.

"They're still next door. Let's go over!"

But Hubie was moving too fast for Jane.

"Whoa, Dad, not yet. Let me get used to being back in town for at least an hour or so, okay? Can I just get freshened up a bit first?"

Hubie nodded.

"That's fine," he said. "Why don't you head over to the house and do what you need to do."

Jane eyed her dad's guns and changed the subject.

"Still love to polish those howitzers of yours, eh?"

"I remember you used to be a pretty good shot, Jane," her father replied.

Jane looked affectionately at her father.

"Truth is, dad, I never liked the damn things. I would just shoot them off because you'd put one in my hands."

"Well, if that governor of yours gets his way, he'll take them all away from us," he said.

"No, he won't Dad. All he wants to do—"

Her words were interrupted again with another loud cough.

Hubie was concerned.

"You all right?" he asked. "That sounds pretty nasty."

But Jane waved him off. She would bide her time. She would sit down with him, and Joanne, at the right moment.

"I'm okay. I, uh, think I'll go over to the house and maybe take a shower, okay? Do you think Joanne will set another place for me?"

"I'm sure she will," he said.

She gave her father another hug, turned and exited the garage.

NINE

Jane emerged from the upstairs shower with a large bath towel wrapped around her and walked across the hall to her bedroom. Beneath her feet, the oak floors creaked loudly as she walked, prompting her to conclude that her childhood home needed work. But that wasn't going to happen; her father was likely quite content to leave it the way it was.

Hubie and Delores rarely ventured upstairs anyway, preferring to let Norma, their housekeeper, run the vacuum around once in awhile. Dee, as everyone affectionately called Delores, was his girlfriend of more than four years now. Although she owned a house not far away, Dee had been a frequent visitor to the Schumacher home. They slept in the large master off the kitchen on the first floor, the same room that Hubie had shared with Donna for three decades. Her father didn't seem to worry whether it was appropriate or not, and neither did Dee. Both felt enough time had passed.

As she climbed into a pair of tight blue jeans and a pale green pullover sweater, Jane scanned her old room. She had spent many untold hours here, but now it was barely recognizable. After their bitter argument, Donna had removed every vestige of proof that Jane had ever set foot in this bedroom. Just as well, Jane thought. Gone, mercifully, were her wretched teenage posters of Blondie and Twisted Sister and Pat Benatar. She smiled, shaking her head.

But where's my poster of Duran Duran? I loved that band, she thought.

Jane noticed the room had now been neutered. Its walls, which once boasted an attractive pinkish hue, were covered with Madras-style wallpaper that had lost its fashion long ago. Who wallpapers any more, she asked herself? She walked to the closet, opened the bi-fold louvered doors and peered inside. Aside from a winter coat that dated back to the Carter administration and a couple of pairs of dust-covered shoes, the closet was nearly bare. There was a lone hanger, sporting a checkered angora sweater.

"Jeez, why does he still keep this crap?" she muttered to herself.

Jane looked up at the top shelf and found what she was looking for—a stack of family photo albums. Stretching high on her toes, she removed several books from their resting place and returned to the bed. She wiped the dust from the albums and began turning the pages.

The albums contained more than a few memories. There were pictures of her and Joanne skipping rope and a photo of them posing on the first day of school. Might have been second grade, she thought. There were shots of them behind the wheel of Hubie's truck, being taught to drive by a reluctant tutor. Then there was a picture of their one and only family mutt. His name was Fred, a simple name for a dog. She had loved Fred but recalled how much Donna bitched and complained about the old beagle spaniel mix and how much he shed. What would she have said about Griz? Well, there would be *no* Griz.

Jane continued turning the pages. One photo attracted her attention. It was one of Joanne sitting at an upright piano that Donna bought at some estate auction when they were little. Donna had snagged the piano with her first paycheck upon landing that job at the Mobil station near their house. Old Mrs. O'Leary on Fifth Street had expired and her children couldn't wait to rid the dusty old barn of their mother's furniture. So Donna decided she'd move things around in the living room to accommodate the aging Baldwin. Of course, Hubie never had a vote. When he enquired how much she had paid for the piece of junk, Donna's droll reply was that she got it for a song. Get it, she asked?

Her mother was determined to learn how to play. After work and when Hubie was fishing or hunting, she'd sit down for an hour or two with Cecil Buchanan, the music teacher at MHS, for a private lesson. Jane and Joanne were too young to hear the rumors circulating around town about the good-looking Donna—then only about twenty-six or twenty-seven—and the divorced, thirtyish Buchanan.

This was Morgantown, after all, and every one of the townspeople knew each other—or if you didn't know them personally—you knew *of* them. Tongues wagged often in this hell hole, Jane thought. Only later, when they were in their teens, was Jane told by a mean and vengeful classmate that there might have been some hanky-panky going on. Who knows what the hell had happened? If it was true, Donna had a lot of nerve telling me to close *my* legs, Jane thought.

Her mother had quickly discovered that she had fingers of stone and mercifully—for everyone within earshot—lost her musical desires. The tortured sounds coming from the old keyboard often forced the girls to flee the scene. Maybe that was why Hubie sought refuge by the river? But Jane shook her head. It was more than bad music that chased her father away.

Fortunately, as Donna's interest in the Baldwin gradually declined, it was picked up by Joanne. Joanne's best friend growing up was Jennie Wong. Her parents had emigrated from China to open a take-out joint in the plaza, behind Donna's Mobil station. Jennie was the smartest kid in school by far, but that didn't stop jealous kids from calling her *Hong Kong Wong*, as if that impolite, even racist, moniker would diminish her skills. By the age of eight, Jennie had become adept at the keys and sat patiently for hours with her friend. Unlike her mother, Jane figured, Joanne had talent.

She continued flipping the pages and came upon one of the girls and their mother sitting at the picnic table in the back yard. "God, this looks like we haven't even reached puberty," Jane smiled. Wait a minute, she thought. There was a pattern here. Flipping back page after page, she saw it. Donna never smiled.

"What did she think? Her face would break?"

Finally, she spotted a photo that stopped her in her tracks. It was a picture of her and Brian Boychuk at their prom; she in a long dress and he in his new deputy sheriff's uniform. He was one good-lookin' rook, she conceded.

Slowly closing the album, she gazed absently around the room and became lost in thought. It had been more than twenty years since she'd set foot in this room and Jane wondered how her life had reached this point. Why had she impulsively returned to this place? What had she hoped to accomplish? Was she really intent on rebuilding her severed relationship with her family? Did she really want to?

After what seemed to be ten long minutes, but was actually much shorter, she gathered herself together. She stood up and returned the albums to the closet shelves. Her Black-Berry buzzed. It was a text from Roberto.

thinkin bout u. hows ur dad? more impt, how'r u? for effing sake call me

She chuckled to herself at Rob's choice of words. It was his attempt at profanity without actually cursing. She stared at his message for a moment before punching the delete button. She'd reply to him later.

Jane was about to leave the bedroom when she heard the unmistakable roar of a diesel-powered truck revving its engine in the driveway next door. She walked to the window and looked out. It was mid afternoon and it had clouded over. A threat of snow was in the air, she thought. It would be dark soon.

It was Denny in his driveway. He was working on the engine of his septic tanker. Her heart instantly skipped a beat at the sight of him and it wasn't one of affection. She knew any return to Morgantown meant she'd have to face her brother-in-law of two decades and she wasn't looking forward to it. But there was no way of avoiding Denny; he was part of one fucked-up family landscape.

Jane continued to stare at the former high school football star from her bedroom window. She watched as he shut the hood of the giant truck and grabbed a towel to clean his greasy hands. Then he limped towards the back steps to his house. It was only an hour away from Thanksgiving dinner, but he was still in his overalls. Even from this distance, she could sense the fury in the man.

Just then, a small car entered the driveway and came to rest behind Denny's tanker. It was her cousins Dan and Marjory arriving for the holiday feast. She watched as Denny halted briefly and, without as much as a wave to the couple, trudged up the steps and into the house.

Jane shook her head.

TEN

A dusting of light snow had begun to fall. Exiting the house, Hubie, Jane and Griz walked down the back stairs and made their way across the large yard towards Joanne's house. Not enough snow to worry about, the old man thought. But silently he pledged to get off his ass tomorrow and install the blade on the front of the truck. He could wake up and find a foot or more, and his customers wouldn't be happy.

Hubie knocked on the back door. He could just let himself in but always wanted to give Joanne and Denny a moment's warning. As they entered the kitchen, Jane saw Joanne near the stove. An apron covered the front of her dark blue pant suit and her long blond hair, dressed in a ponytail, flowed half way down her back. She was removing the turkey from the oven. On the top of the stove, pots were threatening to boil over. Wearing oven mitts, Joanne quietly cursed as she put the bird down and turned her focus to the steaming potatoes and squash.

Her back was to Hubie and Jane.

"I brought my specialty," Hubie said. "Broccoli and cheese."

Without turning around, Joanne said, "Thanks Dad... just put it over on the counter. It should stay hot."

Jane did a quick survey of Joanne's kitchen. The place hadn't changed in years, and it showed. Her appliances were antiques. The sink, chipped in a few places, was one of those form fitting ceramic models that came in one piece. On the floor, the linoleum looked like it had suffered water damage; it was torn and curling in a couple of corners. Counter space was nearly non-existent. Her kitchen had seen better days, but when those days were was anybody's guess, Jane thought.

"And I brought another guest, too, Jo," Hubie said, his voice rising with excitement.

Her back still to them as she administered to her meal, Joanne picked up a cloth and was drying her hands.

"Hi Dee," she said. "I'm glad that you were able to make it."

"Not Delores," Hubie replied. "She'll be here in a few minutes."

Curious, Joanne turned around.

Like her father an hour or so before, she was shocked into silence.

"Hi Joanne," Jane said in a low tentative voice.

Joanne was stunned. She did not know how to react. Her eyes remained frozen, staring at the sister she hadn't seen in years. Jane knew she would elicit this reaction but even she was surprised. Finally, she spoke.

"How are you?" Jane asked.

"I'm in shock, actually Jane...I, I never thought I'd see you in this town again."

"Well, all I can say is...never say never, Jo."

Their eyes remained locked. A moment or two passed before Joanne spoke, her voice becoming edgier, more direct.

"Oh, yeah? I seem to remember a whole lotta nevers. Especially after mom's funeral when you said you'd never set foot here again. And that was—"

She turned towards Hubie.

"—was, when Dad, seven or eight years ago?"

"Something like that, Jo," he said, feeling the tension in the kitchen. "But that was then and this is now. It's

Thanksgiving and I for one am glad to see your sister here today. And maybe you can be too?"

The two sisters continued to stare each other down.

After a few seconds, Joanne relented, giving Jane her approval to be in her home. No words were spoken; it was in her eyes. She put aside her cloth and the two moved forward to embrace.

"I am shocked as hell to see you, sister, but...glad you could make it," Joanne said. "Welcome home...I guess?"

"Thanks, Jo," Jane replied, clearly grateful that the anxious moment had passed. "It means a lot to me to hear those words."

The three stood awkwardly in silence.

Suddenly, from down the hall, Denny arrived in the kitchen, and it was clear that he had still been drinking. At the entrance, he came to an abrupt halt. He too was surprised at the sight of Jane—in his house.

"Well, Jesus-son-a-Christ!" he exclaimed, making no attempt to hide a big smirk. "Look what Griz musta dragged in!"

Jane shuddered.

The moment had arrived. Denny wasn't always a crude man, a concession she allowed herself to think from time to time. But did she believe it? There might have been a time when his roguish, country charm gave him some redeeming value—at least to others who didn't know him as well as Jane did. But when was that, anyway? She couldn't remember. Was it when he played defensive tackle for the Morgantown Marauders with such fire-breathing ferocity that he struck fear into every visiting quarterback?

All Jane could remember was just how fucking crazy he'd get when he donned that uniform. Or maybe he didn't need a uniform?

Maybe he was just fucking crazy.

He was seventeen and, whatever appeal he exuded, Joanne fell for it. He was one of the toughest kids in school, strutting through the corridors, testing anyone who dared to challenge him, much as a hardened lifer would do with a new arrival in the prison yard. Even then, Denny looked at least five years older than he was. He could grow a full beard in two weeks and that made him look even meaner.

It was then that he started drinking heavily and not just at the impromptu parties their gang would hold at secluded spots near the river and away from the disapproving eyes of the sheriff. It was no secret he kept a pint of vodka in his locker at school and would dive into it between classes. His beverage of choice was always beer—he could down as many as fifteen or more on any given night—but Denny always boasted that his asshole teachers never could detect the Smirnoff on his breath.

That he chose Joanne over other girls was never much of a mystery, at least to Jane. Entering high school, her sister was one of the prettiest girls in town and Denny wouldn't settle for anything less. The Marauders' quarterback, Josh Callaghan, was easily the best-looking hunk in school. But Denny, inexplicably, was as big a man on campus as Josh, perhaps for negative reasons. Other tough guys looked up to him, including all the greasers who hung around the town's only poolroom, the Cue 'n Cushion. Denny carried sway, an indescribable swagger and that was probably why Joanne had become smitten.

She likely could have had any of the boys in Morgantown. But she chose Denny. She told everyone she wanted to be Denny's girl.

Denny accommodated her wishes provided she accommodated his needs. You either put out or you moved on, he told Joanne. And so Joanne would. That was the price you paid to be his girl, and she accepted it. Jane never objected to Joanne's willingness to do what she needed to do. But she always questioned with whom, and from time to time Denny would notice the contempt she'd had for him. This irritated the hell out of Denny. His appeal worked on Joanne and, hell, at least a half a dozen others. Why didn't Jane buy it? That always pissed him off.

"Hello Denny," Jane said, coming face-to-face with the man for the first time in more than eight years. She looked him over. He had obviously showered since she saw him working on his truck an hour earlier, but he still looked scruffy and disheveled—not unlike the teenager she'd first met two decades earlier. She noticed that his hair still covered his ears. Once it had been the color of ground pepper, but was now almost entirely gray. His beard, as untrimmed as it was in high school, made him look gorilla-like. For the holiday, a time when most people dressed in finer attire, Denny arrived adorned in an un-buttoned, blue-flannel shirt over a well-worn T-shirt, complete with a breast pocket for his smokes. His blue jeans were tattered at the point where they touched the floor. It was not even four o'clock on Thanksgiving Day and he was already trashed.

"You haven't changed a bit, Denny," Jane said.

Denny shot her another of his sneers.

"Well, thank you, Janey. I'll take that as a compliment."

"You're welcome, Denny. I don't imagine you get many," she replied.

Jane's insult was lost on her brother-in-law, but Joanne caught it. She frowned but said nothing.

"Decided to slum it with us after all these years, huh Jane?" Denny asked sarcastically.

"Interesting choice of words," Jane replied.

Suddenly, Jane heard an inner voice again.

It was her mother's voice.

Take a look in the mirror, Jane. It's your own damn fault!

Jane blinked her eyes and shuddered. Back in Joanne's kitchen, she wondered if the others had noticed her double take.

She heard her sister intervening, admonishing her husband.

"Denny, can you cool it a bit?"

"I asked *her* the question, Jo," he barked. "Not you."

"I wasn't just talking about that. I meant the beer too."

But Denny continued to stare at Jane and ignored his wife's barb. Noticing the strained look on her sister's angst-ridden face, Jane decided to tone it down.

"I just thought it was time to see my family again," she said. "I hope that's not against the law."

Joanne was relieved.

"No, it isn't, and I'm happy you're here," Joanne said. "It's time to eat. Jane, can you help me with some of these dishes?"

Jane welcomed the request. Perhaps it would reduce the temperature in the kitchen.

"Would love to," she said.

Denny went to the fridge and helped himself to another beer. He and Jane locked eyes one more time. Another smirk.

Then he winked at her and vanished from the room.

ELEVEN

Sitting at the old walnut table, Jane couldn't recall a meal in Joanne's dining room, if there ever was one involving her. But she knew she'd been here before. She recognized all the furniture. Without exception, every piece once belonged to her mother and, after Donna died, Hubie had given the entire dining room set to his daughter next door and replaced it with another one. He figured the set would mean more to Joanne than it did to him.

The antique table had arrived the same day as the Baldwin piano. Now with its two leaves deployed, she could see it had sagged badly in the middle. Its unmatched chairs—threadbare and discolored—creaked with every move by its occupants. This caused Jane to wonder if the chair supporting her colossal brother-in-law would collapse under the stress. A well-worn oriental rug, thin as paper, supported the set.

Against the main wall rested a blond maple hutch. It too was out of sync with the rest of the room's decor, but attractive in its own way, Jane thought. Through the hutch's beveled glass doors—one pane was visibly cracked—Jane could see her mother's Our Lady of the Holy Name church plate on display. It was joined by a handful of Uncork New York wine glasses.

Everything was the same as she remembered, Jane thought. Right down to a couple of inexpensively framed prints depicting a scene from some river's edge, perhaps their very own Oswegatchie, but they could have been painted anywhere. The scene was one of ducks lifting off the water's surface, and that too brought back a memory, this time a pleasant one. As little girls, she and Joanne loved to feed the ducks that landed effortlessly on the river near their home. The opportunistic birds, knowing the girls had bread crumbs to offer, swam to greet them. It was only later she had learned their likely fate. That was when the season changed and some trigger-happy imbecile with a sixteen-gauge inevitably ended their graceful lives, and dogs like Griz went to work.

Jane found it sexist that her father seated himself at the end of the table while Denny anchored the other. Joanne, as hostess, was relegated to a place on the side, across from her, and near the kitchen where it was assumed she would be their cook and server. The feminist movement hadn't quite found Morgantown, she thought.

Dee had arrived too and was sitting next to Jane and across from cousins Dan and Marjory. A fit, attractive woman pushing seventy, Dee's most striking features were deep grayish-green eyes and fashionably spiked silver hair. Obviously, she had reached that magical age when smart women could say screw it and give themselves permission to renounce that ridiculous monthly ritual. This woman was beautiful and for a brief, fleeting moment, Jane found herself hoping she'd look this good when she was Dee's age. Yeah, right, she thought. Give your head a shake, Jane. Or as Donna would say, "that's rich!"

Still, she conceded, her dad always had good taste. Donna, after all, turned a lot of heads. Granted, so did her father—in his time. But what did Dee see in Hubie now?

Marjory and Dan were altogether different stories, an exercise in sibling contrast. They were Donna's brother's children, and both were single and childless. And she could see why. The dour-looking Marjory, a short-order cook and waitress at some hash house in Johnsville, a small village about ten miles from Morgantown, was as slender and pale as a poplar. She was in her mid-forties, a lifetime smoker, and it showed. Her hair—long, thick and dark—offered evidence of a purplish dye job gone awry. Then there was Marjory's perpetual frown that Jane remembered from when her cousin was a teenager. It was still there, she thought.

Her brother Dan, three years his sister's senior, was her opposite. Grossly overweight for his squat medium build, his bald head sporting an absurd-looking comb-over, Dan looked like a salesman bellying up to the bar at the end of a busy day. In fact, today he had trouble fitting into one of Joanne's dining room chairs. Jane always knew him to be a guy who smiled most of the time. But his constant state of contentedness perplexed her; why he was so happy was a mystery to her. He was a well-drilling contractor, she remembered, and spent his days operating noisy vibrating machinery in search of elusive new sources of water for farmers and cottagers nearby. As a result, he had become nearly deaf.

An uncomfortable silence enveloped the Lowry Thanksgiving table. Hubie had mumbled something that resembled grace but it sounded half-hearted. His late wife was the religious one in the family, and he didn't practice—or preach—any of the Lord's good works. Jane watched curiously as he passed a bottle of riesling around the table, a predictable choice if there ever was one. The vineyards sprouting up around the Finger Lakes were gathering momentum—even a few accolades—but they'd never be confused with those in Napa or the Central Coast. At least it didn't come from a box, she thought, as she waited to see who would accept his offer. The cousins poured themselves glasses, and so did Dee. Joanne declined, and so did Jane. She'd had enough to drink the night before.

Dishes were passed and cutlery clashed noisily with plates. Simple talk was heard, the perfunctory sounds of an uncomfortable moment. This prompted Jane to believe only a carving knife could sever the tension in the room. Maybe this wasn't a very good idea, she thought. I have nothing in common with *anyone* at this table. If these people weren't related, I'd have nothing to do with them. My being here just makes everyone nervous. Other than Denny, she observed. He was oblivious to just about everything.

With an enormous turkey dagger firmly held in one hand and a giant fork in the other, Denny stood above the bird proudly. He was the man of the house and was fulfilling his one and only holiday obligation. Probably the only time he contributed to a meal all year, Jane figured. Still, she was glad he was focused on the job at hand. Mercifully, it shut him up for a few minutes.

Finally, Marjory, the short order cook and server, piped up. She told the table about an incident at her restaurant. One of her young customers ate the peanut sauce on some fancy chicken satay—a dish that was a "bit too foofoo" for this county, she related—and reacted badly.

"Kid swelled up and almost died!" she exclaimed. "If it wasn't for old Doc Stewart being there—he was havin' his usual Yankee pot roast and smashed potatas—I don't know what woulda happened. Well, Stewart got out some sort of needle and the kid came back. But scarier 'n hell, that's for sure. I blame his mother. She shoulda known better. Is it our fault he can't eat friggin' peanuts?"

Her brother, catching about half her drift, spoke up.

"The kid musta gone into prophylactic shock!" he said, proud of himself. It was all Jane could do to stop from bursting out laughing.

Dee, too, caught it and grinned. She decided to change the subject.

"So, Jane, it must be pretty exciting to work for the governor?" she said.

"The job has its moments, but the hours are long and we're on the road a lot," Jane replied. Denny, his carving duties for the year now complete, sat down and refilled his glass with beer. He decided to weigh in.

"Well, isn't it awful that you pencil pushers down in Albany have to work a little bit now and then?" he said. "I have to work fourteen hours a day myself and no taxpayers are pickin' up the tab for me! Fact is, Foley's in the same business as I am." Denny paused a moment and with a look in his eye that told his family, *wait for it, here comes the punch line*. "Only he shovels more shit!"

Jane inhaled deeply as Donna's voice returned.

The only person you should blame is you, Jane. Just look at yourself!

Her heart skipped a beat. That damn woman! Slowly she returned her focus to the holiday dinner at hand. Denny shot Jane a look that dared her to react, but she didn't bite. Instead she returned his stare with barely hidden contempt. She was not going to dignify his boorish behavior with a response, she thought. Maybe Dad will step in and tell Denny he's being an asshole. But then again, probably not.

Marjory picked up where Dee left off.

"Weren't you a TV reporter before you went to Albany? That is, before you went to work for the governor?"

She turned to Joanne. "Isn't that what you told us, Jo?"

"Yes, Jane worked for a station in Rochester," Joanne confirmed.

Dan looked mystified.

"I didn't know you worked at the *train* station in Rochester, Jane," he almost yelled. "What did you do there? Sell tickets?"

Jane smiled but before she could answer, Marjory waded in.

"Dan, for God's sake, she said *TV station*—not the train station! Turn up your hearing aid!" She gazed across the table. "With all that pounding he does all day, he can't hear a damn thing!"

Jane continued her narrative, uncertain if anyone really cared. She told them that she had wanted to be a journalist since her first year at Oswego State in the eighties. What she didn't say was that she had been assigned to the crime beat and felt she'd observed every murderer, mugger and molester in western New York. There wasn't a scumbag in the city destined for Attica that she hadn't come in contact with or covered. At first, she liked the beat, knowing her stories always gave her top billing on the six o'clock newscast. Crime was the number one interest of her viewers, then and likely now.

But after more than two years of chasing cops and ambulances, Jane knew she had to get out, and when the Albany bureau posted an opening for a political reporter, she lobbied heavily for the job. Politics definitely flowed through her veins and she loved it. But it didn't take her long to discover that she had replaced one criminal element for another. The Rochester criminals were, at least, *honest* to themselves; they knew who they were. There was no bullshit. There were no pretentions. The Albany crooks, on the other hand, smiled at you and patted you on the back. Or on the ass if they thought they could get away with it—before uttering a bunch of lies.

So she began to hope that something—anything—would happen to her that would attract the attention of the *CBS* brass on West Fifty-Second Street. She needed to be liberated. She needed to board that last chopper out of Saigon. But nothing of national consequence ever occurred in Albany. Christ, Dan Rather got promoted to the network because a friggin' hurricane blew through Texas, and they liked his work. Then he found himself in Dallas when Kennedy was shot. Talk about being in the right place at the right time. Hurricanes never happen here. What do we get? Ice storms every hundred years?

Fortunately, when she was thirty-five—a time when most reporters go through mid-career crises—a little known fiber optics millionaire from some downstate town she'd never heard of called her and audaciously told her he was running for governor.

Jane looked around the Thanksgiving dinner table, and for their consumption, resumed her story.

"So, a few years ago, Foley called me to say he needed a press secretary for his campaign for governor, and asked if I was interested," she relayed. "He told me that he needed someone who knew the media and who would be straight with him. I told him I was prepared to serve, and after a couple of long meetings at his home where I got to know him, his wife and his political team, I jumped ship."

Jane noticed that all but Denny were listening raptly to her story. He never looked up from his plate.

"That sounds so exciting," Dee said. "I like Governor Foley. But your father and I don't see eye to eye on him."

"I don't trust him," Hubie grumbled.

"Dad, you don't like any Democrats. Who do you think gave you your Medicare and social security?"

"He's still a socialist," her father grumbled.

Jane stopped and stared at her father, incredulous at what he was saying.

"A socialist?" she asked. "Dad, his company created over five thousand jobs! Socialists don't do that!"

Joanne could see that any political discussion was a non starter at her table and decided to change the subject.

"Jane, Dad tells me there's a guy in your life?"

"Yeah," Denny chimed in, "probably guy number *eighty or ninety* since she left town!" He reveled at his attempt at humor but the rest of the table remained silent in embarrassment. Joanne glanced over at Jane; she could see she was attempting to control her anger.

It wasn't working. Jane reached for the bottle of riesling and poured herself a glass, deciding if there was ever a time for a drink, now was it. She downed it in one gulp, an act that didn't go unnoticed by Denny. He smirked once again.

"Last time I saw you drink like that, Janey, was at that party we had over on the lake," he said. "Remember that? When we just finished high school?"

She turned to him once again, her contempt barely below the surface.

"No...I don't remember that, Denny," she said, haltingly. His intentions were clear, she thought. He was attempting to diminish her in front of her family. To her sorry excuse of a brother-in-law, and many others, she had abandoned Morgantown and had made a success for herself. She was a target of resentment.

The memory of that night was one she had tried to suppress for a long time. But now, at least vaguely, it returned; it was a wild, teenaged romp and a story to which every high-schooler could relate. Still, she wasn't about to give Denny any satisfaction.

He continued.

"Well, I do, Janey. How you and Jack—Jack Daniels, that is—really went to town that night," he squealed with delight. "Looked like you were gonna puke…and that's when you had to find a place to sleep it off. Remember that?"

Jane poured herself another glass of the sweet riesling. God, isn't there anything else to drink but this crap?

Denny noticed, let out another chortle, and turned his attention to Dan.

"See, I'm not the only one who likes a buzz," he said.

Joanne had been following the conversation and decided to weigh in. She had seen her husband behave like this before, and she had to diffuse the situation. Her guests were becoming uncomfortable.

"Never mind him, Jane," she dismissed. "What's the name of your friend? Roberto something?"

"Yes, Roberto…Roberto Alvarez," Jane replied hesitantly. Yet another discussion she was hoping to avoid. "But I call him Rob. He's a lawyer in the city."

Denny piped in again.

"Just what that city needs!" he sniffed. "Another Puerto Rican lawyer!"

Cautiously, Hubie intervened for the first time.

"Denny, why don't you just drop it," the older man said.

But Jane's patience came to an abrupt end. She dropped her knife and fork down and had put up with enough. But she was a professional; she'd remain calm.

"For your—" She paused a moment. There would be no expletive. She would start over. "For your information, Rob is not Puerto Rican," she continued, staring her brother-in-law down. "He came here from Argentina when he was about fourteen or fifteen, but I don't expect you to know where Argentina is. He taught himself English and went to the one of the best universities in the United States. He's a smart, classy man. A very good man."

Satisfied that she might have shut him up, she retrieved her cutlery and resumed her meal.   But Denny wasn't finished.

"Well, the way I see it, a spic is still a spic, whether he's Mexican or Puerto Rican or Argentin-en or wherever he's from. If he's so good, why isn't he sittin' here with you right now? Seems to me that your spic friend probably had some-thin', or should I say *someone*, better to do today."

That was it, Jane decided.   Dinner for her was over. Inside, she was exploding.   But she wasn't about to give Denny the satisfaction of thinking he had won.   She turned and addressed her cousins and Dee.   Then she glanced at Joanne, and their eyes froze before she turned her attention to Hubie.

"I'm sorry but I'm really not very hungry," she said. "And I'm pretty tired too, so maybe I'll just head back to your place, okay Dad?"

Denny, now grinning ear to ear, sensed victory.

"What's the matter Jane?" he said as she rose from the table. "Hit a bit of a nerve, did I?"

The others just sat there, shocked and saddened by his insults. Jane ignored him; immediately, her worst fears were confirmed.   Coming home for Thanksgiving, or any other time, was a bad idea.   She would have to leave.

"Dee, it was very nice to meet you. Dan, Marjory, good to see you again too.   Say hello to Uncle Henry for me.   I'm sorry...but I've got to leave.   Maybe before I say something that I might regret."

Jane exited the dining room.

Joanne arose from her seat and followed quickly behind, catching up with her sister just as Jane was about to open the kitchen door.

"Jane, Jane, wait!" she said. "I'm so sorry."

"I am sorry, too, Jo. But wait for what?" she demanded. "For you to wake up and see what a douche bag Denny really is?"

Joanne, momentarily stunned by Jane's comments, struck back.

"Who the hell are you to come into my house and say that to me? You show up after how many years and have the gall to criticize my life? You're the one who bailed on us, remember?"

Jane glared into her sister's eyes as the two women paused to digest everything that had happened over the last several minutes. There was no use arguing further.

Then she noticed the greenish-black bruise creeping up Joanne's lower neck. It was barely visible above a blouse that had been buttoned nearly to the top. Jane was surprised she hadn't seen it before.

Pointing to it, she confronted her sister.

"What the hell is this?"

"Never mind. It's none of your business!" Joanne replied, pushing her sister's pointing finger away.

A dreadful sinking feeling came over Jane.

Something was very wrong.

"That son of a bitch is hitting you, isn't he?" she screamed. "He is, isn't he, Jo? Admit it!"

There was no response from her sister other than over-whelming sadness in her eyes. That was all the confirmation Jane needed.

"That mother*fucker*!" she cried. "That *is* what he's doing to you! Fuck!"

Joanne's eyes begin to well up. She bowed her head.

"You don't know the whole story, Jane," she said, so inaudibly that Jane had a difficult time hearing her. "How could you?"

Though seething with anger, Jane decided it was not the time to continue the confrontation any longer. She would revisit this topic at another time. Or maybe not. She had enough problems of her own.

But right now, she had to leave the house.

"I need some fresh air, Joanne," she said. "No, fuck that. I need a bath."

And she was out the door.

TWELVE

An hour later, Jane emerged from the shower, the third pelting of the day counting the one she'd had back at her Albany condo. Once again she had allowed the scalding hot water to beat down on her for what seemed an eternity. She needed to rid herself of the physical and emotional demons inside. It didn't work. She was cleaner, indeed fresher, but the morose mood that had enveloped her from the time she left Joanne's house was still there.

This is all I need right now, she thought.

From her upstairs bathroom, she had heard her dad and Dee returning from next door, but she was in no mood to talk to anyone, let alone Hubie. Jane didn't know with whom she was more angry—that fucker Denny or her father. Well, it was no contest, of course. Denny was clearly an evil man. But Hubie *lived* next door to them for more than…how many years? He had to have known what Joanne had been going through.

Hubie may have sensed that Jane was unwilling to talk about their disastrous dinner because it was Dee who arrived at her bedroom door. It was as if Jane was thirteen again and returning from her first date.

Only Donna had never seemed to care if she was all right. She simply used the occasion to berate Jane over something.

But Dee was different.

"Are you okay?" Dee inquired, as she watched Jane pull a large comb through her dark damp hair in smooth, uniform strokes. Jane had always found combing to be one of the most therapeutic things she could do. Especially when she was under considerable duress. Like now.

"Yeah," she said, somberly. "It's been one totally shitty day, and I just needed to be alone. You know what I mean?"

"I understand, Jane," Dee said. "We'll leave you alone for a couple of hours. Your father and I think it best that we spend some time at my place. It's not far from here."

Jane shrugged, signaling her approval.

"I'm sorry I made such a mess of Thanksgiving," she said. "I hope I didn't embarrass you or my cousins too much. It's just that goddamn brother-in-law of mine—"

But Dee just shrugged it off.

"No need to say anything more, Jane," Dee said. "We all have been subjected to his behavior before...unfortunately."

In sympathy, the two women paused as if to absorb the boorish events of Thanksgiving. They retreated into silence. But a moment or two later, Dee made good on her offer to leave the younger woman alone, said her good-byes and was soon making her descent to the first floor.

Jane finished combing her hair and got dressed. But she couldn't escape the notion that Joanne was likely a victim of habitual spousal abuse. Oh, fuck the euphemisms, Jane, call it what it was! Denny was a scum-sucking wife beater of the first order! And it was enough to make her throw up. The tears appeared again, briefly, but goddamn it, she wasn't going to let him or anything else make her cry again. *Fuck*, she repeated. What did Joanne do to deserve any of this?

Jane made her way down the stairs and into the kitchen, where Griz immediately greeted her. She gave him a quick pat and walked to the refrigerator. She hadn't eaten much of Joanne's turkey dinner before the debacle and now she felt she was still a bit hungry. Opening the refrigerator, she saw the leftover broccoli that Hubie had made and thought of him.

Just like dad. She hadn't seen him in eight years and, at the first opportunity, he makes his escape to a safer haven. In the past, it was his bass boat, or that spot down by the river or a friend's hunting cabin. Today it was Dee's house.

Alone, she sat at her mother's kitchen table and tossed spears of broccoli from side to side. Maybe she didn't have much of an appetite after all. Maybe first thing in the morning, she'd pack up and drive to Hunter Mountain and salvage something of this holiday weekend. With everything going on right now, she didn't know if she could deal with Joanne and all her problems, anyway. Joanne has to figure this shit out for herself. Why is it my problem? I have enough of my own. Yes, I'll head over to Hunter tomorrow and be there by noon. Rob would like that and so would I, she acknowledged. I'll call him later when I can get my act together.

She finished picking at the broccoli and decided to throw the rest out. As she was walking to the trash, Jane had another painful coughing bout. Jesus...I thought another hot shower would give me some friggin' relief? But I guess not. She opened up the trash receptacle to find an overflowing bag and silently cursed her old man once again. Can't he even take the garbage out? Should Dee have to do everything?

Donning her winter boots, but still coatless, Jane stepped out into the cold air and noticed that the afternoon's dusting of snow had turned the grounds into a crisp cottony white. Griz followed her out and immediately went to his favorite fence post. The gray, ominous cloud cover that filled the skies over the Adirondack foothills had again disappeared; now a full moon was rising in the east, from the direction of the mountains, and a universe of brilliant blue stars made the snow sparkle. She breathed in the fresh air, and winced. The pain was relentless. Even these fresh northern winds can't help me much, Jane thought.

Suddenly, from the direction of Joanne's house next door, she heard a loud commotion. Even fifty yards away, the sounds were clear and unmistakable. They were the sounds of her sister's screams, followed by crashing dishes and breaking furniture.

Jane quickly made her way across the lawn and peered through the dining room window. Inside, she could see Denny towering over his frightened wife. She could see the fear in Joanne's eyes as she tried to get out of the violent man's way. The room was a mess.

Denny, now raging drunk, was getting meaner and meaner by the second.

"How dare you bring that fuckin' bitch in here?" he yelled, his bellowing voice reverberating throughout the house. "It was bad enough that Dan, that bald-headed, fat ass showed up, and brought his beanpole sister with him. But then, Jane comes!"

Joanne looked frightened and small.

"I didn't know she was coming either, Denny...but it's my house, too," she replied meekly, not knowing how to respond. She had been in this position before and her instinct was to protect herself. And hope that Denny would tire quickly and pass out.

"Your house too?" he questioned. "That's a goddamn joke, and you know it, Jo. What the fuck do you do for this house? You're nothin' but a clerk in a two-bit hardware store!"

Grimly, Joanne tried to avoid direct eye contact with her husband. She knew from experience that it just set him off even more. But she wasn't about to give in—yet.

"I can invite anyone I want to," she said.

"Wrong!" he bellowed again.

With his temper exploding, he grabbed Joanne by the throat and threw her violently against the dining room wall. Her framed prints dropped like lead weights, their glass shattering as they landed on the oak floors. In the hutch nearby, glasses, cups and saucers also fell, breaking into dozens of pieces. The last to go was Donna's prized church plate. It too became a victim, teetering back and forth like a college student on a midterm bender before it finally came crashing down.

"This is my house, and you better not forget it," he continued. "The house that shit built. My shit!"

Reaching over, he grabbed Joanne's ponytail powerfully, jerking her head back in excruciating pain. Forcefully, he yanked her away from the wall and she screamed in utter horror. It was happening again.

"Denny, please—"

She pleaded with her husband to stop.

But Denny ignored her and with one swift backhand delivered a fierce slap across the face and this sent her flying once again. Blood began trickling from her swollen bottom lip.

He moved quickly to his injured and distraught wife and was raising his hand to punch her lights out again when he felt the double barrels of a shotgun jabbed firmly into the back of his neck.

"Hit her again *asshole*, and I'll blow your sorry-ass brains all the way to Buffalo!"

It was Jane, and she had one of her dad's shotguns.

Denny, although still very drunk, was taken by surprise.

"What the fuck?" he exclaimed.

"You heard me asswipe!" she repeated, rage growing in her voice. "Now, get away from her, or I swear I'll blow your *fucking* head off!"

Denny released Joanne and slowly turned around. She moved quickly from her husband and joined Jane.

He smirked.

Suddenly, Jane's inner voice returned. Yet again, another visit from her mother. And she quivered at the haunting memory.

Take a good look in the mirror, Jane. You only have yourself to blame...

Gasping audibly, her heart racing, Jane returned to the horrific scene unfolding in her sister's dining room on Thanksgiving night. A hateful expression remained splashed across Denny's face.

"You shouldn't be stickin' your nose in other people's affairs, *city bitch*!" he said, as he continued to stare down the barrels of the shotgun. She doesn't have the nerve to use that thing—and she knows it, he thought. Fuck, she's been gone so long, she's probably forgotten how.

Jane seemed to be reading his mind.

"Wrong, as you would say, asshole," Jane replied. "My sister *is* my business. And right now, she *is* leaving you—and this house."

Denny focused his attention on his frightened wife.

"Jo, I'm warnin' you, you walk outta here, you don't come back!"

But Jane was undeterred. She gave her brother-in-law a long look of contempt, one that was years in the making. This weapon, she thought, was the great equalizer. Even Denny wasn't that stupid.

Was he?

"You're smarter than I thought," she said. "Not much mind you, since you've always been the biggest dumbass moron I've ever known. But this time you're right. Joanne *is* walking out. And she's *not* coming back!"

The voice of her mother paid another visit.

The way you traipse around...how can you blame anyone?

Jane blinked once again.

"Go ahead, then," Denny said, glaring at his wife. "Get your ass outta my house! You think I need you?"

Joanne remained silent. She was in shock.

"Well, what's wrong? Cat got your tongue?" he demanded. "Have nothin' to say? You're usually pretty lippy, Jo. But with your sister pointing that gun, you gettin' braver?"

That incensed Jane.

"Just shut the fuck up, Denny!"

He smirked at her order. Then he turned again to speak with his wife.

"Well, I don't need you or your fuckin' sister. All you're good for is a fuckin' paycheck, and even then your lousy five hundred bucks a week never paid for shit! And guess what, bitch? I can name five or six local strays who can fuck better 'n you, anyway. Better 'n you ever could!"

Joanne's eyes began to tear up, but she wasn't going to give Denny the satisfaction of thinking he had hurt her—again.

Jane signaled to her sister that it was time to leave. She lowered the shotgun to her side.

"C'mon, Jo...let's leave this fucking loser behind."

They made a half turn, and as they began to leave the dining room, Denny became infuriated.

"I mean it!" he screamed. "You go with that cunt, and you can say good-bye to this so-called house of yours—forever!"

Jane stopped in her tracks. She turned once again to face Denny.

"What did you call me?" she calmly demanded.

"You heard me."

"I probably did, but you might want to say it again?"

His sneer returned.

"What, *cunt*, your ears plugged?"

Jane took several steps forward.

"That's what I thought you said," she replied. Denny looked into her eyes; he knew he'd struck a chord.

Raising the shotgun level with her hips, Jane fired the first cylinder directly at Denny's balls. The tremendous force threw him backwards, slamming him against the same dining room wall that he had thrown his wife against only moments before.

Eyes bulging, he was stunned.

A split-second look of shock, of disbelief, came over him. The bitch actually shot me, the look on his face said. But it lasted only a moment or two as his eyes started to glaze over. He was in grimacing, overwhelming pain.

Joanne screamed.

Denny regained focus, a semblance of consciousness, enough to begin berating Jane once again.

"You fuckin' bitch...you shot me," he said, almost whispering, his knees buckling, his face contorted. As he began to slide down the wall, their eyes locked; his in abject surprise, hers in absolute hatred.

But Jane wasn't finished.

She pulled the second trigger.

This time, her target was clearly and coldly intentional. It was to Denny's chest. The earsplitting blast blew a large hole in his enormous frame. His blue-checkered shirt turned mostly red.

Blood and body tissue splattered against the wall.

Denny fell to the floor, sitting up. His eyes wide open, still in shock.

He was dead.

THIRTEEN

Jane stormed through the light snow between the houses, still carrying the deadly, smoking weapon. Only steps behind her, a rapidly moving silhouette, Joanne was in pursuit and screaming at the top of her lungs.

"Jesus, Jane, you killed my husband," Joanne yelled, as they made their way to Hubie's house.

Abruptly, Jane stopped and turned toward her sister.

"I should have done it—no, make that *you* should've buried that bastard a long time ago, Jo," she yelled.

"But he's my husband!"

"For Christ's sake, Joanne, he was bad! That fucker's been hurting you for a long time! When were you gonna realize that? Huh? When?"

Joanne remained stunned and couldn't find an answer. Their eyes became paralyzed for a moment. Jane's words had astonished her. A few seconds passed, and then Jane turned and continued her journey across the yard.

"I'm getting the hell out of here—now," she announced, and she marched up the porch stairs and into the house.

Joanne stood in the light snow, motionless and in shock.

Her father's house was silent and empty; it gave Jane the eerie, unmistakable feeling that she was very much alone. What the hell had she just done, she asked herself? What the hell just happened?

For a moment, she just stood there, breathing erratically, attempting to find answers. Then she was on the move again. Bounding up the stairs to her second-floor bedroom, she made her decision. She rolled her luggage bag towards the bed and indiscriminately began to throw her clothes inside. She always knew that she was a smart but impulsive woman. But now she wondered, what the hell had made her pull that trigger? If she was carrying a gun, wasn't she prepared to use it? All she set out to do was get Joanne away from that sorry excuse for a human being...that fucking waste of skin.

Shaking her head as if to rid herself of a horrific memory, she knew she had to get the hell out of there. She ran to the bathroom, dropped her toothbrush and other toiletries in her bag and made her way back down the stairs. For a moment, she lingered in her mother's large, country kitchen.

If this was the last time she'd set foot in this room...

All of a sudden, Jane heard her mother's voice again. Goddamn it!

Admit it, Jane, if you hadn't played so fast and loose, you wouldn't be in this trouble...it's your own damn fault...

She scanned the kitchen again.

It was empty.

It had been twenty years. So why was she hearing that voice again? Shivering from fear and shaking her head, Jane grabbed her ski jacket from the rack and flew out the back door. She had forgotten about Griz. He was sitting on the back steps shivering; she opened the door for him and he scooted into the house.

As she made her way quickly to her Mercedes, Joanne's old Explorer suddenly tore into the driveway and braked hard behind Jane's car. The snow from earlier in the day was now turning the driveway into a thin layer of ice. But that was not an issue for Joanne's heavy four-wheeler and its tires.

Joanne jumped from the vehicle, leaving the door open and the engine running.

"Where's Dad?"

"At Dee's," Jane replied. "As usual, made himself scarce."

Joanne looked into her sister's eyes, and Jane could see— for a brief moment—that fire and independence that she once knew.

"Well, you're not leaving without me!" Joanne announced. "I'm going too!"

Jane frowned.

"Oh, Christ, listen to you."

"I'm going!"

Jane rolled her eyes, and it wasn't lost on her sister.

"Don't look at me that way, Jane!" she replied. "You're so damn condescending!"

"You don't even know where I'm going, Jo. Hell, I don't know where I'm headed. I just know that I have to get the fuck out of here."

Joanne paused a moment before responding. Her Confederate blue-gray eyes seemed to be pleading with Jane to understand the situation from her standpoint.

"I can't stay here either, Jane."

"Why not? Just blame all this shit on your crazy, fucked-up sister!"

Joanne raised her head, seemingly to survey the same moon and stars that Jane had enjoyed only a half hour earlier. Then she glanced at her ramshackle house next door. Only a single porch lamp was lit, casting its lonely, orange-colored beam across the lawn between the two houses. She had turned off all the interior lights when she left. Why did she do that? Was it because, maybe—just maybe—they wouldn't find out what had just happened if the house stayed dark? Maybe no one would find out? Well, that was wishful thinking. She knew she couldn't go back.

"Jane, it wouldn't be that easy," she said. "Nobody would believe me. Everyone in this town knows Denny or who he was. And when they find him, half of them will say, 'it's about time' while the other half'll say, 'it had to be his wife.' I don't think they'd believe me even if I said it *was* you!"

Her eyes began to well up and Jane felt her pain. But she remained silent.

Joanne continued. "Either way, I don't want to deal with this right now. So, let's take this truck. That fancy car of yours will just get us stuck somewhere."

Jane took a deep breath. She nodded, reluctantly agreeing with her sister.

"Okay, but I'm driving," she said, reaching for her luggage from her car. She shut the door and started walking back to the Explorer when she stopped abruptly.

"Wait, one more thing," she said.

She returned to her car, opened the back door and retrieved Hubie's shotgun and a box of shells. Joanne stood there, watching in dismay.

"Why are you bringing that thing?" she demanded.

"I don't know," Jane shrugged. "Maybe I'll find a skeet range! Maybe we'll have to eat what we shoot. Maybe I'll have to shoot another son of a bitch who gets in my way! All I know is… I'm not leaving here without it."

Into the dead of an Adirondack night the girls fled the scene. They drove through the town's deserted center and beyond. As they passed row upon row of modest homes built during a distant era, Jane couldn't help but notice that families—*normal people*—were enjoying Thanksgiving the way it should be enjoyed, in a proper and loving way. Not our family, she thought.

After what seemed to be a perpetual silence, but was really only minutes, Joanne rolled the passenger window down an inch and fired up a cigarette.

Jane was not pleased.

"Do you have to smoke in here?"

"It's my truck," Joanne replied.

"But I'm sitting right next to you!"

Joanne frowned.

Taking two quick drags, she rolled her window down further and with her thumb and forefinger together flicked her cigarette out into the night. They resumed their stony silence as Jane guided the truck over the same two-lane road she had traveled earlier that day, a route she didn't think she'd have to traverse again this soon. Finally, Jane looked over at her sister, who seemed deep in thought.

"For how long?" Jane asked. Her voice so low that she wasn't sure Joanne had heard.

"What do you mean?"

"You know what I mean."

Joanne decided not to respond. Instead, she exhaled loudly and kept her eyes on the lonely road. That said it all.

"That long, huh?"

But Joanne was resolute. She wasn't ready to talk about her husband and his long list of sins. Instead, she continued staring out into the wilderness before changing the subject.

"Oh my God...Brent!" she cried. "I have to tell Brent."

Jane was surprised. There hadn't been a mention of Joanne's twenty-year-old son throughout her brief time in Morgantown, and Jane had almost forgotten about him.

"Tell him?" she asked. "Tell him what? That his aunt is a sewer-man killing lunatic?"

Joanne became livid.

"If you're trying to be cute, Jane, you're not! I'm still freaking out about all this. I...I just want to be the one who tells him about Denny. Before...he hears it from anyone else."

"What are you going to say to him?" Jane asked.

"I have no idea, but I have to tell him myself."

"I have my phone. You could call him."

"On a cell phone, Jane? Join the real world, will you? I have to do this face-to-face with my son. Now, turn right up here, near Boonville, and we'll take the Thruway to Syracuse."

Jane realized that there was no stopping her sister now.

They would go to Syracuse.

"Jeez, you know your way around these back roads," Jane said.

It was Joanne's turn to be sarcastic.

"I live here, remember?"

FOURTEEN

Hubie awoke at daybreak and rubbed his eyes before he glanced over at Delores, admiring what he saw. Awake or not, Dee was an attractive woman, and Hubie considered himself a lucky man. Not many women her age managed to look this good, he thought. Hell, most men too for that matter, including me. Dee was not like Donna, although his wife always maintained her inherent physical beauty right up to a few months before she died. Donna's personality, well, *that* was another thing altogether.

The elderly man slowly lifted himself out of bed, donned a pair of pants and a denim shirt before heading to the bathroom. His aching back told him that he needed to make the trek to the chiropractor on Monday. For years, he had looked down his nose at the quacks, as he called them, while increasing his dependence on large bottles of Advil. That was until one day last spring when the drugs didn't work and he could barely walk—or move for that matter. He knew why, of course; he had a bad back simply because he had a bad *front*. The solution was to lose at least thirty pounds. But that would have meant cutting back on his beer.

Reaching the kitchen, he turned the coffeepot on. Dee always tried to make his life easier, he thought, and for that he was grateful. He promised himself that he would make a greater attempt to return her good deeds with one or two of his own. Hubie peered out the window and noted that it had turned clear and cold overnight. Snow in large amounts would arrive soon.

"That plow goes on this morning," he said, talking to himself, a habit that he discovered he was doing more and more each day. "And get some salt and sand loaded too."

He noticed that Jane's Mercedes remained in the driveway. It hadn't moved since she arrived yesterday at noon. She must be asleep. Still, maybe he'd check, and he trotted down the hall and trudged slowly up the stairs. Puffing and panting, he reached her room and found the door slightly ajar. He peaked in. No sign of her. The bed remained made, and she wasn't there. No sign of luggage either. He raised an eyebrow. Where the hell could she be? She was in a foul mood last night when she left the dinner table so quickly. Maybe she went to a motel? But she would have taken her car, wouldn't she?

The retired postmaster returned to the kitchen and glanced out the window again, this time at Joanne's house. Denny's septic truck was parked in the driveway, but there was no sign of Joanne's Explorer. Maybe she put it in the garage last night?

He wrapped himself in his winter coat, slipped on his galoshes, and trudged out the back door with Griz following close behind. Moments later, he was in Joanne's kitchen.

"Hello? Anyone up yet?" he asked. "Jo? Denny? Anyone around?"

No answer.

Hubie removed his boots and continued down the hallway past the living room.

Still nothing.

The house was as tranquil as a church. Only the steady, distinctive hum of Joanne's old refrigerator could be heard.

He stopped and returned to the kitchen, wondering where everyone was. They can't still be in bed, he thought. At the least, Joanne should be up by now. Where was Denny?

Probably sleeping off the beer. But his daughter was always an early riser.

Hubie was about to reenter the kitchen and return home when he noticed out of the corner of one eye a few shards of broken glass on the floor near the entrance of the dining room. There was also an odd, foul-smelling odor wafting through the house. Something really strange was going on, he thought, as he walked slowly down the hall. Reaching the entrance to the dining room, he surveyed the broken glass spread throughout the hall. Slowly, he peered around the corner and into the room where he and his family had dined the night before.

Gasping, he came upon the shooting scene. There was blood everywhere. The horrific sight of his son-in-law propped against the wall, bloodied and blue, sent a thunderbolt through his aging frame. He felt a series of sharp pains across his upper torso, and suddenly another vision arrived. It was as if he was aloft a crowded emergency ward, peering down upon himself, as some overworked intern applied a pair of faulty defibrillators to his chest cavity. It scared him.

As he surveyed the grisly mess, Hubie immediately regretted his curiosity. Denny's eyes were open but he recognized the unmistakable sign of death. He had seen this many times before during his tour of Vietnam, when the convoys he'd led came upon U.S. soldiers ambushed by the Viet Cong. But this was different, well beyond his wildest nightmares.

Hubie never thought he'd witness a death scene like this.

In his own daughter's house.

He nearly buckled over before reaching out to the archway for support. Oh my God, he mumbled, oh my God…

After a few moments, Hubie gathered himself together and made his way back to the kitchen. His heart racing, it took every ounce of his strength to lift Joanne's wall-mounted phone from the receiver and punch in the numbers.

Finally, a response.

"Brian?" he asked, his voice still breaking. "Yeah, it's Hubie. Listen, Brian, you'd better get over here."

He paused to listen to the sheriff's questions.

"It's Denny...it's not good. Get here fast. I'm at their place."

Once again, he remained silent. His sheriff friend continued to bombard him with questions. The older man took another deep breath before answering.

"He's...uh...dead, Brian. Looks like gunshot wounds to me."

Another short pause.

"I'm okay. Just get here, will ya?"

Hubie stood and hung up the phone.

Covering his mouth and chin with one hand, he pulled up a kitchen chair and collapsed, trying to make sense of it all.

He was in shock.

FIFTEEN

The old Explorer was parked on a side street outside a four-storey apartment building that was likely built after the Second World War. The sun had risen but the hilly streets running through Syracuse University were quiet. The campus had been shut down for the holiday weekend, and its students for the most part had dispersed. The day before, the nearby Carrier Dome had been filled to the gunnels for the Notre Dame game, and as usual the *Orangemen* had been shut out by the *Irish*.

It wasn't pretty. They got smoked.

With the exception of a city bus slowly making its way through the campus, the streets were nearly vacant. Inside the SUV, the sisters had pushed their seats back and the vehicle had served as their hotel for the night. Jane's eyes popped open, and it dawned on her where they were and what had happened the night before. Yes, she had succumbed to Denny's provocations. And, yes, she had pulled the triggers. But given her training and skill, not to mention her intelligence, she should have handled it better. Still, an odd feeling of remorselessness enveloped her. She knew she had reached the point of no return. There would be no turning back. It was what it was, she thought. The real question now was: where do I go from here?

But first things first. She nudged Joanne.

"Jo, wake up," she said.

Still wearing her winter jacket, Joanne startled awake. Fear overcame her once again. She was in her truck, and reality was setting in. All she could see was the gray faded ceiling fabric above her and the cigarette burns she had inflicted over the years. Her tongue circled her swollen bottom lip and she tasted a hint of dried blood. The horrific memory of the night before returned, and she groaned.

"Shit, this really is happening," she said. "And it's cold in here. What time is it?"

"Close to eight," Jane replied.

"I think I feel sick," Joanne said.

"Which building is Brent's again?" Jane asked.

"I told you last night!"

"It was friggin' dark! You don't have to rip me a new one, you know," Jane shouted, immediately regretting the tone of her voice. She knew her sister was having a hard time.

"It's that one, right?" Jane pointed to the largest building across the street, one of many brown-brick apartment blocks that were common on campus.

"I think so. I've only been here once myself, last spring," Joanne said, as she gazed almost painfully at her son's sanctuary, his safe haven from the difficult relationship he'd had with his father.

At eighteen, Brent jumped at the chance to leave both Morgantown and his father behind. In the process, however, it seemed he had abandoned his mother as well. Denny had prohibited her from visiting Brent, and only when he'd disappear on an overnight hunting trip was she able to slip down to Syracuse for an hour or two. Once in a while, Brent would text her to say he was back in Morgantown and she'd ask Darryl for an extra hour for a brief encounter. All in secrecy. It was like she was having an affair with a man half her age.

"Well?" Jane asked.

"Well what?"

"Well, are you going in or not?" Jane prodded.

Just then, the front doors of the old building opened and a young couple emerged. They stopped momentarily at the top of the large, concrete flight of steps to survey the weather. The sun was shining and it was a near cloudless day. The young man found a pair of gloves in his leather jacket and put them on. Having zipped her coat, the young woman, blonde and ponytailed, adjusted her earmuffs. He reached for one of her free hands, and they walked gingerly down the ten or twelve steps to the street.

"Brent!" Joanne said, her eyes lighting up at the sight of her son.

"That's Brent?" Jane asked. "Wow, has he ever grown!"

Jane started the engine.

"C'mon, let's catch up with them."

"Wait!" Joanne said.

"Wait? Wait for what? That's why we're here."

"I...I can't, Jane. I just can't."

"Why not?"

"Why not?" Joanne replied, vehemently. "Why not? Just think of what you just said, Jane. What the hell would I say to him? I really don't know what I would tell him."

Jane took a deep breath.

"Well, if you want, I can tell him. After all—"

"No! That's not your job. I'm his mother."

"Oh, I get it," Jane replied. "You'd not only have to explain *what* happened to his shithead father—"

Joanne interrupted her sister in midstream.

"—don't call him that!"

But Jane was undeterred.

"—but *why* too."

Joanne continued to stare out the window. She watched as Brent and his girlfriend walked briskly down the hill before disappearing around a corner. She could really use a cigarette, she thought. But she knew that her sister, the dictator, would force her to leave her own truck to do that.

Joanne broke their brief silence.

"That's not it, Jane," she said. "Brent would know why. He's smart enough to figure it out. He's known for a long time what's been happening."

She turned towards Jane and was now near tears.

"He would know why...and that's what scares me," Joanne said. "Listen, Denny is...well, *was*...an awful man. But he wasn't always that way or at least not that bad. There was a time..."

Her voice trailed off as she collected herself and her thoughts. Jane could see the pain in her eyes.

"I guess...the only thing Denny gave me was Brent. And he's all I have now."

Jane sat there in silence, listening and thinking. Well, that wasn't totally true; Joanne has Dad, and Dee, and me too, for that matter, she thought. But she wasn't about to mention that.

At least not now.

"You could leave him a note," she suggested. "To let him know you were here...that you were thinking of him."

Joanne glanced at her sister and slowly shook her head. If she couldn't discover the courage to speak to her son directly, why would she leave him a letter?

Jane continued. "Or maybe I should? I am, after all, his wacko, absent-from-his-life Aunt Jane. And maybe that would help in some way?"

Sensing her sister's approval, Jane grabbed a piece of yellow paper from the glove compartment and composed a note. Folding it, she jumped from the truck, crossed the street and entered the foyer of the apartment building. She stood there, scanning the tenant listings and found 'Lowry 2-C.' She jiggled the main door but it was locked. She was ready to give up when she spied another young couple about to leave the building and waited until they opened the door.

Riding the small, single-door elevator to the second floor, Jane walked the long hallway until she found Brent's apartment. She shoved her note under his door and, as she was about to retrace her steps, another young man delivering flyers passed her. She nodded politely and made her way back to the front entrance.

Crossing the street, Jane could see Joanne leaning on her truck, smoking. Without a word, she nodded to her sister. Joanne dropped her cigarette on the ground beside the truck and stepped on it. They opened their doors, jumped in and pulled away.

SIXTEEN

Police vehicles barricaded the Lowry driveway, and Boychuk had ordered a yellow police tape installed from the front of the garage, around Denny's truck and ending at the front door of the house. A paramedic vehicle had arrived, but only to serve as a hearse. From up the street, a television news truck was making its way to the house. Not much ever happened around Morgantown, and this was news.

As Dee looked on from the kitchen window, she could see several of Hubie's neighbors—bundled up to deal with now sub-freezing temperatures—standing on their lawns across the street, wondering what was going on. From her vantage point, she could see multiple sets of human tracks in the snow between the two houses.

Inside the Lowry house, Hubie was standing with the sheriff in the hallway at the entrance to the dining room. They both watched in silence as his investigators went about their business. It was a surreal moment.

"Can't say I'm surprised, Hubie," the sheriff said finally. The older man just nodded in agreement.

"Where are your girls?"

"Don't know, Brian. I woke up this morning and they were both gone."

Boychuk turned to face Hubie. The smiles and camaraderie of the previous morning in his garage were nowhere to be seen. Today was all business. Still, he was worried about the elder man. Hubie looked terrible, his face ashen and pasty, and the sheriff wondered if his office would get a 911 call some day about him.

"Gone? I saw Jane's car over there when I arrived," he said, tilting his head in the direction of Hubie's driveway where Jane had parked her Mercedes less than twenty-four hours earlier.

"Her car's here, she isn't. And Jo's truck isn't here either. She normally parks it beside the pumper. When I came in here this morning, I called for them but there was no answer."

"Any idea where they are?"

"Nope, not a clue."

"Well, we're gonna have to find them and talk to them," the sheriff said.

"You think they're responsible?"

"No idea, Hubie."

The father in him emerged. His girls couldn't be murderers, could they? Like her mother, Jane had a fiery temper and proved last night that she could blow her cork. But could she do this? He refused to believe it. And Joanne, well, he knew she wasn't very happy. But no, he didn't think she could have done this either.

"For the life of me, I can't figure any of this out, Brian," Hubie said. "You know as well as I do that Denny never would've won any popularity contests around here. And I always suspected he was a stay-out. Maybe an ornery husband?"

Boychuk shrugged.

"Possibly. I'm not ruling anything out."

"It's a mess, for sure," Hubie said, solemnly.

The sheriff continued. "My people will give me better information, but it looks like there was a pretty good fight here last night," Boychuk said, pointing to the broken glass, fallen pictures and upset dishes in the hutch. A dining room chair had been upended.

"It looks as though Joanne didn't even finish clearing the table when the fracas broke out—assuming, that is, that she always did everything at mealtime. Did Denny ever clean a dish in his life?"

Hubie shook his head.

"Well, if he ever went anywhere near the goddamn sink it was probably to clean a fish."

The sheriff tapped the shoulder of one of his investigators and asked her to move over so he could take a closer look. He bent over to inspect Denny's body. After the blast, his large frame had come to rest upright in the sitting position against the wall. His head had slumped slightly, and his eyes remained open. He looked as if he was about to pass out from yet another wasted night.

"Looks to me like old Denny here got blown away from close range, maybe less than three or four feet, and judging from the amount of blood on the wall and on the floor, it was either a twelve or sixteen gauge. Likely a twelve."

He surveyed the dual wounds and winced at the blow to the groin.

"Two shots, too. The first one wouldn't have been fatal... but would have hurt real bad, that's for sure. And it would have changed his behavior—permanently. But it might not have killed him, at least not right away. Oh, he would have bled to death, eventually. Now—" He pointed to Denny's chest wound. "—the second shot was clearly meant to put him away. No doubt about it."

Hubie said nothing as Boychuk turned to look up at him.

"Have you checked your rack?" the sheriff asked.

"Not yet."

"You'd better."

SEVENTEEN

Joanne and Jane were sitting at the counter of a quiet road-side diner, eating breakfast without making much of a sound. The former Burlington Northern railcar was one of those silver liners that had carried wealthy Manhattan social-ites to and from the Thousand Islands or Saratoga Springs in the twenties and thirties.

Today, the only tracks evident were two parallel rails sup-porting the liner on a bed of gravel. Inside, the modest eat-ery was nearly empty. From the far end of the counter, their waitress, a woman in her late fifties with a plumpish face and dirty blonde hair coiled tightly in a bun, walked over and offered them a refill.

"More coffee?" she barked. Both sisters nodded in appre-ciation but without comment. Behind the counter was a window to a small, cramped kitchen where Jane could see the cook toiling away. Unshaven and unkempt, he was wearing a grimy, three-quarter-length apron and a Mets cap. Past the window, on an extended wall, a television rested on the top of a stainless steel milkshake maker. The TV was on, but the sound was muted.

Driving east out of Syracuse, the sisters had retraced their route from the night before. Jane noticed how dispirited Joanne had become and decided to leave her to her thoughts. She had simply fired up the Explorer and pointed it away from the city. After about forty minutes, they exited the Thruway near Rome and picked up Route 365 and were soon rolling through a string of hamlets before spotting the lonely diner.

Jane's breakfast was interrupted by another ferocious coughing fit, and it alarmed her sister. "That's the second or third time I've noticed that," Joanne said. "That's a heck of a cough. What's up?"

Jane put aside her coffee, opting for a long drink of water. "Nothing. Just bronchitis."

"You sound like shit."

"Thanks," she said. "Feel like shit too."

They resumed eating their breakfast in silence and watched as several hunters decked out in fluorescent orange gear arrived and sat down at one of the three booths at the end of the railcar. Their waitress, trudging slowly, followed the hunters to their table. She dropped a couple of menus in front of them, turned their coffee cups over and filled them. Obviously, they were regulars. Few words were exchanged.

In the absence of conversation, Jane stared absent-mindedly at the silenced television. A young weather girl was pointing at a map of New York and New England. Then a graphic came on-screen to inform viewers that the entire northeast could expect as much as a foot of snow. Jane frowned. Just what we need, she thought.

Finally, she wiped her mouth and turned towards her sister.

"You know, you might not believe this, but I think you've done a great job with Brent," she said. Joanne shrugged, accepting the compliment.

"I don't know where he got his brains, but thankfully he won that scholarship," Joanne said.

"Well, I know where he got them," said Jane, "and they didn't come from Septic Sam."

Jane's comment elicited a faint smile from her sister. Joanne knew what Jane was talking about, however. Like their mother, Joanne had breezed through high school, earning

high marks in sciences and math simply because those sub-
jects came easy to her.

Jane had thought she wasn't that hungry until she sat
down. Now, she was ravenously attacking her breakfast. But
she wanted to continue her conversation and turned to look
at her sister, who was sipping her coffee.

"You may not believe this either, Jo, but I've always been
a bit envious of you," she said.

"Envious of me? Boy, that's a good one," Joanne said,
raising her eyebrows. "You? My-name-is-Jane-and-I'm-
going-to-the-White House-Schumacher?"

"It's true."

"How?"

"Well, Brent for starters. I haven't seen him very much, I
admit, but he's obviously turned out to be a smart young guy.
One who knows that his future is not in Morgantown, too."

Joanne was taken aback by her sister's praise.

Jane continued.

"And you made a good decision and look what you've
got? You've raised him to be a wonderful kid. Well, really
he's no kid any more. But you made a good choice. I, on the
other hand—"

Suddenly Jane was interrupted by pictures flashing on
the muted television behind the counter. The news channel,
still broadcasting in closed captions, was showing dramatic
pictures of Joanne's house. Videotaped images of the police
investigation were being flashed across the tiny screen. Paramedics were wheeling Denny's body from the house, a sheet
covering the entire stretcher. Yellow police tape was everywhere.

Alarmed, Jane nudged her sister, and flicked her brow
towards the television. They began reading the captions now
appearing on-screen.

...POLICE IN MORGANTOWN ARE INVESTI-
GATING A THANKSGIVING NIGHT DEATH OF
A LOCAL MAN. DEAD OF GUNSHOT WOUNDS
IS DENNIS EARL LOWRY, FORTY...

The news channel then flashed a head-and-shoulders picture of Denny taken about nine years earlier. Joanne recognized it from a family photo that hung in the hallway of her home, a picture that included her and Brent. Her son was about eleven or twelve when that picture was taken, she remembered. They must have cropped her and Brent from it. It was taken during a brief time when Denny was clean-shaven and not bad-looking. He clearly was forcing a smile, a far cry from both his appearance and attitude over the past couple of years. They continued to read the captions.

POLICE ARE GIVING OUT NO DETAILS, BUT
ARE TREATING IT AS A HOMICIDE. THEY
HAVE YET TO ANNOUNCE ANY SUSPECTS IN
THE CRIME.

Jane quickly scanned the diner to see if anyone else was watching. The hunters at the corner booth were oblivious to what was happening on-screen, seemingly engrossed in a playful argument about who'd drop the first deer in its tracks. A farmer was propped on a stool at the opposite end of the counter, but the angle of the television prevented him from watching. He was eating his breakfast alone.

Jane dropped her cutlery and reached for her purse. She removed a twenty-dollar bill, slapped it down on the counter and started zipping her coat.

"We have to get the hell out of here!" she announced to Joanne who was still staring at the television screen, although the news had moved on to other items. The image of Denny being wheeled from the house unnerved and nearly paralyzed her. The sound of Jane's voice, demanding a departure, snapped Joanne from her stare.

"Where the hell are we going?" Joanne asked, thinking she could use another smoke.

"We're heading to the hills," Jane replied. "Placid, I think. I know of a hotel there where we can hang. We can go there and figure this thing out. And I have some unfinished business…" But as she attempted to reach for the keys to the SUV, Joanne beat her to them.

"Okay, but I'm driving," she said, and they marched out the door towards the truck.

Joanne turned the ignition over and their journey continued. Soon one northern route merged imperceptibly with another one, and she began to relive the events of the last twenty-four hours. That damn crime scene in her driveway was now being splashed all over the news. It had unnerved her. Over and over in her head, she wondered how it all got so out of hand. It was a friggin' nightmare and, once again, it was all coming back.

Horrible.

Denny's drunk…

His hand…all I can see is the back of his hand…the brute force of it all…the pain…so sharp and so excruciating…

She was so embarrassed…so humiliated…her dishes were breaking…her pictures shattering…the hatred in his eyes…

His insults…his never-ending put-downs…she couldn't believe how cruel he was…and…

And then there were the shots…she'd never forget those shots… they shook the house…

The neighbors must have heard them, didn't they?

What the hell was happening to me?

She shook her head and snapped out of her daydream. She didn't have any answers to her nightmarish questions.

One thing was clear: like Jane, she wasn't ready to return to Morgantown and face the music.

Miles passed as Jane idly watched the countryside rolling by. Often, between the woods and the streams, a large farm would appear on a hillside, its livestock grazing lazily in the fields, its summer crops of corn and hay now harvested. Another bridge crossed another stream, and the northern New York landscape gradually became more mountainous and rugged. In the great distance and through the many valleys, she recognized the familiar peaks that surrounded Lake Placid. They were the lasting monuments to the international triumphs of nearly thirty years before.

Jane looked over to her sister. She knew Joanne was hurting badly and that she had to say something...anything. She wanted to assure her sister their journey would end soon, but she didn't think that would ring true. Jane had tried to tell Joanne to stay home but, oddly, was glad that her sister was with her.

Most of all she wanted to tell Joanne that she wasn't responsible for Denny's death. But, in a roundabout way, her inaction—really, Joanne's chronic inability to make a decision over the years—just gave him *carte blanche* to keep up the abuse. Wife-beaters like Denny displayed a common behavior; as long as he was able to get away with it, he wouldn't have stopped. Jane knew this from her time covering the crime beat in Rochester. She had seen a few like him in her career. Oh, maybe Denny would have eventually paid for his acts. Perhaps his penchant for violence would have spread. Possibly an angry husband with a weapon of his own would have dealt with the son of a bitch.

But today, while Jane simply wanted to say that things would work out, she had no idea. One thing was now certain: they were in this together.

"I know what you're thinking, you know," Jane said.

"Oh, you do, do you Jane?" Joanne said, snapping out of her deep funk, her voice rising, a touch of anger evident. "I didn't know you had become such a mind reader too. You really know what's going through my puny little head right now?"

"Your head was never puny, Joanne, so don't go there," Jane admonished. "But I have a sense of what you're thinking... that I've really fucked up your life—"

Joanne interrupted her.

"Can you *stop* using that word?" she barked.

Jane was perplexed.

"What word?"

"You know what word!" she cried, her turn to admonish. "The F-bomb! I hate it! It was Denny's favorite word and I can't stand it!"

But before Jane could respond, her BlackBerry sounded loudly. Almost relieved, she reached into her purse and retrieved it. It was Roberto on the line and she decided to take the call. But she would keep it short. She was in no mood to talk to him.

"Hello there, Argentina," she said.

Roberto was sitting in an overstuffed chair next to the fireplace at his law partner's cabin in the Catskills. Through its picture window, he could see huge snowmaking machines creating at least the illusion of winter for the growing number of weekend skiers and snowboarders on Hunter Mountain. The Catskills were not the Adirondacks, not even close. But these mountains had long won the battle of geography; their proximity to New York City enabled the wealthy—the hedge fund managers, the media moguls, the orthopedic surgeons alike—to take full advantage. Not to mention Wall Street lawyers like Roberto. Today, he and many others were here. It was a holiday weekend.

"Jane, you're there!" Roberto was excited. He sat up in his chair, not expecting her voice on the other end of the phone.

"I am indeed, Rob."

"Jane, what the hell is going on? I haven't heard a thing from you in two days. Where are you?"

Jane glanced again at Joanne behind the wheel.

"I'm with my sister, Rob, in her truck."

"Where are you going?"

"Just out for a drive."

She could tell that he wasn't pleased with her evasiveness, but it was all he was going to get—for now.

"How's your dad? Was it a stroke?" His questions kept coming.

"Not as bad as we figured," came Jane's cryptic reply.

Roberto's frustration was evident. He sensed he was getting the brush-off.

"And you never told me about your doctor's visit," he continued. "What did she say?"

"Just as I told you," she replied, continuing her dance of deception.

"Told me? You haven't told me a thing! You've ignored my texts, and you haven't called. What the hell is going on?"

"My sister and I are just taking a nice drive through the hills," she said. "I don't think I'll have much of a signal soon, so we'll likely get cut off at any minute. I'll call you later, okay?"

But Roberto was unmoved. He didn't like what he was hearing.

"Well, answer me one more question. When are you returning to Albany? I could meet you there."

"Don't know, Roberto. Got to go. Bye," she said abruptly, and hung up.

Joanne, who had calmed down, was listening to her sister's conversation, at least one side of it.

"Your Puerto Rican friend?"

Jane smiled and nodded.

"Yeah, my personal Puerto Rican. Jesus Christ!"

"You met him, where? The Caribbean?"

"Yeah, Jamaica, last year," she replied. "I don't know how to define what or who we are...since we're not shacked up or anything. He works in Manhattan and I spend most of my time in Albany or on the road with Foley. And so we don't get to see each other as much as we'd like. Or at least as much as *he* would like anyway."

Joanne continued, "So, is he number eighty or ninety?

Jane burst out laughing.

"Fuck off!"

EIGHTEEN

A few hours had passed. After the call from Roberto, Jane didn't feel like reopening her previous conversation with her sister. She was mentally and physically fatigued and her chest ached. To the steady humming sounds of the truck's snow tires, she soon felt herself dozing off. It had been less than forty-eight hours since she departed Albany, and most of that time had been spent in a car or an SUV or on back roads that she had never traveled.

Joanne was exhausted too and envied Jane's ability to rest, especially after the events of the previous day. The front seats of her Ford Explorer weren't exactly a Best Western, or even an EconoLodge for that matter. But she would press on. She would find out soon enough just how much stamina she had.

She saw the sign for the village of Speculator, and remembered her dad, a big boxing fan, describing how the heavyweight fighter Gene Tunney would train there in the twenties, before his epic battles with Jack Dempsey. Tunney would charge millionaires from New York fifty cents each to watch him work out and then donate the money to the Catholic Church in Lake Pleasant. She didn't even know who Gene Tunney or Jack Dempsey were until Denny—glued to the sports channels every Friday night, at least on the Friday nights that he had made it home—began watching *Famous Fights*. He'd liked the fights; it was the only television show he'd watch.

Speculator was approaching and she needed to make a decision. Either she would follow a course that would take them through Eagle Nest and Blue Mountain Lake, eventually ending up in Lake Placid. Or she could choose roads further to the east that passed through Oregon and Sodom, not far from Pudding Hollow. She made her decision; it would be the former. It was a more direct route, and besides, Jane was asleep and didn't know where the heck they were anyway.

Twenty minutes later, Joanne arrived at a small bridge that appeared to have been built with creosoted railroad ties decades before. On one side, resting in a fast-flowing stream, a small crane sat idle. The ancient overpass was clearly under renovation but in her fatigue she had missed the signs to slow down. Suddenly, she hit a pothole hard and Joanne could feel the front tires swerve. She felt she was losing control of her vehicle. Braking hard, she struggled with the wheel to control the truck. The violent bumps startled Jane, and she awoke from her brief restless nap.

"Shit, I think we have a flat," Joanne said, negotiating the remainder of the bridge and pulling the Explorer to the side of the road. It came to a halt.

"Damn it, what else can happen to us," she said. Just the previous week, she'd had her old winter tires installed on the truck, hoping that she could eke out another season with them. But no tire can fend off a foot-deep crater in the road.

Jane, blinking awake, surveyed their situation, and it was clear they were in the middle of nowhere. Make that the end of nowhere.

"I have a spare on the back," Joanne said.

"You ever fix a flat?" Jane asked.

"Yes, haven't you?"

Joanne glared briefly at Jane; the look on her face said everything.

"Triple-A all the way, right?"

Jane shrugged. Yeah, she thought.

"Are you sure you weren't adopted?" Joanne asked.

Joanne jumped from the truck and walked to the rear of the vehicle. Opening it, she released a loud sigh when she spied Hubie's shotgun. It lay conspicuously on its side, its box of shells nearby. Annoyed at the sight of the weapon, she grabbed a blanket and covered the gun, but only partially. Its black oak gunstock was still visible as she reached under the floorboards to retrieve a tire iron and the vehicle's rusting jack. Her spare was attached to the Explorer's rear door.

After a few minutes, despite her self-proclaimed savvy at fixing flats, Joanne was having problems. She had managed to place the jack behind the truck's front frame and get it cranked it up without the vehicle crashing down. That was an achievement in itself, but she was nowhere near replacing the tire. Helplessly, Jane watched, her arms crossed to preserve warmth.

Joanne was struggling with the wheel nuts, her frustration evident. She grunted loudly with every attempted turn of the cross iron.

"We could still call a tow truck," Jane said. "Better than doing this."

But Joanne would have nothing to do with that suggestion.

"And wait here for two hours before a tow truck arrived? The nearest one is likely over at Schroon Lake, on the Interstate. But by the time it got here, it would probably be dark."

She sighed again with resignation.

"These damn tires were just changed," she added. "Why can't I get the lugs to move?"

"Because maybe they put them on with drills?" Jane asked. Her sister shot her a 'you're not helping here much' look. Jane caught it.

"Well, I've *seen* tires being changed."

The bridge behind them was located at the end of a long straight stretch before the road began a gradual incline. Jane estimated it was probably two miles or more in length to the top of the hill. Ten or twelve minutes had passed. Not another vehicle had approached in either direction. Finally, from over the hill, a white pick-up truck slowly made its way towards them. It came to a halt across the road from the sisters. The driver's side window rolled down and a man sporting a red bandana and silver earrings peered out. Jane couldn't decide whether he was a native of the Adirondacks or Appalachia.

"You ladies look like you're having some trouble there," the man said. "Need some help?"

Joanne, crouching and bent over the tire, looked over her shoulder suspiciously.

"No, we're all right," she replied.

"No, we're *not* all right, and yes, we *could* use your help," Jane quickly countered. Joanne shot her sister a nasty look, but Jane ignored it. The man exited his truck, his cowboy boots making loud, distinctive clicking sounds across the pavement, and walked towards them. He introduced himself.

"I'm Matt...Matt Booker," he said with a smile. Jane quickly studied him. A man of medium build, he looked to be in his early forties but a youthful face might have masked his true age. Despite the brisk temperatures, he wore only a black leather vest over a denim shirt. His sleeves were partially rolled up, and Jane could see a tattoo on his right arm. He was a decent-looking guy. A mountain man.

Jane extended her hand, confident that Matt was no ax murderer. And even if he was, who'd mess with her?

"I'm Jane, and she's—"

"—pissed off," Joanne replied, curtly.

Matt took it all in stride.

"Okay…Miss pissed off…whaddaya got here?"

Joanne reluctantly stepped aside and Matt assumed control of the situation. In short order, the cowboy proceeded to remove the wheel nuts and replace the tire.

"Just needed a little elbow grease, that's all," he announced, as he rolled the tire towards the rear of the vehicle. He was about to return the tire iron and jack to their proper places when he spotted the butt end of the shotgun peeking out from under its woolen hiding spot. An eyebrow shot up. He paused briefly and then rejoined the sisters.

"Where you ladies from?" he asked.

"Morgan—" Jane was interrupted by her sister.

"—Syracuse!"

His eyes skated back and forth from sister to sister.

"Syracuse, huh?"

"Yes, my son and I live there," she lied. "He goes to SU." Joanne glanced at her sister but Jane didn't say anything to contradict her story.

"You have a college kid?" Matt asked. "I mean a *college-aged* kid? I wouldn't have guessed that."

Joanne wasn't sure how to take his compliment, offering only what resembled a sheepish shrug. Other than Darryl, who flirted harmlessly once in a while, Joanne wasn't accustomed to men saying nice things to her.

She changed the subject.

"Is there a motel around here?"

"Yup. Happen to know a nice little one a few miles up that way," he said, pointing towards the hill. "Called the North Star…across the road from the lake. Not exactly an original name for a motel for these parts, but it's a good, clean one though."

"Does it have a bar?" Jane asked.

"That it does. With some fine entertainment...most nights."

"Thanks for helping us, Matt," Jane said. Joanne nodded in agreement but said nothing. "We appreciate it."

"No problem," he replied. "You gals take care now, okay?"

They watched as he opened the door to his pick-up and drove away.

NINETEEN

Jane was wrapping up an electronic transaction at an ATM when Joanne exited the convenience store. It was getting late in the afternoon—the flat tire had set them back more than an hour—and they decided their travel day was over. Three hundred bucks ought to do it for now, Jane thought.

The North Star Motel was right where Matt said it would be, but upon arrival, Jane noticed some semblance of civilization a bit further up the road. They pushed on for another half mile to fill the gas tank and get some cash. Joanne also said she was hungry but didn't want to stop at another roadside restaurant.

Joanne was about to reenter the Explorer when Jane whipped out her BlackBerry and dialed a number. She was calling directory assistance.

"Morgantown, New York," she told the operator. "I'd like the number for the sheriff's office."

Joanne overheard her sister's telephone conversation and became alarmed.

"What the hell are you doing?" she demanded.

"I'm calling Boychuk."

"What? Why?"

Jane waved off Joanne's protests and continued her mission. As press secretary to the governor of New York, she knew a little about damage control. Foley was a smarter politician than most and didn't find himself in much trouble. He didn't keep a mistress on the side or consort with hookers. He preferred a dirty martini over a single malt, and sometimes quaffed a few beers with his Ivy League sons. But he wasn't a drunk and never tasted nose candy. Sure, he had smoked—and inhaled—a little weed at Dartmouth. Who didn't?

Nor was he a closet gambler, or lived his life *in* the closet, either, because Jane knew his affection for his classy wife of twenty-four years was genuine. Hell, she suspected that he and Maureen liked to tear one off in his office from time to time. When Jane had met the high-tech mogul, she immediately assumed that he'd had opportunities; after all, he was tall and fit and good-looking. Not Hollywood handsome, mind you, but he ruggedly filled his tailored suits and crisp white shirts. His jet hair was throwing hints of gray at the temples and, at fifty-three, he more resembled a Big East basketball coach than a politician. But a fool-around? No, she had concluded; he was not the adulterous type. His ambition was more powerful than his libido.

As a reporter who had covered more than her share of politicians, Jane knew she'd heed the number-one rule when faced with a crisis: get out ahead of the story, take your lumps and control the message. If this wasn't a crisis, Jane thought, what the hell was it? She would manage it.

The operator came back on the phone, told her she had the number and would connect her. A female voice at the other end of the line answered.

"Morgan County sheriff's office," the voice said.

"Brian Boychuk, please," Jane replied.

"Who's calling?" the woman barked. It was not a polite question; it was a demand, and Jane thought that Boychuk had some work to do in training his staff on phone etiquette. This was the Morgantown Sheriff's Department, for Christ's sake, not the NYPD. New Yorkers expect rudeness from their cops and are disappointed when they don't receive it. But up here?

"Tell him it's Jane Schumacher," she said.

Several moments passed before Boychuk came on the line.

"Jane!" he exclaimed. Gone was 'Shoes,' the colloquial nickname he had fondly given her when they were teenagers and the one he had used to address her only the day before. Today, he was all business.

"Chucky, how are you?" Jane decided to have some fun with the good sheriff. After all, if she couldn't do it, who could?

"More important question, Jane—where are you? And where is Joanne?"

"That's two questions, Chuck," she said. "You just said you had one important question."

But the sheriff was in no mood for games. He had everyone on his case over Denny's shooting, including the troopers, the mayor and a few nervous townsfolk. Murders didn't happen in his county, or at least they were rare. And he wasn't going to waste time.

"Jane, don't mess with me. Where are you?"

"Here and there, Chuck. Not relevant right now."

"I have a feeling that you girls are in a heap of trouble," Boychuk said, immediately regretting using the term 'you girls' as soon as it came out of his mouth. The Jane he used to know would have slapped him upside the head for any sexist, condescending thing he'd say, and he expected it now. But he was surprised; she didn't interrupt him, and he continued.

"Your brother-in-law is dead. One of Hubie's shotguns is missing. You and Joanne have gone AWOL. It's all starting to add up, Jane."

"Add up, Brian?" she asked. Now, she too was addressing him by his real name. Boychuk always knew that when Jane called him Brian she wasn't joking around anymore.

"Add up?" she repeated. "I seem to remember you flunking tenth grade math...so don't start telling me you think things are starting to add up."

"We did a lot of things in high school, Jane," he said, "some of which meant skipping a class once in a while. You know what I'm talking about."

"I have a fond memory or two of high school," she replied.

"Really?" he asked.

"No, not really," she said, almost cruelly.

She decided it was her turn to get to work. It was time to absolve her sister of all of her alleged crimes and do it now. Jane looked over at Joanne, who was eating from a bag of tortilla chips. She was leaning against the truck and had been listening to Jane's one-sided conversation. Jane noticed and began walking away from the store. To her surprise, Joanne didn't follow her.

"Brian, let me get to the point. This story's got a lot more legs than the Rockettes at Radio City!"

"I have no doubt, Jane, and I'm hoping you'll tell me what happened," he replied. The sheriff knew he had to keep her talking. Not that he could trace the call—it was a cell phone after all—but instinctively felt he could persuade his ex-girlfriend to give herself up.

"I've known Denny for a long time. As long as you have." Jane snapped.

"I know you've known *about* Denny for a long time too, Brian!" she yelled. "I suspect the whole fucking town has known *about* him! Goddamn it, why didn't you do something?"

That put Boychuk on the defensive.

Jane was right; he had known about Denny's drinking, his late night visits to the Paddle Inn and his sordid reputation for screwing every willing barfly who walked in the door. Moreover, his switchboard had received more than a few noise complaints from Joanne's neighbors. But each time, as Boychuk dispatched his deputies, Denny would answer the door to assure them nothing harmful was happening.

Just a little bickerin' goin' on, deputy, he would say. Just a little argument 'tween me 'n the wife, that's all. You know what I mean? Joanne was usually nearby when they'd call on the Lowry home. That true, ma'am? The cop would ask Joanne. And without uttering a word, she would nod in agreement to the skeptical police officers and the situation would be diffused. And each time they would leave.

Indirectly, Boychuk had raised the issue with Hubie from time to time, but the older man had shrugged it off. Now he'd wished he had been more direct with Hubie. He should have asked him directly about the rumored troubles next door. Been less roundabout.

"What could I have done, Jane?" he asked. "Arrest him on suspicion? Joanne never issued a complaint."

Jane's voice was cracking mad, so angry that it set off another coughing fit that briefly interrupted her.

"Are you all right? You sound terrible," he said.

"Never mind me, Brian, didn't you see the evidence? It was all there in fucking black and blue!"

"She still had to press charges, Jane. Simple as that."

"Simple as that, eh? Well, you know very well she wouldn't have done that, Brian," she said, now lowering her voice. "I wish she had."

"Me too, Jane. Me too," he said, pausing a moment to digest the emotional and violent events of the last twenty-four hours.

"Listen, why don't you turn that truck around? Come in and see me?"

There was another long silence at the other end of the phone as Jane pondered the sheriff's request. It was something she had considered all day as they drove through the Adirondack foothills.

"Jane, are you still there?"

"I'm still here...I'm listening," she said, finally, her voice breaking. "But it's time for you to pay attention to me now, Brian. Joanne had nothing to do with what happened to Denny. Nothing!"

"I half expected you to say that, Jane," he said. "But believe me—and I say this as a friend—it'll just get worse for you and for Joanne if you girls—" He quickly corrected himself. "—if *you and Joanne* keep running."

Another long silence.

"Understood, Chuck...understood. Gotta hang up now."

Jane ended her call and, turning toward Joanne, signaled that it was time to go. Her sister said nothing during the short time it took to drive back to the North Star, a ten-unit motel with its office attached at one end. Across the parking lot sat a separate, log-sided bar with a red neon sign above the entrance. It was called The Adirondack Road House. How apt, Jane thought. Only a few vehicles, mostly pick-ups, were parked in front.

Exiting the Explorer, Joanne finally broke their silence.

"I can't believe you did that, Jane," she said. "What did you say to Boychuk?"

Her emotions still brewing, Jane replied, "I asked him if he needed a date to the Policeman's Ball."

TWENTY

Marcia Bell peered out of her fourth-floor office window and began to feel sorry for herself. It was the Friday afternoon of Thanksgiving weekend, for God's sake, and she was stuck in the governor's office. She had hoped to spend a few days in Stowe to grab a few runs down Mount Mansfield before the real election season had started.

Admonishing herself, she quickly got over her self-pity. There would be time later in life for skiing. The opportunity in front of her was simply too good, too promising, to turn her back on it. Soon she would begin to work on her first presidential campaign. Foley would travel to Roosevelt's home in Hyde Park, on Pearl Harbor Day no less, and they'd begin an adventure that should take them all the way to the steps of the U.S. Capitol in about two years. Like Jane, Marcia was a student of American history; as FDR himself would say, it would be a date that would live in infamy. She was excited.

Two days ago, only minutes before she had left for her doctor's appointment, Jane had asked Marcia to put in an extra hour or so in advance of the candidate's weekly strategy meeting. It was held every Saturday morning—regardless of whether it was a holiday or not. That meant she'd be stuck in Albany, at least until that afternoon, and she had wondered if it was worth it to drive to Vermont.

Jane got the chance to play while she and the rest of the political team had to work. Marcia had guessed that Foley felt sorry for his hard-working press secretary and gave her the weekend off. Who's running this damn show anyway, Marcia asked herself. She knew the answer, of course; Foley was his own man. But that didn't detract from the fact that Jane was one of the most powerful political assistants today. And Marcia liked that.

Even the governor, who had decided to spend the holidays at the mansion with his family, would be there tomorrow, she thought. New York governors were notorious for their absences from the capital and especially avoided the sprawling, Victorian-era house set aside for the state's top dog. But she knew that despite his protestations, despite his acclaimed love for a *real* city further south, Foley enjoyed the mansion for a number of reasons. He reveled in its views of the Hudson. He'd stroll through its grounds, taking in the history of the place. And he enjoyed playing touch football, Kennedy-style, with his sons and their friends when they arrived for the holidays. All in front of curious and willing camera crews alerted by her, of course.

Years removed from the White House, the Democrats were itching to regain the levers of power. One beltway pundit, not necessarily a Foley fan, said the Democrats sensed their party was leaving the political wilderness behind. Thus, he wrote, they sent a request down to central casting and up popped Foley. An inaccurate assessment, Jane had told Marcia, but one she vowed to change. Foley was substantive; his brand would have a long shelf-life.

The party's establishment had been courting the lawyer and self-made millionaire for years. Hailing from a wealthy, educated town about ninety minutes north of the city, Foley was considered a rising star, an heir apparent or simply the 'next' one. But he had bided his time, turning down offers for State Assembly, for Attorney General, for Congress. If he was going to make a political run—well, was it ever in doubt?—it was going to be the big time and nothing else. The governorship of New York was simply a means to an end, the lower step on a two-rung political ladder.

Besides, if there was ever a moment for a charismatic politician, this was it. The war, conceived on a bed of bald-faced lies, was going badly for Americans. The current administration was crony-filled and incompetent, prompting voters in the mid-terms to throw the bums out. Jane had said she wasn't sure it was public anger or just the inevitable electoral cycle that was behind the shift to the left. But no matter; their party had regained control of Congress, and was to be led by an über-liberal, signaling that change was in the air.

Of course, they were the recipients of some good luck too as the election season was hit by a few juicy sex scandals. First it was that southern congressman and his dalliances with male interns. And then it was that unctuous religio—*le grand fromage* of evangelicals—admitting to a gay affair while professing a curious affinity for crystal meth. Talk about manna from heaven! That the country was fed up was an understatement. But the middle-aged preacher, an apostle of hypocrisy, helped independent voters realize their errant ways. Christ, if they couldn't win the White House with all this shit going down, they never would.

Marcia was about to head down the hall to the photocopier when her phone rang. On weekends and holidays, it was standard operating procedure to have all incoming calls redirected to Marcia's desk for action. And if she wasn't physically in the building, the switchboard knew where to find her. She always carried two cell phones in her purse on orders from Jane, who didn't believe in call waiting.

She picked up the phone, thinking it might be her pharmacy-school boyfriend wondering when she was returning to their apartment. Instead, it was Jack Davis, the head of the governor's security detail and a senior officer with the New York State Troopers. They spoke on a daily basis as she scheduled political events.

"Marcia, it's Jack. Are you sitting down?"

"No, I'm at the copier, Jack," she replied.

"Well, better find yourself a chair."

Moments later, Marcia—stunned at the news—was racing through the empty offices in the direction of Claudia Raymond's corner suite. Claudia was Foley's chief of staff, political director, senior advisor, campaign guru and all-around fixer. She was even more powerful than Jane, if that could be possible.

She arrived at Claudia's office and was greeted by Gloria Chaput-Hughes, the governor's personal secretary since his days in fiber optics. A robust sixty-year-old grandmother of French-Canadian descent, Gloria was a self-described political junkie and totally dedicated to the cause. She would do anything short of a felony to elect Foley president.

She looked up.

"You're stuck here too, Marcia?" she asked with a bit of a grin. "What's Thanksgiving anyway? An overvalued event, in my opinion."

Gloria immediately realized that Marcia was not in the frame of mind for small talk. She saw the pressing, frantic look on the younger woman's face.

"What's up?"

"I have to see Claudia and the governor right away," Marcia said. She thought her head was going to explode.

"Marcia, they're both on a conference call. Can it wait?"

"No, I need to see them both right away," the press assistant said, excitedly.

"It's about Jane. And it's urgent."

TWENTY-ONE

Jane opened the motel office door and stepped in. Right behind her was Joanne, who couldn't wait another minute for a hot shower and a change of clothes. She was still wearing her blue pantsuit from Thanksgiving night, which had come directly from the racks of the Salvation Army store back in Morgantown. The motel lobby was empty save for a rack of glossy brochures promoting a few of the mountain region's tourist destinations. She recognized some of them. One summer, Donna and Hubie had whisked a pair of eight-year-olds off to Santa's Village before trekking further north to the Ausable Chasm. That was the extent of their one family vacation.

There was no one in sight. Over in one corner, a Coke machine stood against the wall, next to the ice maker. Behind the desk and next to a curtain shielding the lobby from what Jane figured was the manager's office, were individual keys to the motel units. She waited briefly to see if anyone heard the office door opening. Then she noticed a call bell on the counter and punched it down hard. These things are annoying as hell, but effective, she thought. From behind the office curtain appeared Matt Booker. Both Joanne and Jane did a double take in surprise.

"You!" Jane said, as their roadside savior smiled. The bandana he had been wearing earlier was now removed, and she could see a full head of wavy black hair. It had grown well past his ears but his brushed-back style was attractive. There wasn't a hint of gray to be found, prompting Jane to surmise that he was in denial to the evils of aging. Well, who wasn't, she thought. Get in line, Booker.

"Uh-huh, it's me," he said.

Joanne said, "You work here?"

"I guess you could say that. I own the place."

"Ah, that's why you gave it such a glowing recommendation," Jane replied. "In my business, that's what we call a conflict of interest."

Matt smiled, a bit embarrassed.

"I wasn't lyin'," he said, throwing his palms in the air. "This here's a nice place. Nothing fancy but clean. Can I get you gals settled in?"

"I'm sure you'd love to," Jane replied.

"Yes, I'm tired and I need to clean up," Joanne said.

Joanne dug deeply into her purse and pulled out a small metal Beechnut tobacco can. She pried it open, revealing a modest wad of twenty-dollar bills wrapped tightly with an elastic band. She looked at her sister, who was witnessing the cash on display. She became flustered.

"My Christmas Club," she said, as she pulled a handful of bills from the band. She turned to Matt, who was also watching.

"How much for a night? No, make it two nights, because I don't want to see the inside of a car for a while."

"It's still off-season," the innkeeper replied. "Forty-two-fifty a night, plus a seven-percent tip for the governor."

"Can't neglect the governor," Jane piped in.

Joanne paid Matt and he handed her a key to a unit. "Number six, about halfway down," he said. As Jane reopened the office door, she turned and addressed him again.

"That bar next door. Yours too?"

"Yes, ma'am. Good food. Cheap beer. Great singer tonight, too!"

She looked back at him with amusement, and he responded in kind.

They exited the lobby.

Joanne kept walking to their unit while her sister jumped in the truck and drove it the short distance to the unit's door. They entered the room and Jane fell face down on the first bed she saw. In minutes she was out cold. Lord, Joanne thought, she really is exhausted. She can fall asleep anytime, anywhere.

In what seemed to be an hour later, but may have been longer, Joanne emerged from the shower to find her sister still curled up on her bed, sleeping. The cut on Joanne's bottom lip was healing quickly and was now barely noticeable. The healing powers of the mouth, she thought. I wish the bruise on my neck would go away this fast. She climbed into a clean pair of jeans and a red sweater before grabbing for her coat.

She needed another smoke.

It was late afternoon, dark and markedly cooler. It gets cold fast in these higher elevations, Joanne thought. The moon had risen above the tree line and now loomed large above the lake across the road. Its bluish-white reflections danced delicately across the water. In a matter of days, or perhaps hours, a layer of black ice would cover this pond, followed by drifting snow brought on by a nor'easter blowing through the Adirondacks. The season, like her life, was changing.

Joanne took another drag on her Salem menthol cigarette and continued to let her mind wander. She pictured herself in her bright orange snowmobile suit, steering one of her father's sleds over the endless, tunnel-like trails that began at the end of their road and continued across the frozen Oswegatchie. A day on the Ski-Doo was a wonderful way to get through winters around here, she thought.

Those machines meant freedom...wonderful freedom.
Freedom?

Now that's a joke, Joanne thought. Get a grip, girl. How can you think of riding snowmobiles, or returning to the store, or worse—going back into that damn house?

How can you plan to do anything now?

She suddenly thought of her money stash and her tobacco tin. Why did she have to show Jane and that friggin' motel owner who fixed our friggin' tire that tobacco can? Just showed how stupid she was! Like she was a kid again, hiding babysitting money from everyone.

She heard Denny's voice again.

Another Friday night before the fights came on TV.

Where's your paycheck, Jo? You know you don't know a fuckin' thing about managin' money...and someone's gotta pay the bills. And that's me...you couldn't do a fuckin' thing if I wasn't around.....

"Jesus," she muttered as she flicked her butt to the ground and crushed it under her shoe. She reentered the motel room and heard Jane in the bathroom. She was coughing again, and Joanne could hear the water running.

Jane finally poked her head out from the bathroom.

"Jo, I'm starved," she said. "Let's head over to that bar."

TWENTY-TWO

After his conversation with Jane, Sheriff Boychuk decided another visit to Hubie's house was in order. He dreaded the difficult chat he would have to have with his friend of more than twenty years, but this was one issue that could not be dealt with over the phone.

From the moment he saw Denny's bloodied, crumpled body on the floor of the Lowry dining room, Boychuk knew that Joanne was involved in some way. Forget Hubie's wishful thinking that the shooter might have been some pissed and vengeful husband getting even; this was clearly a case of a battered wife who'd had enough. At least that's what he had thought until he spoke to Jane. She had confessed, sort of. But Joanne was now an accessory, and that was still serious.

He knew Hubie would take it hard.

Pulling into the Schumacher driveway, the county sheriff knew that the crime scene would still be fresh and cruel. His yellow tape still surrounded the house. He had assigned watchful deputies for the last twenty-four hours while his investigators gathered the last bits of evidence. That job should be finished tomorrow, he thought, but we can't let anyone mess with the place.

Meanwhile, Denny's body had been removed to the morgue, and he had no idea when—make that if—Hubie would hold a funeral for the man. He wondered if Joanne would want to eulogize him and, if so, what she would say about her husband.

All this was done, Boychuk regretted, in full view of television cameras. Dealing with the press was one of the things he hated most in his job. If it was left up to him, he'd just as soon ignore the bastards, even though they were useful from time to time.

Inhaling deeply, Boychuk put his Chevy cruiser in park, retrieved his hat and walked up the back steps to Hubie's home. This was not going to be much fun, he thought, as he knocked on the door. Dee appeared and greeted the sheriff. She knew there would be many of these visits over the coming days and weeks.

"Hello Sheriff," she said.

"Afternoon, Mrs. Killian, I hope I'm not interrupting anything?" he said. He had known Dee since Hubie had introduced them at the VFW where they met a few years before, and he liked her. He remembered thinking just how different Delores Killian was from Donna.

"No Sheriff. We're just waiting for Brent and his girlfriend to get here from Syracuse," she said. "Hubie didn't want to do it, but he called Brent this afternoon."

"How'd the boy take it?" Boychuk asked.

"Not good, but I'll let Hubie tell you himself," she said. "Come on in."

The sheriff entered the kitchen; it was a very familiar room. He recalled how anxious he had felt when he finally got up the nerve to ask Jane out. Not about his first meeting with Hubie, but with Donna. Jane had told Brian that her father was not like other dads...you know, the kind of guy who'd eye you up and down? Trying to figure out what kind of punk you were and what your plans would be for his daughter? No, Hubie's not that kind of guy, Jane said.

Now, my mother's another piece of work. I have no idea
how she'll react. Just do me a favor and don't piss her off,
Jane had warned.

From the central hallway, Hubie arrived and shook hands
with the younger man.

"Well?" Hubie simply asked.

"Pretty clear what happened, Hubie," Boychuk said.
"We've put out a warrant this afternoon, right after Jane
called me. From where, I do not know."

"She called you?"

"Yes, to tell me specifically that Joanne had nothing to do
with Denny's shooting. She called me on her cell phone and
our conversation lasted only about two minutes. I asked her
to come in and see me, but she made it plain that she had no
intention of doing that—at least not yet."

Hubie sighed at the grim news and looked to Dee for
support. She just shook her head, sadly.

"Did you speak with Joanne?" he asked.

"No. But I assume she was with Jane."

"I'm having a bad time with this, Brian."

"I know."

"And you have no idea where they are?"

The sheriff clenched his lips and shook his head.

"Not yet, but we've put out an APB. News like this
gets around fast, even in these parts, and it won't be long
before we pick them up. I'm just hoping they haven't left the
county, because then it'll be out of my hands. The troopers
will take over."

Hubie felt weak and sat down at his kitchen table. He
felt another twinge from his chest and breathed in deeply.
The discovery of Denny's body had shocked him. But the
realization that his daughters were responsible for the shooting was overwhelming. He didn't know how to feel.

"I just can't believe that Jane would do something like this, Brian," he added. "I kind of figured that Jo might snap at some point, but Jane?"

Boychuk paused before he replied to his friend.

"Hate to say this, Hubie, but Jane's been a stranger to you for a long time. You really don't know her."

Hubie said nothing, but the sheriff could sense that the older man agreed with him. It had been eight years since he had seen his rebellious daughter. She had arrived, reluctantly, to attend her mother's funeral. His wife's illness had progressed from diagnosis to death in a matter of weeks, or at least it seemed that way. It was more like four months, but all he knew was that she went fast.

Jane had carried a grudge for many years, but for the life of him, he didn't know why. Of course, Donna and his daughter had had that big fight in the driveway when she was a teenager, but people can get over things like that, couldn't they? In Jane's case, apparently not. But after he had reached her at her desk at the TV station, informing her about Donna's condition, she showed up surprisingly at his wife's bedside. He decided to leave them alone in the hospital room for an hour. But when Jane departed—in one hell of a hurry—she was crying, almost uncontrollably.

Ten days later, Jane had returned for the funeral. But this time there were no tears. Hubie wondered what had happened at Donna's bedside only days before. Were they tears of sadness—or of anger?

After delivering the grim news, Boychuk felt sorry for his friends. They didn't deserve any of this, he thought. Their lives will never be the same. So tonight, at least, he would leave them be.

"I'll be running along, folks," he announced. "As you can expect, we'll be burning a bit of midnight oil over this investigation. I hope we can convince your girls to come in and deal with everything, but who knows?"

Hubie rose from his kitchen chair.

"I'll see you out, Brian," he said morosely.

"Good night, Mrs. Killian," Boychuk said.

"Good night, Sheriff. Thank you for coming over."

Hubie reached for his coat and followed Boychuk out the door and down the back steps. He whistled for Griz to join them. The two men were walking to his squad car when another vehicle pulled up beside the cruiser and came to a halt. It was Brent and Tracy, their faces full of sadness and despair. Leaving the front door of his car open, Brent got out and walked towards his grandfather and the sheriff. Tracy was a few steps behind. Close to tears, Brent threw his arms around his grandfather.

"I had to come home, grandpa," he said.

"I know, son, I know."

"It's just been...so unreal," Brent said.

He regained control of himself, and gestured toward his girlfriend.

"Grandpa, you remember Tracy?"

"Yes, of course, nice to see you again, Tracy," Hubie said. "Sorry you had to be part of this."

Tracy grimaced, acknowledging Hubie's welcome.

"I wanted to be with Brent tonight," she said.

Hubie gestured towards the sheriff, who was witnessing the difficult but tender reunion.

"Brent, you remember Sheriff Boychuk?"

"Yes," Brent said, shaking hands with the police officer. "Good to meet you again, Sheriff."

"Brian here has been updating us on what's been going on, or at least what he knows so far," Hubie said, and he

proceeded to recap what Boychuk had told them a few minutes earlier, including details of Jane's phone call.

"Tell me, Sheriff, you can't believe that my mother had
anything to do with my dad's death, can you?" Brent asked.

But Boychuk simply shook his head.

"Sorry, Brent, can't do that. Wish I could, but I can't.
Your mom's involved, we're sure of that. Her sister seems
to be taking responsibility, but your mom's a part of this in
some way. Till we bring them in, we won't know the full
story."

Sensing the seriousness, Brent stared at the sheriff for a
few moments, biting his bottom lip so hard that he thought
it would bleed. He began to lose it again. He turned and
walked back to his car, slamming the door shut with such
force that the entire vehicle shook. Hubie thought there
would be broken glass.

Tracy followed Brent into the car, and in an effort to con-
sole him, wrapped an arm around his neck.

"Jesus fucking Christ!" Brent swore.

Tracy said nothing and continued to hold him tightly.

He turned towards her.

"You know, Trace, my mother took my old man's shit
for years. She'd never admit it, but I knew what was going
on. But look at her now? She gave up everything for that
bastard, and, now…now, they're gonna lock *her* up! And for
what? Why couldn't she just walk away? Why?"

"I don't know, Brent," she said, barely whispering.

"I don't know."

TWENTY-THREE

The troubled sisters walked across the motel parking lot and entered the roadhouse. For a Friday night on a holiday weekend, there were few patrons in the cowboy joint, but it was still early, Jane thought. Aside from a few beer drinkers, dressed mostly in denim and munching on peanuts in the shell at the long, polished oak bar, only two or three elderly couples were eating dinner quietly at tables along the windows. A pool table, near the bar, remained unused.

Jane scanned the dance floor and the accompanying stage. Guitar in hand and sitting on a stool before a lone microphone, Matt was belting out what she recognized as a Jackson Browne song. A soft yellow spotlight zeroed in on him, and he appeared to be lost in his music. To his rear, she could see a set of drums perched against the wall. Next to the drums sat a baby grand piano. None of the customers appeared to be paying much attention to him, but it didn't seem to matter.

Matt noticed the girls entering his saloon. He raised an eyebrow in recognition but continued his tune. Jane lifted a hand to wave to Matt, but Joanne simply averted her eyes and headed to the bar. They were greeted by a female bartender painted to the eights, if not the nines, and dressed in a short, white skirt. Despite the season, she wore a matching low-cut pleated blouse that was tied in a knot at her midriff. Jane noticed a belly button ring peaking out for all to see. A bar towel was slung over her shoulder, nearly masking what appeared to be a name tag attached to her blouse. The only thing thankfully missing was chewing gum, Jane thought. The bartender approached the sisters with a couple of menus.

"Evenin' ladies," she said. "Are you here for dinner?"

Jane read her name tag.

"Tammy is it? Yes, we understand the food is good here...at least that's what that guy over there tells us," she said, pointing to the stage singer.

"Not fancy, but decent," Tammy replied, placing the menus in front of them. "Can I bring you something in the meantime?"

"Bud Light draft for me," said Joanne.

Jane looked over Tammy's shoulder at the roadhouse's liquor collection resting on elevated glass shelving in front of a bar-long mirror. Not a great selection; a lot of the usual rot-gut in fact. But then she spotted what she was searching for.

"Johnny Walker Red on the rocks with soda water on the side," she said. "Make that a double and hold the soda."

"Got it," Tammy said and turned to reach for the Scotch.

Joanne raised her eyebrows at the order and looked at her sister.

"Someone's on a mission," she said.

Jane let out another loud cough.

"Nothing like red to cure a blue, sister."

Over on the stage, Matt wrapped up his set, placed his guitar on its stand and sauntered over to the bar.

Jane asked, "That's it? That's all we get?"

Matt climbed aboard a barstool next to Jane as Tammy brought the drinks. Seeing Matt arrive, she brought a small bottle of mineral water and placed it in front of him, as if it was a silent or unspoken ritual.

"Oh, I'll get up there again later," he said with a grin.

"Well, there's always the jukebox," Jane said, snidely. Joanne came to his defense.

"He wasn't *that* bad, Jane," she said.

Matt feigned a look of hurt and humiliation. "Not *that* bad? Such a ringing endorsement!"

"You know what I meant..." Joanne said. She was in no mood for small talk. If she had her way, they'd eat a little dinner and get back to the room. She was exhausted from the events of the last twenty-four hours.

"I know, I know," Matt replied. "I was just jammin' ya. So, how's the room? Clean enough for ya?"

"It's fine," Jane said.

"So, what're you ladies up to tonight?"

"You're looking at it," Jane replied, downing her Johnny Walker in one gulp before catching Tammy's eye for a refill. Matt noticed.

"Ah, that kind of night," he said.

Joanne wasn't paying attention. Instead, as her eyes perused the old roadhouse, she concluded that it was remarkably similar to the one she worked in after Brent left for Syracuse. Every drinking hole around here looks the same, she thought, although she was the last woman to know much about bars. Denny never took her out, but she'd join friends from time to time. Once, one spring evening, she and Hong Kong Wong decided to have a drink at one of the bars along the river. They weren't there five minutes before a couple of softball players, much younger than them, tried to hit on them. Jennie wasn't amused but Joanne was mildly flattered. When was the last time any man paid any attention to me?

So three years ago, she took a night job at the Wishbone Café downtown, the one next to her father's post office. She began serving tables and occasionally helped out in the kitchen. Denny had always said her store paycheck didn't pay for shit, and that she could look for a second job to bring in some extra dough. Denny didn't care how or when. If he stayed home on Fridays, it was only to watch the fights on television and drink. If he didn't make it home by supper time, she knew he'd be out until the wee hours of the morning. The next day, Saturday, was a day he kept for himself too. For fishing, hunting—anything to stay away.

Though she was on her feet all day at Turnbull's, her night job at the café was satisfying, almost liberating. During the day, Joanne played cashier to plumbers, carpenters and husbands with long honey-do lists. At the cafe, it was a different clientele, families out on their one night a week, maybe a trucker or two. Besides, the tips were good. On a good night she could make forty-five or fifty dollars, socking away a twenty or so in that tobacco can in the laundry room under a stack of old sheets. The laundry room was a perfect hiding place. Denny never set foot there.

An hour later and after nibbling at a Chicken Caesar salad, Joanne noticed the roadhouse was beginning to fill up with younger couples, as well as single men whose options for entertainment in the mountains were limited. Most of the tables were busy, the remaining bar stools occupied. Matt had left the bar and was again on stage, switching smoothly between country hillbilly and classic rock. A few couples were enjoying his music. He was pretty good, Joanne thought.

Starved, Jane plowed down on the baked haddock special and continued to order double Scotches. Before long she had joined a few couples on the dance floor, alone, swaying to what Joanne recognized as a Bruce Springsteen song. Finally, Matt took a break and the dancers dispersed. All but Jane. She scooted to the jukebox and deposited a handful of quarters. As another song came to life, Matt joined her at the Wurlitzer.

"Come on Mellencamp, dance with me!" she commanded, and soon the two were all over the floor, moving to a slow tune, her arms draped over him. Over at the bar, still sipping draft beer, Joanne noticed Tammy's reaction.

"Your friend is really goin' to town, huh?"

"She's my sister, and she's just letting off a little steam, that's all," Joanne said.

"Well, looks like more than that to me," Tammy replied, as she ran glasses over soap brushes in the sink before dousing them in a basin of grayish-looking rinse water in need of a change. Her towel was still slung over her shoulder. Joanne began to catch the bartender's drift.

"You and Matt an item?"

"You could say that...at least I like to think so."

Joanne shrugged, dismissing her fears.

"Don't worry, sweetheart. She's harmless."

"I'm not so sure," Tammy said.

Joanne continued to watch as Tammy glanced over her shoulder at Jane, dancing to slow songs with the singer.

Tammy's frown told her she was pissed.

What the hell am *I* doing here? Joanne asked herself.

TWENTY-FOUR

The next morning, Roberto entered the key into the lock and Jane's condo door opened. After his brief, unsatisfying call with her and a sleepless night in the Catskills, the New York attorney decided it was time to figure out what was going on. Leaving his skis behind and grabbing a coffee at some rundown joint on Route 23, he left Hunter just after dawn, turning his Infiniti north on the Interstate at speeds the troopers wouldn't appreciate. An hour or so later, about the time it took to listen to the greatest hits of Bob Marley on his iPod, an album he had downloaded after he and Jane met at Negril, Roberto found himself in front of Jane's building in downtown Albany.

Of course, he had been here before. After Jamaica, they had exchanged keys to their apartments. Unlike Jane, Roberto didn't particularly enjoy the drive from the city to Albany and had tried to convince her to fly to and from New York more often. Still, he was familiar with the capital, especially when corporate clients needed him to meet with their lobbyists or curry favors with the legislators. But he blamed their long-distance relationship on the Democratic governor. Why not, isn't that what politicians are for? If her boss hated Albany as much as Jane *said* he did, or as most of his predecessors did, why didn't he just move his office permanently to Manhattan? Jane wasn't entirely innocent either, he thought. She's the one who convinced Foley that he had to *appear* to be governing the Great State of New York, while coveting a higher office.

Roberto liked Jane. No, it was much more than that. He was convinced he was in love with her. But he sometimes wondered why. She was clearly the most intelligent woman he had met since his divorce four years ago. Her sense of humor—no, make that her sense of sarcasm—was one of her most endearing traits. He'd never encountered a woman like her, or any man for that matter, and he lived in New York, the veritable center of the sarcastic universe, the capital of snide, the hub and habitat of the impolite.

He knew she liked New York City and secretly hoped she would forsake politics to resume a broadcasting career. She was a natural on television; her on-air presence was magical, not at all like the current crop of phony, trash-talking celebrities that populated the airwaves today. Really, he thought, she could do anything she wanted in the media. Perhaps join a big advertising or PR firm on Madison Avenue. Or edit a magazine. Or, at the very least, launch a political blog. Anything to keep her closer to him. But he knew that wasn't going to happen as long as her boss remained as popular as he was. It looked like the District of Columbia was in the cards.

But New York was his kind of town. It had been home to Roberto since he was in his early teens, first in the Bronx when he arrived from the slums of Buenos Aires with his parents and his four sisters, and then eventually Manhattan. His father, Ricardo, had been a cook on an old navy frigate in the early eighties. But when the Brits kicked Argentina's ass in the Falklands, he and his wife Rosaria decided enough was enough and they packed themselves and their kids on a slow boat to the Bronx—in a way trading one slum for another. America, they felt, held out a greater future.

He didn't speak a word of English but that didn't deter young Roberto from succeeding in New York. He was a quick study. By the end of his first school year, the tenth grade, Roberto had conquered his fears and had become fluent. But not without insult, heartache and pain. Other kids in the Bronx, mostly immigrants themselves, were brutal; even the Puerto Ricans called him a spic. But by the time he was sixteen, he was six-two and nearly two hundred pounds. Nobody messed with him.

Roberto also discovered that he was smart and that academics came easy to him. So effortless, in fact, that his full ride to Columbia eventually led to law school and, after finishing in the top ten percent of his class, to one of Lower Manhattan's most prestigious firms for the past dozen or so years. After months of choreographing one of Wall Street's biggest mergers, the twinning of two giant HMOs, he agreed on a whim to his secretary's demands that he flee the city and head to Negril. There, she told him, play some tennis, waste your daylight hours on pulp fiction, demolish some piña coladas—and get laid. Those were her specific orders, particularly the last one. By his second day at the resort, when he and Jane met at the swim-up bar, he had accomplished three of his four goals.

Why that pool bar near the beach popped into his head as he entered Jane's building, he didn't know. But those concrete barstools, hidden discreetly underwater, had started it all. They'd had a wonderful week and could have left it at that. But whatever they had going, it dawned on both of them that they should probably continue their adventure in New York.

Sometimes, however, Roberto wondered what that "whatever" was. For the first few months after Jamaica, their relationship was laugh-filled, intellectually stimulating and hot. And sometimes rough, very rough. Their sex was the best he'd had, but she sometimes seemed to lose it. One time, to his shock, she bit him on the nipple and drew blood.

But when he asked what the hell she was doing, she simply professed her remorse and feigned innocence. You bring this out in me, Argentina, she'd say. But to Roberto, that answer seemed disingenuous, even insincere. He couldn't tell if it was simply passion, escape or sexual release. Or a power play to demonstrate she was equal—even superior—to men? Maybe she had become possessed or something? What the hell did he know? He was a lawyer, not a shrink.

Once in a while, she'd throw him a bone, hinting that maybe, just maybe, they had something real going. However, when he'd return the signal, in a determined attempt to make warm, she'd tossed him cool, sabotaging his emotions. She kept her distance, and not just figuratively. Theirs was an I-87 romance, and Roberto feared the Interstate would grow longer—at least metaphorically—if she graduated to the White House.

Entering her apartment, Roberto didn't know what to expect. But any clue to her suddenly weird behavior would be welcomed. From the beginning, he had doubted her "my dad is sick" story. It just didn't jive with the woman he knew. Roberto flicked on the hall light but quickly realized it wasn't necessary. The faux-wood blinds in her living room were open and the bright, morning sunshine illuminated the flat. He strolled slowly through the condo and surveyed the mess from the night before. She had always been an untidy woman; keeping a spotless place wasn't exactly a priority. Now, reams of reading material were strewn throughout the apartment.

But Roberto knew that Jane wasn't always this cluttered or chaotic. It was clear that she got out of Dodge pretty fast, he thought. He turned toward the kitchen and saw the empty bottle of Scotch. On the counter opposite sat the last remnants of the Irish cream, next to her prized White House mug. Jesus, she really hit the sauce before she left, he muttered to himself. On the couch was her briefcase. That was odd. Jane never went anywhere without her briefcase.

What the hell is going on? Maybe her dad really is sick? But why did she come back to her apartment? Why didn't she just drive directly to Morgantown? He wondered about her father, since she rarely spoke of him. Why the sudden desire to see a man she always described as a failure? He knew Jane had a twin, but had no idea what she looked like. Scanning the apartment, he remembered there wasn't a single family picture.

Roberto decided to investigate further. He opened her briefcase and started to rifle through her papers and briefing books. He didn't care if he was spying on state secrets; he just wanted to figure it all out. But the search came up empty. He walked over to her coffee table and picked up magazines and newspapers. Still nothing. Then he noticed the blinking red light on her telephone on an end table beside the couch. Now there's a machine that Jane rarely used, he thought. Why she had a landline, he didn't really know. She didn't need it. Her BlackBerry was her life-blood, her link to the world, and God help her if she lost that device.

The red light meant she had messages. He pressed the play button.

'You have two new messages', it annoyingly squawked, and it spit out the first. It was some telemarketer, and he quickly erased it.

The second message rocked him back on his heels. It was a bombshell.

Ms. Schumacher, it's Dr. Schaefer's office calling again. We know it's the holiday today but you left the office so upset last night that we couldn't set up your treatments. We'll

try your cell, too…but call us. We need to set your schedule
as soon as possible. Monday morning is wide open. So is
Tuesday afternoon. Please call us at—

Alarmed, Roberto memorized the number and pushed
the erase button. He took another long look at her apartment before walking towards the door, figuring he'd be back
here before he knew it.

But now was the time to hit the road, again.

Opening the front door, he noticed Jane's copy of the
Times-Union sitting face down on the hallway floor. It must
have been delivered only minutes before. He picked it up
and was about to throw it inside her apartment when he read
the large headline splashed across the front page.

"Jesus Christ!"

TWENTY-FIVE

Joanne stirred in her bed at the North Star Motel. It had been a fidgety, unsettled night for her, and she awoke a number of times. In past sleepless nights, and there were many in the twenty years she was married to Denny, she had always managed to rid herself of busy-brain by playing tricks on herself. She would imagine herself mounted on her father's snowmobile, racing over the winter trails at breakneck speeds, testing her skills...always testing...always pushing herself. She didn't have to count sheep; her thoughts of high-octane racing over the trails and through the woods usually did it and she'd be fast asleep in minutes.

There was no doubt about it. She was a hardcore sledder.

But last night had been different. The only thing racing was an overactive mind.

Then she remembered her dream.

During the night, she had been startled awake and it was a real doozie. She couldn't decide if it was a nightmare or a premonition. Whichever it was, like most dreams, it was bizarre and inexplicable.

She was with Denny again. They were riding in his septic truck, and he was driving carelessly, fishtailing over loose gravel, down some anonymous road in the country. No words were spoken, but occasionally he'd glance at her with a sneer that told her, as always, he was in charge. His eyes said it all.

Suddenly, Denny lost control of his huge truck and it plunged over a bridge and into the river. Joanne felt the vehicle filling quickly with dark, deadly water. But strangely she didn't panic. Calmly, almost methodically, she rolled down the passenger-side window, and holding her breath, she removed her seat belt and escaped. She pushed herself to the surface of the Oswegatchie, or at least she assumed it was the river at the end of her street.

She also assumed Denny did the same, but apparently he did not because—in this dream—she heard her husband shout for help. Why won't you save me? He demanded. But as his pleas grew louder, Denny was not in sight. She continued to dive—again and again and again—below the surface but to no avail. It was all in vain. She couldn't save him.

She could only save herself. An odd feeling came over her. She wasn't cold. She didn't even feel wet. Then she woke up and realized where she was.

What the hell was that all about? His voice! Those sounds! She knew she'd never forget them. Why don't I feel something? He was my husband forever, for God's sake!

Propping herself up in the motel bed, she looked over at the small digital clock on the dresser. It read eight-fifteen. Oh, maybe she got some sleep after all. The morning sun was peeking through a small crack in the room's curtains, and it was enough to lighten an otherwise drab and lonely unit. She raised herself on both elbows and looked over at Jane's bed next to hers. Her bed was still made.

She was not there.

"Ah, shit," Joanne said.

She jumped out of bed, and after a quick visit to the bathroom, was soon marching past the other units towards the motel office. At the lobby door, through the glass, she looked in and saw only an empty counter with no sign of life. She continued on across the parking lot, where she could see lights on in the bar. Matt was there; he was sweeping the floors. She stormed in, slamming the door behind her.

Matt looked up to see who was entering his bar and smiled.

"Good morning," he said, leaning on his broom. But he quickly realized she was in no mood for small talk.

"Damn it, Matt!" she yelled. "I turn my back and you're all over Jane? Is that what you mountain men do? Jump the drunk city chicks after they get wasted in your bar?"

Alarmed, Matt shook his head.

"Whoa, whoa, girl!" he replied. "What're you talkin' about?"

"Jane!" Joanne was livid, and it showed. "Where is she? Back in your unit, sleeping you and the booze off?"

Matt threw up his arms in defense.

"Joanne, slow down. She's okay, probably pretty hung over, but okay."

Joanne remained unconvinced, and it was not lost on Matt.

"Jane's on my couch in the office," he said. "If you had peeked in, you mighta seen her. After you left last night, her supper didn't agree with her. And when I tried to bring her back to your room, she wanted a glass of water. So, we went back to my office, and while I was getting her water, she passed out. A nuclear charge couldn't have lifted that gal from the couch last night. I just threw a blanket over her and said nighty night."

He raised his right hand as if he were swearing on one of those Gideon Bibles that were beside every bed in his rooms.

"That's the God's honest truth," he concluded.

Joanne eyed him suspiciously for a moment before responding.

"Nothing else?"

"Nothing else, Mom," he said, grinning widely, as if he were pleading for absolution.

Then, with two fingers together, Boy-Scout style, Matt saluted her.

"Barkeeper's honor!"

He had calmed her down.

"Buy you a cup of coffee?" he asked.

TWENTY-SIX

Brian Boychuk was at his desk, poring over the reports of the murder investigation assembled by his forensic experts. Preliminary tests from the buckshot taken from Denny's chest cavity and groin were "consistent" with shells found near Hubie's gun rack. When he retrieved the weapon, and he would, there would be no doubt. It was a pretty cut-and-dried case, he thought. Still, the shooting and Jane's subsequent admission of responsibility had shaken him. Never in his twenty-year career did he think he'd be heading up an investigation such as this.

The townsfolk were upset when they heard the news too, and more than a few of the big county's ninety-five-thousand inhabitants were signaling their displeasure. He had instructed Judy, his daytime switchboard operator, to reroute all the calls to him since he knew he could persuade voters that Denny's death was a crime of passion, not the beginning of some nut on a murderous rampage. The APB, and his discussions with the media, calmed most fears—especially from those in and around Morgantown who knew Denny or the kind of man he was.

Still, his brief conversation with the girl he once knew was unnerving and saddening. He tried to reconstruct what had happened. Denny must have been slapping Joanne around something fierce when Jane showed up, armed to the teeth with Hubie's shotgun, waiting for that piece of shit to provoke her. If he did—hell, he must have, knowing what a big yap Denny had—it was the stupidest thing he ever did. And the last thing too.

But whatever Denny had said, was that enough for Jane to shoot him in the gonads? Why in the balls, Boychuk wondered? Goddamn that must have hurt! And then she blasted him again, in the chest, knowing full well that that buckshot would kill him doornail dead. She's smart; she didn't need to fire that weapon to save Joanne from Denny's grip. So why did she pull that trigger—twice?

His ex-girlfriend was always a hothead and a "difficult filly to corral," as his rancher father liked to say when he and Brian would train horses on their farm outside Morgantown. Even when they were teenagers, Brian and Jane would lock horns over many things. She was never short of an opinion, and theirs was not exactly a love-hate relationship, he remembered. More like an "I-love-you-but-can't-stand-you-sometimes" kind of courtship.

Throughout most of their senior year in high school, Brian had watched Jane from down the corridor as they fidgeted at their lockers, sorting school books and talking with friends. She was one of the foxiest girls in high school. But he didn't know if he'd get out of the batter's box, let alone make it to first base. There were at least three, maybe four other guys on the football team who'd she'd choose before him, he thought at the time. But peering as inconspicuously as he could, trying not to get caught, he didn't see any other boys near her locker for weeks. Awkwardly, Boychuk had mustered up the nerve to approach her. Before he could utter a word, however, she had signaled who would be in charge.

"It's about time," Jane said, with a smirk and without even turning in his direction.

"I'm sorry?" he said, surprised. "I don't know what you're talking about."

"Don't bullshit me, Boychuk!" she barked. "We both know you've been looking my way all term. It's about time you came over to say hi."

Sheepishly, he had agreed. It was very difficult for him not to notice her. With her long auburn hair, sometimes tied in a bouncy ponytail, but usually streaming down her back, Jane Schumacher was the finest specimen at Morgantown High.

And that's how it all started.

She had agreed to accompany him to the school dance that Friday night, and from that moment on, he and Jane were nearly inseparable. At Jane's request, he would agree to double-date with Joanne and Denny for a night at the drive-in or when the carnival came to town. Though they were teammates on one of the state's best high school football squads—he was a fleet running back while Lowry was a defensive tackle—they never cared for each other. Joanne was pretty awesome back then, too. But more than once, Boychuk had caught Denny eying Jane up and down. And it bugged him.

Boychuk often wondered what Joanne saw in Denny. Granted, as a teenager, Denny was tougher than an Amish mule; he liked to pummel the living shit out of opposing players, especially those who carried the ball. He guessed this toughness—and the possibility of a pro football career—might have been the basis of Joanne's attraction to Denny. But when Denny got hurt during his senior year, ending any hope for a rich sporting life, his anger levels exploded, bitterly swinging out at everything and everybody. And that's when he started drinking like a Bills fan at a tailgate party.

Of all the dates that he and Jane enjoyed, Boychuk remembered their senior prom the best. He surprised her that night by showing up in his new deputy's uniform and remembered her lukewarm response. Oh, she told him he was a hunk, and looked good, but he never forgot her tepid, almost indifferent reaction. Still, it had been a wonderful night. Jane was tall, dark and beautiful in her prom dress. They had partied till the sun came up.

That spring and summer of 1985 was nothing short of electric. He had felt they had a future together. She had received her acceptance at Oswego State but there seemed to be an unwritten agreement—college or no college—that they were meant for each other. But by the Fourth of July or a bit later—he couldn't remember the precise moment—something had happened that changed everything between them.

Jane had turned inward and quiet, not at all like the vivacious, outspoken girl he'd known. She wouldn't talk to him. She ignored his telephone calls. One day, unannounced, he paid a visit to the golf course where she worked but she refused to see him. She just pushed him away and, reluctantly, he decided to give her some space. Then about six weeks later, in a cloud of dust, she drove into the driveway of his father's ranch and declared profanely that she had no intention of staying one more day in this armpit of a town—or engaged to a *fucking cop,* no less.

Without giving him as much as a moment to react, she jumped into her old Datsun and disappeared down the road. She simply vanished. When he pressed Hubie and Donna for answers, all they would say was that they thought Jane had left for good. He was heartbroken. It was only much later that he learned through the grapevine that Jane had been spotted living in the mountains.

The phone rang, and it snapped him from of his daydream.

It was Jack Davis on the line. Not only was he the head of the governor's security detail but an assistant commissioner of the New York State Troopers as well. Boychuk had known Davis from their days at the police academy in the eighties.

"Jack, how are you?" Boychuk asked, knowing full well why the senior trooper was on the line.

"I'm fine, Brian," Davis said, but the county sheriff figured he probably wasn't. Jack Davis was a busy man. He wasn't exactly the type to pick up the phone to make idle chitchat with a one-time colleague.

"Listen, Brian, I'm getting more than a bit of heat from the governor over that murder up your way and, of course, that press secretary of his. I'm just calling to find out what's new, so I can get Foley off my back."

Boychuk knew this call would come sooner or later. If the sisters had left Morgan County, and he had a suspicion they had, he would have to turn the investigation over to the troopers and the state bureau of investigation. But he wasn't ready to relinquish ownership.

"Trust me, Jack, I know she works for Foley, but I've got this handled," Boychuk reassured his friend. "I've spoken to Jane Schumacher, and I have every reason to believe she's not far away."

"How do you know that Brian?"

"Well, I don't, Jack but I've known Jane and her sister a long time, and I don't think they'd go off very far. Frankly, I think they're just holed up in some goddamn motel near here trying to figure it all out. I have every reason to believe she'll call me again today or hell, show up on my doorstep. I asked her yesterday to come in and see me, and she didn't say she wouldn't. Jane's a smart gal and knows that she's just getting herself and her sister in deeper shit if she stays away."

Davis wasn't buying it.

He knew this murder investigation was bigger than any sheriff of any upstate county. That his friend knew these women personally was another issue, politically, because the shit was about to hit the fan. Jane Schumacher was not your run-of-the-mill suspect. She was one of the governor's senior aides. However, Davis knew that as long as the women didn't leave Morgan County, he could only offer assistance to the local authorities.

Just then, one of Boychuk's deputies arrived at his desk. The sheriff cupped the receiver so the trooper couldn't hear him.

"Jack Davis, as predicted," Boychuk whispered to his deputy.

The deputy nodded. It was no surprise to him.

Davis continued.

"I hope you're right, Brian, for all our sakes," the governor's chief cop said. "Listen, do you need any help? Can your department get this done, bring them in?"

"I've got this handled, Jack," Boychuk said. "But if I need anything, you'll be the first one I'll call."

The sheriff bid his good-byes and hung up the phone.

"Our fine governor and future president wants the Gestapo to take over," Boychuk said. "Whatcha got for me?"

The deputy smiled, waving a piece of paper.

"I have good news and not so good news," he said.

"Give it all to me," the sheriff replied.

"Well, the good news is that it seems Miss Jane used her ATM card," he said. "The not so... is that they're three counties over."

TWENTY-SEVEN

Still in her blue jeans and sweater from the night before, and covered with a heavy, woolen blanket, Jane looked around the room and wondered where the hell she was. Jesus, she thought, third night in a row. One of these nights I'll take my clothes off *before* I go to bed. It was a small room, lit only by a lone, dust-covered window near the ceiling. There was a curtain behind her and another door at the opposite end of the room. Looking around, she saw a picture on the wall and figured out where she was.

The motel office!

Her eyes continued to scan the room. A large, antique oak desk was pushed against the wall, and an old computer monitor—its face lined with orange, red and green Post-IT notes—rested in one corner with a small, silver lamp in the opposite end. On the wall, a cork bulletin board was cluttered with what Jane guessed were invoices thumb-tacked over each other, perhaps to avoid payment if they remained sight unseen. Under the lamp sat a framed picture of Matt with an elderly couple, presumably his parents. On the wall to the right was another photo of a rock band. In both pictures, he was wearing one of those crazy horse cowboy hats. He didn't look bad at all.

Now a few memories of the previous night returned, and she cringed. After that gal—what was her name? Pammy?—delivered the third or fourth double Scotch, she couldn't remember much else. She hoped she didn't do anything stupid. But then she remembered the wooden dance floor covered with sawdust and peanut shells. She could see Matt up on the stage, singing. Oh, Christ, there was more...the jukebox...scrambling for quarters to play a few songs...some slow dancing. It was coming back.

But not all of it. How in hell did she end up here? Jesus, I feel like crap again. Slowly she lifted herself from the couch and walked towards the lobby. Good, there's nobody here. Jane spied her ski jacket on the back of a chair and exited through the curtain, around the counter and from the office. She hoped that Joanne was in the unit because she didn't know where the hell her key was.

Joanne was propped up against the pillows on her rumpled, unmade bed when Jane walked in. The television was on, but Joanne wasn't paying much attention. She was engrossed in a *Times* crossword puzzle, and she barely acknowledged her sister's arrival. She had just lit another cigarette.

"Nice of you to finally surface," Joanne said, dryly.

Without answering, Jane noticed the cigarette and became incensed.

"Oh fuck, you're smoking again!" she said. "Goddamn it, that thing's stinking up the entire room!"

Joanne quickly doused the smoke but wasn't happy about doing so.

"Jesus, I didn't know you became such a friggin' tyrant," she said. "And you thought *Mom* was bad."

"Well, go outside if you want to smoke!"

"It's too cold!" Joanne protested.

"Tough shit. I'm not going to sit in here and inhale that crap."

"Well, I'm not sure I wanna stay in here and take *your* crap!" Joanne said, her voice rising in frustration.

Jane marched to the bathroom and slammed the door loudly behind her. Peering closely into the mirror, Jane didn't like who and what she saw. She knew she had been wrong: red was not a fucking cure for the blue. The booze wasn't working. She felt worse now than she ever did.

Look in the mirror, Jane!

That summer…that summer of 1985…and the memory of the knock-down-drag-'em-out battle she'd had with her mother in the kitchen returned. It was an incident that set the stage for the rest of her life. She'd been dealing with this for…well, forever it seemed.

Donna's voice came back.

That shrill and accusatory voice of hers…rising with every word, growing louder and louder. She was relentless.

That's just great, Jane, that's just fine!

How stupid can you get?

If you hadn't played so fast and loose, you wouldn't be in this trouble…

Admit it…

Look at yourself. The way you dress?

The way you flaunt yourself around?

Skirts up around your ass?

How could you blame him?

You can't blame him…just take one long look in the mirror, Jane.

It's all your fault, and you know that…

…just take one long look in the mirror, Jane…

"Goddamn it!" Jane screamed. She hated mirrors.

How could a mother—any mother—say things like that to her daughter? Did she hate me that much? Jane breathed deeply, and it hurt. She began splashing cold water on her face, thinking it would be enough. But it wasn't. She finally decided to strip down and have a shower. As the steaming water poured over her, so did the tears. Again.

Forty minutes later, she emerged from the bathroom. Through the unit's window, she could see Joanne outside on the covered stoop having another cigarette. Jesus, she's going to have to stop that habit, Jane thought. But it's up to her, not me. I can't get her to stop. Only Joanne can do that herself…

Then she shook her head, disgusted with herself. Fuck, will you listen to me? I have to lay off her for awhile.

The shit she's put up with?

Still wrapped in a large motel towel, Jane was trying to decide what to wear—I'm running out of clean clothes, she thought—when her BlackBerry rang. She picked it up and scanned its blue-lit screen.

It was Foley. She decided to take the call.

"Hello Governor," Jane said, guardedly.

"Jane! You're there! I haven't been able to reach you."

"Why, Wendell, you know I'm at your service twenty-four-seven," she said.

"That's not true. Your phone's been off. But I'm not talking about that, Jane. How are you?"

"I'm fine, Wendell. Just enjoying the holidays with my family," she replied.

Foley was seated at his desk in Albany. When Marcia stormed into his office the night before, he had assembled his political team and asked Jack Davis to brief them. This was serious. But he had known Jane a long time and he wasn't about to let the media—in their chorus of condemnation, smelling red meat—control the agenda. He would delay an official reaction until he got the chance to speak with her. He wanted to give her the benefit of the doubt. But after Davis's briefing, Foley knew that benefit was *in* doubt.

"That's not what I understand, Jane," Foley said. "From what Marcia has told me, from what Jack Davis says, the world as we know it has been turned upside down."

Jane sighed.

It had been thirty-six hours since she broke up that fight in Joanne's dining room—a strange way of putting it, she thought, *broke up* a fight—and she knew this call from Foley would come, and soon.

"How about I call Marcia and have her release a statement saying, 'Governor Foley's whacked-out press secretary has lost her mind but that's no reason to believe her boss can't run for the White House.' What do you think of that, Wendell?"

Foley was in no mood for Jane's glibness.

"Not a laughing matter, Jane," he scolded.

Just then, Jane had another loud coughing fit.

"Jane, are you all right? That cold, or whatever you have, sounds like it's getting pretty bad."

Jane recovered.

"I'll be okay, Governor," she said, her voice still raspy.

"I'm not so sure, Jane. Let me help you. Where are you?"

"I told you, Governor. Out for a ride with my sister."

"Jane, this is serious. You have to give yourself up. Jack tells me that some upstate sheriff says he has it under control, but I'm not buying it."

"That's Chucky for you!" Jane said.

"What? Who?"

"Sheriff Boychuk... of Morgan County. An old friend," she said.

"Well, that just makes things worse, and I don't like what I'm hearing, Jane," Foley replied. "If your sheriff friend doesn't handle this right, Jack will take over. I'm giving them twenty-four hours to do so...which is about twenty-three *too many* in my judgment."

He paused for a moment.

"Jane, why don't you just come in?"

"Everything will be resolved soon, sir," she said ruefully. "I have something to do before that happens, though. Whatever, I promise I won't embarrass you much longer."

Jane started making a garbled sound into her BlackBerry. It was on purpose.

"Oops, losing my signal, Wendell. Wendell?"

And she hung up.

TWENTY-EIGHT

It was shortly before noon when Roberto pulled into Morgantown. As he traveled the same roads that Jane had journeyed only days before, his mind was a cauldron of emotions. Shock, anger, disbelief—you name it. Forty-eight hours ago, life was pretty good. Today, he didn't know.

He had planned this weekend in the Catskills for weeks and was ecstatic when Jane said she could join him. For months, she had been working non-stop for Foley and the governor had agreed to a three-day pass. They would squirrel away in the hills, do a few obligatory runs, enjoy a rare Malbec and dine on a little *asado de tira*, perhaps some *chivito* or *empanadas*, sweetly followed by a little *dulce de leche*—all Argentinean delicacies. His father, the navy cook, had taught him at an early age that women liked men who weren't afraid of a kitchen. This was fine with Jane; her most ambitious recipe was a bizarre, curried rice dish that she tore out of a magazine at the dentist's office.

This weekend would be extra special, he told himself. He was going to surprise her. And it wasn't just the transfer he had engineered to the firm's Washington office shortly after Foley had secured the nomination.

Roberto realized his dire predictions about Foley's prospects were only wishful thinking. Jane's boss was a smart, charismatic guy, and if he didn't screw it up, would likely be the next occupant of 1600 Pennsylvania Avenue. We could do worse, he thought, a lot worse. He's not your typical liberal who never met a social program he didn't want to expand.

As a Latino, Roberto had bucked the Hispanic trend toward the Democrats. He was a Republican. But he knew the GOP's gig was probably up; the Congress was swinging left-of-center and there wouldn't be another Republican in the White House for some time. His party was politically bankrupt, lacked a single good idea and was leaderless. He was saddened by the state of affairs.

Over and above all that—and despite Jane's protestations— Roberto had remained a Republican. He was a capitalist. A free-enterpriser who clawed his way to the top. He was the very embodiment of the American dream and he wasn't about to give it up.

Still, he was resigned to a Foley victory. The governor would win.

But that never stopped Roberto from raising Jane's ire.

"I'm not just a pretty face, you know," he had teased her. "Immigrants like me sometimes know more about your history than you do."

Jane always had a quick retort.

"Immigrant, my ass, Argentina," she cried. "Don't give me that 'I-just-fell-off-the-freighter' crap. You're as American as apple pie, baseball and deficit spending!"

He remembered this conversation when he had spoken to his immigrant mother, Rosaria. His mom had pleaded with him to come home for Thanksgiving and be with his family, and would he please bring Jane?

"She is welcomed," Rosaria had told her son over the phone last week, her broken English evident. It was a language with which she and her husband still had difficulty despite the fact that they'd been in New York for twenty-seven years.

After the Falklands fiasco and recognizing Argentina's penchant for tin pot generals, dictators and rogues—usually under the beret of the same man—they knew they had to leave. On arrival, Ricardo found a job in a popular, upper-Manhattan restaurant while Rosaria put a sign in their apartment window advertising her sewing skills. It was enough to feed their family in their adopted land.

Ricardo was hard-working, skillful and smart—traits that Roberto and his sisters inherited. Within three years, his father was managing the place and, by the early nineties, was able to convince a bank that a vacant store a few blocks away deserved a fine dining establishment serving the delights of Buenos Aires. Putting in eighteen hours a day with the help of his kids who bused tables, took out the garbage and swept the floors, his new venture, *Ricardo's,* was an immediate hit. As a consequence, the restaurateur's only son learned to cook—and liked it.

"Mom," he timidly said to his mother several weeks ago, "I'm sorry, but Jane and I can't make it home for Thanksgiving." Since his first year in high school, Roberto had only spoken English to his mother even when she'd revert to Spanish when she got excited, and this was one of those times. Rosaria revered Thanksgiving, her favorite American holiday, and its special meaning for immigrants. It meant her large grown family could be together at least once a year.

Breaking the news, he expected his mother to be disappointed and she didn't let him down. In her mother tongue, Rosaria let him have it, delivering the verbal equivalent of double barrels. How could you do this to me? How could you do this to your mother and your father and your sisters and your brothers-in-law and your nieces and your nephews? How could you, Roberto?

But listen to me, he said in English, always in English. Listen to me. I have news. I have good news. Do you know where I went last week? Do you know where? I went down to 47ᵗʰ Street, Mama. You know what's on 47ᵗʰ Street? Yes, Mama, that's right. It's the diamond district of New York. She smiled. Everything was okay. Rosaria liked Jane.

Yes, Roberto thought. This weekend *was* going to be special.

Past tense, he now thought.

His GPS system easily found Hubie's house and he pulled his Infiniti into the driveway. Immediately he noticed Jane's Mercedes parked in front of the garage. Next to her car was what he guessed was her dad's pick-up truck with the large snowplow mounted on its front. For a few moments, Roberto allowed his eyes to gaze around the property and towards the dilapidated home next door. That's where it all *happened*, he thought. That's Jane's sister's place.

He looked over to his passenger seat and retrieved Jane's copy of the *Times-Union*. Roberto didn't know how many times he had read and re-read the lead story, implicating a senior Foley aide in an upstate murder. Lifting the newspaper and resting it on his steering wheel, he looked again at Joanne's house. Then back to the newspaper. Then back to the house. Then back to the paper and its wire service photos on the front page. There was Denny being wheeled out on a stretcher in a body bag. Another photo, inset, was a shot of Jane looking impressive and official with the governor at their news conference the previous day.

As he stepped from his vehicle and mounted the back stairs to Hubie's house, he couldn't help but think that his life was now one of front pages and news bulletins. But never mind me, he thought. He was peripheral to the horrific drama unfolding in Jane's life. Where was she? What was she going through? How was she doing? And then he remembered his call to Dr. Schaefer. He had called the number on Jane's answering machine, and to his utmost surprise, the doctor herself came on the phone.

Roberto reached the door and knocked.

Hubie answered with a puzzled look on his face. There was a strange man on his back steps.

"Can I help you?" Hubie asked.

"Mr. Schumacher?"

"Yes."

"I'm sorry to bother you. My name is Roberto Alvarez and I'm a friend of your daughter, Jane," he said.

Hubie was momentarily surprised to meet Roberto and didn't know how to respond.

"May I come in?" Roberto asked.

"Yes, yes, of course," the older man replied, and opened the screen door.

TWENTY-NINE

Matt had almost finished filling the tank in his nine-year-old Silverado when the sheriff's cruiser pulled into the parking lot of the Valero station. It was early afternoon; he'd had a few errands to run before he was needed at the road-house for what he had hoped would be a busy Saturday night. Business wasn't bad, but it could be better, he thought. Ski season will be here soon.

He loved the Adirondacks, but for the longest time, he'd almost forgotten how much. In his late teens and early twenties, he and his touring band made stops in every hamlet in upper New York and New England, even venturing into Canada from time to time. They had knocked on the doors of every biker bar and country-and-western joint they could find, pleading with owners to play for their patrons. Then, thinking that he'd had talent, he decided to move to points south and west—to Nashville and Los Angeles and back—in search of country music's holy grail, a recording contract.

His fifteen years of touring were exhausting and frustrating, if not self-destructive. Of course, there was more than enough Jack to float a party barge, not to mention assorted powders that went up his nose. Along the way, he'd met a woman named Janelle and they had a daughter together. His little girl's name was Jamie. That forced him to get his act together for a while. But two years ago, Jamie, by now a whiny, mutinous thirteen-year-old, moved with her mother to Albuquerque. When Jamie called him—that is, *if* she called him—it was for...what else? Money.

That was when he took stock of his life and declared it a mess. He had cut a few albums, but sales were negligible. What was he thinking? There was no recording career and probably never would be. Then Hillary, his beloved mother, died suddenly of a hemorrhagic stroke. Her death was followed six months later by Jake's, his pop, who probably had no more use for life. That was the wake-up call that Matt needed and he made up his mind to return home. He took the small chunk of cash he'd inherited from Jake to buy the motel and bar in the mountains, and packed up his Silverado one last time. You can't go wrong in these hills, he thought.

After a moment of fidgeting with the gas cap, Matt watched as the police cruiser came to a halt in front of the store. That's a bit strange, he thought. It had a *Morgan County* insignia on its side, and he immediately wondered why a sheriff from two or three counties over was in this part of the state. Two officers got out and entered the store. Matt tightened the gas cap on his truck and followed the cops through the door.

The sheriff was showing mug shots to the clerk behind the counter. Matt, waiting his turn to pay for his gas, stood behind the sheriff and his deputy. He couldn't help but recognize the pictures the cops were showing.

"Are you sure you haven't seen this woman?" Boychuk asked, referring to an eight-by-ten picture of Jane Schumacher. "Think real hard, okay?"

"Can't say that I have, Sheriff," the teenaged clerk replied, pushing her multiple shades of spiked purple hair to one side, then another. A gold earring was affixed to one eyebrow and another protruded from her nose. She smacked a large wad of chewing gum of what Matt guessed was Dubble-Bubble, judging from the tennis ball-sized pops she was creating and destroying under the sheriff's brimmed hat.

Boychuk frowned. This kid was annoying the crap out of him.

"We know she was here yesterday at this time," he said, his voice demonstrating frustration. "You were on duty, right?"

"Yeah, I was here. I'm always here."

"Well, we know she bought gas and got money from your ATM," the sheriff continued. "And you're saying you can't remember her?"

"She don't ring a bell…sorry."

Matt chose a magazine from a nearby rack and pretended to be reading.

Then he spotted Joanne's picture.

"What about this one," Boychuk demanded. "Seen her? These gals are in a lot of trouble and any help you can give us would be appreciated."

The clerk, blowing yet another loud bubble, looked over the picture and a light went on, if only a dim one. The sheriff figured it might have only been a candle.

"Yeah, I did see this one," the clerk said, excited to be of assistance to the sheriff. "She bought some smokes, soda and stuff. And a lottery ticket."

Boychuk was astounded

"A lottery ticket?" he asked. "She bought a lottery ticket?"

"Yeah," the clerk said, pointing to her tray of tickets under her glass counter. "One of these scratch and sniffs… ah…I mean, scratch and *wins*. That's what my dickwad brother calls them. I remembered her because she had this long, stringy blonde hair with gnarly roots."

Matt decided he would interrupt the conversation between the cop and the clerk. Feigning impatience, he dropped a couple of twenties on the counter.

"Forty for the gas, right?" he asked.

"That's fine," the clerk said.

As he was exiting the store, he heard the sheriff once again. "You wouldn't happen to know where these gals could be?"

"No idea, Sheriff," the young clerk said. "We get a lot of customers in here every day."

Matt decided his errands could wait. He jumped into his truck and drove the mile or so back to his motel and bar. As he drove up, he could see Joanne's maroon Explorer still parked in front of their unit. He was about to walk over and knock on their door when he looked through the porch windows and into the roadhouse. He decided to check in first, see how it was going and went in. Lunch hour was nearly over and the tables were emptying. A few stragglers were sitting at the bar and Tammy was making small talk with them.

He was about to leave when he heard sounds coming from the direction of the stage. He turned to look. It was still darkened; the dance floor lights were out. But he could hear soft, musical sounds coming from his piano. A female singer, her back to him, was playing.

It was Joanne.

He recognized the tune...it was a gentle Sarah McLaughlin song.

Matt looked around the nearly empty bar. A couple of his regulars were there, drinking draft beer, flirting with Tammy. They were oblivious to the sounds coming from the stage. Tammy looked up and saw Matt enter the bar. Their eyes made contact briefly before one of her customers diverted her attention, ordering another round. Without Joanne seeing him, he sat down quietly at a table in the corner.

Far away from here...from this dark, cold hotel room...and the endlessness you feel...

Joanne continued, alone in her music, alone on the stage.

Matt sat there nearly in awe. He glanced back towards the bar. There was nothing but disinterest in what was unfolding on stage. *These dumb fucks probably think it's the juke box.* Leaving sophisticated, urbane and tempting Los Angeles eighteen months ago was bittersweet; he loved California but knew he had to move on. His decision to return to the hills, however, meant he'd have to deal with people who didn't know the difference between a guitar pick and an ice pick.

Listening to Joanne, at the piano, he was enraptured.

Spend all your time waiting for that second chance...

This chick is good, he thought. *She can really play. Can sing too.*

There's always some reason to feel not good enough...

She couldn't have had any real training, could she? Obviously, she's playing by ear. Not bad at all. Nice vocals... good range.

In the arms of an angel...I'll find some peace tonight...

At last, Joanne wrapped up her song and for a moment remained transfixed, almost spellbound. She was basking silently in her accomplishment. From his table, Matt rose and started walking to the stage, clapping. His hands paused between each clap for emphasis. Surprised and uncomfortable, Joanne whipped around. Someone had actually been listening. Not just someone. It was Matt.

She'd never had an audience, any audience.

"Very nice, little lady," Matt said.

"How long were you here?"

"Long enough," he replied. "And that was one bitchin' song!"

"You really think so?"

"I do. It was great."

"Just something I've enjoyed, or used to enjoy...when I figured no one was paying attention," she said.

"Used to?"

"Yeah, a gazillion years ago...when things were different."

"Well, I don't know where you learned to tickle the keys like that, or sing, but you're really good."

"Thanks," she said, their eyes locked for a few moments. He signaled for her to join him at a nearby table.

"C'mon, I need to talk to you," he said.

Perplexed by the change in the tone of his voice, Joanne followed him as they made their way back to a table in the corner. She looked over to the bar and saw that a few additional customers had arrived. Above the red-felt pool table, a stain-glassed Tiffany-style lamp had now been switched on. A man who looked to be in his thirties was racking the numbered balls; his partner, in overalls, was leaning on a cue waiting to break.

She nervously joined Matt.

"Listen, it's none of my business, but are you and your sister okay?" he asked in a concerned voice.

"Yeah, well she's not feeling very good today, but that's partly your fault," she said. "Why?"

"Well, I don't mean the booze...lemme tell you what's on my mind. You know, when I was fixin' that flat of yours, I couldn't help but see that shotgun in the back of your truck."

Joanne immediately became defensive.

"It's my dad's," she said anxiously. "Hunting season, you know."

"I figured that. But there's more. I was over at that gas station today. You know the one, down the road?"

She nodded.

"Well, I was just there, and...uh...some sheriff was there, askin' a whole lotta questions about the two of you."

"Oh, yeah?" she asked.   A terrible feeling came over Joanne. Boychuk was closing in. It wouldn't be long before we'll have to face the real music, she thought.

"Yeah. Now, I'm tempted to ask you what's goin' on because I like you both," he continued. "But then I thought all of this is really none of my affair. Know what I'm sayin'?"

"Maybe."

He reached into his vest pocket and pulled out the keys to his pick-up truck. He offered them to Joanne.

"And even though it's none of my concern—what you girls mighta done or not—I might be so bold as to make a suggestion," he said. "You wanna hear it?"

Joanne said nothing but her eyes told him that she was open to any of his ideas.

"Okay, I'd like to suggest that you and your sister borrow that truck of mine outside and high tail it outta here as soon as you can. Don't worry…I'll put your SUV in a safe place, where it'll be looked after. How do you like my suggestion so far?"

Joanne's eyes turned toward the roadhouse's window. The early afternoon light was streaming in. It was a beautiful day.

She knew *he* knew—about the mess they were in.

"But won't that get you into trouble?"

He smiled.

Trouble?

Compared to the time he and his band got busted at the Canadian border? Their Ryder truck loaded to the nuts with musical gear, they had crossed the bridge at Detroit with about a pound of weed hidden in an acoustic guitar. Now talk about *dumb* fucks! That was *real* stupid. He and his group spent two days in that hoser jail before his dad drove over from Seneca Falls to bail them out.

"Naw, my truck's been stolen three times!" he said, shrugging his shoulders. "Well, not here, in California, but ripped off nonetheless. But fact is, if anyone asks, that's what I'll tell 'em, and they'll buy it. Now, where might you be heading?'

"Sure you want to know?" Joanne asked.

Matt nodded.

"Jane wants to drive up to the Lake Placid area."

"Well, again, I don't want to throw kerosene on the campfire, but my dad left me a cabin up there. It isn't much...but you're welcome to it. The key to the place is on that chain."

Joanne smiled at Matt's offer. Did I misjudge this guy? Or was it that she just didn't trust most men?

"One final thing, though," he said, grinning widely.

"Don't forget your dad's double-barrel. Even though I'm just a redneck from these mountains, I don't have any use for 'em myself."

THIRTY

After Roberto left Morgantown to return to his cabin in the Catskills, Hubie told Dee he needed some time to think. He reached for his winter coat, Griz's collar and whistled for his dog. The late November day still had a couple of hours of light, and fresh air was what this old man needed. Dee said she understood. Her plans were to go home for a few hours; her friend needed to deal with this news by himself.

She had never seen him so distraught. She had never seen him so close to tears. It was becoming a bit clearer now, Dee thought. Why Jane did what she did. Dee had always hated guns and would never go near Hubie's collection in the garage. But she was starting to understand Jane's motivation. That didn't excuse her from taking the law into her own hands. But she knew what Joanne had been going through with Denny.

Bundled up, Hubie followed Griz as the dog trotted down the stairs and down the long driveway. The light dusting of Thanksgiving Day snow had disappeared but he could sense that more was on the way. The clear, cold days since Thursday night were coming to an end; a new front was moving in. Before Roberto had arrived, he was able to mount the plow on his truck and was prepared for winter.

He'd be busy soon.

At the end of the driveway, he picked up the pace as he walked briskly down the road. Griz knew the route. They were heading to their favorite path along the Oswegatchie, the lazy and winding river nearby. Hubie's doctor, a fellow

Army vet, had bluntly told him he had to do something about his bulging beer gut and the best way was to stop drinking. Knowing that was out of the question, the old military doctor had ordered daily walks. Not just a leisurely stroll either.

He had to get the old pump going.

A week after he was discharged from the Army, Hubie and Donna had made the two-storey house on Seward Drive their home. He couldn't believe that was more than forty years ago. His plan was to stay in the Army, retire with at least a twenty-year pension and figure out what the future held in store. He had been only twenty-six but already had eight years under his military-issued belt, and felt he had many good years of Army life ahead.

That was before he met Donna at some Watertown bar. At nineteen, she was stunning, easily the most beautiful girl he had ever seen. It was the spring of 1966, and not surprisingly, she had that beatnik look about her, adorned in a loose-fitting, floral dress whose hem ended abruptly above the knees, giving Hubie and his warriors a chance to witness the finest pair of legs in the room. Her long, glossy reddish-brown hair flowed airily down the middle of her back, aided by a gentle breeze emanating from a pair of French doors that opened widely to a large, outer deck. With warm weather upon them, revelers were eager to jump the seasonal queue.

There she was at the long bar, now filled to capacity sitting beside a thin, hook-nosed woman who Hubie assumed might have been a co-worker. Immediately, Donna reminded him of Grace Kelly—only as a brunette—when the starlet played opposite Cary Grant in *To Catch a Thief*, the first feature he saw as a kid at the old Allegheny Theater back home.

But Donna was neither a hippie nor an Army groupie. Far from it. She wasn't influenced, let alone impressed, with the hordes of hard bodies that would drop into the town's beer joints like paratroopers landing in Normandy, looking to get laid before they shipped out to the jungles of Southeast Asia. Maybe her friends were willing participants, but not her. Let them stake out a future husband, a man of their khaki dreams who could offer a life of exotic travel to posts like Pearl Harbor, or Guam, or Germany—even California. But not her. She was determined to get an education and build her own life.

At least she thought so.

But against her better judgment one night, Donna agreed to have a beer with her friend Joyce after work. She was bored and work that day and every day was tedious. Her life was deadly dull.

"One beer, and one beer only," Donna warned.

"All right," Joyce had said. "I'll take what I can get from you, honey. Better than you staying home all the time. It's nice out. The days are getting longer, and if you play your cards right, so will your nights!"

But Donna wasn't buying it.

"Joyce, if I want to pay the freight at Cortland this fall, you know I have to put in a ton of overtime at the plant," Donna said. "So don't start waving beers at me on a work night. Besides, The Arsenal is always filled with those fucking morons from Drum, staring at us all the time, undressing us from across the bar."

"And that's a bad thing?" Joyce smiled.

There she was when Hubie and his pals walked in. Perched on her stool, feeling sexy in her favorite dress, she sat there smoking her long-filtered Buckingham's that her brother Henry, the long-distance trucker, smuggled in from Canada. By now, a second and third Genesee had disappeared and she was working on a fourth. So much for her pledge of abstinence.

The young men arrived triumphantly. They might have been dressed in buttoned-down, embroidered shirts reminiscent of Key West during Hemingway's time, tight blue jeans, and of course cowboy boots, but there was no doubt they were Army. Their lean, muscular bodies betrayed all things military. Minus their berets, their crew cuts made them look like Roger Maris the year he belted sixty-one home runs.

The pointy-nosed Joyce noticed them right away. Dismissing the others, she instantly fixed her eyes on Hubie. This guy's different, she surmised; he's reserved, almost shy. His body language was unusual, almost as if he was apologizing in advance for his horny, childish friends. Almost too modest.

Joyce winked at Donna, tilting her head in Hubie's direction. Her friend, now enjoying a mild beer buzz, caught her drift; don't even *think* of going there, she warned, I'm not getting involved with a freakin' soldier. Even if he looks like a real stud, Joyce asked? Even if he has that Steve McQueen look about him? That caught Donna's attention. She glanced again.

The Arsenal was now elbow deep with customers. A local rock band had set up in one corner and their tunes had attracted a number of dancers to the hardwood floor opposite. At the nudging from one of his friends, who made a 'if-you-don't-I-will' gesture, Hubie decided he had to make his move.

He practiced his introduction.

"You from around here?"

Without looking up, Donna took another gulp from her Genesee draft and, with her defenses down and libido rising, just laughed.

"That's the best you can do army boy?" she asked. "That's your best line? You've been standing there for a half an hour and that's all you can come up with? Pretty lame."

"Yes, ma'am," he said, embarrassed. He was a polite soldier and that was how he was supposed to address a woman.

Something *had* happened that night and it had changed both their lives. She still hated the Army and its jugheads, as she had called them. But the prospect of some summer fun before heading back to Cortland was overpowering.

Carelessness, however, established their fate and by the end of June, a life of domesticity lay ahead. The flower child was no more, if it was ever there in the first place since he soon discovered more rigidity in the woman than recreation. There would be no second year at Cortland State for Donna, or a third or fourth for that matter. She learned she was pregnant, likely with twins. She was Catholic, and it was the sixties. There was only one option.

Hubie continued to walk along the peaceful waterway. Griz was now in full sniff, and Hubie was convinced the damn dog had to have had some hound in him. The big, brown animal darted about, often disappearing into the high brush that grew rampant along the river's shore. Hubie could hear him trampling over fallen leaves and dead branches. Dusk was rapidly approaching and from where he stood, Hubie could see across the treetops and into town. The streetlights had started to illuminate in the distance.

He would soon whistle for Griz and head back, but not before a moment of rest on the hemlock. It was his favorite spot, a rare straight stretch on a black, cold river where the century-old tree lay. It had crashed to the ground during an ice storm years before. It had fallen parallel to his well-worn path, and there it stayed in perpetuity, rotting, graying but still majestic. He recognized the fallen tree for what it had represented: the renewal of life. The giant hemlock had generously stepped aside, sacrificing its existence so that future generations of maples and spruce, with their insatiable need for sunlight and nourishment, could thrive.

When he and Donna were having problems, which was early and often in their marriage, he'd come to this exact spot. He'd bring a couple of beers, a sandwich and a pole, and toss a bobber into the river. Maybe snag a smallmouth or northern or two. Here he would sit for hours, wondering where it all went wrong and how he could make his wife happier. He remembered coming here the day Donna was diagnosed.

And again the day she died.

Today, he came once more in search of some comfort and consolation, and perhaps an explanation for what was going on.

THIRTY-ONE

"I hope he gave you a refund for the second night," Jane said, smiling over to her sister at the wheel of Matt's white Silverado as they traveled through the higher elevations towards Lake Placid. The clear skies they had enjoyed were now history; the temperature gauge on Matt's truck read twenty-five degrees, and clouds were moving in.

There would be snow.

"Christmas is coming, after all."

Joanne looked over and returned her smile.

She knew that Jane was only kidding. But it hurt just the same, since she never had any money that she could call her own. After Brent was born, and for the nearly six years she spent at home before he started school, a twenty-dollar bill in her purse was a small fortune. Of course, there would be grocery money but Denny doled that out like a war-time paymaster. There was never any cash for clothes—for *new* clothes anyway—and what she did wear came straight from the racks at the Salvation Army store. She was always broke.

It was the same for her hair. When it got too long, she'd pull her scissors out and park herself in front of a mirror, hoping she wouldn't suffer the butchered look. As she grew older, she'd had to color her hair. Peroxide was one product that Denny didn't mind her buying because he seemingly liked her as a blonde—at least earlier in their marriage. Later, she wondered why he cared; he rarely touched her anymore. Once in a while he'd come home drunk and want some quick action, but she'd feign exhaustion or illness. But God forbid if she bought a lipstick, even a cheap one. Denny would tell her to knock it off. No wife of his would go around looking like a slut.

After a while, Denny somehow convinced Hubie to co-sign a loan for fifty grand to buy the septic pumper and start him in the shit business—his words, of course. Only when Brent entered first grade did Denny allow Joanne to go to work at the store, nearly fifteen years ago.

Allow her?

More like an order.

He told her she had to work because he paid all the bills. That was why all her paychecks disappeared. You couldn't balance a checkbook in a month of fuckin' Tuesdays if you tried, he told her. *Not if you tried*, he'd always say...

The sisters continued their journey north in virtual silence.

Finally, Joanne spoke up.

"He thought I was good," she said, her eyes glued to the winding and narrow road.

"Who?" Jane asked.

"Matt."

"What are you talking about?"

"Matt thought I was good," Joanne replied. "On the piano."

"You played his piano?"

"And sang too."

"No shit!"

Joanne smiled.

Jane stared at her sister admiringly. She had remembered how much Joanne had loved that old upright piano, still gathering dust in Hubie's living room. So much so that her sister would reject Jane's pleas to join her and their friends outside just to practice on the old Baldwin. In fact,

Joanne had wanted nothing to do with her and her mischievous ways; she was never the shit disturber that I was, Jane thought. She never rocked the boat. She just wanted to play the damn piano.

As they continued their journey into the mountains, Jane smiled as she remembered how good Joanne really was.

"No shit!" she repeated as they sped over darkened blacktop, the never-ending double line illuminated only by the high beams from Matt's truck. A few flurries had started to blow across their path.

"It's been a long time since I remember you at Mom's piano," Jane said. "Well…I'm sorry, 'cause all I remember is how bad Mom was. Not how good you were."

"Well, there was a time when I wasn't bad," Joanne mused.

"I agree. Have you played much lately?"

Joanne shook her head.

"I can't remember the last time I sat down," she recalled. "Oh, once in a while, when no one was listening or watching, I'd play a little. Either at Mom's or at the VFW where I'd volunteer once in a while. Or at the Grange Hall. They had a piano there too, always off-key but I'd stay after the bake sales. But only if I knew no one was around."

Jane was surprised.

"Why? Why wouldn't you want anyone to watch or listen?"

"I never thought I was any good," Joanne replied. "But that was okay. It was my way of escaping…and I didn't need an audience."

Her voice trailed off for a moment or two before resuming.

"Besides, Denny never cared. Once or twice, he'd catch me playing and just give me one of those sneers, those ugly sneers of his...and tell me not to give up my day job...or my night job too, as it turned out."

A silence came over them once again.

Jane allowed her sister's words to sink in. She couldn't believe the pain that Joanne had endured and for so long. She had been absent from Joanne's life for years and had no idea of the existence that she had led. She had failed her when Joanne needed her the most.

Joanne seemed to sense Jane's reflection. She knew all her talk about Denny was affecting Jane, but that wasn't her intention. She wasn't looking for sympathy. It was her problem, nobody else's. Enough talk about Denny. What was the point, anyway? She didn't know *why* she let it happen.

Joanne's thoughts slowly returned to her magical moment today, and how exhilarated, how animated, she felt on stage. After watching and enjoying Matt's singing the night before, as he delivered such a powerful solo performance, she returned to the bar and was inexplicably drawn to the stage—to the baby grand.

"Somehow I knew the music," she said softly, her eyes still glued to the road. Snow was now blowing swiftly over the undulating highway. She looked at the speedometer and noticed she was doing about forty-five, a safe and comfortable speed for these roads.

"I somehow knew the words too," she continued. "Matt just happened to come in and listen. He said I was bitchin', so I guess that meant he thought I was good. Such a pretty song too, so beautifully written. I guess I had memorized it because...well, you know...I still can't read music. But somehow, I knew I could play it and sing it. It was like it came out of a dream...something that's been locked up inside for a very long time. Do you understand, Jane? Do you have any idea of what I mean?"

Joanne diverted her eyes briefly from the steadily worsening weather and looked over at her beaming sister.

Jane's eyes said it all.

Jane understood.

THIRTY-TWO

As darkness fell over the capital, Wendell Foley decided he needed a break. He had ordered his entire political team, nearly twenty-strong, to the mansion for an emergency strategy meeting, and it wasn't going well. So he ducked out to be alone in his thoughts, and to contemplate his immediate plans. The media was having a field day with the Schumacher murder story, and now his campaign could be crippled before it was started. His political future would be determined by how he'd deal with this stunning news.

But for now, he'd get some air. And this was the perfect place to do so.

Unlike many of his predecessors, who preferred a condo or apartment in Albany when the legislature was in session, Foley was in awe of his official residence. He loved the history of the place, its Victorian pyres, its sweeping and wraparound porches, its dignified and manicured grounds, its view of the city, the panorama of the river.

Many times, when he returned to Albany to babysit the legislature—Jane's words, not his—he would walk the perimeter of the property alone, deep in thought, contemplating his future, sketching his political plans. He would imagine what it was like in the late fifties when a retired Harry Truman would pay a courtesy call, dropping in on the august Averill Harriman to plant a sugar maple. Or he'd stroll through the modest apple orchard, ordered sowed by Hugh Carey, and pick a piece of fruit. Often, when he had grown tired of the gym, he'd meander to the back of the

mansion and do a hundred laps in the FDR pool, installed by
the great man in 1929 to help him deal with his nightmarish polio. Later, someone turned the pool into a greenhouse.
Thank God, Cuomo restored it.

Sometimes, when Maureen remained in Pleasant Valley,
he would roam the hallways of the ornate house, trying to
envision how Teddy enjoyed the home, if he did. The first
Roosevelt served barely two years as governor before being
tapped by McKinley to be vice president. Well, everyone
knew what happened then. Foley tried to imagine what
Rockefeller was thinking when he personally oversaw reno-
vations made to the mansion after the '61 fire. Or whether
Charles Evans Hughes, the governor turned great jurist,
marched across these same oak floors as he too weighed his
chances for the White House in 1916? Even cranky, old Grover Cleveland—the union buster and corruption fighter, and
a two-time winner—could be a role model.

Foley was schooled in the events of the past. He knew just
how different it used to be. Before the Internet and the five-
hundred channel universe, a single interview with Cronkite
could reach millions. JFK knew that. By pouncing on the
power of the televised image, he had invented the modern
presidential campaign. Foley would be the new JFK. He
would learn by his example. Well, he'd be Kennedy, *minus*
the bimbo starlets and gangster girlfriends, of course. But
emulate him he would. He'd get the country moving again.

The battle for the nomination would be fierce. His oppo-
nents—like that pint-sized congressman from Ohio, for
starters—had enjoyed nipping at his heels, criticizing him
for signaling his presidential ambitions so soon. There were
others as well, including that beefy, bilingual governor from
the dusty mesas who never refused a cable interview. Or those
senators from the northeast who forgot that Clinton whupped

them in the early nineties. They were making noises again. Talk about lifetime politicians! They didn't stand a chance.

Foley knew that his party was its own worst enemy, but he was confident that he could corral his loony left, the Ivy League latté sippers, the gays and feminists, the friggin' trade unions and trial lawyers, and of course Hollywood elites. When the time came, they would support him. They would raise gobs of cash for the campaign. They would put up signs and knock on doors. They'd shuttle voters to the polls. After all, what choice did they have?

Since he was a teenager, Foley knew a political life was in his future. He was a natural leader, head of the student union, valedictorian and star of the basketball team. He chose Dartmouth for his undergraduate studies and, subsequently, enrolled at Cornell's Law School. Forget Harvard, he said at the time. It was overrated. But he knew he had been born with a silver spoon firmly embedded in his mouth and that he needed a taste of the real world. So, forsaking the tempting money of Wall Street, he accepted a job with a storefront legal aid group in the Bowery. He would help those who had nothing. Maybe later he'd take the corporate route.

It all went to hell, of course.

After being admitted to the New York Bar, Foley quickly discovered that he hated being a lawyer. Despised it, in fact. Even storefront law, while commendable, was just an elaborate hoax foisted on those elements of society who were dispossessed and cast aside. It was a ruse, he concluded, and a scam. He and his altruistic colleagues soon discovered that no matter how hard they battled on behalf of the poor, theirs was a losing cause. They discovered quickly their struggles with wealthy land developers and financiers were for naught. Their foes' true intent was to evict tenants from their slums and they usually won.

A year in the dangerous Bowery opened his eyes to another America. It was an experience that told him there were millions of people in this country who worked hard, played by the rules and still didn't get ahead. If he ever was in a position to make a difference, he promised himself he would.

But first things first, he thought. He needed to build a career. So, at the age of twenty-six, Foley—his tail tucked sheepishly between his legs—abandoned his legal vocation and landed back in his hometown.

One night after a pick-up basketball game, he accepted a buddy's invitation to be the chief financial officer in a three-person start-up that was developing fiber optics technology. He had no idea what a CFO did nor what fiber optics was. But within months, he felt he'd made the right decision. He rose to become chief executive of the growing firm, and when a little-known Silicon Valley firm introduced something called a browser, the Internet had arrived for the masses. And fiber optics was the global answer to connectivity.

He made millions.

Foley, munching on an unlit Cuban cigar, watched as the bone-chilling Hudson River continued its journey to the sea. He allowed himself a smile; Maureen detested tobacco and refused him permission to light up—in her presence or not. He knew he was technically breaking federal law. But he vowed to end that ridiculous 1960s-era embargo with Cuba, whether Castro was alive or not.

Snow was definitely on the way, he thought, as he pondered the political crisis before him. His thoughts returned to Jane. What had happened was unfathomable. What had caused her to change her weekend plans to return home? What possibly could have propelled her to do what she did?

Only days ago, she and I were joking and planning and loving this business, Foley remembered. She was lecturing me to be careful about what I said and how I acted in front of the great unwashed.

Now he didn't know where Jane fit in. But he wasn't prepared to throw her under a bus. Despite the protests of his senior team, including the brilliant Claudia, tonight wasn't about his image or his campaign. It was about Jane, a woman he had respected since her television reporting days. She was his straight shooter, his connection to the real world, his ground wire.

More importantly, however, this was also about Jane, the person.

Her disturbing telephone call yesterday provided him no answers, but he had known her a long time and knew instinctively that there were reasons for what she did.

He was not going to bail on her now.

From his porch, Foley could see the large klieg lighting being set up at the entrance to the mansion. Marcia had informed the press that a scrum would take place in about twenty minutes. He threw his cigar into the shrubs, took one last look at the majestic Hudson and returned to the living room of the mansion. The room became silent. All eyes were glued to the candidate as he reentered the house.

"Okay, people, let's do this, let's get it over with," he announced.

"Governor, are you sure you want to go through with this?" Claudia asked. "You've heard what the cable shows are saying. The blogs are having a field day at our expense. The Sunday talk shows are leading with this Jane issue. Tomorrow's *Times* is coming out with—"

Foley cut her off.

"Yes, Claudia, let's do this."

THIRTY-THREE

The scattered flurries had turned into a howling blizzard, and Jane knew her sister was battling to see what was left of the road. The salting and sanding crews, anticipating the coming storm, were clearly working the highway. But visibility remained poor. Better than having black ice, Jane thought, especially with the sorry-assed vehicle that Booker had loaned them. How long has he lived here? Couldn't he at least have remembered to refill his windshield-washer fluid? It's a fucking nightmare.

Jane gave her head a shake.

Listen to me, she thought. Booker was decent enough to hand over his truck and the keys to a shack in the mountains, and I'm bitching? If it wasn't for him, we'd likely be in the back of Boychuk's cruiser, heading to a slammer in Morgantown, awaiting exposure and embarrassment.

Still, next time loan us a decent vehicle, will you Booker?

She smiled to herself.

Yeah, next time.

Moments later, they saw signs of the approaching village. If she remembered correctly, the road to Matt's cabin was a sharp left off Route 86, another two-lane road that eventually led to North Pole and Wilmington. Jane couldn't wait to get there. Joanne would put on a fire and they'd warm up. She was so tired; her lungs hurt like hell, and she was doing everything to suppress her chronic cough.

Earlier, when Joanne had returned from the bar, Jane had immediately shot the idea down. But on second thought she had realized that Matt's puzzling act of generosity was their one and only option. The shooting and her connection to Foley probably made her a sizable story by now and she wondered whether Wendell had disowned her yet. She hoped so, since his campaign was more important than any twisted member of his staff. Every campaign had to be prepared for a scandal of some sort, and this one was the size of Gibraltar.

But her suspicions were just that, and right now she wasn't about to call the governor to find out. At the motel and roadhouse, she had completely lost sight of the outside world. She hadn't glanced at a television screen, a newspaper or even her BlackBerry. It was very extraordinary for someone who had always been in command. Perhaps she didn't want to know the kind of political damage she was creating? No, that wasn't it; every bone in her body—every fiber of her being—was urging her to find out. But her mission now had changed. She would speak with Foley when the time was appropriate and not a minute sooner. Still, for the first time in her adult life, she was unaware of what was going on. It felt weird.

Taking refuge at Matt's cabin would be a good idea. Boychuk would soon catch their scent. Surely he knew about her connection to Lake Placid, didn't he? And by now he'd likely enlisted the aid of the local cops to start banging down the doors of every bed-and-breakfast for miles around. Brian was taking this investigation personally. He was a proud man who was going to solve this problem. It was only a matter of time before he would put two and two together and come up with more than four. That's why the cabin was their only option.

Minutes later, they were cruising through the village. It was her first return to Lake Placid since she was a teenager and it hadn't changed. The resort tried awfully hard to be

America's Innsbruck, or St. Moritz—its Olympic cousins—and for the most part it worked, though most Americans had probably never heard of those European ski destinations, let alone visited them. Placid was modest yet never inexpensive. Quaint but strangely world-class. Homespun though uniquely historical. Her past treks to Austria and Switzerland came to mind. Placid may not have been on par with those exotic locales, but it wasn't far off either.

A thick, snowy blanket covered the village, and Jane considered how lucky she was to see it again. It was beautiful. This town knows how to welcome winter. Christmas lights had been installed and were sparkling from every telephone pole on the strip. Behind the old brick edifices on Main Street lay tiny Mirror Lake. Summer tourists confused it for the *lake* in Lake Placid, but winter's ski bums knew better. In the now sub-freezing temperatures, Mirror had formed a thin layer of dark ice, and wisps of blowing snow were forming on the surface. Across the lake she could see the well-lit façades of the large vacation hotels. Now, those places knew how to throw a party.

Most of the shops were nearing closing time, and the streets were filled with weekend warriors hopping from store to store proudly displaying their latest Obermeyer, Marmot Uptown and Roxy Corvette skiwear. Jane felt a twinge; she loved to ski and remembered all the exciting, almost dangerous, runs she had missed during the first and only winter she stayed here. Famous Whiteface Mountain was only a few miles away, but for her, in her state at the time, it may as well been on the moon.

Suddenly, as if on cue, the slamming sounds of her parents' screen door returned. Her mother's voice was paying another visit as Jane knew it would.

If you leave now, Jane, you leave for good! You know that!

She did leave, and it was for good.

That day, in the heat of the moment, Jane had thrown a bag into the back seat of her Datsun and pointed it in the only direction she knew—and that was out of town. It was fate that made her turn left instead of right, even though—at eighteen—she didn't know the true significance of the word. But providence played a role and she ended up in Lake Placid, not Syracuse or Rochester or even Rome—or somewhere further south. That she turned left instead of right determined who she would later become.

She had arrived in Lake Placid at the end of a muggy Labor Day weekend. It was one of the busiest tourist days of the year, and the traffic was surprisingly thick for a town whose resident population never exceeded twenty-five-hundred. She had money; her purse was stuffed—literally—with her tips from the golf course where she had driven the beer cart from hole to hole, flirting shamelessly with the ill-dressed men. It didn't take her long to figure out how to make some real dough. Just wear a low-cut tank top and cut-off denim shorts. Flash your boobs once in a while and compliment the old boys on making a great putt. And the money flowed in. Jesus, those guys were saps.

She had arrived in the village unsure of what she would do. For the first time in her life, she was alone, really alone. But strangely, she felt neither lonely nor scared. A bit apprehensive, yes; uncertain, sure. But what could happen to her in Lake Placid?

Her first task was to look up the address of that clinic that her high-school nurse had told her about. She would see a doctor and go from there.

Correct that.

Seeing a doctor would have to be her second or third undertaking. Her first mission was to find a place to live because sleeping in her car was not an attractive option. Well, really, wasn't that how she got into this trouble in the first place? She proceeded slowly down Main Street and drove through the village streets. After only a few minutes, she saw a sign in Victorian lettering that read *Edna's Rooming House.* A second sign on hooks below read *Rooms Available.* She pulled her car up to the curb, went in and met Edna.

"Forty-five a week, but that includes meals, and I'm a decent cook," the matronly woman behind the counter had said. "There's a hotplate in every room, but please don't burn the place down. Plus a fridge. I make breakfast and dinner, but for lunch you're on your own. I only have three rules here; no men, no booze, no drugs. Well, four rules, I guess. Absolutely no smoking. Understand that, dear?"

It was not really a question.

"I understand, ma'am," Jane had replied.

"Good, then we'll be fine."

After laying down the law, Edna told Jane that she would probably like it at her house since there were others her age staying there as well. Many were summer workers who'd decided to remain for the tip-rich foliage season. Others were snow bunnies arriving early for what they'd hoped would be five or six great months on the slopes. They're about the same age as you, Edna had said. And they're probably in the same boat as you, too, dear.

I doubt it, Jane thought.

She climbed the stairs to the second floor and found her room. It was everything that Edna had promised: simple, surprisingly large, clean. The walls were papered in a floral design, perhaps their third or fourth layer since the big house was last renovated. A couple of cheap prints hung neatly on the walls. As Edna had pledged, a small bar fridge sat in the corner beside a four-drawer mahogany dresser. On the opposite side of the room was a closet; it was empty except for a single shelf and a rod with three or four steel hangers. There was no television, but a scratched and dented RCA Victor radio sat atop a small, green table. A lone wooden chair was tucked under the table.

Jane let out a big sigh. This is my life now, she thought. She threw her bag on the small, single bed and went to the window. Maybe it comes with a view of the mountains or the lake, she thought. No, just the back alley. Well, whatever, I won't be here that long. If I can get a job at a restaurant or a bar waiting tables or as a hostess, I can find a small apartment somewhere.

Jane decided that her search would start immediately and left the rooming house for the short walk towards town. It was busy and crowded. She could see young couples not much older than her holding hands, perhaps on their honeymoons. There were parents too, annoyed and tired, who were dragging their pre-teen children down the street, likely in search of a burger stand. Across the street, she noticed a group of middle-aged men, maybe twelve in all, fresh from the golf course and looking for a steak. And some night action, no doubt. They could have been my customers this summer, she thought.

For more than two hours, she walked the entire length of Main Street, both sides, and halfway around the lake. At one corner, realizing she hadn't eaten all day, she spotted a pizzeria and was about to stop for a quick bite when she noticed a *Help Wanted* sign in the window of a building only yards off the main drag. She turned down the lane and looked up at the weathered letters of the sign above. It was the office of the *Lake Placid Tribune*, the village's weekly newspaper.

She tried the door and to her surprise—on a Sunday—it opened. She looked around but there was no one in sight.

The décor was Prohibition, with no apparent desire to move on. Hung from the rococo-styled cathedral ceilings were large wooden fans, spinning slowly to condition the stuffy, late summer air. Two enormous oak desks sat back-to-back and each was graced by a black Underwood typewriter.

She continued to scan the room. Steel filing cabinets, their tops cluttered with stacks of newspapers, lined the walls on both sides of the room. Above the cabinets were *Tribune* page-fronts from the past—Jane guessed it might have been a daily back then—commemorating an end to the War, reporting sadly on JFK's demise, proclaiming that man had stepped on the moon, and of course, announcing the nation's first and only presidential resignation. Large photos of the opening ceremonies for the XIII Winter Games were prominent. At the front, a small counter welcomed visitors. Jane knew she was stepping back in time.

From a backroom came a squat, disheveled man whom Jane guessed was in his late sixties. A blizzard-white moustache spilled well over his upper lip as he chomped down on an unlit pipe. He was milling about his office as if he was searching for something and had forgotten what the hell it was. He was oddly-dressed for a hot day: adorned in a tweed jacket with leather patches at the elbows, he looked like a college professor nearing retirement. The collar of his soiled, white shirt was open, his tie askew. All that was missing was a fedora.

Later, she would recount her experience to Roberto.

"Do you remember that Duke Wayne movie?" They were at a restaurant in the east seventies one night, enjoying grilled Pacific salmon and a glass of Jordan. "Jimmy Stewart was in it too. What was it called? Oh, yeah, 'The Man Who Shot Liberty Valance.' Do you remember that movie?"

Just as Roberto attempted to say no, he hadn't seen it because…well he was too damn busy busing tables at *Ricardo's,* or boning for a Columbia exam, Jane continued her story, undeterred.

"Well, in that movie, the editor of the *Shinbone Star*, his name was Dutton Peabody. It was one of the greatest scenes in journalism!"

"You mean *movie* journalism?" Roberto corrected her. "It wasn't real—"

But Jane waved him off. Her eyes sparkling with excitement, her voice rising, she began to recite the scene from memory, word-for-word.

"Good people of Shinbone! I…I'm your conscience! I'm the small voice that thunders in the night! I'm your watchdog who howls against the wolves. I…I'm your father confessor! I…I'm… What else am I?"

Now nearly coming out of her seat, Jane delivered the punch line.

"And John Wayne—I can't remember his character's name but it didn't matter, he always played John Wayne— well, Duke turns to Peabody and says, *'Town drunk?'*"

She roared with laughter.

"Well, Dutton Peabody was my first boss in the news business, and he worked in Lake Placid! He was everything Peabody was, except a drunk. Oh, he wasn't exactly a teetotaler, but I never saw him drunk."

Jane stood at the counter waiting for her Peabody to notice her. Minutes later she discovered that his name was really Walter Matheson. Befuddled, almost shocked to see anyone in his office on a Sunday, the elderly man looked up and asked, "Can I help you?"

"I'm here because I saw your sign," she said, pointing to the window. "You're looking for help?"

The next day, Jane began her career in journalism.

Her job was to cajole merchants into buying ads and to run pages to the printer, and when she found the time, to speak to the cops and write up whatever they said. On Friday nights, she'd be assigned to cover high school hockey and football. She worked seventy hours a week and made about five hundred a month.

And she loved it.

As the sisters drove their borrowed pick-up through town, Jane looked to see if the *Tribune* was still there. It was. Nothing had changed.

She had heard that her Dutton Peabody, old Walter, had passed away a few years ago, and that saddened her then— and now.

A *Help Wanted* sign was in the window.

THIRTY-FOUR

Boychuk was sitting at a booth in a roadside restaurant and was about to order breakfast when his deputy entered. In front of him was a copy of the *Times-Union*. He was reading about the governor's attempt to play down the Schumacher murder story. What piqued his interest was Foley's comment about the investigation—that it was "in the hands of the police"—without mentioning whether his troopers were involved.

He knew Foley didn't need this mess. The governor was the nation's leading political figure and wanted to avoid any story that hinted at scandal, or in particular, that he was bungling a murder case involving his press secretary. Jack Davis had told Foley that it was the county sheriff's responsibility to run the show as long as the suspects hadn't fled the county. If this was true, the troopers could offer only nominal support while hoping that the local gumshoes didn't screw it up.

Boychuk also knew it wouldn't take long for the press to get wind that the leading investigator on the case—some county sheriff—was a personal friend of the family. A former boyfriend to friggin' boot! The sheriff had not informed Davis about that, or that Jane had used her ATM card a couple of counties over, or that the Valero clerk had confirmed they were there. He knew he was skating on thin ice. He was no fool. He would call Davis this morning to tell him what he knew and ask reluctantly for his support. He didn't want his dalliance with Jane twenty years ago to put an end to his police career. If he discovered where they were, his first call would be to Davis and they could share the glory, if that was the proper word.

Still, he had no intention of dropping his pursuit; he would continue the chase. In a matter of days—maybe hours—Davis's people would move in and relieve some of the pressure facing the governor. The troopers would take this over. But Boychuk felt he owed it to Hubie to continue. He knew Denny and what he was like, what he did to Joanne for so many years.

He also wanted to treat Jane properly. The woman he remembered was an impulsive hot-head; this shit with Denny had landed her in serious trouble. But she clearly had reasons for doing what she did, and he wanted to hear her side of the story. Obviously, there would be charges and she'd go on trial for murder—second-degree at most. Or maybe her case would be reduced to manslaughter. But it wouldn't be cut and dried; there were mitigating circumstances. He'd have discussions with the district attorney over this case.

After grilling the clerk at the Valero station, Boychuk and his deputy had decided they would stop at every motel, gas station or Amish farm—if need be—to find the Schumacher sisters. The law officers spent the afternoon doing just that, first by heading south in the belief the girls might have decided to find refuge in one of the cities along the Thruway. He had hoped they were still in the vast, sparsely-populated mountainous region, but feared they may have preferred the easier anonymity of Rome, Utica, even Albany.

Boychuk shook his head. Even Jane wouldn't have returned to her apartment. She was an intelligent woman. She knew he'd have an APB out on them and that meant a couple of Albany cops staking out her place. Maybe they were heading to Syracuse? Maybe Joanne wanted to see her son? But Joanne would have known that Brent had returned home, wouldn't she? If they went city-side, it would be much tougher to round them up; there were so many more places to hide. In a city, few people would notice them, especially if they split up. Individually, these girls could remain on the run for some time—and time was running out for him. Instinct told him, however, that they would stay together.

But before he'd throw in the towel and call Jack Davis, Boychuk decided to turn around and retrace his steps along this thinly-traveled highway that eventually led to Lake Placid. He'd head north again, past the Valero where Jane used her bank card and further if necessary. He knew that Jane had spent some time in Lake Placid after they had broken up, but he didn't know for how long or what she did. One thing was for sure: unless they were holed up in a private residence, there were fewer places to hide in ski country.

A mile or so up the road, passing the gas station once again, Boychuk spied a sign for The North Star Motel and pulled his cruiser into the parking lot. He spotted the bar in the corner of the parking lot.

"Jimmy, why don't you wander over to the office and see if there's anyone there that knows anything," the sheriff said, "and I'll head over to the bar. Maybe Jane needed a drink."

His deputy jumped from the cruiser and headed to the office as Boychuk approached the roadhouse. It was late Saturday afternoon. He scanned the nearly-filled parking lot for Joanne's maroon Explorer, but there was no vehicle matching that description. Still, maybe they're here, he thought. Or if they were here and had left, maybe someone in this cowboy joint would remember them.

He walked in. Immediately, heads at the bar turned towards the cop walking through the door, always an ominous event for beer drinkers who knew they would have to remain on their toes if they wanted to avoid a breathalyzer later. But the patrons needed not to worry. It was clear that this cop had other things on his mind. Carrying a manila envelope, Boychuk approached the bar. Tammy looked up and smiled at the sight of the good-looking sheriff in front of her.

"What can I do for you officer? Are you hungry? Or can I get you a beer?" she asked, knowing fully what his answer would be.

"Not today," he said, noticing her name tag pinned to her denim shirt.

"Tammy, I'm Sheriff Brian Boychuk of Morgan County," he said, offering his hand to the bartender. "Were you on duty last night or earlier today?"

Reaching out across the bar, Tammy shook the sheriff's hand.

"Yup, worked 'til close, which was around two or three in the morning," Tammy replied.

"Well, in that case, I need to talk to you about something." Boychuk looked down the bar and noticed that Tammy was working alongside another server. She looked a bit younger, a lot prettier, and she too playfully talked with the men at the bar.

"Can she work the bar while we have a word?" he said, pointing.

Tammy nodded and got the younger bartender's attention.

"Cindy, can you cover for me?" she asked, winking. "This handsome policeman wants to talk to me. Maybe he has a pair of handcuffs to show me."

Boychuk rolled his eyes.

These bar chicks are the same everywhere, he thought. They'd flirt with anyone, even cops, if it meant a few good tips. He directed Tammy towards an empty table, where they sat down. He opened his envelope and spread the eight-by-tens of Jane and Joanne across the top.

"I need to know if you've seen these gals?" he demanded, now all business.

Tammy looked at the photos carefully. She knew those freakin' girls were trouble, especially when she caught a glimpse of them on television earlier in the day. They're famous, she thought, and they were in my bar.

"Yeah, I've seen them on the news," she said, her eyes darting back and forth from mug to mug. "...and yeah, they were here last night. Dark-haired one got really trashed. The stringy blonde one just sipped a few beers."

Boychuk's spirits rose quickly.

"Were they staying at the motel next door?" he asked.

"As far as I know, yeah. But I don't have anything to do with the motel. I have enough to do here."

"How long were they here?"

"They came in for supper, sat at the bar," she continued. "Dark hair had the fish. It was Friday, after all. But really, she was more interested in fancy Scotch than fish. Drank doubles all night and got pretty drunk. Not many people around here drink that iodine 'cause they can't afford it. This is mainly a beer and bourbon joint."

That sounds like Jane, the sheriff thought. Beer was her favorite beverage when they were dating, but that was a long time ago. He assumed her palate had improved, leading to more expensive tastes over the years, especially since she started moving in high political circles.

"What about the blonde one? What did she do all night?" he asked.

"She just sat at the bar and watched Matt sing," she said. "Matt's the owner of the bar and used to be in bands down south. He's pretty good."

She smiled, mischievously. "And hot too."

"What else happened?"

"Well, the uppity one got drunker and drunker, and the next thing I knew, she was dancing with Matt between sets. Putting money in the juke box and wouldn't let him outta her sight."

"This guy Matt and the brunette were dancing? Did they know each other or something?"

Tammy shrugged.

"No idea. But she was all over him for a while on the floor and I thought it was embarrassing—and I told him that this morning. Well, I didn't pay much attention to them after blondie paid the bill…I got too busy to keep my eyes on those chicks."

Just then, the deputy sheriff entered the bar and joined his boss and the bartender at the table.

"Sheriff, our twins stayed here last night," the deputy said.

Tammy interrupted them.

"They were twins?" she asked. "Didn't look like no twins to me."

"They're fraternals, Tammy," he replied, annoyed at her intervention. He wondered if she knew the distinction but didn't care. He returned his attention to his deputy.

"Go on, Jimmy."

The deputy continued.

"Well, the clerk tells me they checked out earlier today. The owner of this place is a guy named—" He checked his notes. "—Matt Booker. But he's not here. At least I can't find him. The clerk said they checked in under the name of Joanne Lowry. Can you believe that? She checked in under her own name."

"Makes sense to me," Boychuk replied. "Joanne probably feels that she didn't do anything wrong. Has nothing to hide. What else?"

"Well, the clerk has no idea where they were headed. And this guy Booker, she doesn't know where he is right now, either. I knocked on his apartment door—his place is behind the motel—but there was no answer."

Boychuk nodded his head in appreciation.

"Thanks Jimmy," he said. "This young lady here," he continued, turning his attention again to Tammy, who clearly appreciated the 'young' part since the difference in their ages was only about five years, "says they were here last night too."

"Tammy, how tight was this Booker guy getting with the dark-haired one?" he asked.

"Pretty tight," she said. "But as I said, she was drunk and falling all over him. I don't know what happened. I was too busy."

Her curiosity was aroused.

"Are these girls in a whack of trouble, Sheriff?"

Boychuk nodded, rising from the table. He scooped up the pictures and placed them back in the envelope.

"Now, Tammy, give me the straightest answer you can give me," he continued. "Do you or don't you know where these ladies went? I have a hunch you know more than you're telling me."

Tammy stood and addressed the sheriff. He's not a bad-looking guy, she thought, but a bit of a pain in the ass.

"Not really," she replied.

"Now what does that mean, not really?"

"I have my suspicions," she said.

Boychuk was growing impatient with this woman. The ignoramuses he had to deal with, he thought.

"Well, do you care to *share* those suspicions with me?"

"Well, Matt has this cabin near Lake Placid," she said. "They might be there."

"Now, why would they be there?"

"Just as you say, Sheriff, just an idea," she said. "He and the brunette got pretty cozy last night. Today, I saw blondie over at the piano, playin' and singin'. And he was speaking to her too."

Boychuk's eyes focused squarely on Tammy. This might be it, he thought. He may have found them.

"You happen to know where this cabin is located?"

"Yeah, been there once."

THIRTY-FIVE

Joanne awoke first and was stoking the fire in the large woodstove when she heard another loud cough coming from Jane's bedroom. It had been a rough night for her sister. She was hacking all night. While Joanne got to work starting the fire and priming the water pump, Jane had retreated to one of the cabin's two bedrooms and pulled down the bed covers. She had passed out in her clothes—again. Joanne sensed there was more to Jane's claim that she was suffering from bronchitis. But she didn't know what. When Joanne had enquired, Jane simply brushed her off.

Near the end of the village strip, they had stopped briefly for a foot-long submarine sandwich before paying a visit to the convenience store next door for a few groceries. They continued for a mile or two before they saw the road that led to the cabin. At least six inches of fresh snow had fallen, but the plow operators had included the country road in their route. Joanne simply had slammed the truck into four-wheel mode and gunned it up the hill.

Now Joanne listened again.

There was no sound from her sister's bedroom. Jane must have fallen back asleep. Good, she thought. She's a mess and needs her rest. She finished loading the stove with several slabs of dried birch and turned towards the counter to pour herself a second cup of coffee. Matt had said there was likely some food left from the visit he'd made a month ago and that they should help themselves. She began making breakfast. Her sister couldn't sleep all day.

Joanne peered out the kitchen window and noticed that it had finally stopped snowing. Matt's truck was layered in white. On the far side of the property stood a second, outer building that Joanne had guessed was a small workshop or sleep camp. Overnight, the fierce winds had created a drift half way up its low-hanging roof. In front of the building, close to the road, Joanne saw a snowmobile that appeared ready for the new season. It looked like an Arctic Cat. She'd loved those machines as much as her father's Ski-Doo. She wondered if the keys were in the ignition. She'd welcome a reprieve, a distraction really, from the events of the last seventy-two hours.

Through a break in the towering, cumulous storm clouds, the sun was attempting to make an appearance. But the overcast sky shed sufficient light to deliver a postcard of incredible beauty, a winter wonderland of snow-covered spruce and pine clinging to the mountain cliffs nearby. Last night, in the pitch dark, Joanne had had no idea there was such a spectacular vista below. Today, however, was a different story. From where she stood, Joanne could see the entire village below, linked only by the twisting road they had traveled only hours before. The village looked busy; she could see the plows continuing their work, especially on the thoroughfare that surrounded Mirror Lake. A change of seasons had come to the Adirondacks.

Her eyes once again turned to the dormant snowmobile, and Joanne allowed her mind to wander back ten or twelve years. She was aboard her father's Ski-Doo but this time as a passenger. Brent, only eight or nine years old, was driving the big machine—laughing and hollering—as mother and son enjoyed a long winter ride. As they steered through the trails at high speeds, Joanne pleaded with her son to slow down but to no avail. He loved the breakneck pace, and she always let him have his way. Denny spent little time with Brent. It was left to her to raise her son, and that was what she was doing. Technically, they were a family. But Joanne felt more like a single parent.

The creaking sound of a bedroom door opening awoke Joanne from her daydream. It was Jane, who had risen and was on her way to the bathroom.

"Are you hungry? I'm gonna put a few eggs on for breakfast," she announced to her sister after hearing the toilet flush. There was no response. Instead, she listened as Jane emitted a series of horrific coughs. Finally, the door opened and Jane emerged. Her face was pallid, her shoulders drooped, and she appeared almost too weak to walk. Alarmed, Joanne rushed to her side.

"Oh, God, let me help you." Joanne said as she led Jane to a chair in the kitchen.

"I'll be okay, Jo, I just need a little java."

Joanne went to the coffeepot and poured her sister a cup. She reached into the fridge for the carton of milk.

"You're *not* okay," Joanne said. "Let me warm up the truck and take you to the hospital."

"No, I said I'll be okay," Jane said.

"I don't believe you."

Jane stared blankly at her sister and perhaps felt that a moment of truth was at hand.

"I'll be fine, Jo," she replied. "I do need to go into town, though."

"Then let's go see a doctor," Joanne demanded. "That bronchitis you say you have is getting a lot worse. You coughed all night! Let me take you to emergency and get it checked out."

But Jane, now sipping her coffee, shook her head.

"Think about what you just said, Jo," she replied. "The hospital would have Chuck and the troopers on us pretty damn fast...and I'm not ready for that. At least not yet."

Joanne knew Jane was right. But she also knew they'd have to stop running from the police. The last couple of days were her first tastes of freedom after so many years under Denny's control. Still, her instinct, as always, was to do what was right. She looked again at her sister, searching for an answer to the central question.

"What the hell are we doing, Jane?" she asked. "Why don't we just go home?"

Jane looked deeply into Joanne's blue eyes.

"Get cleaned up sister, we're goin' to town."

THIRTY-SIX

An hour later, Jane and her sister were sitting in Matt's truck downtown, diagonally parked in front of a fashionable ski shop. It was late Sunday morning on Thanksgiving weekend, and the stores were opening their doors to winter shoppers. Jane knew firsthand how busy Lake Placid was in winter and how shop-owners took advantage of the first holiday of the season. If snow had arrived, and it certainly had last night, the merchants would be happy. The village's main drag would be busy. And today, it was.

Jane remembered her first Thanksgiving in Placid. After landing her *Tribune* job, she'd had little time to find an apartment of her own. Her life was a constant state of motion, helping old Walter and Nora, his wife, keep the venerable rag afloat. Almost immediately, Jane realized she *was* the staff. She was saleswoman and receptionist, errand girl, phone operator, window cleaner and sidewalk sweeper. She washed the floors, drove the paper's van and filled the street side boxes. When she played her cards right, she would become a reporter.

Old Walter was a tolerant man with an impatient employee. He knew she preferred writing over street sweeping. Well, who wouldn't? He knew she didn't care for the mundane tasks that burdened every weekly newspaper. From the moment she walked in declaring she'd do anything at the paper, he took an instant liking to Jane. She was a teenager who was mature beyond her years. He later figured Jane had been born old. She never complained, not once, and Walter liked that. So he'd send her off to cover anything—a boating accident on the lake, a broken chair-lift on the slopes, a charity garage sale—anything. He'd remind her constantly to take her camera.

Don't screw it up Schumacher, he'd say. Pay attention. Get the story.

Walter knew almost immediately that Jane had what it took to be a journalist. She was curious, articulate and skeptical—all the qualities needed to be a success in this business. He started teaching her the trade, editing her prose ruthlessly with a big, black pencil, leaving mischievous notes in her story columns.

"Remember old Walt's rules, Jane...rules that every writer needs to know. Memorize these! They have to be cast in granite!" His lectures never ended; his impish grin ever-present. He'd test her to see if she was paying attention. He'd have some fun at her expense.

"First, remember to *never* split an infinitive," he'd say, knowing that Jane wouldn't know the difference between an infinitive and a dangling modifier. But he suspected she would look the terms up. He knew she had to know.

"Second, take the bull by the *hand* and don't mix your metaphors either."

"Third, avoid clichés like the plague!"

"Fourth, stop using exclamation marks!!!"

And then Walter would burst into laughter.

Later, Jane would remember his lessons and smile. Walter was a demanding boss who worked her so hard that she'd collapse into bed at night, exhausted.

Edna, too, was a kind and considerate woman, someone who Jane later recognized as a strict but fair custodian who ran more of an orphanage than a rooming house. Many of "her kids" had come from troubled backgrounds or were runaways. Or they were college drop-outs, free spirits or simply just alone in a small town. She was their den mother. But she never violated their privacy.

Their Thanksgiving dinner that year was a feast and not just in the culinary sense. An old-style New England liberal, Edna started the conversation by railing about the excesses of the Reagan Administration, rising to an almost apoplectic rage about an ancient president who was so hopelessly out of the loop. And she wasn't shy with her words.

"That old son of a bitch…that *bad actor*…is dangerous," she'd cry, her voice rising according to plan. "Did you know he has two red buttons on his desk? One says 'launch' and the other says 'lunch!'"

Of course, she would howl with delight, knowing that she had kick-started a debate that her young tenants loved.

"We'd better hope that his staff delivers his meals to his desk before the old bastard gets hunger pangs!"

Now parked in front of the ski store, Jane snapped out of her daydream. She and her sister continued to sit in silence. After another hot shower, and feeling marginally better, she had announced she was ready to go into town. She was still in a great deal of pain, but the coughing had subsided. The coffee had helped and so did Joanne's breakfast. At last, after a few minutes of watching shoppers on a Sunday stroll, Joanne broke the silence.

"Is there a reason why we're sitting here?"

"Yes," Jane replied. "There is."

"Well, do you mind sharing it with me?"

Jane pointed to the ski shop.

"There's someone in that store who I need to see," Jane said, continuing to gaze straight ahead. She studied the stylish store's window now filled with the latest sporting gear. All the major brands of skis, boots and clothing were prominently displayed. This store could be on Fifth Avenue, Jane thought.

"Who?" Joanne asked.

Jane shifted in her seat, paused and inhaled deeply before letting out a deep sigh. A look of seriousness came over her.

"Someone I've known about…a long time, Jo."

She paused again, before continuing.

"Jo, you know why I left town when we were both eighteen?"

"Yeah, what about it?"

"Do you remember what I said just before I left?"

Joanne was confused. She recalled the bitter argument Jane had had with their mother and how it resulted in her leaving Morgantown for good.

"What do you mean?" Joanne asked.

"You knew I was pregnant, like you?"

"Yes, we knew. Or at least I found out eventually."

"Then you remember what I told Mom I was planning to do?"

Joanne nodded.

"But Jo, I didn't do it. I couldn't."

"Are you saying what I think you're saying, Jane?"

"Uh, huh…I didn't have the abortion, Jo…I *had* the baby."

Her mouth agape, Joanne was flabbergasted. She couldn't believe what she was hearing.

"What?"

"I had the baby. A little girl. Nobody, not you, Mom or Dad, ever knew."

Joanne was now blown away by the revelation. She was speechless. She sat there in shock.

"Oh, Jane, we knew you were pregnant, but we all thought…" Her voice trailed away for a moment or two. "This is incredible. I can't believe it!"

Jane knew her news would be almost too much for Joanne.

"Neither can I, sometimes. I've told no one about this… till now. When I left, after that big fight with Mom, I was planning to end it…end my pregnancy. Have an abortion. But the clinic I went to, well, they said I had another option. They introduced me to a couple who couldn't have kids…and well, they took care of me after I couldn't work any longer. They're the ones who helped me through college too."

Joanne placed her hands to her face as if to shelter her emotions from her sister and anyone else who might see her.

"Oh my God," she said, not sure how she should react or think.

Jane watched her sister's reaction without saying anything. Finally, she spoke.

"She's in there, Jo," she said. "She works in that ski store. Her name is Makenna."

"Really?"

Jane nodded.

"Makenna? That's an unusual name but pretty just the same," Joanne said.

"I think so, too…but I didn't name her. She's nearly twenty-one now."

"Brent's age."

"Yeah, Mom and Dad must have been real proud of us, eh? Here we are, teenagers, and we both get knocked up! Well, like mother, like daughters, I always said. Anyway, the deal I had with Makenna's parents was that I wouldn't have any contact with her. I've honored that deal all her life. I've spoken to her mom from time to time, and they've told me a few things over the years. About her love for skiing, and for this town. Once, earlier this fall, her mother let it slip that she was working in a nice ski store when she wasn't in college."

Her voice trailed off for a moment.

"Well, right there—" she pointed to the store in front of them, "—is the nicest store in Lake Placid. That's why I think she's in there. But that's it. No other information."

Joanne was stunned at the news, that Jane had been a mother all these years and that she had a niece she never knew she had.

"Don't most kids in this situation want to know about their real parents?" Joanne asked.

"I don't even know if she knows about me, Jo…or that they've told her she's adopted," Jane said. "That would account for her never contacting me. Or maybe she knew and didn't want to meet me. I don't know."

The sisters continued to gaze at the ski shop, taking a few moments to digest Jane's disclosure. Both knew this was further evidence that their lives had turned upside down. Finally, Jane made a decision.

"I have to go in, Jo," she said. "I have to meet Makenna."

"Didn't they say never to contact her?"

"Well, as I say, never say never…besides, I'm going to jail anyway," Jane said. "What does it matter?"

Joanne opened the door and beckoned her sister to join her.

"Well, you got that partly right, Jane," Joanne replied. "It's more like we're going to jail first—forget the two hundred dollars—and then straight to hell. Lead on, sister!"

THIRTY-SEVEN

The women entered the ski store. Inside, it was everything its elegant window displays advertised. Forget Fifth Avenue, Jane thought. This charming little shop could be located on the Magnificent Mile or even Rodeo Drive. Slowly they made their way through the aisles, casually perusing the ski jackets and sweaters. Jane checked out a tag on one item. Beverly Hills *prices* too, she thought. But then skiing would never be confused with bowling or bocce ball. Only well-heeled folk arrived in Lake Placid each winter, including more and more affluent Europeans. The foreign invasion had started and this upset the locals.

Their secret was out. Their sleepy village had changed.

As Joanne held back, Jane spotted a young sales girl behind the counter. She was pulling sweaters from a large cardboard box and placing them neatly on display. Posing as a customer, Jane walked slowly over to the counter. The sales girl, a tall, muscular-looking woman about twenty, looked up and smiled. Her legs looked so powerful she could have been the captain of an Olympic bobsled team.

"Good morning," she said.

"Hello," Jane replied.

"Can I help you at all?"

Jane's eyes darted to a name tag on the sales girl's lapel. It wasn't Makenna; it read "Kelly." A brief feeling of disappointment came over her.

"Uh, well, not really. We're just looking," she said.

"Well, feel free to look around," the girl replied. "As you can see, we're getting a lot of beautiful clothes in now."

Kelly tilted her head towards the snow-filled streets.

"Overnight, winter arrived! Isn't it wonderful?"

Jane returned her smile. From the corner of her eye, she could see Joanne milling about the store, not far from the counter. Their eyes met, briefly.

"Yes, it is. I had forgotten just how nice Lake Placid is in winter."

"Your first time back in a long time?" Kelly asked.

"Yes. Used to live here, years ago. I've been to a lot of ski resorts, but not many can compare with Placid."

"So I've heard. Unfortunately, I've never been outta the northeast and so I can't compare it…but it's my plan to ski 'em all, one day."

Jane smiled again and was about to turn around and continue through the store when she got up the nerve to ask the question. She wasn't about to leave without enquiring about the daughter she'd never met.

"Uh, by any chance, does a Makenna work here?"

Kelly nodded.

"Yes, she's out back. Want me to get her for you?"

Jane hesitated. She didn't want to be seen to be too pushy, too inquisitive or too obvious. But before she could answer, a younger version of herself emerged from the backroom.

It was Makenna.

Jane stood there, stunned. She was five foot nine or taller, with long, silky brown hair tied in a ponytail that bounced to and fro as she entered the room. She had the gait of a graceful athlete at the top of her game. As she walked towards them, Jane was immediately struck by the young woman's quick powder-blue eyes and porcelain skin. She was exquisite.

"Kell, did that shipment of Rossignol bindings arrive yesterday?" Makenna asked. "I can't find them anywhere."

Jane continued to witness the interchange between the two athletic young women and thought of herself at that age. By the time she was twenty, she was in her sophomore year at Oswego State and had won spots on both the softball and soccer teams. On skates since the age of seven, she became a power forward on Oswego's women's hockey team as well. She had been in superb shape.

Three days after landing a job with Walter at the paper, Jane summoned the courage to visit the small clinic in Saranac Lake. Mrs. Kirkland, the nurse at her high school, was a supportive and discreet woman in her late fifties whom Jane felt she could confide. Jane noticed the nurse was a golfer, and had taken her aside one day at the course. She could tell her about her suspicions and that, well, it's been more than six weeks, and well…you know. She'd also told her about Donna and how news like this would freak her out.

Mrs. Kirkland understood. Jane's situation wasn't new or original. She had helped many young women over the years, first in Brooklyn and then Schenectady before settling in their upstate town. The city girls were mostly Puerto Ricans and African-Americans, all poor, not knowing where to turn. But she didn't judge them. She didn't criticize or lecture them. They were in trouble and they needed her assistance. God forbid if this country regressed, she thought.

Jane came to love old Mrs. Kirkland. The wise and wonderful nurse told her about a small clinic operating in the mountains, and maybe, just maybe, she could go there for help.

As Jane watched Makenna—now a confident, young woman making her way in the world—she remembered that late summer day when she entered the Saranac clinic.

Her intention was to rid her young body of this invasive species. She wasn't about to become her mother, riddled with a lifetime of unhappiness, never achieving her goals. She was only eighteen, after all, and didn't know what she wanted in life. But one thing was certain; she wasn't going to be Donna.

An Adirondack version of Mrs. Kirkland took her aside. She suggested an alternative plan. You have another option, Miss Schumacher, the clinic nurse had said, a more positive option. You don't have to do this. I know a nice couple. I can introduce you to them. They're about ten years older than you...

Well, the nurse convinced Jane, and they met. With her anxious husband looking on, the woman had looked into Jane's eyes, tearfully explaining their love for children and the pain of her infertility. She pleaded with Jane to reconsider.

Jane did, and she was glad she did.

Now she was watching intently as the two young store clerks worked together. Jane could sense a strong bond of friendship between them.

Kelly continued.

"Yup, the Rossies came in yesterday," she said, pointing in the direction of the storeroom. "The UPS guy stacked them in the far corner...on the far side."

As Makenna turned to head back to the room, Kelly interrupted her.

"But *Ken,* hold on. This lady's been asking for you."

Kelly shifted an eyebrow in Jane's direction, and Makenna switched gears. She looked over to the older woman, curious.

"Hi, I'm Makenna. Can I help you?"

Jane became a bit flustered. She could feel her face turning crimson.

"Uh, my sister and I just came in to have a look around."

Makenna looked puzzled.

"Do I know you?" she asked. "Or should I know you?"

"No, not really. I knew your parents a long time ago, when you were just a baby."

"Really, how?"

"I once interviewed them," she lied. "I was once a reporter for a TV station."

"Really? I don't remember Mom or Dad saying anything about that."

"Well, as I say, you were just a little girl then, and I can't even remember the story I was working on or why I spoke with them," Jane said, growing more and more uncomfortable with a narrative she'd made up on the fly. She decided to extend her hand to the young woman before her.

"My name's Jane Schumacher."

"Hi…nice to meet you. I'll mention you to my parents when I head back to Plattsburgh for Christmas. That's where I'm from."

Of course, Jane knew exactly where her parents lived.

"Oh, they probably won't remember me," Jane replied. "We just struck up something back then."

Affectionately, Jane continued to stare into Makenna's eyes.

"You've really grown into a very lovely young girl…well, not a girl anymore."

Makenna became slightly unnerved by the compliment.

"Thank you," she said hesitantly.

"Do you work here full-time or…?" Jane asked.

"No, just on weekends and some holidays like this one. I go to Clarkson. I'm in my final year in environmental engineering."

"Clarkson? That's a good school," Jane said.

"Yeah, I like it. But the skiing's better here than in Potsdam," she shrugged. "Well, there's not much skiing in Potsdam. Pretty flat place. Do you ski?"

"Some, when I can find the time. Environmental engineering?"

"Yeah, the world's going green and so I thought I'd go where the jobs are going to be," Makenna said.

"You must be a whiz at math."

"I get by...I just hope there's a job out there with my name on it when I graduate."

Jane nodded. She glanced over at Joanne, who was witnessing the exchange. Makenna noticed too; the younger woman and Joanne made brief eye contact. For a moment, Jane considered calling her sister over to introduce her to Makenna but decided against it. She sensed that Joanne approved.

Jane resumed her conversation with her daughter.

"It's a tough job market, for sure," she replied. "But smart people always find a way."

"You said you were a reporter?" Makenna was growing more and more curious, wondering who this woman really was. "You look familiar. Have I seen you on TV?"

"Maybe...but it's been a while since I was a journalist."

Makenna realized she had work to do and started looking for an exit to this conversation.

"Well, it was nice to meet you, Jane. But if you don't mind, I have to get back to the storeroom and find those bindings! The season's upon us."

"Of course...Makenna. Very nice to meet you, too."

Makenna smiled, turned and disappeared through the storeroom door. Jane looked over towards Joanne. Reveling in the moment, recognizing the significance of the meeting, both were close to tears.

Joanne placed her arm around her sister.

They exited the store in silence.

THIRTY-EIGHT

Boychuk and his deputy sat in their cruiser in the corner of the parking lot at The North Star Motel. He had spoken to Hubie and had made his decision.

"Are we calling in the troopers?" Jimmy asked his boss.

"No, not yet."

Jimmy grimaced. It was a look not lost on the sheriff.

"Sheriff, Placid's at least two hours away, maybe more. Besides, we don't have the juris—"

Boychuk cut him off.

"Don't argue with me, Jim! We're gonna see this through."

The senior police officer knew he was entering forbidden territory, and the look of determination on his face said it all. And Jimmy knew it too; he had seen that expression before. It was what made Boychuk a good cop. But the deputy was still skeptical.

"All right, Sheriff," he conceded. "You're the boss."

Boychuk heard the doubt in his deputy's tone of voice. He knew he'd have to mitigate the situation.

"I know what you're thinking, Jim," he said. "My wife is wondering why we're still here too. Thinks I'm obsessed with this case."

In their decade of marriage, Boychuk had never mentioned Jane's name to Susan. His wife had met Hubie several times as they'd prepared for one of their hunting or fishing trips. But she didn't know—till now—that the retired postmaster had had two daughters. Moreover, Boychuk's pursuit of the women—over "hell's half-acre and beyond" she told him on his cell phone—had puzzled her. Why didn't he just turn the investigation over to the troopers, and come home? Someday, he'd tell his wife about his first love.

But for now, his mission was clear.

Like Susan, Jimmy was also ignorant of his past history with Jane. The sheriff was a private man; he rarely shared details of his personal life with his team. But this case also perplexed the deputy. The shooting had taken place in Morgan County, and it was clear the two officers were outside their county's boundaries. This case should have been earmarked for the state police days ago.

Maybe Susan's right, Jimmy thought.

But Boychuk was adamant. He told his deputy they would head to Lake Placid and check out the situation.

"These sisters have gotten themselves into a helluva mess," Boychuk added. "But Jane Schumacher is *not* stupid. She told me she still had something to do, whatever that is. But I think we'll find that out today."

"You think so, Sheriff?" his deputy asked. "All we have is a hunch from that barmaid who thinks they're in Lake Placid at some cabin."

Boychuk nodded. The Lake Placid destination made sense to him. Jane had connections there.

"They're there. I'm positive," Boychuk replied. "And besides, we're closer to this thing than Davis and his people are. Hell, Davis doesn't really care about this case. To him, it's cut, dried and fried. He's just trying to avoid further embarrassment for the governor."

"Okay, you're the boss," Jimmy repeated.

"Trust me on this. I think I'm right."

Boychuk put his cruiser in reverse, backed up and peeled away from the motel, pointing their vehicle north.

His Tahoe had barely disappeared over the long hill and beyond the lake when a vintage Lincoln Continental pulled into the motel lot. It was Matt. After he offered his old pickup to Joanne and covered the Explorer in a garage behind the motel, Matt had disappeared himself. He had fired up Jake's old car and driven over to Glens Falls for the night. He had a drummer pal there and decided that it was time to drop in. He knew the sheriff would eventually find the way to his bar and start asking questions. But he wasn't prepared to deal with cops.

Matt knew he was courting trouble. Probably big-time shit. His decision to loan his truck—not to mention the keys to his cabin—to a couple of fugitives was going to cause him problems. He knew that when they were picked up or surrendered, the police would pay him a visit. Maybe he could profess innocence, tell the cops that he had no idea what kind of trouble they were in. Or he could say their SUV broke down and they needed to borrow a vehicle. That he was just helping out a couple of women down on their luck, the kind of man who was common around these parts, a salt-of-the-earth type of guy.

He smiled. He'd dredge up every cliché in the book. But it was true. People here actually *do* things for other people. They don't expect to be paid for simple things and are almost insulted if you offer them money. Maybe they'd be pissed if you don't offer them a beer. But that was it. It was one of the reasons he had returned from California; the fuckers out there would rather point a nine-millimeter Glock at you than offer to help.

No, there was something about those gals that made him—in that moment, after listening to Joanne's pretty song—hand over his keys. What was it? Was it the good-looking one, Jane, the sassy one who was so grateful to me for fixin' their tire? He'd never forget that twinkle in her eye. She was somethin'…oh, for sure on a mission to get wasted… and she liked to dance. Or was it Joanne, the quiet one, who ripped him a new orifice for thinking that he'd violated her sister? He liked that. Very protective. Or maybe it was her singin' and playin'? Blowin' his mind with raw but real talent? She too could be a fox, he thought…if she worked at it a bit.

Well, he put it out of his mind for now. Maybe Joanne would back him up when she got nabbed. Tell the cops he was just a hillbilly, a nice but not very smart son of a bitch.

Matt put the old Lincoln in park and entered the bar. It was just before noon, but he knew Tammy would have opened the saloon an hour earlier. Legally, he could open earlier but that was a bad idea. It was hard enough to get his regulars to leave at night.

Tammy was pouring a draft for one of the pool players as Matt walked up to the bar. He knew she was havin' a hissy fit about something, and it was probably because he paid so much attention to Jane and Joanne. For a moment or two he sat at the bar and watched her go about her business.

When Jake died, and left him a bit of cash, Matt bought the bar and motel—and Tammy came with it. She was a fixture; she'd worked the roadhouse for years, and from what he could tell, the locals liked her. Well, hell, they'd like *anyone* who flashed her tits as much as Tammy did. Not long after he took over, Matt discovered she was divorced and had a young son, but wasn't raising him much. She was limited to supervised visits with the kid after ending up on the losing end of an ugly verdict. Her ex knew she was slutting around, but that wasn't enough for the judge to take away her son. No, the determining factor in the judge's decision was when she found out Tammy had left her six-year-old alone on more than one occasion. To go drinking.

Matt had known a lot of Tammys over the years. After all, he and his band had played joints like this since he was nineteen. He knew it was a bad idea to swim off the company pier but in a moment of weakness he had succumbed. After California, he was lonely. The wars he'd had with his ex-wife had exhausted him. That he had been unsuccessful in rekindling some sort of relationship with his daughter had also hurt him bad.

He returned upcountry nearly two years ago, in the thick of winter, and surrendered to Tammy's raw charms. Now, of course, he regretted it; Tammy was like the other women in his life who felt there should be something more to their *soirée* than the sex. They always did.

After pouring another beer, Tammy finally sauntered over to where Matt was sitting and put a mineral water in front of him. She knew his drink of preference; it had been a couple of years or more since he'd had his last Jack 'n Coke back in Bakersfield, or was it Oxnard? That was how bad it got; he couldn't remember. Well, whatever, it felt like a long time ago.

"Some sheriff paid us a visit today," she said, resisting the urge to demand why he'd been absent for nearly twenty-four hours.

Matt wasn't surprised. He knew the cops would continue their search up and down the quiet highway leading to the mountains.

"Yeah, what'd he want?"

"Oh, I think you know full well."

"Humor me."

"Well, if you want to remain coy," she said, the word sounding more like 'coe-way', with two syllables. That was one thing he could never figure out. If people around here never left upstate New York in their lives, why did some of them sound like they'd been born in Tennessee or Alabama?

"He was lookin' for those twin sisters, although they didn't look like twins to me. Apparently, if you don't know this—but I'm sure you do—they're wanted for that murder over in Morgantown. They're sayin' one of them put away her husband with buckshot!"

"Is that right?"

"Yup, and I knew they were trouble the moment they walked in here. I just knew it!"

Matt was getting pissed.

"Why, because one of 'em got drunk and started dancin' with me?" he asked, his voice rising.

"Well, yeah, she was all over you, Matt. It was clear to me and half the bar," she said. "The boys here thought you made an ass of yourself."

"The boys, huh?" he said, sarcastically. "Not what you thought, though, was it?"

Tammy continued her glare.

"Well, it was none of their fuckin' business and none of yours too," Matt said. "But, more important, what did you tell this cop?"

"That I didn't know where they were...other than a wild guess I had."

"Yeah, and what was that guess?"

She smirked.

"That I thought they might—just might—be at that cabin of yours in the mountains. You know...the one you took *me* to once?"

Matt was now livid. He never despised anyone as much he did Tammy right now.

"Jesus Christ!" he bellowed and jumped from the bar stool. Watching him march to the door, Tammy decided to go for the jugular.

"What's the matter, Matt?" she yelled out. "Miss your chance to *do* it with twins?"

Just then, Cindy, the younger bartender, arrived for her shift. Matt greeted her at the door.

"Cindy, as of right now, you're in charge of the bar," he said. "Can you handle it by yourself until I figure things out?"

"Sure, Matt, if that's what you want," Cindy replied.

"Yes, it's what I want."

He turned and walked back to the bar and faced a still smirking Tammy.

"You're through here. You don't work here anymore. Get your things and get the hell out of here—now."

THIRTY-NINE

"She's beautiful, Jane...inside and out," Joanne said as she and her sister stepped over a snow bank as they exited a small liquor store carrying a six-pack of Bud Light and a pint of Scotch. It had been an emotional moment for both of them and perhaps a few beers and some high-test might settle their nerves. Besides, it was also a moment to celebrate, though Joanne knew it was a bad idea to drink in a vehicle after a major snowstorm—or anytime for that matter.

She had always frowned when Denny drank beer at the wheel of his septic pumper, but she gave up long ago trying to change him. Secretly, she'd hoped the cops would nail him. That would teach him a lesson. But then she thought about it. If he lost his license, how would he work? That would just put more pressure on her. More than that, he would've become meaner and meaner.

But who cares now, she thought. If she wanted a beer at noon on a Sunday in her truck, well, she'd have one.

"That she is, Jo," Jane replied, wistfully. "That she is."

"Like her mom," her sister replied, shooting an affectionate glance to Jane as they entered Matt's truck.

Jane smiled.

Summoning the strength to meet her daughter for the first time had been painful. No, it had hurt like hell, because in the space of three or four minutes she entertained the notion that Makenna could have been a part of her life over the years.

Well, perhaps not, she thought. She would still have honored the deal she had made with her parents. It was exhilarating just the same. Bigger than the biggest high she'd ever had—and she'd strolled through the corridors of power. That Makenna didn't know who that strange woman was or why she approached her didn't matter. What was important was that Jane had now been vindicated. The decision she'd made twenty years before was the best one. Jane was happy to have created such a wonderful human being, and one that was going to be a success in this world. That was all that mattered today.

At the same time, she had answered the most critical question of her life. Who was this young woman she had brought into the world? What was she like? What had she become? She'd experienced a lifetime of second-guessing— really a nagging sense of doubt—throughout her adulthood coming to grips with those questions. But today those feelings were put to rest. An enormous sense of elation came over her.

Continuing through Lake Placid, Jane began to reflect on the remarkable string of events that had overtaken her life since Wednesday. One minute she was plotting the launch of a presidential campaign, setting the stage for months of mudslinging politics that promised to end in triumph. The next minute she found herself parked in a rundown Silverado in the mountains looking to get drunk, again.

And, oh yes, wanted for murder. Did she forget to mention that?

She rolled her eyes. Well, to paraphrase her late brother-in-law, shit happens. All the more reason to drink, and with one hand on the wheel, Jane opened her bottle of Johnny Walker and took a healthy swig.

She noticed her sister watching intently.

"How can you drink that stuff?" Joanne asked.

"Haven't had a beer in twenty years, Jo. Even the smell of that crap makes me puke. And beer breath is worse!"

"Oh, I'll make it a point to open my window," Joanne replied. "I wouldn't want to offend you. But I seem to remember you drinking a lot of 'em then."

"Well, that was then," Jane replied, reaching into her purse to remove a bottle of Tylenol. Popping a couple of pills into her mouth, she reached for Johnny once again, tilting her head back to swallow.

"How many of those are you going to take?" she asked, as her sister guided the truck through the village.

"This bronchitis is awful."

"Those aren't antibiotics. Those are Tylenol. Shouldn't you be on penicillin or something to kill the bugs?"

Jane said nothing. Instead, in her rearview mirror, her eyes were peeled on the police cruiser on their tail. It had been following them since they had turned the corner from the liquor store. She arrived at an intersection, and she decided to turn left for a route around Mirror Lake.

The cop followed them.

"Oh, oh," Jane said.

"What?"

"There's a member of the local constabulary on our ass," Jane said. Alarmed, Joanne whipped her head around to see the police car not far behind them.

"Probably just some Barney Fife from the village," Jane said.

"How long has he been there?"

"A couple of blocks…but don't panic, I'm not giving him any reason to stop us. I think he's just kicking tires."

They continued to drive the speed limit around the lake. Earlier, when they had left the cabin, this road was snow-packed. But now, a mixture of sand and salt had been applied and the narrow thoroughfare had turned a slushy brown color. In less than twenty-four hours, Mirror too had thickened in the fifteen-degree weather. It was now a rippled sheet of white.

Suddenly, the gumballs on the cop car behind them began to flash, and the car's siren let out a short, piercing wail. He was pulling them over.

"Oh, Christ," Joanne said, her voice signaling her rising fear.

"Relax…as I said, he's probably harmless, and besides, I work for a politician, remember?" Jane handed her bottle to her sister and stopped the truck on the side of the road. She considered popping a piece of gum into her mouth, but rejected the idea; he won't be able smell my breath, she thought.

"But tuck the booze under the seat."

The young cop, sporting a brimmed hat and a pair of bright-orange sunglasses, stepped from his cruiser and approached the Silverado. Making a fashion statement, Jane thought, as she rolled her window down.

"Afternoon, ladies," he said.

"Hello, officer."

"Is this your truck?"

"No, no, it's a friend's. We just borrowed it…to move some furniture today."

"Is that right?" he said.

Despite his glasses, Jane could see him trying to stare her down. She figured he was one of those young cops who loved his uniform. But if this particular guy thinks he's going to outsmart me, he's wrong, Jane thought. She'd learned a long time ago how to win an argument. A smile here and there works wonders. She once got out of a speeding ticket in Napa by smiling innocently at a motorcycle cop and apologizing for still using her "New York foot."

She'd deploy that strategy now.

"That's right, officer. However, I didn't think we were speeding, were we?" She put the question directly to him, knowing the answer. He continued to stare, wondering what he had here. But he was succumbing to the attractive woman's magic.

"No…but did you know you have a broken tail-light?"

Thanks, Matt, she thought. First an empty windshield washer and now a busted light. Wait till I see that cowboy again.

"No, I'm sorry, but we didn't know, officer," she replied. "But thank you for telling us. We'll get her fixed first thing tomorrow morning, okay?"

She flashed the cop another smile.

"By the way, I like those Serengetis you're wearing. I assume you got them in the village? I've been looking for a pair myself. "

The young cop became flustered, and it showed. He was unsure just how to deal with the flirtatious woman. After a moment, ignoring her question, he regained his composure.

"You ladies from around here?" he asked. "Have I seen you before somewhere?"

"Don't think so, officer. First time in Lake Placid. We're from the city…a friend of ours has a cabin over there." She pointed in the direction of Matt's place. "—and we're helping him move some stuff…maybe get in a few runs later. Maybe have some fun in this nice town of yours. We're sure there's a lotta fun to be had here—as long as we don't drink and drive. Is that right, officer?"

She smiled at him again.

The cop stared for a moment further. Then he relented.

"Yes, that's right," he said, returning her smile ever so slightly. "All right...now I could write you up, but you'll have to get that light fixed as soon as a garage opens up tomorrow, you understand?"

"We will, officer. Thank you," she said, flashing another smile.

The cop nodded, tipped his hat with courtesy and returned to his car. Glancing in her side mirror, Jane watched as he started his cruiser, pulled a U-turn and drove towards the village. Joanne heaved a huge sigh of relief before looking over to her sister. She reached for her can of beer and handed Jane her Scotch. Then they broke into wide grins, followed by a burst of laughter.

"Man, you're good!" Joanne said.

"Works once in a while, Jo," she said, still laughing. "Haven't been put in jail...well, at least not yet. But all this got me thinking. Do we deserve some friggin' fun, or not? And I know exactly the right place."

She placed the Silverado in drive and peeled away. Minutes later, off a back road leading to Saranac, Jane stopped the truck at the gates of a small amusement park and miniature golf course. When she worked for the *Tribune*, Jane had visited this park often and was happy to discover it was still there.

In summer, it was a tourist attraction, providing tired parents an opportunity to entertain their rambunctious kids for a few hours before dinner. Or allow them to blow off some steam afterwards. The park boasted the usual fare: shooting galleries, a Ferris wheel, tea cups and of course a carousel. In summer's opposite season, it was buried under heaps of snow.

The sisters exited the truck and Joanne was perplexed.

"This is your idea of fun?" she asked.

"Jo, don't you remember when we were kids and loved the fair?"

"Yeah, it was the only thing we had to do in summer—" She slipped into a backwoods accent that Darryl her boss would have been proud of. "—other than tippin' cows...or drinkin' at tractor puuulls."

Jane laughed.

"We both worked there one summer and rode the rides at night. You remember the time we double-dated?"

"Yeah, don't remind me."

Joanne approached the fenced property and surveyed the park. It was deserted and dormant, a far cry from that July evening when she and Jane, joined by their football-playing boyfriends, took in the fair. Joanne had pleaded with Denny to join them and he reluctantly agreed after she promised him a night to remember. Only she wasn't referring to the fair.

For a night, Boychuk had put aside the animosity he'd held towards his Marauder teammate. The future sheriff knew what Denny called him behind his back. He was "nothin' but a bohunk farmer," Denny would say.

But Jane had convinced him to go.

That was before that fateful day later that summer when so much had happened. Within weeks, Jane would be gone; to where, Joanne wouldn't find out until much later. Brian would be off to the police academy, only to return at Christmas as a rookie officer. And Denny...well, Denny would be looking for a job to support a new wife and the baby they'd conceived.

Denny once had prospects; he might not have turned into a bitter sewer man. But he'd just had a few bad breaks— literally, Joanne thought. That was before a drunken, midnight chase put an end to his football career, first a scholarship at either Boise State or the University of Michigan, and then perhaps a stint in the pros. There was a time that Joanne thought she'd make a good wife to a professional football player.

But in a flash, his life came crashing down, and he never recovered.

Joanne remembered it as if were yesterday. The early morning call she got from the hospital. It was Denny, angry and hysterical. He related how his mother's asshole boyfriend—a nasty, tough-as-nails prison guard named Dominick—ran Denny out of his own house, waving his snub-nosed revolver in the air, firing it into the night and pursuing the boy across the yard and into the woods. Well, at eighteen, Denny was hardly a boy. At six-two, he was a man, thoroughly hardened by his three years as Morgantown's All-State defensive tackle. He had been toughened also by the constant beatings he had suffered at the hands of an alcoholic father before the old man upped and left about four years before.

Anyway, when Denny arrived to find his mother sobbing, he took matters into his own hands, only to find that old Dominick—one of many Dominicks in his mother's life after his old man disappeared—had plunked his prison-issued handgun down on the dresser. He told Dominick to stop hurtin' his mother, stop slappin' her around or...or...

Or what kid, Dominick asked?

Or I'll bust your chops, you bald-headed old bastard, Denny cried. But it proved to be an idle threat, since Dominick wasn't about to take any shit from this kid. The old lady gave him enough already, and he wasn't about to take it from her kid too.

The first shot was for effect as ceiling plaster crumpled to the bedroom floor. Denny's mother, Adele, now wrapped only in a bed sheet, screamed at the top of her lungs.

The second shot came a lot closer, in fact too close for Denny's comfort. He could almost feel the bullet fly past his ear. This fucker's a lunatic, he thought, as he fled down the back steps of their double-wide two at a time and towards the woods. Another shot rang out, and as Denny looked over his shoulder, he didn't see a decaying tree stump a few feet in the distance. He tumbled hard and felt a distinct pop. His leg was broken in three places. Writhing in pain and close to tears, all he could hear was Dominick's hateful laughter mixed with Adele's shrieks.

The snow covered amusement park brought all of Joanne's memories back. There once was a time, she thought...

"Jane, even if we could get in and get rid of some of this snow, I don't know if we could even fire up the rides—"

Suddenly, Joanne was interrupted by the sound of a thunderous gun blast. Alarmed, she turned around. With Hubie's shotgun again in hand, Jane had blown away the locks to the gate, and flung the doors open. A wicked grin came over her as she moved to the next victim—the park's green power box.

She pointed the twelve-gauge at the locks and let loose the second barrel. It exploded, ripping a hole the size of a softball in the steel. She opened the power box and flicked the main breaker. The entire park roared to life.

"Let's go! I know how to run these babies!"

Taking another big gulp of her beer, Joanne laughed.

"You're insane!"

FORTY

The sisters looked like star-crossed adolescents on their first date to the movies, wild-eyed and holding hands. Firing up the enormous Ferris wheel, its lifts bouncing and shaking, Jane and Joanne sprung into action. The ride's chairs once boasted lovely, gay-nineties-styled murals; today, the decorative designs had faded and the ride was in serious disrepair.

But that didn't matter as they sat in their chosen car, shrieking with laughter. They were lost in the moment. They were kids again at the fair. If they tried hard enough, they might have seen hundreds of others there, reveling in a warm summer night so long ago. They would have joined the traveling roadies, the vendors, the obnoxious but lovable carnival barkers as they hawked their red-hots, cotton candy, stale popcorn and watered-down soda.

Jumping from the wheel, their ride complete, they bolted for the tea cups—the silliest of attractions—and once again, Jane instinctively knew how to operate them. It didn't matter that many inches of snow had fallen. The spinning mugs functioned as designed and round and round and round they went, exploding with laughter each and every time their cup narrowly avoided a collision with the next one. How could they not crash? They came so close! It didn't matter to Jane that she was rapidly losing steam or that her chest muscles ached. Or that the constant circular motion was almost making her barf. She was having a ball.

Their final ride was the merry-go-round, simple and dependable, everyone's favorite. To Jane's disbelief, this ride worked too. But as it moaned and groaned under the heavy new snow, the distinctive sounds of a classic carousel came alive. It was a tune that Jane imagined—rightly or wrongly—may have echoed across Coney Island after its famous carousel began offering five-cent rides in the late nineteenth century.

Or maybe she was recalling something different? Maybe old Walt was right; she was born old. From movies, or newsreels perhaps, she recalled the resonant sounds of organ grinders, the dirt-poor immigrants on the New York street corners, joined by their white-topped companions, the clever Capuchin monkeys, eking out a living during a much tougher era. Everyone could recognize those sounds, couldn't they? Well, whatever...it didn't matter at this moment in time. Nothing mattered. She and Joanne were determined to mount every smiling steed and stallion, chasing each other until they were exhausted with joy. Round and round they rode, clinging to the poles, knowing their destination.

Suddenly, Joanne saw another police car coming up the long road. She tapped Jane's shoulder and both let out a loud roar. With the carousel still in motion, its music reverberating throughout the entire park, they jumped from its circular platform and raced to their truck. Soon they were zigzagging their way over a back road and away from their latest crime scene. They had made their getaway.

Laughing...hooting...whistling all the way.

Joanne popped another Bud Light as she guided the truck through the back streets toward the cabin road. She glanced at Jane who smiled in return. It had been an emotional yet thrilling day. Having witnessed Jane's poignant reunion with her daughter, Joanne now felt a loving appreciation for the sister she had relegated to a troubled past. For as long as she could remember, at least since they had ascended into adulthood, Jane was the sibling that simply didn't exist.

Today, she was part of her life. Again.

But she couldn't lock their painful past away in some distant vault, not anymore. Her mind returned to that summer, after they both had graduated from high school, and wondered how it all went so wrong for them. She never understood her sister's decision to leave town so abruptly, so angry, so bitter. Aside from their last, brief reunion—their mother's funeral eight years before—they hadn't spent any time together. For a reason that Joanne could never fathom, Jane severed her connection to her family.

She knew Jane despised their mother's need to control their lives and how Donna had smothered them. But there had to have been more to it than that, wasn't there? What the hell was it? As they traveled up the long road, she decided to break their silence. She would ask the question.

"Do you ever think about her?"

Jane looked over at her sister, surprised by the question.

"You talking about Mom?"

"Yeah."

Jane sighed.

"Not if I can help it," she replied. "Oh, she pays me visits from time to time. Too often for my liking and, I have to say, my memories of her are not fond...not kind."

"Do you miss her?" Joanne asked.

"Do I miss her?" Jane repeated the question as if she were searching for an answer from deep within.

"No. Well, at least not until all of this shit started going down. Over the last few days, I've wondered how she could have helped me—us really—through this mess. If she even *had* the capacity to help us. Who the fuck knows?"

She corrected herself, knowing Joanne's distaste for her swearing.

"Oops, I'm sorry..."

Joanne shrugged.

She knew her sister wasn't about to change her habits. Jane, sensing absolution, paused for a few moments before resuming her train of thought.

"Do you...do you remember how she made all our clothes?"

"Yeah, I do," Joanne replied.

"Well, I knew they never had much money, but we were fourteen before I had a store-bought blouse and one different from yours. She always had to dress us the same! How sick was that? Well, I'll tell you what I think. It was because she wasn't happy with who we were...she always seemed to be disappointed in us. Look at our names, for Christ's sake? Joanne and Jane? They're names that parents give *identical* twins."

Joanne couldn't disagree with her sister.

"She was always envious of Janet Snider and her twins over on Oak Point Road," Joanne agreed. "They were identicals."

Jane laughed at the memory.

"But they were *boys!*" she shouted. "They were fucking boys!"

Joanne noticed it had started snowing again. She smiled at the absurdity of their conversation. Jane continued.

"I know what it was. It was because Mom had to control every friggin' aspect of our lives, and she never gave up."

She looked over at Joanne once again.

"I'm going to tell you something you probably never knew," she said, her voice so low that Joanne could barely hear her. "Once, not long after I started going with Brian, I caught Mom reading my diary. Not in person, but I caught her. I suspected she was reading it because she started behaving so weirdly. So one night, I purposely left a couple of strands of my hair on my diary. The thing was hidden! In my closet...covered by a few boxes. But Donna found it! I think she spent her days scouring our rooms for evidence of our teenaged depravity, for Christ's sake!"

Joanne was listening, intently. "You set a trap for her?" There was more admiration than accusation to her question.

"Well, in a manner of speaking yes, because I suspected she was nosing around. And yes, I put a few strands of my hair on it...and sure enough, the next day the hair was gone. She knew where it was. And I *knew* she read it, regularly I suspect. So, in my next entry, that night, I left her a nasty message, and I know she got it because she acted pretty embarrassed around me for a few days—guilty even, that I caught her in the act."

She peered at her sister, searching for a reaction.

Joanne was shocked. "Really, Mom did that?"

"She did...I always suspected she was spying on me," Jane said. "Probably wanting to know how many times Chucky and I screwed. Wanting to know everything I did. And maybe about you too, but me for sure. And she wondered why I left when I did."

"You never told me that, Jane," Joanne said. "Why not? Why didn't you?"

Jane grimaced. She was exhausted and in pain. All she wanted to do was return to the cabin and go to sleep.

"I don't know, Jo...I don't know," she replied. "Maybe it was because I always knew you were closer to her than I was. Maybe it was because I was more of a pain in the ass, too. I never liked being ordered around. It seemed all she wanted to do was make our lives miserable. And she was hardly a great role model. She got knocked up too!"

Joanne reluctantly agreed with Jane, but said nothing. And it was clear that Jane wasn't finished.

"Why couldn't she accept us for who we were, Jo?" Jane asked. "Goddamn it! You know, I went through life thinking it was *our* fault that she fucked up *her* life! That it was our fault."

Jane's voice trailed off for a few moments.

"You know, there was one time...one particular time... that I would have liked a hug...just a friggin' hug...instead of yet another accusation. But it never happened. So... case closed!"

Jane collected herself. This was too good a day. She was not going to let Donna ruin it—for her, or for Joanne.

They continued their drive up the winding road. The snow was drifting more heavily, and Joanne knew she had to get Jane back to the cabin. The day had taken too much out of her, and she needed rest. Finally they arrived, and Joanne looked over at her sister. Jane was a mess. She seemed to have aged years in a matter of days. But that didn't seem to deter her.

"This was one helluva day, wasn't it, Jo?" Jane asked, smiling.

"That it was, city—"

She caught herself before repeating what Denny had called her.

"—that it was."

"I'm pretty tired and am not feeling well. Pretty crappy, in fact, so I think I'll just go in and lie down, okay?"

"Okay, don't yell at me, but I'm staying out here and have another dart."

Jane nodded, and through her sadness, smiled.

"I'm never going to yell at you again, Jo."

She opened the truck door and walked toward the cabin. Joanne watched her sister disappear inside before lighting a cigarette. From her view high above the village, she could see a pair of snowplows making their way up the hill. They were working in tandem, their blue flashing lights illuminating the newly-fallen snow. Soon she'd have to find a shovel and clear a path for the truck.

She took another drag on her Salem Menthols and turned her attention to the snowmobile parked near the outer building. Now that machine wouldn't have any problems in this weather.

A few minutes passed. Suddenly, from the front seat of the truck, Joanne heard the unmistakable sound of Jane's BlackBerry going off. She wished she hadn't forgotten her cell phone in the rush to leave her house on Thanksgiving night. Maybe she would've gotten up the nerve to call Brent. Well, yes, she'd cussed her sister out for even suggesting that a phone call—on a cell, no less—would suffice. But now she changed her mind. She missed her texts from Brent. She cherished the daily contact she'd had with her son, including a message on Thanksgiving morning wishing her a good day and apologizing for not coming home. That was only four days ago, but it felt like an eternity.

The ringing continued.

Curious, she opened the truck's passenger door and retrieved the handheld device. She read the screen and answered it.

"Dad!"

FORTY-ONE

The Morgan County sheriff and his deputy arrived in Saranac Lake and proceeded to the local state police barracks. Having second thoughts, Boychuk had relented and called Jack Davis in Albany and briefed him on his suspicions that the Schumacher sisters were in the mountains. If the information he got from that bartender was right, and instinctively he knew she had every reason to tell the truth, they were only about ten miles away.

Boychuk knew he was straddling a fine line and that Davis would be pissed; the head of Foley's security detail would likely want to know what Boychuk knew about the location of the girls and when he knew it. But to his surprise and satisfaction, the trooper didn't ask those questions. He told Davis he had been returning to Morgantown when he got a tip that they were in Lake Placid and decided to pursue it. Boychuk knew his horseshit would be tolerated as long as the sisters were picked up soon.

Davis had given Boychuk some rope. He realized his friend had a personal reason for rounding up the suspects. But as long as there was no further violence, Davis would look the other way because he knew Boychuk was a good cop. Foley's political problem would soon be over provided that the governor was smart enough to wash his hands of Jane Schumacher. That is if he didn't want to risk his chances of landing the big job.

The police in Saranac Lake were expecting them. So were the local Lake Placid police, who had been alerted as a matter of courtesy. Since the murder took place several counties over, this was clearly a case for the troopers and both Davis and Boychuk didn't want the locals attempting to pull rank. They were confident that wouldn't happen; every small-town chief knew better than to pick a fight with the troopers.

Boychuk and his deputy were greeted by Staff Sergeant Roland Bouchard and met the chief of the Lake Placid department, whose name he soon forgot. Boychuk felt this meeting was a total waste of time but he had told Davis that procedure would be followed. His mission was to find Jane and Joanne, and this stop in Saranac was useless, possibly detrimental. What was preventing the Schumacher sisters from fleeing the area once again?

They weren't there more than a couple of minutes when they learned that a local cop had pulled the girls over earlier that day and failed to recognize them. Boychuk was incredulous. No wonder there are so many real crooks on the loose. Now, that was a strange thought. *Real* crooks? He had never considered the sisters to be dangerous, at least to others.

"You mean to tell me that one of your people stopped two women earlier today for a tail-light—women who fit their exact description—and he let them go?" he demanded. The local chief squirmed in his seat.

"Yes, Sheriff, I believe that's correct."

Boychuk frowned, shaking his head.

"He didn't ask for their license and registration?"

"No. He felt it wasn't required."

"Isn't it standard operating procedure to ask for this shit when you pull anyone over for any reason?"

The embarrassed chief nodded.

"Yes, normally," he replied.

"Normally," Boychuk repeated, his sarcasm dripping. This would have been over by now if that cop had just done

his job. He'd have had the girls in custody and the paper-
work completed to transfer them back to Morgan County. If
that guy worked for me, he caught himself thinking, I'd have
his balls for bookends.

"But in this case, he didn't. Any reason why?"

The chief continued to fidget in his seat.

This wasn't going well. He didn't appreciate the dress-
ing down he was receiving from some sheriff, especially in
front of Bouchard. He and the Saranac trooper had worked
well together in the past, and he'd have to do so in the future.
This sheriff was just trying to score points, he thought.

"He felt it wasn't warranted, Sheriff," he replied. "They
weren't speeding or drinking. It was only a tail-light."

Boychuk's anger was rising.

"Doesn't anyone watch the news in these parts?"

"Or pay attention to the bulletins?" Jimmy interjected.
Boychuk shot his deputy a disapproving glance. He'd handle
this guy.

The chief continued to defend his department's behavior.

"Sheriff, we do pay attention to APBs, but this particular
officer reported to work and went directly to his cruiser without entering the office," he said. "In addition, the truck he
stopped was not a maroon Explorer. It was a white Silverado
pick-up."

"A white Silverado?" Boychuk asked.

This was news to him. He didn't see this coming. That
peroxide blonde back at the roadhouse didn't say anything
about a change of vehicle. Goddamn it, he cursed under his
breath. She hadn't told him that, and now he was wondering
if she'd been bullshitting him all along. No, he was sure she
wasn't. He could see in her eyes that Jane had pissed her off
when she danced and drank with her bar-keep boyfriend.

Nothing like a jilted lover...

The local chief detected an opening. This had caught the sheriff off guard. This Morgan County prick seemed surprised.

"Yes, it was a white pick-up, Sheriff and not an Explorer," he said. "Could it be we're talking about two different cases?"

"No!" Boychuk bellowed. He looked over at his deputy. "Jimmy, call that cowboy bar again and get that bartender on the phone. Find out if her boss, uh...what's his name again? Booker?"

"That's right, Sheriff...Matt Booker," Jim replied.

"Well, find out if old Matt owns a white Silverado. If he does, then our girls are not far from here. And if he does, Jack Davis needs to know about that. Booker'll be in a bucket of shit, too."

His deputy scurried off to a phone at the end of the room. Sergeant Bouchard was listening to the conversation and decided it was time to get to work. In a matter of minutes, he'd be rounding up a couple of his Chevy Tahoes and heading over to that cabin where the Schumachers were believed to be located.

But before he could wrap up the meeting and coordinate the raid on the mountain cabin, the local chief piped up again.

"Sheriff, I have to tell you about another incident that happened about ninety minutes ago or so that might or might not be connected to your case."

"Pray tell, Chief, whaddaya got?" Boychuk asked. His impatience was evident.

The chief related how his department got a couple of calls from residents saying that they heard gunshots coming from an amusement park on the edge of town. The officer that was dispatched discovered the break-in. The lights were on, the Ferris wheel was operating and the carousel was spinning. There were fresh footprints in the snow.

"The locks were shot off?" Boychuk asked.

"Yes, the locks to the gate and to the power supply box."

"What was used? What kind of weapon?"

"From the damage done, looked like a shotgun, probably a twelve-gauge," the chief said.

Boychuk raised his eyebrows. A look of determination came over him. He clenched his lips and with his right hand waved a fist in the air. A victory fist. He knew the girls were at hand.

"Gotta be my ladies!" he said. "Sounds like they wanted a day at the fair!"

He turned his attention to Sergeant Bouchard.

"We're wasting time here, Roly," he said, thinking he could call the trooper by a colloquial handle, a gesture of camaraderie even though the two officers had met only minutes before. "How soon can you get your guys together? We know where that cabin road is. It can't be more than about half an hour from here."

"Maybe less, Sheriff," Bouchard said. In comparison, he was all business. "Let's go. Chief, you can accompany us to the cabin, but we'll take it from here. Thank you for your input."

Jimmy returned.

"Sheriff, that bartender we met with the other day no longer works there," he said. "Apparently, she's been relieved of her duties."

"She was fired?" Boychuk asked.

"Apparently," the deputy replied. "But another bartender, some woman named Cindy, told me that Matt Booker does own a white Silverado. And she hasn't seen it for a couple of days."

Boychuk smiled.

"Let's go!"

FORTY-TWO

Joanne ended her call with her father and barged into the cabin. Jane was curled up on the couch and sleeping soundly. Clearly upset, she couldn't decide to wake her sister or not. Pacing around the cabin, she was shaking with emotions she couldn't identify.

Was it anger? You're damn right!

Was it sorrow or disbelief?

Was it all of the above?

Jane opened her eyes and noticed her sister's frenzied state.

"What's wrong," Jane asked. "Is Boychuk here?"

Joanne remained silent. Her heart was racing, her eyes fixed in a piercing glare. Finally, she spoke.

"Tell me, Jane, do you...do you have any *more* secrets you wanna keep from me?" she demanded. "Is there anything you want to tell me, Jane?"

Jane released a loud sigh.

"Jo, I'm tired, and I feel terrible," she replied. "What are you talking about?"

Their eyes locked.

"Jane, I just got off the phone with Dad. He called your cell phone a few minutes ago, and I answered it. It seems that Roberto paid him a visit."

She paused for a moment before continuing.

"And, it seems Roberto spoke to your doctor in Albany."

Jane sat up on the couch. Biting her bottom lip, her eyes scanned the small cabin interior. Through its front windows, she could see the menacing snow storm continuing to pile drifts across the property. Finally, she looked directly into her sister's eyes.

"How much did Dad tell you?"

"Not a lot...but enough to say—"

"—that it's not good, right?"

Joanne nodded, grim-faced, her eyes welling up.

"Lung cancer!" Jane said, her voice betraying more anger than pity. "Can you believe it? Lung cancer...of all things! I've never smoked a day in my fucking life. And this happens to me?"

Joanne shook her head. Everything was now more clearly in focus.

"I should have suspected something," she said. "All that coughing and hacking you've done. And I thought I saw blood in the sink today, too."

"Guess I didn't clean up too well, huh?"

Joanne was now fighting back the tears and losing the battle.

"Well, it all makes sense now, Jane," she said. "Coming home for Thanksgiving... after all these years of staying away. Then you shoot Denny, when maybe you didn't have to—"

Jane exploded.

"I'm not sorry I blew that asshole away!"

"Jane!"

"Well, I'm not..."

"You could've walked away, though, right Jane? *We* could've just walked out the door and never come back. But, no, you shot him. Twice. Made sure he was dead."

Exhausted, Jane remained silent.

"It's all coming into focus now," her sister continued. "After what your doctor told you, you had nothing to lose, did you? That was it, wasn't it?"

Jane said nothing. There wasn't much more to say. Joanne filled the void.

"Then, this whole trip here to Lake Placid…and our visit today with Makenna? The daughter you've never seen? And maybe you thought you had to meet her before it was too—?" Joanne couldn't find the courage to say the final word.

Jane simply shrugged. She couldn't—or wouldn't—argue with Joanne.

"I guess it all started with me thinking I'd come home, maybe make some peace with you and Dad…and tell you that I was sick. But then I saw for myself what that bastard had been doing to you…beating the hell out of you…and then when he called me a—"

Jane couldn't repeat the word. Never shy with profanity, even she wouldn't stoop to Denny's disgusting level. She would *not* repeat a word that was universally considered as the worst in the English language. But she continued.

"Well, I just lost it. I just couldn't stand by and let him hurt you again…or *me*, for that matter."

Joanne took a step back.

"What? What do you mean—you?"

Jane rose from the couch and walked slowly to the living room window. She knew Joanne's eyes were glued to her. Once again, she watched as the raging storm whipped wildly outside.

Joanne would have never put this puzzle together, and now was the time to level with her sister. Joanne was right; Jane never intended to kill Denny, only to save her from his abuse. But he'd had provoked her, taunted her, that goddamn wink in the kitchen! Called her names. Dared her to recall a memory of a night so long ago of a brief, violent and violating moment. Nearly twenty-one years ago.

"Jo, you came in here asking if there were any more secrets," she said, her voice almost trailing off to a whisper.

She drew a breath so deep that she could hear her lungs wheezing desperately.

"Well, there is...something else...something that happened a long time ago..."

She turned to face Joanne, and once again, their eyes locked.

"Do you remember that party at the lake? That Fourth of July weekend, after we graduated from high school?"

Her painful flashback began.

She could see herself. She was eighteen again.

A large party was at its zenith. It seemed that every senior in tiny Morgantown was there, perhaps sixty in total, and Jane was its leading participant. She saw herself, again. Dancing to a Billy Ocean hit on the turntable. Her hands in the air, one of which was clinging to a half-empty bottle of Jack Daniels.

From where she was in the living room, she could see Joanne with her drink of choice, a beer, with their friends on the far side of the deck. Brian was there, as well, along with most of the football team. Happy teenagers, breaking the rules, celebrating their high-school pasts, toasting their college or working futures.

Suddenly she felt dizzy and began to stagger. She felt herself passing out...and started down the hallway for a bedroom to sleep it off.

In the kitchen, a pair of male eyes. They were following her every move. They watched as she entered the last bedroom. Inside, almost instantly, she flopped on to her back and passed out. Looking behind him to see if anyone had noticed, the young man continued to follow. He quietly entered the room and bolted the door behind him.

Half asleep, she felt her jeans being pulled down past her knees and then past her ankles before they were removed. Her panties followed suit. Despite her intoxicated state, she somehow knew there was something very wrong. Something bad was happening to her. Though the room was hot and dark, a trickle of light eased its way from under the pine-paneled door. Though the enormous frame in front of her was in silhouette, Jane knew who it was.

It was Denny.

He moved quickly, looming large over her. For a brief moment, he watched his girlfriend's sister, clearly innocent, there for the taking. Joanne was easy, almost too easy. Jane was not. For fuck's sake, he was *Denny Lowry*, football star. Why couldn't he have her too?

Well, he would have her.

"Hi Janey honey...I've been watchin' you...all night."

But before she could react, Denny was cupping her mouth. From nowhere, emerged a knife. With a clicking sound that Jane would never forget, the six-inch blade snapped open, and he pressed it to her neck. Suddenly, she had nearly sobered up. Her eyes said it all. Feelings of horror and helplessness came over her.

But Denny would tolerate few, if any, sounds. He would shut her up.

"Quiet now, sis...and I won't hurt you. But I will if I have to. Or if you tell anyone about this, I'll come back and kill you... and you know I will. Besides, you'll like this as much as me...why should the bohunk be allowed to have all the fun?"

Powerfully, forcefully, Denny mounted her.

He was just too strong, too overwhelming, for her to resist. As dizzy as she was, and nauseous from the Jack Daniels, she understood what was happening to her, a private, unbelievable nightmare from which she had no escape. There would be no respite or rescue. She couldn't or wouldn't fight back. He pushed himself on her, thrusting, entering...and his *breath*...that unmistakable smell of stale beer...

"You know as well as I do, the way you've been wigglin' your ass around here, nobody'll believe you, Janey...not even Jo...am I right?"

Of course, with his knife at her neck, she couldn't answer. She couldn't respond.

Jane finished her story and buckled once again, landing heavily in a kitchen chair. Exhausted, depleted...and defeated.

Stunned into silence, Joanne, too, stumbled to the couch and collapsed. Her hands covering her mouth, she stared off into an unknown distance.

She began to weep.

"I'm...I'm so sorry, Jo. I should have told you about this long ago," Jane said, finally.

Joanne looked up from her spot on the couch, her emotions shattered, her life as she knew it broken.

"I needed to be told, Jane. Why—?"

"I don't know...I really don't know why. Maybe I was afraid that Denny was right...that you wouldn't believe me...that maybe you'd think I wanted it too... Jesus, you were so much in love with him. Well, it was only weeks later that you had run off and eloped...because you were pregnant with Brent."

"You still should've told me, Jane..."

Jane nodded slowly in agreement.

"Yeah, you're right. But shoulda, coulda...didn't...and I've been living with this all my adult life. Jo, I'm so sorry. I have no excuses."

Joanne stared into her sister's eyes.

"You told no one of this...all these years?"

Jane blinked. She was biting her lip so deep that she thought it might start to bleed.

"You're the second person I've mentioned this to...in twenty years."

Joanne became alarmed. She jumped from the couch.

"What do you mean? *Second?*"

Jane paused, not sure if she could continue.

"Mom. I told her about it too."

Joanne raised her head, and her moment of grief turned to anger.

"Mom! Mom knew about it too and didn't tell me? Oh my God!"

Jane nodded once again.

"I went to her, Jo. I needed my mother to help me... but she blamed me! She blamed *me* for what Denny did. She thought it was all my fault...the way I was dressed. Wearing those short skirts...and that I brought it all on *myself*. What kind of fucking mother would blame her own daughter for—?"

"Oh my God!" her sister screamed. "You mean to tell me that Mom knew about Denny all those years and said nothing—to me? Goddamn it! I can't believe this is happening."

Joanne swung around and dropped heavily into a kitchen chair, gazing absently out the window and into the blizzard blowing outside their doors. Jane, clearly upset, her frail body trembling, rose from her chair, staring sorrowfully at her sister. Her words had hurt Joanne. But now the man was dead and didn't Joanne deserve the truth?

Suddenly another thought occurred to Joanne. Her eyes exploded with fury mixed with disbelief. She was thinking the unthinkable.

"Then you found out you were having a baby too, Jane!" she yelled. "Don't tell me—"

The sisters were abruptly jolted by a loud ringing coming from Jane's BlackBerry. The device was still in Joanne's hand. She looked at the screen and then looked back her sister.

"It says North Star Motel!" she said. She knew who it was but discovered that she was nearly paralyzed with shock. One ring was followed by another. And another. Finally, she answered.

"Joanne...it's Matt. Are you still at my place in the mountains? Is Jane with you?"

"Uh, huh." It was all she could mutter.

"Listen, little lady, I just found the number to Jane's phone. My bartender, well, my former bartender, Tammy, she ratted on you! The cops know you're there. They're on their way now."

FORTY-THREE

Escaping the cabin with Jane's arm draped over her shoulders, Joanne saw the flashing lights of the Tahoes racing up the mountain toward them. She knew the troopers deployed their huge, four-wheel drive vehicles for a reason. Those damn trucks could navigate this road under any conditions.

Jane's condition had deteriorated quickly. She was barely able to don a winter coat and wrap a scarf around her neck before collapsing in a chair, gasping for breath. But Joanne knew they had to leave, and she scoured the cabin for more winter clothes. On a shelf, she found an old woolen tuque and a pair of mitts, and dressed her like Jane was a little girl on her first day of kindergarten. She lifted Jane to her feet. She had to get her sister to the hospital, fast.

"Come on, Jane, they're coming," she yelled. "You can make it!"

"I don't know, Jo…I'm so tired and I think I'm gonna be sick."

Joanne took another glance at the cruisers and had a decision to make.

"We can't use the truck!" she shouted. "They'd have us in a minute and I'm not gonna let them take us to jail—not yet, anyway."

Joanne carried her sister toward the Arctic Cat parked near the outer building. Its cover was laden with more than a foot of snow, which she quickly swept away. Jane stood beside her and nearly collapsed but her sister caught her before she fell.

"Come on Jane. You're not leaving me yet!"

"Jo, I'm so tired. Why don't we just wait for Brian to get here, and let him take me?"

Joanne shook her head.

"We don't have time to explain anything, Jane. Do you understand? Besides, I'm not ready to give up and neither are you. Not after all we've been through! Okay?"

Through her pain, through her exhaustion, Jane smiled.

"Okay."

Joanne smiled in return and then turned her attention to the snowmobile. She ripped the cover off the machine and noticed the keys still in the ignition. Thank God, she thought. Well, actually, she thanked Matt. God had nothing to do with it. Right now she was pissed at God.

She hopped on and after a couple of cranks it came to life. Jane climbed on behind her.

"Don't tell me you know how to drive these damn things, too!" Jane yelled, over the loud guttural sounds coming from the Arctic Cat.

"I'm the sister you never had!"

Joanne could see the police advancing up the hill. They couldn't be more than a half a mile away now. She made her second major decision. There must be trails that inevitably led to the village. She was sure they existed and probably could find them. But the quickest route to the hospital was straight down the mountain, exactly in the direction from where the police were now coming.

"How are we getting out of here?" Jane yelled into her sister's ear.

"Watch and learn, sister! Hold on!"

Joanne gunned the snowmobile into action and it picked up speed and into the path of the oncoming cruisers. Now, less than a quarter of mile apart, Joanne didn't let up on the accelerator.

Closer and closer they came, with Joanne pushing the machine hard at the first cruiser coming up the hill. That's probably Boychuk in the first vehicle—knowing him, she thought. And right about now he's probably thinking we're friggin' crazy. Let him think what he wants. We're going to that hospital.

They were only yards away, now. But the lead cruiser was the first to blink, swerving at the last moment to avoid a direct collision. Joanne had the same instinct too; she angled the machine up a freshly-minted snow bank on the left, and came perilously close to losing control, nearly flipping them over. Her superb driving skill took over, however, and their machine passed the first cruiser with a thud to the snowy road.

The first truck braked hard, causing it to slide sideways through the snow before it came to a halt. Joanne looked back, and indeed it was Boychuk at the wheel. For a brief moment, their determined eyes locked before she continued on at breakneck pace. He would be hard to lose, she thought.

Boychuk was only the first of her worries, however. She still had to deal with the remaining cruisers. This time, she decided to increase the stakes and see what would happen. Fortunately, the second truck was following too close to Boy-chuk's vehicle, forcing its driver to brake hard and bail in an opposite snow bank. The third truck—also following too close behind—lost control and crashed hard into the rear of the second cruiser.

That left one final Tahoe.

Witnessing the collisions ahead, the cop in the fourth cruiser slowed to a halt and turned his vehicle ninety degrees, creating a roadblock. Joanne's Arctic Cat was now no more than fifty yards away. She made another quick decision; she'd ignore the blockade. She thumbed her accelerator hard and aimed her machine towards the towering snow bank on her right. Using it as a ramp, she flew the machine through the air and over the hood of the last cruiser, bouncing heavily on the mountain road. To her surprise, the freshly fallen snow offered them a stable landing, and they were able to speed away. Their mouths agape, the troopers watched helplessly as the sisters escaped.

Joanne let out a loud victory hoot.

Weak with exhaustion, Jane held on for dear life but smiled as well. But the race was still theirs to lose. Looking behind her, she saw Boychuk's vehicle in close pursuit. He had regrouped, fishtailed around the other disabled vehicles and followed the snow machine as it picked up speed.

A minute or two later, Joanne reached the bottom of the hill. She entered the village at high speed, barely missing oncoming cars. Horns blared and cars nearly slammed into each other as drivers attempted to avoid a snowmobile seemingly gone berserk. Sitting behind her sister, barely holding on, Jane feared she might lose consciousness.

"Joanne," she yelled as the machine made its way into town. "I'm not feeling so great."

"Hang on, honey. I think I know where we have to go!"

At high speed, Joanne continued through the village. Fortunately, it was a quiet Sunday afternoon and there was little traffic. From behind, she could see the flashing lights of what she presumed was the sheriff's lead cruiser following them through town. Then Joanne saw the blue hospital sign pointing off to the right, and she abruptly turned the Cat ninety degrees in the direction of the medical center. Boychuk's cruiser kept pace. Damn it, she thought, why couldn't she lose that sucker?

But in this high stakes-game she held better cards and she gunned her machine full speed ahead. Attempting to keep Joanne's snowmobile in his sights, the sheriff let his vehicle skid hard on the turn, ramming his truck into another snow bank. Steam poured from under the hood. They'll have trouble catching us now, Joanne thought. Trucks are no match for a machine like this.

Knowing Jane was in serious trouble, she continued straight down the road and soon—through the driving snow—saw the bright red emergency sign over a covered entrance.

Joanne drove the Arctic Cat right up to the sliding, automatic doors and waved frantically to a couple of attendants inside.

She had accomplished her mission.

FORTY-FOUR

Alone outside the intensive care unit, Joanne sat and waited. The adrenaline that had surged through her veins during the high-speed race had subsided and she too was exhausted. She had gotten Jane to the hospital. Now, however, she cradled her head in both hands in despair. Reality was setting in. What else could happen to her? And to Jane?

Her thoughts returned to the cabin that they had shared only an hour or so before and Jane's revelations. Bombshells, really. Actual, pardon-my-*effing*-Polish bombshells, she thought. From the moment her dad called, she thought she had the answer to the riddle. Jane's crazed, impulsive behavior in Morgantown was driven by her cancer. She simply had nothing to lose. And their subsequent trek to Lake Placid to seek out a daughter she'd never met was motivated by Jane's knowledge that she had little time left.

But now it was more than that.

Jane's confession—that Denny had violently raped her—had shaken Joanne's heart and soul. She was so stunned, so dazed, that she felt violated as well. And so hurt. It meant her entire life with Denny, and their twenty years together, had been a big lie. Denny had married her, fathered their beautiful son and together they had lived a lie. And now she knew why Jane didn't just walk away that night when she could have...when Denny called her names. She had the gun and was in control. We could have walked out of that house and away from Denny—forever. Instead, she turned and shot him in the balls. Before finishing him off.

It was simply payback time.

And the bastard deserved it.

Another fearful thought entered her mind. Oh my god, what if Denny *was* Makenna's—?

She was suddenly interrupted.

"Mrs. Lowry?" Joanne looked up and met a slight, bony-shouldered physician in her mid-thirties standing over her. Dressed in a white lab coat, with a stethoscope around her neck, she looked to Joanne to be East Indian or something. Her umber, empathetic eyes struck her immediately.

"Yes."

"You're Ms. Schumacher's sister?"

"Yes, I am," Joanne replied.

She extended her hand, and Joanne accepted it.

"My name is Saabira Akram," she announced. "I'm the doctor who is treating your sister."

Joanne was nervous. But she found instant solace in the woman. Months later, she discovered Saabira meant "patient" in her native Afghanistan from where she, her siblings and her parents had escaped just after the Soviet invasion in 1979. A very appropriate definition of the woman, Joanne had thought.

But she was bearing bad news.

"I'm afraid your sister is not doing very well. She's resting now but it's clear she's suffering from a lot of things and exhaustion is one of them. May I sit down?"

Joanne signaled her approval.

"What can you tell me?"

"Well, I just got off the phone with your sister's doctor in Albany, and I'm afraid the prognosis isn't very good," the doctor said.

"What do you mean?" Joanne asked.

"Your sister didn't tell you?"

"Not much," she replied sullenly.

"Well, your sister has what we call S.C.L.C. It stands for small cell lung cancer. Unfortunately, it's the fastest growing and most lethal form. Does your sister smoke?"

"We've been a family of smokers," Joanne replied. "But in Jane's case, never." She remembered why not.

It was a summer night when they were about twelve. Joanne had been on look-out duty, checking to see if the coast was clear, even though she had been a reluctant co-conspirator in the heist. In this case a pack of cigarettes from Donna's purse.

But steal them Jane did, and the two—joined by three of their schoolmates, including, to their surprise, Hong Kong Wong—dashed off to the small lumber yard behind their house with their ill-gotten booty. That they failed to realize their foolish choice of a hiding spot was obvious; the whole damn yard could have gone up in smoke. That didn't matter to Jane, of course. She was always a risk-taker. And she knew heavy smokers—like their mother—would never miss a pack. Donna always kept an open carton around the house.

Jane was the first to strike the match, almost burning her fingers and cursing loudly in the process. She took the first drag of the pilfered menthols deep into her lungs before exhaling. But within moments, she became nauseous and started vomiting all over the ground. The next day, undaunted, Jane convinced them to try again. And she threw up once again. That was her clue, an unmistakable signal that cigarettes might not be for her. Joanne's stomach, unfortunately, never rebelled but she often wished it had. She discovered that she had liked smoking. Most smokers do.

"We see that sometimes," Dr. Akram continued. "It's uncommon. About ten or fifteen percent of lung cancers involve non-smokers. And it's even rarer among women. But it happens, unfortunately."

Joanne was becoming overwhelmed with bad news. She put her head in her hands once again before returning her attention to the gentle, caring physician.

"So, what can you do?"

"Chemotherapy, with some radiation likely," she replied. "But not here, though. We'll probably med-evac her to Albany as soon as she's ready to go."

"What about surgery?" Joanne asked.

She shook her head.

"Surgery is likely out of the question, but I don't think they'll know for sure until all her tests are done," she said, pausing for a moment. "Unfortunately her cancer has probably spread. But as I said, we don't know that for sure. What we do know is that she should have started treatment weeks, perhaps months, ago."

This was the most distasteful part of her job, the doctor thought.

"I'm sorry, Mrs. Lowry," she said. "I hate to be the bearer of bad news, but that's what it is. I'm sorry."

Joanne collected herself.

"Can I see her?"

"Yes, but make it a short visit, okay? She really needs to sleep now. I'll check in with her a little later."

The caring physician had barely exited the ICU's waiting area when Joanne burst into tears. She'd been crying often on this trip. How many more tears did she have in her? How much more bad news could she take?

At last, she was able to gather her strength and looked up to find Boychuk standing in front of her. Strangely, as their eyes met, she was happy to see him. She rose and threw her arms around him.

"How bad is it?" he asked.

"Very bad, Brian....very bad. Did you talk to that doctor?"

The sheriff nodded grimly.

"Just for a minute or so. She told me about Jane's condition, but not much else and only after I told her the situation."

He tried to lighten the moment.

"I had no idea you could drive a sled like that, Joanne," he said, forcing a smile.

"I had to get her here, Brian...she's really sick."

"I understand, Jo, but you could have let me do that."

"Maybe, Brian...but I couldn't be sure you'd know just how bad she was and how she needed to be brought here fast."

"I understand ...I really do. Have you been in to see her yet?"

"Not yet. I'm afraid I'm too emotional right now. Maybe you could go in?"

Boychuk looked away as if he was weighing her suggestion. Heeding his request, the troopers had remained in the waiting area of the emergency room. Boychuk knew he'd have to make a strong case to return them to Morgan County, but there were no guarantees. A judge might just keep them here until the local DA dealt with the issue.

"What's gonna happen, Brian?" Joanne asked.

He grimaced. He knew this question would be asked.

"Well, the troopers are likely going to take you back to their barracks in Saranac where they'll want to talk to you about it all. Now, you don't have to say anything—"

"I have nothing to hide!" she cried.

"I know. I know," he said. "But you do have rights. You can wait until you get a lawyer by your side."

A look of despair came over Joanne. She was crestfallen; all this talk of police and lawyers. She knew she'd have to face the consequences of her actions. But her immediate thoughts were of her sister and her failing health.

He sensed that.

"But all that can wait a while," he said. "Why don't you sit and rest here while I go in and see if Jane's awake? Okay?"

Joanne nodded and sat down.

Gently, the county sheriff pushed the door to Jane's room open and walked over to her intensive care bed. A sturdy, well-built nurse in her mid-forties was busily adjusting Jane's intravenous tubes. Jane's eyes were nearly shut and it appeared to Boychuk that she had been heavily sedated.

She turned her head and saw him standing beside her bed. She smiled faintly. The sheriff turned to address the nurse.

"Can I speak with her a moment?"

"Yes, Sheriff, but make it short," she replied.

"Will do," he said, turning his attention to the patient. At first glance, Jane seemed to have aged about five years in the past four days. Her face was drained of color and she now looked gaunt.

They stared into each others' eyes for a moment or two before he broke the silence.

"I can't honestly say that it's good to see you, Shoes. In here I mean," he said.

She smiled again.

"Well, Chuck, right now, I guess it's better to be seen than to be viewed."

"Now, don't get too far ahead of yourself, Jane," he replied.

"*Far ahead* are two words that are not in my current vocabulary, Sheriff."

He feigned surprise.

"Sheriff? When did I become Sheriff?"

"You've always been my sheriff, Brian. Ever since the twelfth grade. You chased me then and you chased me now."

He laughed.

"But this time, you let me catch you."

Jane paused and turned her attention to the hospital room window. It was getting dark but she could see that the snowstorm outside had begun to diminish. Perfect night skiing weather, she thought. What I would give to get over to Whiteface, she thought.

She turned to face her police officer once again.

"I'm not sorry for what I did to Denny," she said.

"Ah, that man put the *ass* in the words 'no class,' Jane," he replied. "But that didn't give you an excuse to do him in. Joanne could have pressed charges, and I promise you that he would've done time."

Jane was about to answer when a severe coughing fit overtook her. She grimaced with pain. Boychuk looked on, sympathetically. He noticed a glass of water with a straw on her side table. He reached for it and passed it to her.

She took a big sip.

"Well, with the way I am now, at least I won't have to do much time anyway, right?"

He frowned.

"Now don't go saying that!"

"It's true."

Boychuk stared at his former girlfriend. Despite her frail state, he still believed she was the most beautiful woman he'd ever met. She had ditched him before he left for the academy, but he'd never fallen out of love with her.

He had waited until he was thirty-three before marrying; it wasn't a priority, his police career was important. His union to Susan, a high-powered school board official, came about almost apologetically. It had seemed like an act of necessity for both because, well, that's what people like them did. They had always assumed there would be children, but they somehow never got around to the conception and rearing part. Guess we were just too busy with our lives to think about kids, Boychuk had admitted to Hubie once or twice. The older man thought different. After Jane, though they were just teenagers at the time, no other woman could invoke such passion. No woman could live up to Jane.

Now standing beside Jane's hospital bed, in spite of what had happened over the past four or five days—or the past two decades—his affection for her had returned. But he knew this was foolish in so many ways, and his official train of thought returned.

"Well, Jane, it's probably out of my hands now," he said. "The troopers have taken it from here. They're downstairs."

"Remember what I told you, Brian, that Joanne had nothing to do with what I did."

He shook his head. "Unfortunately, it's not that simple."

Jane was fading and it showed.

"I'm getting pretty tired now, and I'm having trouble staying awake."

"Right, get some rest. Feel better, okay?"

"I'll try."

She closed her eyes. Boychuk turned and began to exit her room. But before he reached the door, she called his name.

"Brian?"

He turned to face her once again.

"Yes, Jane?"

"There's something I need to talk to you about. But it can wait...see you later."

FORTY-FIVE

Even with the blowing snow, the late model Infiniti had easily navigated through Saranac Lake and was on its last leg to Lake Placid. The storm seemed to be easing up a bit. When Roberto got the call from Jane's father, he had abruptly turned his truck around and motored back to Morgantown. Together, they decided to drive to Lake Placid.

For Hubie and Roberto, the call from the sheriff was a call to action. They couldn't stand idle as Jane and Joanne were apprehended and then wait for them to be transported to some Morgan County jail. No, they had to act. That they were likely holed up in some mountain cabin was reason enough for them to go, never mind the disclosure from Jane's Albany doctor that she was really sick. They would drop everything and head to Placid.

Hubie had liked Roberto the moment the young Argentinean knocked on his back door a few days earlier. He felt that Jane was right in describing him as a good man. Of course, Hubie had known only one other guy in his daughter's life, and that was Boychuk. Now this imposing man from Manhattan had entered the picture. He would have been proud to have either as a son-in-law.

But now, after he had received the painful news about Jane's cancer, all those thoughts had disappeared. Hubie's first concern was for Jane and the intensively personal battle she seemed to be fighting alone. She didn't deserve this fate regardless of how she'd turned her back on her family all these years. Maybe now he could be the father he had never been. He hoped it wasn't too late.

Their trip from Morgantown had taken more than three hours, or about double the normal time. For long stretches of the trip, they drove in awkward silence, breaking it only to comment on the weather or to reflect on the surprising lack of traffic on the highways. But a simple question to Roberto about his upbringing in the Bronx opened the floodgates.

Hubie learned about Roberto's long trip aboard a soybean-laden freighter from Buenos Aires to New York in the early eighties. He learned how the kid spoke no English until he was fifteen, but how his curiosity and determination took over. Here was a man, Hubie thought, who was born dirt-poor but made something of himself. Hell, Roberto was more *American* than most native-borns. Over too many beers at the VFW, Hubie and his cribbage-playing buddies blamed the woes of America on immigrants. Now, after getting to know this young man, he realized how wrong he had been. America was built on the backs of young people like him. Maybe, Hubie now thought, he should learn to shut his mouth.

It was evident just how much Roberto loved his daughter and how the younger man had hoped that he and Jane would have a future together, despite the current circumstances. Hubie listened as Roberto had reflected upon his relationship with Jane and how she would push him away at times.

"So, I don't really know the score," Roberto said. But then a smile emerged from the handsome Hispanic. "But I don't give up easily, Mr. Schu...I mean...Hubie."

Roberto's candor was refreshing, even contagious. Why he opened up to the young man he had just met, Hubie didn't know.

But he did. And it felt good.

He described his girls lovingly; they were smart, both had been excellent athletes and both could have succeeded in anything they had wished. At least until they neared adulthood when "some mistakes were made," as Hubie said.

"They were very cute as kids," he continued. "Donna liked to dress them in the same clothes and the girls *loved* that. But to tell you the truth, Rob—can I call you Rob?—I wasn't always there for them. Donna, well, she was the one who raised them…and maybe she went overboard once in a while, but she meant well. Once in a while I tried to intervene, but Donna pushed back…told me to go fishing. So, I did…and now I regret doing that."

Hubie stopped his story short. He wouldn't tell this man everything he remembered about Jane's mother or about their problems. Donna always blamed him for destroying her life's dreams. She had cursed him for their shotgun marriage and for ruining her life. It meant an unpleasant union for many years, but it was their daughters who were the ones who lost out. He didn't say that to Roberto.

So he resumed his tale about Jane. That Roberto should have known her when she was a teenager, he said. She was a real pistol, always shooting her mouth off.

"That sounds like Jane today," Roberto laughed.

"Not surprised," the older man simply replied.

His voice trailed off and for the next ten or fifteen miles, they drove in silence. As the two men reached the outskirts of Saranac Lake and continued east toward Lake Placid, they were uncertain of what they would discover. Roberto's mind came into focus, carefully weighing what his line of defense would be. He wasn't a criminal lawyer. But he knew what to do. He'd have a few things to say to the local police and district attorney. There were mitigating circumstances.

The good news? Their trials would be held in Morgan County, where the shooting occurred, and where a jury of their peers would be chosen. From among the same people who might have known Denny, or about him.

Roberto glanced over at the older man beside him and sensed that Hubie was thinking the same thing. He paused to consider his next words.

"She's facing a lot of legal problems, Hubie," he said. "She'll be charged with Denny's murder. Likely second-degree...because it wasn't premeditated. Maybe we can get that reduced to manslaughter with extenuating circumstances. As for Joanne, well, she'll probably face accessory-after-the-fact, which means she didn't know that Jane was going to shoot Denny but helped her get away."

Hubie tried to digest Roberto's words.

He couldn't believe it had come to this. If only he had stepped in when he suspected that Denny was beating the hell out of his daughter? How often did he believe that? But how many times did Joanne tell him to mind his own business? He didn't have enough fingers and toes...

Roberto's mood darkened.

Jane's legal troubles were the least of her worries. All his brave talk about reducing the charges, all his thoughts about manslaughter and mitigating circumstances, were really secondary to the bigger crisis that Jane was facing. During his brief conversation with her Albany doctor, Schaefer had been cryptic yet clear; there was no doubt about her prognosis. Her doctor was adamant. Just get her back.

The last leg of their trip over the snowy Adirondack roads was interrupted by the sound of Dee's cell phone. Hubie didn't have time for those goddamn things, and even if he did, who'd call him? But she had loaned him the phone for their trip. Just in case.

Now was one of those times. Hubie answered the call.

"Hubert?" She always called him Hubert.

"Yup, hello Dee. What's up?"

"Sheriff Boychuk just called," she said. "He's found the girls, but the news isn't good."

FORTY-SIX

Her hands cuffed behind her back, Joanne was being escorted out of the hospital by two New York state troopers. A shift change was occurring at the small Adirondack hospital and the wards, hallways and nurses' stations were naturally hectic. Since she and her sister had escaped the horrors of Thanksgiving night, Joanne knew this moment would come. But she didn't think it would be this public. She was now a perp, she thought. An aider and abettor, an accomplice...and a criminal. But, damn it, she wasn't going to be embarrassed. She held her head high, making eye contact with curious bystanders, almost defiant.

Boychuk had bought her some time and she appreciated her old friend for doing so. As the Morgan County sheriff left the intensive care unit, he asked the troopers to delay Joanne's arrest for an hour to enable her to be with her stricken sister. But he told Joanne that Jane was losing consciousness fast, and she'd better get in there.

Sure enough, Jane was out cold. The nurses had her wired up to an assortment of monitors and intravenous tubes, and the sight of her pale, exhausted sister shocked Joanne to her core. Joanne couldn't believe it. Only four days earlier, Jane had arrived at her kitchen door for the first time in more than eight years looking very much like the vivacious and confident woman she had seen only on television for years.

Jane was the woman that Joanne had so detested for so long yet secretly admired from afar. Many of their peers had married and settled within the same zip codes as their parents and grandparents. But Jane Schumacher's life had been one of a romance novel; she had escaped the small town, educated herself and clawed to the top. She was a talented woman in great demand by rising politicians and media stars. She had been chauffeur-driven to private tarmacs and to fancy hotels. She had walked the halls of power, hob-knobbing with national leaders, world figures and opinion-setters.

But now she was facing expulsion and dishonor. Her last ride was on the back of a snowmobile, frail and fatigued, the object of pity and perhaps scorn. Often she had accepted police protection. Now she was in police custody. It was an enormous fall from grace.

Joanne was beginning to figure it all out. For more than twenty years, Jane had been burdened by a violent past. There was a reason for her two-decade-long family rupture. That it took a serious illness for the truth to see the light of day was very sad. But that didn't mean she could forgive her sister for staying silent for so long. And she had no idea how she'd handle the memory of her mother now. She would deal with all that later, she promised herself. Now was not the time.

An hour before, standing by Jane's hospital bedside, Joanne had decided not to disturb her. She found comfort in a leather chair in the corner and collapsed. Within moments, with overpowering exhaustion, she fell fast asleep.

Thirty minutes later she was awakened by the sounds of Jane's voice.

"What, no room at the inn?"

Joanne stirred. Her eyes came into focus. She smiled.

"I guess I just passed out," she replied. "How long have I been here?"

"No idea...but it's dark outside now," Jane said, glancing at the window. The lights of the village were evident. "You look like hell!"

Joanne shook her head.

"You're no Easter lily yourself, sister. Better not ask for a mirror."

"Fuck you!"

"Well, fuck you too!" Joanne replied, and they both broke into laughter.

"I thought church ladies like you didn't use words like those," Jane said.

"I don't...but in your case, I'll make an exception."

"That was quite the ride we had."

"I've always liked fast sleds," Joanne replied.

"I wasn't talking about last night...I was referring to the last four days."

"That it was city...*girl*. That it was."

The hospital door opened. A middle-aged nurse with a stern look on her face announced that Joanne would have to leave the room.

"Your sister needs her rest," she commanded. "And besides, there are a couple of policemen in the hallway who would like to speak with you."

The sisters exchanged glances and smiled once again.

"Don't say, it Jane!"

"Okay, I won't say I told you so," she said. With her thumb and forefinger clenched together, she made a zipping motion across her lips.

"Good call," Joanne said, smiling.

Slowly she approached her sister's bedside. She raised Jane's left hand—the one not wired to intravenous tubes—and caressed it gently. For a few moments they stared silently into each other's eyes before Joanne bent down and kissed her sister's forehead.

Both knew their carousel ride had ended.

Joanne turned and left the hospital room. She was greeted by a boyish-looking trooper who might have been a corporal fresh from the 10th Mountain Division's latest deployment, the same unit that sent thousands of fresh faces to the battle theaters. A second policeman, even more cherubic than the first, remained stoically silent.

Another memory returned, and this time it was of the pictures of her dad at that age during the mid-sixties. These men could have been brothers of another time, Joanne thought. Almost apologetically, the policeman informed her of the charges and read out her Miranda warning. He told her that she would have to accompany them to their offices in Saranac Lake and produced a set of chrome-plated handcuffs.

"Just standard operating procedure, ma'am," he said.

Joanne and the young cops exited the hospital through the same emergency unit doors she had entered only hours before. Through the glass doors, she saw a Chevy Tahoe cruiser parked under the entrance's concrete awning. Its lights were flashing, its motor running. There were several other police officers milling about, prompting Joanne to wonder if these were the same guys she left behind so easily during their high-speed snowmobile chase. She greeted them with a half grin. The crazy chick on the Arctic Cat was not so easy to catch, huh boys?

Seeing Joanne and her escorts arriving, one of the officers opened the Tahoe and was about to place her in it when a voice rang out. They halted in their tracks, looked around and Joanne recognized her father with a tall Hispanic man standing next to him. This must be Roberto, she thought. Instantly she realized why Jane was so attracted to him.

"Dad!" Joanne said, her eyes lighting up at the sight of her father.

"Hi, Joanne," he replied, noticing her hands in cuffs. He was shocked at the sight. How could they do this to my little girl, he thought?

Hubie put his arms around her but realized the cuffs wouldn't allow her to reciprocate.

"We're here for you," he said. It was an emotional moment for both.

"We finally made it. How are you?"

The lead trooper interjected.

"Are you Mrs. Lowry's father?"

"Yes, officer, and we'd like to speak with her," Hubie replied.

The trooper nodded, signaling his approval. He turned his attention to Roberto standing beside the elderly man.

"Who are you?" the young officer asked.

The Argentinean stepped up and spoke.

"My name's Roberto Alvarez, and I'm Mrs. Lowry's attorney," he said, handing the trooper one of his business cards. "Where are you taking her?"

The policeman scanned the card and handed Roberto a piece of official-looking paper.

"Back to the barracks in Saranac Lake," the cop replied. "That's a warrant for her arrest for accessory. We just finished serving her sister as well, and she's under hospital arrest. We'll take further action when it's...appropriate."

Roberto finished reading the warrant and turned his attention to Joanne.

"Joanne, I'll follow you and the police to the barracks. We'll be able to talk there."

"Thanks, Roberto," she replied.

"How's she doing, Joanne?" Hubie asked.

Joanne shrugged. Her face was fraught with resignation and despair.

"Not good, Dad," she said. "She's very tired and having a lot of problems breathing. They have her in the intensive care unit...with round-the-clock nurses looking after her. It looks as though they'll send her back to the hospital in Albany soon, too."

Hubie and Roberto listened and both were stunned.

"But Dad, the nurses told me they were allowing no more visitors tonight, okay?" she asked. "She's just not in very good shape."

Hubie looked disappointed but understood.

"Okay, I'll get Roberto to drop me off at a motel down the road," he replied, nodding towards the handsome New Yorker. "I'll try to see her tomorrow, but...Jo, you're in good hands with this young man."

With Roberto looking on, Hubie kissed his daughter good-bye. Then the trooper nodded and placed Joanne in the back seat of the Tahoe. He walked around the cruiser, jumped in and pulled away.

FORTY-SEVEN

Not long after the sun rose over the Hudson River, Marcia Bell was at her desk in the governor's office. It was the Monday after Thanksgiving and the youthful press assistant had spent the holiday weekend at work. Since Jack Davis's call Friday morning, she had shuttled between her downtown office and the mansion as the Foley campaign's crisis communications team went into high gear. The only times that she found herself at her apartment was to catch a few winks, shower and to change clothes. To think that she once had plans to drive to Stowe for the holidays and get in a few runs too. A fleeting memory now.

That, of course, was before the shit hit the fan. All weekend, Marcia struggled with her emotions. She was torn between her devotion to her mentor and leader, and the loyalty she had for the governor and the entire campaign team. Unfortunately, Jane's news hit like a meteorite on Thanksgiving, traditionally one of the slowest news weekends of the year. The cable channels, the blogs and every talking-head in politics had focused on the Schumacher murder story. Nothing but a continuous loop of video was running. It showed the yellow tape surrounding Joanne Lowry's home in some unknown New York town, pictures of the Lake Placid hospital and Jane's past televised appearances. Cable must think the world's problems have been solved, she thought. Scandals, especially those of a spicy and salacious nature, often trumped substance in the news business. Jane had taught her that.

Marcia spent Saturday and most of Sunday fending calls. The governor's decision to hold a scrum Friday night and defend his press secretary was a good one. He had resisted calls from the media and the party to throw Jane to the mountain lions, but she knew that line of defense couldn't last long. He had given her the benefit of the doubt, while maintaining a neutrality of sorts by declaring it was a matter for the police.

That was all Marcia was allowed to say to the bloggers and other reporters who called. She wasn't even allowed to go off-the-record. No speculation of any kind, Claudia had ordered. If there was any spinning to do, she'd do it. Now was not the time to twist the story in any way. In fact, our goal is to disown it, Claudia warned.

But Marcia knew that Foley would have to cut her loose. No staffer was bigger than the candidate, the message, the campaign.

Jane had taught her that too.

If she thought things were bad seventy-two hours ago, she had no idea how the rest of the story would unfold. All it took was another call from Jack Davis, who asked the redoubtable red-head to put him on hold and march down the hall to the governor's office. He needed to hook up with Wendell and Claudia immediately.

Both were there and they took the call.

"Evening, folks," Davis began. "Well, I have news... good and bad."

"Well, let's have it all," Foley said.

The good news, the senior trooper recounted, was that Jane and her sister had been apprehended and that there had been no further violence. The bad news was that she was very sick, and he informed them of Jane's prognosis.

Foley let out an audible gasp while Claudia and Marcia consoled each other. Davis knew the news wouldn't go down well but continued his narrative, a sad climax to a puzzling blockbuster of a story.

"But our suspicion—and I admit it's just that right now—is that Jane was told she had terminal cancer and that she acted as though she had nothing to lose."

The governor interrupted the senior trooper.

"Well, we don't really know that, do we Jack?"

"No, Governor, we don't, but I've spoken to the Morgan County sheriff and that's how he sized up the situation. He has been a friend of the family's for years. At the same time, it doesn't make sense. We all know Jane Schumacher...how disciplined a woman she is. The sheriff told me that it must have taken one hell of a provocation for her to do what she did. Remember, Governor, she could have walked away. She could have taken her sister out of that house. She could have put the gun away. But the sheriff thinks the brother-in-law probably said something. He knew Jane's sister's husband very well, after all, and she lost her cool. Maybe she felt that her illness gave her immunity from prosecution. But I don't know if we'll *ever* know the real reason."

Still fighting her emotions, Marcia realized she had known there had to have been more to Jane's constant coughing than bronchitis. It had been going on for weeks and Jane just refused to see her doctor until Marcia threatened to bring the physician to the governor's office. Of course, Marcia had no idea if she could have pulled it off. Doctors don't make house-calls any more...even if the governor himself had called on her behalf. Well, maybe if the governor called.

She listened as the head of the protective detail spoke. That's a plausible explanation, she thought. The Jane Schumacher she loved was a strong woman, and if she knew she was dying might have done something like that. But the more she considered the possibility—that Jane simply had nothing to lose—the more it seemed that it wouldn't have been enough. Sure, Jane had a temper; she saw it emerge often, especially when she dealt with all the assholes in the media.

However, Jane's overriding goal was to elect Wendell Foley the next president of the United States; she was motivated by one thing—winning. But while she was as partisan as anyone in politics today—she fiercely believed that the country desperately needed Foley—Jane had always put her country first.

So Davis's theory just didn't add up. There had to be something else behind it, and maybe someday she'd learn what it was. Jane was just too smart to give up on her life's ambitions so quickly, no matter how much the abusive prick provoked her.

Abusive prick...

Just listen to me. Jane's influence had rubbed off.

Before hanging up, Davis told the governor his office would be issuing a press release today and that they should expect a flood of calls from the media. Not only would the statement say they had caught the murder suspects but that Jane was suffering from a life-threatening illness and was under hospital arrest.

"Thanks, Jack," Foley said. "Please extend my congratulations to your colleagues and to that county sheriff too for their good police work."

"I will, Governor...I'm sorry to be the bearer of such news, though," he replied. "I know how close you all have been to Jane Schumacher. This is tragic...very sad."

Foley agreed, said good-bye and Claudia ended the call. For a few quiet moments, the three of them just stood there, stunned at the news. Foley had given Jane the Thanksgiving weekend off, and had fully expected to see her in the office today. Weekend polling, before the Schumacher murder story broke nation-wide, indicated that Americans liked what they saw from the New York governor. His ultimatum to New York legislators had especially produced high marks.

His message that he was one Democrat who could play the fiscal card better than any Republican in the land seemed to be gathering resonance. He had planned to assemble his political team this morning, including Jane, and put the final touches to the launch strategy. On December 7th, he would announce from Hyde Park his intention to run for President of the United States. Now Jane wouldn't be part of that announcement.

After a long pause, Claudia spoke.

"Governor, the media will descend on that hospital in Lake Placid like locusts—if they haven't already," she said. "All the networks will be sending their correspondents to the mountains and so we have to issue our own statement, now. To get ahead of the cycle."

Foley nodded and looked at Marcia.

"Marcia, can you draft something quickly?" he asked. "Short and to the point, though. That this is a matter for the police and ultimately the courts. But I also want to say something personal."

"Like what, Wendell?" Claudia asked.

"Like…I've known Jane a long time. That the Jane Schumacher I've known is a smart, principled and moral person and that I'd like everyone to pray for her full and speedy recovery. And that I'm looking forward to her resuming her duties."

Claudia was flabbergasted.

"You can't be serious, Governor!" she said. "You want to say that you want her back?"

"That's right," Foley replied, suddenly on the defensive.

"You can't say that, Wendell," she protested.

"Why not, Claudia? She hasn't been convicted of anything yet."

Exasperated, Claudia continued her case.

"Governor, think about it," she continued. "Didn't she basically admit to that sheriff that she was guilty of these charges? And to you on the phone the other day, too? Granted, she was defending her sister but she did admit she pulled the trigger—twice for God's sake—and killed the husband? No matter what happens with her cancer, if she beats it as we all hope she will, she still sounds guilty to me. And the courts will likely confirm that. If it gets that far, that is."

The governor turned and stared into the light of a cold Albany morning. He knew that Claudia was right. No matter what happened, Jane's job on the campaign was over. But he didn't want to admit that, now. Jane Schumacher's skills, her knowledge of the national media, her instinct for the political jugular, her ability to frame an issue, her talent for jockeying, messaging and spin were unparalleled.

But she was more than a smart political operative. She was a good person who had believed in him from the start. She gave him an unvarnished view of the world that every president needed to be an effective leader. He could not do this without her—or always thought so.

Claudia's words rang true, however. The cause was more important than any one person. Every member of his staff was potentially dispensable, and now Jane Schumacher was one of those people. He knew Claudia was right.

"Okay, I hear you. But we just learned that she's not just fighting an election campaign—she's fighting for her very life. Do you understand that?"

Both Claudia and Marcia nodded. He took a deep breath.

"All right, I won't say I am looking forward to her return. But I do want people to know the real Jane Schumacher, the woman I know and trust. I am *not* ready to give up on her!"

Claudia understood.

She looked over at Marcia and then back to the governor.

"Wendell, I think we can convey a message of hope and friendship in your statement today. And we can deal with the ultimate question about her political future with you...at an appropriate time...later."

FORTY-EIGHT

Hubie glanced at the clock on the dresser in his Lake Placid motel room. It read half-past-eight, and he was glad that he had gotten back to sleep. About five hours earlier, he awoke with a startle and groaned, thinking he'd never get any shut-eye. But after a requisite trip to the bathroom—one of the two or three nightly visits he had been making over the past six or eight years—he had collapsed back in bed. The next thing he knew, the sun was up.

Roberto had dropped him off at the nearest motel, and after booking a couple of rooms, the elderly man had walked across the street to a family restaurant for some chow. Hubie had been hoping Roberto would return from the troopers' barracks in Saranac with some good news and that a semblance of normalcy would return to their lives. Maybe Joanne would win her freedom, at least for now, and perhaps they could see Jane before she was sent back to Albany for treatment.

But Roberto hadn't returned. And so he had decided to dine alone.

As he was finishing his club sandwich, alone at a booth, Dee's cell phone had sounded once again. She had asked Hubie to call her as soon as possible and now he felt pangs of guilt. But when Joanne had warned him of her sister's exhausted and tenuous condition, Hubie was in no mood to talk to anyone. He had decided he'd call Dee later. To his surprise, it wasn't Dee calling.

"Hubie, it's Roberto."

"Hi Rob," the elderly man had said, becoming more and more comfortable in abbreviating the young Hispanic man's name.

"Where are you?" Roberto had asked.

"Well, I got us a couple of rooms and now I'm having a bite to eat," Hubie had replied. "What's up on your end? What's happening with Joanne?"

As Roberto began to explain the situation, Hubie's mood had darkened further. The attorney told how he had met with the police and a young assistant district attorney at the troopers' offices in Saranac Lake. He had hoped he could convince the DA that Joanne's bail should be modest in nature and that aside from shoplifting a candy bar from the now-defunct five-and-dime store at the age of eight, she'd never been in any trouble.

Despite a promise that Joanne would be in court when the time came, the DA had disagreed. Accessory-to-murder was a serious charge, he had said, and he was planning to ask the judge in the morning for a fifty-thousand-dollar bail.

"It's ridiculous!" Roberto had thundered. "I know hard cons in the city who committed worse crimes than Joanne's and got lower bail. That is, if Joanne committed a crime. Who does he think she is? Bonnie Parker? Hell, she's not even Martha Stewart! But because of who Jane is and who she works for, this is not your run-of-the-mill case, Hubie. You should see this DA. Some kid named—"

He had checked his notes.

"—Justin Cochrane."

"Johnnie Cochran?"

"No, not Johnnie," he had replied. Roberto had laughed at the mention of the late celebrity lawyer involved in the O.J. Simpson case a decade before. "But I admit I had the same thoughts. He probably thinks he has a great future in litigation, or that his name will sound perfect when he's named to the Supreme Court in thirty-five years. But right now he hasn't started shaving yet and he strikes me as a kid who likes cameras. Wants his five minutes in the limelight. So, unfortunately, Joanne will have to spend the night in Saranac before I can post her bail and we can take her home."

"She has to spend the night in jail?" Hubie was incredulous.

"Yes, unfortunately."

"Goddamn it," her father had cursed. "It just gets worse, doesn't it, Rob?"

"We'll get it worked out, Hubie, don't worry."

"But what about this fifty grand? I can call my bank in the morning...maybe get an emergency loan on my house? Or put up the house itself?"

"That's unnecessary, Hubie," the lawyer had said. "I'm going to ask the DA to reduce that number by at least half. And don't worry, I'll post it myself, and we'll be able to spring her. She's so *not* a flight risk. All she wants to do is go home."

Hubie had almost become overwhelmed with emotion. Here was a man whom Joanne hadn't met before today and was now willing to post a huge bail for her. He was choked up.

"Hubie...Hubie, are you still there?" Roberto had asked.

Finally, the older man spoke.

"I am, Roberto...that's very generous of you. I can't tell you how much I appreciate this."

"Forget it, Hubie, it's the least I can do. Joanne's a good woman. I know that. She's Jane's little sister, after all. Besides, she won't jump bail and as I said, I'm hoping we can take her home. She might have to wear an ankle bracelet for now, but we'll get her home. I put in a call to the Morgan

County DA about ten minutes ago. We'll get this worked out."

As he lumbered out of bed, Hubie remembered his conversation with Roberto the night before. My girls are lucky to know this guy, he thought. He went to the window and peered through the curtains. Roberto's Infiniti was parked in front, and Hubie figured the younger man had made it back to Placid. He wondered how long he had had to stay in Saranac Lake, arguing with the cops and that prosecutor.

He quickly showered, got dressed and was out the door. He would catch up with Roberto later; right now, he needed to see his daughter in the hospital. He had called the motel desk and asked for a taxi, and about twenty minutes later the old snowplow operator entered the hospital.

Throughout their trip to the mountains, Hubie had avoided discussion about Jane and her behavior on Thanksgiving Night. Roberto had tried several times to broach the subject but soon realized the older man was uncomfortable doing so. It was a topic for another time, perhaps another place.

Jane had just reentered Hubie's life. Today their reunion would be under the most painful of circumstances. He couldn't believe that he was here. The last time they had laid eyes upon each other was when she stormed angrily from Joanne's dining room table after a loud and profane argument with Denny. Now he was about to enter her hospital room. It was almost too much to bear.

Reaching the floor where the intensive care unit was located, Hubie emerged from the elevator and approached the nurses' station. He stood there for what seemed an eternity before a nurse raised her head.

"I'm here to see Jane Schumacher," he said. "My name is Hubert Schumacher, and I'm her father."

She checked her charts as if she was having an internal debate; would she or wouldn't she grant him permission to see her. These people like to hold power over other people, he thought. Finally, she spoke.

"Two doors down on the left, Mr. Schumacher," she replied testily. "But please make it short. She stabilized overnight, and we're getting her prepped for her trip to Albany today."

He nodded his appreciation but not his thanks and started walking down the hall. Maybe Jane's head nurse thought she was both judge and jury? Perhaps she had concluded that Jane was just another criminal and not a cancer patient? She could use a lesson in bedside-manner, he thought.

Hubie hadn't set foot in a hospital for eight years, and to him that was still about eleven too many. These damn places were all the same, he thought. Antiseptic walls, always off-white with cracks showing in the plaster. Hard terrazzo flooring, too. Everyone scurrying about, trying to look important. At the end of the hallway, some poor son of a bitch was groaning on a gurney, still waiting for a room of his own. Don't go to a hospital if you really get sick, he often admonished his friends. Have no use for these places.

Years ago, Donna's diagnosis had been a shock. But like most ovarian cancers it was already too late before it had begun. From discovery of the disease to death encompassed only a matter of months and she was gone before he knew it.

Now he felt the same dreaded feeling.

Or maybe worse. It was his baby girl in there.

At last, he arrived at the ICU and found Jane's room. A trooper was stationed outside her door, and after identifying himself, Hubie entered. He was unsure of what he would find. Jane's eyes were closed, but as he approached her bed, her eyelids fluttered and she turned her head towards him. A faint smile.

"Hi, Dad," she said, drowsily.

"Hi, Jane. Howya feeling?"

She shrugged. Her eyes told him that she'd been better.

"They're gonna move me out of here today, I think, and I'll be taking a nice, leisurely drive back to the bright lights of Albany—my favorite town," she said. Even in her sickbed, Jane couldn't resist a moment of sarcasm. "Too bad, too. Just when I was making plans to finally tackle Whiteface."

Hubie smiled.

"Well, don't go selling your skis just yet, dear," was all he could think of replying.

Jane turned her head to look across the village and gazed upon the white-capped mountains nearby, recalling memories from her eleven-month stay in Lake Placid so long ago. She remembered its first snowfall and the excitement it brought as skiers arrived in droves, but knowing she couldn't join them. She was pregnant with Makenna, and old Walter wouldn't give her time off, anyway.

She turned and faced her father once again.

"Guess I messed up pretty good, didn't I, Dad?"

"Truth be told, Jane, it was me who messed up—not you."

She stared into his eyes. Some of her anger was returning.

"Dad, why didn't you *do* something?"

"I don't know," he replied, without conviction.

"You don't know? You've lived next door from them for years. You must have seen something, because it was going on for so goddamn long!"

Hubie knew this conversation would occur but was still unprepared for it. He paused before responding.

"I never saw him hit her, Jane."

"Well, that fucker must've left some evidence over the years, Dad," she said. "That's not good enough!"

"I did have my suspicions…I mean, I saw how he could be with her…how mean and belligerent he could be, especially when he was drinking. I think a lot of people did too. But when I'd say something to Jo—and I did, often—she'd say, 'it's between me and Denny, Dad. It's between me and him.'"

Jane listened but wasn't buying her father's story.

"That's all she said? That she wanted you to butt out?"

He nodded. It was now his turn to peer out the window for a few moments. He wasn't proud of himself.

"But I should've been the one to intervene…not you," he said sadly. "Hell, I should've shot the bastard myself."

Jane smiled.

"Well, I beat you to it…"

She was interrupted by another fierce coughing fit that forced her to sit up in bed, wincing with pain as the intravenous bottles rattled and shook. Helplessly, Hubie watched his exhausted and spent daughter. Finally, after the coughing subsided, she dropped down again on the bed and changed the subject.

"With you here, who's doing your plowing?" she asked. "It must have snowed like hell in MoTown too."

Hubie welcomed the change.

"I asked Armstrong to cover for me."

"Armstrong? Wayne Armstrong? Big guy? Nice, too, if I remember correctly?"

"That's him."

"Didn't he have a thing for Joanne a long time ago?"

He smiled.

"You're asking me? Well, maybe, but he probably wouldn't have gotten past your mother."

Jane laughed.

"Ah, yes, he probably would have failed the gauntlet like so many guys," she said. "Only Boychuk and our good friend, Denny, were able to gain Donna's approval. I could see Brian winning Mom over, but that asshole?"

"Joanne was in love..." Hubie simply replied.

Jane nodded. Almost all her strength had been sapped; her eyelids were drooped and crestfallen. The medicine Dr. Akram had prescribed was working.

"Will you come and see me in Albany?" she asked. Hubie felt his heart skip a beat; his Jane was back. But this time she looked about eight years old.

Hubie nodded, affectionately. He bent down and kissed his daughter's forehead. Jane's eyes began to tear up, but she held back.

"I'll be there," he replied.

FORTY-NINE

It was half past nine when Roberto pulled his SUV into the parking lot of the police barracks. He had knocked on Hubie's door at the motel, but there was no answer, and the Manhattan lawyer figured he was already on his way to the hospital. The night before, after his call to Hubie, Roberto had decided to eat dinner in Saranac Lake before driving the ten miles back to Lake Placid. His negotiations with the DA and the police had been frustrating and pointless.

He was still pissed at the prosecutor when he arrived at the barracks, and soon he found out why the district attorney insisted that Joanne spend the night in jail. This was a big political story and, across the parking lot, were five satellite trucks from television stations as far away as Plattsburgh, Syracuse and Albany. News that the sisters had been apprehended spread quickly, and this suited the young prosecutor nicely. The DA wanted to tell the world that Joanne was in custody pending bail, and he wanted to look tough. A grandstander, Roberto thought, even up here in the freakin' woods.

Since he'd started seeing Jane, Roberto had learned a lot about how the broadcast news media operated. All the big cable networks would have sent correspondents and producers overnight, but they relied on local television stations to provide the news feed back to New York, Atlanta, or wherever else. Now they were setting up their gear outside the barracks, pointing their enormous satellite receivers to the southwestern skies. The weather was cooperating this

morning. This allowed them to mount a phalanx of microphones outside the station, with the New York State Police
insignia behind them. As Jane had always said, these morons
need visuals. They have to tell their stories in pictures.

He pulled his Infiniti into one of the last parking spots,
and began walking towards the entrance of the barracks.
One of the reporters must have been forewarned that Joanne's
attorney would be paying a visit and soon Roberto found
himself in the middle of a scrum. He couldn't begin to count
the number of microphones now thrust under his chin. But
he was no rookie; he was an experienced spokesperson on
many corporate bids, and knew the drill. He'd have to throw
them a bone or they wouldn't leave him alone.

"You're the Schumacher lawyer, right?" one reporter
screamed.

"Yes, that's true. My name's Roberto Alvarez," He knew
he'd have to identify himself at some point, but he wondered
how long it would take for the media to figure out that he
was more than Jane's attorney.

The reporters jostled for position.

"What can you tell us, Mr. Alvarez?" another asked. So
far, he didn't recognize any of the personalities who infested
the cable networks but he was sure they would be here, soon.
In the meantime, the networks would take their feeds from
the locals. Little did they know they'd have to decamp from
the Adirondacks soon and head to Albany if this story had any
stamina. They would have to be content with interviewing
the police, the prosecutor and perhaps the chief of medical
staff at the hospital because they weren't getting anywhere
near his clients.

Another reporter yelled out a flurry of questions.

"What's Jane Schumacher's condition? What about her
sister? Is she going to post this huge bail?"

Roberto threw up both hands, effectively signaling an end to the inquisition. He'd answer their questions if they could show some civility. That's asking a lot from this bunch, he thought. These people are congenitally rude. No, that would mean they were born this way. More like habitually or chronically impolite.

"People, as the New York state police announced yesterday, Ms. Schumacher is under hospital arrest in Lake Placid. My client, Joanne Lowry, Ms. Schumacher's sister, is in custody here, pending bail. That's where I am headed now. To post her bail and let her go home...to her family. When all the facts emerge, everyone will know that Mrs. Lowry has faced a terrible ordeal and I believe the police and the district attorney will realize that."

Another reported piped up.

"Counselor, what about Jane Schumacher? Now charged with murder?"

Roberto wanted to end this scrum right now, and started walking towards the entrance to the barracks.

"I'm not prepared to speak about Ms. Schumacher, other than to say her immediate future is in the hands of her doctors...and so if you'll excuse me, I have to meet with the officials here. Thank you."

He turned, opened the door and entered the police station. He was immediately greeted by Sergeant Bouchard, the same trooper who had joined Boychuk in the convoy up the mountain the day before. Bouchard escorted Roberto to the conference room where the young district attorney was seated with a man who appeared to be at least seventy. This guy could be the kid's grandfather, Roberto surmised, but he was likely the local justice of the peace. His request to have the judge present had been granted. Roberto wanted the matter expedited as soon as possible.

"Good morning, Mr. Cochrane," he said.

The DA rose and greeted Alvarez.

"Good morning. Let me introduce you to Judge Engle-
hart. He'll be making the decision on my request for bail for
Mrs. Lowry, and I have to tell you, he shares my belief that it
should be substantial given the nature of this crime."

Interesting, Roberto thought.

This prosecutor might think he was shrewder than he
really was. He had obviously leaked the bail story to the
people outside—to prove he was a tough-on-crime kind of
guy. But his attempt to put words in the mouth of the local
justice of the peace was manipulative, to say the least.

Time to release my inner Bronx, Roberto thought.

"Good morning, Judge, nice to meet you," he said,
shaking hands with the old duffer. This man was more
accustomed to dealing with building code violations than
accessory-to-murder charges.

"Gentlemen, let me get to the point," Roberto said,
unleashing a torrent of details of Joanne's victimization at
the hands of a violent alcoholic and how these facts would
be dropped onto the laps of a sympathetic townsfolk like a
truckload of frozen venison.

It was a monologue. Truly one-sided. He told his young
friend that he'd feel obligated to go before the assembled
scribes outside and inform them that Mrs. Lowry had never
been busted for as much as a parking violation as she drove
her ten-year-old Explorer to her cashier's job at the local
hardware store for ten-fifty an hour. He described it as a
place where the boss and every drywaller in town loved her.
He talked about her charity work—the bake sales and what
not—where she raised a few bucks for the cancer campaign
in Morgan County. Her mother died of cancer at the age of

fifty, did you know that? Oh, and yes, don't forget her weekly trips to the Grange Hall to cook suppers for the elderly.

So, gentlemen, do you understand what I'm saying? Do you know how this so-called case will go down when the public finds out you're prosecuting a woman—a wonderful, law-abiding citizen, let me remind you once again—who was beaten to a pulp with regularity but decided to keep it silent to protect her only son? I think the cable networks will eat this up, don't you think?

Maybe Oprah, too?

The old judge listened without uttering a word.

When Roberto had finished, the judge asked him to step outside while he conferred with the prosecutor. Shouldn't be more than a few minutes, he said. The last words Roberto heard before he shut the conference room door came from the judge. "Son," he heard the older man say, "I think you'll have to reconsider..."

Within twenty minutes, Roberto had managed to reduce Joanne's bail to five-thousand dollars based on his personal pledge to drive her back to Morgan County and ensure her court appearance in ten days. There was no need for an ankle bracelet.

Roberto was waiting in the outer room when Sergeant Bouchard brought Joanne in. Looking haggard, her hair unkempt, she forced a smile as she walked towards him. He had known this woman for less than eighteen hours. But he knew she needed a hug, and they embraced warmly. The gratitude on her face read like a neon sign in Times Square.

"Thank you, Roberto," she said. "I really appreciate this."

Alvarez raised his hands in protest.

"You're welcome, but I've heard enough," he replied. "Let's just get you out of here and over to the hospital."

"You're a nice man, Rob," she continued. "My sister is a lucky girl."

"Well, I'm not sure she'd agree with you right now, Joanne."

Pausing for a moment, she stared into his deep, round eyes. "I meant…to have you in her life."

FIFTY

The sleek Gulfstream executive jet glided through a few low hanging clouds that hugged the mountain tops before touching down safely in Lake Placid. A weekend low-pressure cell that had produced more than eighteen inches of snow had moved on to Maine and Nova Scotia, and it was a mostly clear, cold day in the Adirondacks. Fortunately for the pilots, an airport crew consisting of one man, a truck and a plow had sufficiently cleared the forty-two-hundred foot tarmac, enabling the jet to land safely.

There was no regular service offered at this small airport. If locals needed to fly somewhere—say Boston—they'd have to drive the ten miles to the next town to catch their only air connection to the outside world. The operators of the Gulfstream knew Saranac Lake was the more logical destination, but not this time. This plane's passengers wanted only to land, top up the fuel tanks, pick up some important cargo and get the hell out of there. Placid's smaller field was also very private. The plane's occupants hoped the media hordes in town were staking out the larger airport and would ignore the tiny mountain strip. Upon landing, they realized their gamble had paid off. Theirs was the only action around.

After taxiing to fuel tanks located about a hundred yards from the small bungalow-sized departure lounge, the pilots were greeted warmly by a heavy-set man of about fifty. He was wearing a Ford Diesel cap and a half-length ski jacket; it was clear he was in charge. In quick fashion, he unraveled his fuel hose and connected it to one wing of the Gulfstream and pulled the lever. Refueling would take less than ten minutes.

In the distance, the pilots could see their cargo arriving in a red-and-white ambulance. As ordered, there were to be no sirens or flashing lights. This transfer was to be done as quickly and inconspicuously as possible. The emergency vehicle entered the gates of the airstrip and pulled up beside the executive jet. The airport operator watched as the side door to the plane opened. There was no need for a ramp; the paramedics had obviously done this before. Jumping from the truck, they wheeled the stretcher towards the plane's door, and after pushing a few buttons, the hydraulics began to function as designed, lifting the patient into the jet. A nurse, managing the I.V. stands, accompanied the stretcher inside. Seconds later, the aircraft's door closed. The pilots watched as the operator disconnected the fuel lines and gave them a thumbs-up signal. They were ready to go.

Inside the jet, its occupants greeted their new passenger. She was still groggy from the painkillers and barely awake, but that didn't diminish the surprise on her face.

"Governor!" Jane exclaimed. "What the hell are you doing here? Claudia, you too!"

The governor of New York beamed. His chief of staff stood nearby, with virtually the same expression on her face.

"I guess you can't run this state without me, huh?" Jane asked.

"Warren Buffett couldn't run this state, Schumacher," he replied.

Despite her heavily-drugged condition, which was not entirely nullifying her pain, Jane smiled back. When she had opened her eyes this morning, Dr. Akram informed her that she had called Albany's leading oncologist and that a transfer back to the city would occur today. But instead of driving back to the capital by ambulance, a journey that would have taken a minimum of two-and-a-half hours over a bumpy, winter-rugged I-87, there was a change in plans.

She would fly back. And she was leaving right away.

Dr. Akram told her it was important to start her treatment quickly, and that an air ambulance to Albany had been ordered. Jane had mixed feelings about the urgency of her situation. She'd said good-bye to Hubie in her room, and he promised to visit. But she was saddened that Joanne and Roberto hadn't returned in time. She had especially hoped to see Roberto. She had so much to say to him, to tell him she was sorry and to thank him for. Hubie had told her about Roberto's efforts to gain Joanne's freedom and that, briefly, planted a smile on her face. That's my Argentinean, she thought. What a good man. Then Dr. Akram then arrived and told her it was time to ship out. The tiny Afghani physician looked deep into Jane's eyes and wished her all the best.

As her stretcher was being wheeled out of the hospital, Jane knew that cameras awaited her outside. More than a few enterprising reporters would have been apprised of her impending release and transfer. Jane took no pleasure in the fact that she'd become the central story line in the governor's embryonic presidential campaign. Of course, that had happened the moment she pulled the triggers of her father's shotgun. But she was going to rectify that. This story was going to end.

Exiting the hospital, even Jane was surprised by the mob assembled at the emergency doors. There had to be at least a dozen television and still photographers clamoring for position and at least that many more reporters lying in wait. All to catch a glimpse of the governor's press secretary-turned-assassin. Some hoped they'd get lucky; she might even say something for the record. Others had a more ghoulish motive. Maybe they'd witness a once vivacious and powerful woman on her deathbed.

All were disappointed.

Dr. Akram, two solidly-built orderlies, a nurse and three of Bouchard's biggest troopers accompanied Jane's stretcher through the media cordon, surrounding it as they wheeled it to the emergency vehicle.

Now aboard Foley's plane she was face to face with her boss for the first time in nearly a week. How their world had turned on its ear in that short time was beyond belief, she thought. She was pleased to see the governor. This was consistent with the man she knew—and the Wendell Foley she had hoped to introduce to the country.

"So, now you want to run an even more dysfunctional government, right Wendell?" She attempted to suppress a laugh that she knew would hurt. "But you didn't answer my question, really. What are you doing here?"

Foley took her by the hand and gripped it. Then he smiled.

"Don't flatter yourself, Schumacher," he said. "Claudia and I both felt that you've had enough time off for Thanksgiving and decided it was time for you to return to work. And if the only way to get you back was to fly up here and get you ourselves, we thought we would. Besides, it was a nice day to see the mountains…and get some fresh air. God knows, in this business, I'll need a lot of fresh air."

Jane wasn't buying it.

"You're a terrible liar, Wendell, and that's one of the reasons you might make a half-way decent president," she said.

"Half-way decent, eh? Such high praise! What do you think, Claudia?"

Claudia nodded.

"You're being overwhelmed with adulation, that's for sure," Claudia said. "But we both wanted to see you, Jane. Get you back to the city as soon as possible and get you the care you need."

The Gulfstream had finished taxiing to the end of the short runway. The louvered cockpit door opened and the retired Air Force pilot—a barrel-chested man in his sixties sporting a short, cropped goatee—peered out.

"Wheels up in three minutes folks...so you'd better get yourselves strapped in," he said. "Weather's good. We should make Albany in about forty minutes."

Foley thanked his pilot, and he and Claudia took their seats next to Jane's stretcher. Her nurse, bolting the steel-reinforced bed to the floor, sat down as well.

"So, how are you feeling, Jane?" the governor asked.

"Well, last night, I have to admit, it wasn't very good," she replied. "But today, a bit better...in other words, same old, same old..."

She paused a moment.

"Guess I really screwed up, didn't I Wendell?"

"Same old, same old," he replied, sardonically.

"Well, everything they say about me is true."

"Everything but why, Jane...*why* you did what you did."

Jane grimaced. She knew she'd need another hit of morphine from the intravenous tubes attached to her, but that would have to wait until they arrived in Albany. The damn drug made her drowsy and that was one condition she wanted to avoid right now.

The executive jet was now at full throttle, and a moment later was airborne. Thinking it might be the last trip she'd make to the Adirondacks for quite some time, she glanced out of one of plane's small porthole windows and saw the snow-capped mountains glistening in the noonday sun.

"Well, that's not important now, Governor," she said. "What is important is that I am—or presume I am—still on your payroll."

"You are, and I'm not doing anything to change that," Foley said, though it sounded as if he himself was not convinced.

Jane smiled once again.

"I appreciate that, Wendell. The only thing hemorrhaging more than my lungs is my American Express bill...but what I...what I was going to say was that we're gonna have to part company. Just look at the story I've created. I'm a terrible drag on your campaign."

Foley winced and Jane noticed it.

"Yes, Wendell. You know I am. And you know that you have to get rid of me. It's true, and both you and Claudia know it. We all know that I'll be resigning—today. I don't even want the media to find out about this flight!"

The governor frowned and turned his head as the jet banked over the mountains, turning south for the brief flight to the capital. He didn't like what he was hearing. Jane Schumacher was one of his closest confidants, his brilliant media strategist, his friend. He couldn't imagine a run for the presidency without her.

"You know I'm right, don't you Wendell?"

By his silence, Jane knew Foley had agreed with her.

"Now, with me being the superb media manager that I am, let me call a few friends and leak this news. I think I still have a few friends. I'll tell them that you will miss me, but that it was necessary to place me on indefinite medical leave. And I'll tell them that it was your decision, given my condition. They might not believe it, but tough. That will be the line of attack. I want you and the campaign to move on."

Jane paused a moment to let the news sink in.

"Okay?" she asked.

Foley nodded.

"And now you can give my job to Marcia, at least for the campaign. Hell, she's smart, knows the media well, and has a great candidate."

"She's impressed me and Claudia, even this week," he replied. "But Schumacher, Marcia doesn't have your experience."

"I know that, Wendell, but she's a very quick study, and besides, like me, she's drunk the Kool-Aid."

The governor held Jane's hand, stroking it. He knew this would be a difficult decision to make today. And he was having a problem accepting it.

"Are you sure?" he asked.

"Hell no," she replied, her voice filled with sadness. "Down deep I'm fighting this with every fiber of my diseased body. Nobody wants to be with you more than I do as you kick ass in the primaries and in the election too. But that'll be a breeze—"

"Won't be a breeze, Jane, they'll put up one helluva fight—"

Jane shook her head.

"Remember who the other side will put up?" she asked. "If you can't beat that relic—that *Luddite*—then you don't deserve to be president."

Foley smiled.

"You're still bustin' my—"

"—yup! Someone has to."

She paused, turning her head towards the executive jet's windows. The mountain tops, fresh from their first brush with winter, had disappeared and only a few clouds had taken their place. Before she knew it, she'd be in another hospital and her real battle would enter another phase.

"But we all know this is how it has to be."

FIFTY-ONE

Hours later, as darkness set in, Roberto's Infiniti pulled into the long driveway. The return trip to Morgantown seemed to have taken forever despite the lack of traffic over the now cleared highways. That they had missed Jane's departure from the hospital by about twenty minutes saddened Roberto, but he understood her health took precedence. Still, he really wanted to see her, look into her eyes and tell her ...well, he didn't know what he would have told her. It had been less than a week since they were together in Manhattan, but it felt much longer. And given what Hubie and Joanne had told him, Roberto wasn't sure if he wanted to see his girlfriend in her current condition.

Hell, what was he thinking?

He wasn't even sure if she was his girlfriend.

Their trip to Morgantown was also a mostly silent one. After Roberto gained her release from jail in Saranac Lake, Joanne had returned to the motel for a shower and a change of clothing. Once again, he silently cursed the actions of the young prosecutor who wouldn't release her the night before. Totally unwarranted, he thought.

More than once, Roberto glanced in his rearview mirror to see how Joanne was coping with the drive back. She looked shell-shocked and fatigued. Twenty minutes into the journey, he watched as she pulled out a pack of cigarettes and popped one into her mouth. As a non-smoker, he objected to anyone wanting to light up in his vehicle. But for Joanne, he was prepared to make an exception given the stress in her

life. To his surprise, she stopped short, stared at the cigarette for a few moments before rolling the back window down
and throwing it, the lighter and the entire pack out onto the
highway.

Moments later, she was fast asleep. And soon after, he
noticed Hubie nodding off as well, resting his head against
the front passenger window. It had been one hell of an ordeal
for this father and daughter. They didn't deserve any of this,
Roberto thought, but from what he had learned of Denny,
maybe they were better off.

All of this was set aside as they drove up Hubie's
driveway.

"Are you sure you don't want to come in?" Hubie asked
Roberto, as the older man and his daughter exited the vehicle. "You've done a lot of driving over the past twenty-four
hours. We have lots of room here, too...if you want to stay."

Roberto smiled. "No thanks, Hubie. I have to get back
to New York. There's a lot of work waiting for me back in
the city. But I appreciate your offer."

The older man nodded and smiled.

"Well, it's me and Joanne who have you to thank,
Roberto. I can't tell you how much we appreciate everything
you've done for us."

Roberto glanced at Joanne. She simply smiled, confirming what her father had said.

"You're welcome, but it's not necessary. You're Jane's
family, and we all have to do what we need to do."

Hubie understood. This was a man of integrity and
honor, he thought.

"Are you stopping over in Albany?"

"Not today, Hubie," he replied. "I'm going to let Jane
see her doctors and get her treatments under way first. But
I'll fly up there later this week...when the time is right."

Hubie outstretched his hand to Roberto. He thanked him again and bid the Argentinean good-bye. After his SUV disappeared down the road, Joanne peered through the darkness in the direction of her house next door. Except for a lone, orange-colored light over the entrance of the garage, partly illuminating the snow-laden yard, the property looked cold and abandoned. The yellow police tape that she'd seen on the diner's television set only days before had been removed. Over to the side, Denny's pumper truck sat parked, a bitter reminder of events past. She guessed she'd have to deal with that truck, and her house, eventually.

But not tonight.

Not tomorrow or the next day either.

Maybe never, if she had her way.

She turned her head away, and together she and her father entered his house. They were greeted by a smiling Dee working in the kitchen, preparing dinner. The two women looked at each other warmly and hugged. Griz rose from his makeshift winter bed, a cushion from a summer deck chair, to greet them as well.

"It's good to have you back, Joanne," Dee said.

"Thanks Dee, but I'm not sure how I feel right now."

"Totally understandable, dear," the elderly woman said. She sensed the pain that Joanne was suffering. She turned her attention to Hubie; he'd finally called and updated her on Jane's condition and her abrupt departure by air to Albany.

"How was the drive?"

"Uneventful," he said. "Roberto was kind enough to bring us back. I invited him in but he said he had to return to New York."

"Well, you both must be hungry," she said. "By the way, we have—"

Dee was interrupted by the sounds of footsteps in the hall near the kitchen.

"—company," Dee continued.

From the hallway, Brent walked in.

"Something smells real good, Dee. I'm—" He stopped in his tracks, clearly not expecting to see his mother standing at the kitchen door.

"—starved."

Joanne and Brent locked eyes.

"Hi, honey," she said after a moment, awaiting his reaction. She had been dreading this reunion for days, uncertain how he would treat her when they met again. Her worst fears materialized. His eyes seething with anger, Brent turned on his heels and stomped back down the hall.

Dee was watching it all unfold.

"Jo, I'm sorry, I was hoping to warn you."

Heartbroken, Joanne slowly removed her winter boots, hung her coat on a hook and without saying a word, followed Brent down the hall. She found him, arms crossed, slumped on the couch in front of the television. He was staring blankly at a hockey game when Joanne entered the living room.

"Can I join you?" she asked.

Without looking up, Brent shrugged as if to say it was a free country. In painful silence, she sat down and started watching the game.

"Sabres and who?" she asked.

"Boston," he replied.

"Who's winning?" she said, not knowing what else to say.

"Three-*fucking*-one, Bruins," he barked. "Can't you read the screen? Jesus Christ!"

Joanne was stunned by the anger, not to mention the profanity.

"I don't think I deserve that, Brent," she said.

"Oh, yeah, Mom?" he asked. "What do you deserve, then? How about this question then? What did you do with my mother?"

Joanne took a moment to answer.

"I'm right here...where I've always been..."

"Well, from where I sit, right fucking now—"

"Brent!"

"Oh, you don't want to hear me swear, Mom? What the hell do you want me to say? That I'm ecstatic about my mother going to jail? Is that what you want me to say?"

Joanne continued to stare in silence at her son.

She knew she would face his anger but wasn't prepared for the hatred in his voice.

Brent continued to stare at the TV screen. A moment or two passed.

"Did it all have to come to this, Mom?"

"Well, no, I didn't plan any of this, Brent," she replied.

"Really, Mom? Then what exactly was your plan? To keep having the shit beat out've you forever? To let that asshole keep doing what he was doing before you found the guts to leave?"

Joanne attempted to defend herself, but knew her son had a good case against her. She had put up with Denny's violence for too long.

"That isn't fair, Brent" she said, turning her attention as well to the television. She noticed that Buffalo had scored, making it a closer game. "You don't know the whole story."

"Oh no, Mom? Well, as I see it, you didn't pull the trigger but you may as well have. Or should've. No, it took Aunt Jane to do your dirty work—someone who I haven't seen since I was about twelve goddamn years old!"

Joanne leapt to the defense of her stricken sister.

"Your aunt Jane didn't know she was going to do what she did either, Brent," she replied. "She did what she did to save me. You just don't know the full story."

Brent was still furious.

"Yeah...she knew she was dying, so she probably said to herself, 'what the fuck? I'm not going to be around next week—'"

"Brent!"

"—so she said, 'why don't I just blow old Denny away? He's just a shit-for-brains anyway. And that way, my sister doesn't have to make a decision!'"

Joanne was speechless. She didn't know how to respond to her son, and he knew it. He jumped from the couch and started to leave the living room.

"Tell Dee I've lost my appetite."

FIFTY-TWO

A heavy mist covered the East River like a shroud. Roberto's limo had edged its way down East 60th Street and was crossing the Queensboro Bridge. With any luck, they would soon be on Northern Boulevard, and since it was still early, maybe the heavy afternoon traffic en route to LaGuardia could be avoided.

Roberto knew he was in good hands with Edward, the firm's diminutive seventy-two-year-old chauffeur. Edward knew every trick in the book. A former New York City taxi driver who could have been a leprechaun in another life, there wasn't an expressway, avenue or back alley in Gotham that he hadn't mastered and conquered. He would get Roberto there in plenty of time for his flight to Albany.

After he had dropped Joanne and her father off in Morgantown two days earlier, Roberto had made his way back to the city. As a partner in the three-hundred-lawyer Wall Street firm, he knew his colleagues would cut him some slack. They would let him manage this high-profile Schumacher case. His personal profile—and that of the firm's—had shot through the stratosphere as the media circus continued its show under the big top. But he also realized his role would soon end; his representation of the sisters was fleeting. An hour after returning to the office, Roberto recused himself for conflict of interest. He called on one of the firm's top criminal litigators to take over.

Jane Schumacher was big news, or at least was until yesterday, Roberto thought. At breakfast, he had read a piece in the *Daily News* quoting sources close to the Foley campaign that Jane had resigned from the campaign due to serious illness. A few more details on the Thanksgiving Day shooting emerged, too. Those same sources told a story that Jane may have intervened in a domestic dispute between her sister and her abusive husband, prompting favorable blogs to speculate that she shot him to save her sister. What she did was wrong, the story continued. But there was little remorse; feminist writers from across the country had sided with Jane. Not surprisingly, the gun-loving, radical right also leapt to her defense.

Three hours after the newspaper story hit the Internet, Roberto's office television was tuned to *Fox News*. He watched as the governor publicly accepted her resignation and spoke warmly of his long-time press aide as he tearfully wished her a speedy recovery. Even Roberto, a Republican, thought it was a masterful performance by the Democratic contender. Foley had put the issue behind him.

The mist had now turned into a black, pelting rain. Edward's Lincoln Town Car arrived at LaGuardia and pulled up to the curb at the US Airways terminal. The flight to the state capital was a short hop and would take only an hour or so. This was the trip that Jane should have taken more often, he thought. But she had insisted on driving her Mercedes up and down the Hudson Valley.

"There you go, sir," the elfish Edward said as he opened the trunk to the limo. "With forty-five minutes to spare, too."

"I wish you'd stop that, Edward," he replied. "If anyone should be called 'sir' around here, it's you, my friend."

Edward lifted Roberto's roller luggage from the trunk and smiled.

"Whatever you say...*sir*," he said smiling.

Roberto shook his head, returning his smile.

"There's no one better in this town than you."

"Thank you, sir. Give my regards to Ms. Schumacher, okay?"

"How did you know that I was going to see her?"

Edward smiled again.

"You forget. She's been a passenger in this car many times. I just put two-and-two together. Old hacks like me are experts on human nature."

Roberto looked at his chauffeur with affection.

"As always, you're right again, Edward," he said. "And I will...give Jane your best. Thank you. I'll see you tomorrow night, at this time."

"Have a good flight...sir."

A couple of hours later, Roberto's taxi arrived at the Albany hospital. He was apprehensive. He wasn't sure how this reunion with Jane would go or if she was in any condition to see him. Or if she *wanted* to see him. After all, she had repeatedly shunned his offers of help.

He entered the hospital and asked the lobby attendant for Jane's floor. Emerging from the elevator, he made his way to the nurses' station and was told where to find her. She was in a private room and was stable, he had learned, but very weak from her treatments. There were no troopers in sight. Governor's orders.

Roberto slowly pushed the door open. To his astonishment, Jane was awake and gazing absently out the window at the city below. She seemed miles away, but alert. Beside her bed sat her laptop computer, as well as the latest editions of the *Times*, *Daily News* and *Times-Union*. Her BlackBerry sat on the side table.

Jane had taken no joy in reading about the latest fatality numbers coming from the war with another fifty people killed the day before. What a goddamn mess! Now her boss will inherit all this shit, she thought. How incompetent could one administration be? Surely the worst we've had in a hundred years! But even her party couldn't avoid its terminal stupidity; there was yet another item about that southern congressman being re-elected even though the cops had found nearly a hundred grand in cash in his freezer? Jesus!

At the sound of the door opening, she turned and smiled at her handsome Hispanic.

"Argentina!" she said. "Now, why did I know you'd be coming soon?"

"That's because you know me so well, Schumacher."

He approached her bed, bent down and kissed her on the lips before retreating to gaze warmly into her eyes. It was followed by a longer, loving kiss that reminded Roberto of their splendid seven days in Jamaica the year before.

That he was shocked by her physical condition was a massive understatement. Stunned even. The woman before him was a far cry from the Jane who had left his apartment only a week or so before. She appeared almost ravaged, her complexion pasty. Her auburn hair, once vibrant and thrilling, was now lusterless. Her eyes—Jane's sparkling hazel eyes—looked exhausted and dull.

But in an instant, Roberto felt a fresh emotion envelop him. Her appearance mattered little to him. Actually, nothing mattered. He only wanted to be with her. His memory returned to that day down on East 47th Street before Thanksgiving. To the diamond district. And to the apologies he had made to his mother, Rosaria, for missing their family holiday in the Bronx. He'd had a mission then and that was to be with Jane. Somehow the memory of that assignment returned today; it had all come back into focus. Somehow, it all became clear.

Jane, the mind-reader, sensed what was going on. She looked deep into his eyes.

He kissed her again.

"Why didn't you say something to me, Jane?" he asked. "Why didn't you include me in your struggles? I would've been there for you...you know that."

She nodded. Their eyes remained locked.

"I know that, Rob," she replied, softly. "I do know... now. You would've been there for me...but I guess I needed to deal with this, with everything, by myself. I've always dealt with stressful things by myself. But strangely, things happen for a reason."

"What do you mean?" he asked.

"Well, think about it. If I had shared my diagnosis with you...that night before Thanksgiving or the next day, I might not have gone to Morgantown. We might've just stayed in Albany or at Hunter, crying our eyes out. But then I never would've found out about Jo..."

She paused for a moment. Her words were sinking in with Roberto.

"I know I handled it all wrong, Rob," she continued. "I know I could've taken her out of that house. I was impulsive. I didn't have to shoot the bastard..."

"But you're not sorry, are you?"

"No...I'm not."

She allowed herself a hint of a smile before continuing.

"And not just because of who Denny was or what he was doing to Joanne. But also because I got to know her again. We connected again. Can you understand that, Argentina?"

He nodded. He came from a large family. He knew what it meant to have loving relationships with siblings.

"But when this happened, I wish I would've asked you for help, to have you more in my life."

Roberto smiled but remained silent.

Jane continued.

"All I can say is that I regret a lot of things I've done."

"Well, don't, babe..." he replied.

She looked puzzled.

"That word...*regret*...Jane," he continued. "Don't use it. It's the most useless emotion we can experience. What's done is done. We can't do anything about it...all of it is behind us now...all we can do is move forward."

She was determined not to cry. She knew that he was always a supportive and loving man but hadn't fully appreciated him until now. There was no one else like him in her world.

"My dad told me what you've done for Jo," she said. "Thank you so much, you wonderful man you!"

Roberto tightened his grip on her hand and shook his head.

"It's not necessary, babe. Besides, Joanne's case is such a slam dunk that any DA worth a mail-order law degree would recognize that right away. No jury in the world would find her guilty. And as for your case, Jane, I've asked—"

Jane interrupted him.

"—let's not go there either, okay? That's the last thing I want to discuss with you...here...and now. I just want to enjoy you here with me."

He nodded.

Her legal problems dwarfed the crisis she was now facing. She was smart; she knew exactly what lay ahead.

"Our first priority is to get you better and out of here."

FIFTY-THREE

Joanne had returned from work and was in the upstairs bathroom at her father's house when Jane's ambulance turned into the driveway. She watched as the paramedics opened the vehicle's rear doors and wheeled her sister out. Another lake-effect snowfall had hammered the region but Hubie had cleared and sanded his driveway in anticipation of his daughter's arrival home for Christmas.

Lying on the hydraulic stretcher, Jane was protected from the elements. But from her window, Joanne could see her sister's head wrapped in a yellowish turban. My poor sister, she thought. She's lost her beautiful hair. Over the past few weeks, Joanne and her dad had made the trip to Albany several times to see Jane, but the visits were always cut short. Her treatments prevailed. They always did.

As Dr. Akram had predicted, there would be no surgery.

Their worst fears had materialized.

Hubie greeted the paramedics as they approached the house and guided them through the back door. The week before, anticipating the big day, he had shown up at Joanne's register, his cart laden with pressure-treated lumber and boxes of nails. He was determined to build a ramp beside the steps to provide access to the house for a stretcher. Perhaps later, in spring when the snow disappeared, the ramp could be used for a wheelchair.

Darryl, her corpulent boss, had been supportive upon her return to the store. He acted as if nothing had happened, other than to say that it was about time she got back to work.

After all, Jo, you know Christmas is coming. It's the best time of the year. Just love Christmas, Jo. The store looks so nice...and sounds nice...all the carols and all. It's just great. Well, boss, she'd replied, you certainly like the sounds of Jingle Bells coming from my register, that's for sure. But Darryl, feigning insult and injury, just gave her that "you-just-kicked-my-puppy" look and asked her, how could she say he was so callous, so cold-hearted, so Ebenezer-like?

They had both laughed.

For the most part, her regulars welcomed her as well. At first, a few looked her over cautiously, perhaps in judgment. But after their subsequent visits, they would joke and laugh as Joanne punched up their bills. The violence of late November was the great unspoken topic around the small town, but she had sensed that they knew what Denny was like, and perhaps most felt he got what he deserved. She detected neither pity nor disapproval in their voices or in their eyes.

Joanne was back in her routine, if that's what anyone could call it. Since returning from that jail in Saranac Lake, she had gone about her business without complaint. She was relieved when Roberto told her that an ankle bracelet wasn't required. But she still had to obtain permission to visit her sister in Albany. Other than that, she couldn't leave town.

Which, to her, was stupid. Where would she go, anyway?

Every day, as she left Hubie's house for work, she had trembled when she'd glance across the yard to her house. Her father had kept the driveway plowed, and the pumper was still there. Once he'd said that he could probably find a buyer for it when she was ready to make that decision. After all, Denny's customers had moved on, he said, and maybe you should too?

There was no business left. May as well sell it, he said.

Hubie also mentioned, almost apologetically, that he had given the undertaker permission to have Denny cremated as well. But this brought no response from Joanne. When he raised the subject of a funeral service—you know, dear, sometime down the road, we might think?—she had snapped at him.

He knew not to go there again.

From the upstairs bathroom, Joanne could hear Hubie and the paramedics roll Jane into the house. He had rearranged his den on the first floor to accommodate her bed because it was closer to the bathroom. He replaced the room's ancient tube-styled television with a flat-screen model that he had bought on sale at Turnbull's. And he had moved a large La-Z-Boy from the living room into the den so Jane could put her feet up, read the papers or work on her laptop. Maybe catch a nap when she wanted. His daughter was going to be comfortable.

Joanne thought of all this earlier in the day as a steady stream of customers pushed their carts towards her register. She was glad that Jane was coming home, but she wasn't sure how she felt about the coming Christmas season. Peering out at the parking lot, she noticed how the snow had been piling up. But that nice lady from the Salvation Army had lifted her spirits. She had been there all day, freezing, ringing her bells and smiling to shoppers entering the store. Joanne couldn't help but admire the elderly woman. She didn't lay on any guilt if they decided not to contribute a quarter or two to her charity kettle. She simply smiled and wished them a Merry Christmas.

Only four days to go, she thought, and still no word from Brent. She had hoped he would call. That he'd announce that he and Tracy would be coming to Morgantown. But that was only wishful thinking. In the past, Denny had chased him away. Now, it seemed she was doing the same thing. After their bitter argument nearly a month before, he had stormed out of her dad's house and bolted for Tracy's parents' home in the Finger Lakes, forsaking the final weeks of the fall term at the university. Except for a single email from his girlfriend telling Joanne where they were, she had heard nothing from her son. Not a phone call. Not a text. Nothing. She hoped he hadn't quit school. He was only one semester away from graduation, after all.

The sounds from the first floor abated. Joanne looked out the bathroom window once again. The paramedics were returning to their vehicle accompanied by her father. They shook hands with Hubie, jumped in the truck and drove away. She walked back to the mirror and for the longest time stared at her reflection. She had paid a heavy price for her stress. Her blonde, wiry hair had become dry and bland and much too long; her roots were showing again. There were lines on her face that she thought didn't exist before. Or had they? Maybe she hadn't been paying attention. Had she'd aged and didn't notice? God, she couldn't believe that she'd turn forty in less than a month. I look fifty, she thought.

Joanne took one last long look at herself. She remembered her sister downstairs. Then she opened a side drawer and removed an electric trimmer.

She fired it up.

Minutes later and without saying a word, Joanne stood at the entrance to Jane's new bedroom. With her back to the door, Jane had climbed from her hospital bed and into the chair. She had removed her yellow turban, revealing only a quarter-inch of brown stubble where her fine stylish hair once had been. A dark brown wig rested on a cabinet next to her bed.

Now she was leaning forward and scanning the room's photographs of the twins growing up in Morgantown. They were the same pictures that she had perused at Thanksgiving. The girls skipping rope. Their first day at school, dressed identically. With Fred, their mutt. And that picture of her and Boychuk at their graduation; she, in her long, floral-print dress, beautiful; he, in his uniform, gorgeous.

She smiled.

"Had to have been Dee," she muttered out loud, unaware of Joanne standing behind her.

Joanne spoke up.

"No kidding," she said. "Dad couldn't find a picture on a driver's license."

Surprised to hear the sound of her sister's voice, Jane turned to greet her. She took one look at Joanne and burst out laughing. Joanne, sporting a Marine-style brush cut, stood there with a broad grin pasted across her face.

"You are one great chick, do you know that?" Jane said.

Joanne nodded.

"Yes, I do," she replied. The grin widened.

"Welcome home."

FIFTY-FOUR

The next day, Jane awoke to sounds coming from the kitchen. She looked at her digital clock and it read nine-twenty. Jesus, all I do is sleep on these damn drugs, she thought. Glancing outside, she saw that it was snowing again and knew her father was likely on his second round of service calls across town. Joanne had left too. Her shift at the store had started before nine. There were only a few days remaining before Christmas, and shoppers would keep her busy.

Wrapping herself in a housecoat and plunking herself in her wheelchair, Jane opened the door to the den and rolled herself down the hall and into the kitchen. When Jane had arrived back in Morgantown, Dee had moved in. Her father was affectionate and even attentive at times, but was next to useless. It was Dee who assumed a good deal of the responsibility for Jane's day-to-day needs when she wasn't at her day job at the VFW.

There was Carol too. She was the stern but supportive hospice worker who arrived every day to make sure Jane was taking her meds, mostly for pain but also to hold any infections at bay.

Dee was finishing a few dishes at the sink when Jane arrived. A kitchen towel was draped over her shoulder. She turned and smiled.

"Good morning," she said.

"Hi, Dee, how are you?"

"Well, it's a beautiful morning again, Jane," the elderly woman said.

Jane looked out the window and cringed.

"I almost forgot just how much snow we get up here in upper-butt-crack county," she said. "I guess I've been spoiled a long time."

Dee laughed. Over the past month, she had come to enjoy Jane's ribald sense of humor. Jane had spent a lifetime in the presence of powerful people, mostly men, and wasn't shy with an expletive or two. Dee also liked how she'd put Hubie in his place with a well-timed remark.

"What can I get you for breakfast?"

"Maybe just some coffee for now, Dee, thanks," Jane replied. She knew what was coming, however. She knew that Dee would tell her soon that she needed to eat something. Maybe she'd have some cereal in a few minutes.

As Dee poured Jane a cup of coffee and retrieved the cream from the refrigerator, Jane took a long look at her father's girlfriend. This woman was fit and stylish—striking even. She was sixty-seven friggin' years old but didn't look it. What was it about Dad? How did he attract women of Dee's caliber? Well, he'd always had an eye for beautiful women, because Donna after all was stunning in her time.

"You know, Dee, I think this is the first time we've been alone since I got back. And I've wanted to say thank you for everything you've done for me—and for Joanne. And, of course, for my father."

Dee put her hands in the air.

"You're very welcome, dear, but it's not necessary," she replied. "You girls are like daughters to me. You know, I never had any daughters."

"Dad said your boys...one's in Seattle and the other is where? Denver, I think he said?"

Dee nodded.

"Yes, Jeff and James are a little older than you girls and are doing well. I'm a grandmother three times over now too, but I don't get to see them as much as I'd like. Both my sons and their families came here last year for about ten days, and it was very nice. We lived in Utica for years, but after my husband died, I decided to come home. I was born here, after all. Got the office manager's job at the VFW. That's where your father and I met."

Jane smiled at the older woman.

"You're so different from my mother, Dee," she said. "And it's clear to me that you and Dad get along well."

"Well, your dad is a good man, Jane...when you get to know him—"

Dee stopped short. She'd realized that she may have gone too far. But Jane wasn't insulted.

"I'm sorry," Dee said.

"That's okay. I have been AWOL for a long time, and it's true, I don't know my father as well as I should."

Dee took a seat at the table.

"Well, that might be true, Jane," she said. Maybe now was the time to speak up, she thought.

"You know, there are a couple of things you should know about your father," Dee said. "One is that he respects other peoples' privacy, and I think that's what he did in your sister's case. He and I both had suspicions about Denny and saw how mean he could be to her. But Hubert felt—rightly or wrongly—that it was between them. That he shouldn't intervene...I think he regrets that now, though."

Jane listened intently, trying to understand her father's rationale—or excuse might be a better word—for failing to step in. Perhaps she'd never understand why her father had never intervened. But Dee's explanation made some sense.

"And the second?" Jane asked.

Dee paused. Jane knew she was carefully crafting her words.

"The second, in my opinion—and this is only my opinion and so you can take it for what it is—is that your father was a defeated man, Jane. Now...I'm not here to disparage your mom. I would never do that. I have no ulterior motive in this. Your father and I are good friends, and I'm not looking for anything more from him. But from all our conversations, it was clear to me that he lived with a very controlling, dominant woman. It's been a long time since she's been gone, and if he says anything, it's usually something nice. But he was a browbeaten guy for a long time, and when I would ask about it, or why he didn't leave, he'd just say that he would never have inflicted a divorce on you girls...or break up your family."

Dee took a long look at Jane. She wondered if she was getting through to her. She had touched many nerves but had hoped she wasn't out of line.

"In many ways, your dad lived a life of quiet desperation, Jane," she said. "I think that's why he went off by himself to fish or hunt, especially when you and your sister were very young. He told me that every time he tried to be a father, Donna would step in and put an end to it."

Jane's head had dropped. She was now staring at the kitchen floor. The older woman continued.

"I'm sorry, Jane," Dee said. "I guess I'm out of line."

"No, you're not...Dee," Jane said, finally. "You're simply confirming what I figured was true all along. Some crappy memories..."

Jane remained silent for a few moments, digesting what Dee had told her. It was making some sense to her now. Her father was a victim as well. Donna was a shrew, and Jane didn't know whether she could forgive her or not. She had pulled the triggers on Denny. But was she finally dealing with her mother too? An awful thought, but could it be true?

"I'm starting to understand, Dee," Jane replied. "But I wish he could have found a little backbone somewhere along the line…that's all."

Dee returned to the refrigerator and removed a frozen casserole from the freezer. She knew her words had resonated with Jane. But the younger woman let it go. Instead, Jane changed the subject.

"I feel bad for Joanne," Jane said. "Brent's taking all of this pretty hard, and I feel responsible for it."

"Don't beat yourself up, dear," she said, and Jane sensed that she too felt no sorrow for Denny's fate. "What's done is done."

Jane took another sip of her coffee. The conversation switched to the bitter reunion between Joanne and her son a few weeks before. As Dee recounted Brent's vitriolic tirade, Jane wished she could sit down with the kid and knock some sense into him. She would set him straight; it wasn't his mother's fault and Brent shouldn't make her pay twice.

"She hasn't gone back into her house, has she?" Jane asked.

"No, but Hubert has. To get her a few things. Too many memories, I suppose. When she got home from the mountains, I heard her mumble something like, 'where can I get a can of gasoline?'"

"I don't blame her," Jane said.

Jane shifted in her kitchen chair. The pain in her chest had worsened, and she sensed she was losing the battle. No telling what will happen in the coming days or weeks, she thought. After a long pause, Jane spoke.

"Dee, when I was in the hospital, I asked one of my nurses to wheel me down to the gift shop. I have something in my room that I'd like to show you. Can I ask you a small favor?"

FIFTY-FIVE

It was shortly after seven by the time Joanne got home after a long day on her feet at the store. She entered the kitchen and was greeted by her father and Dee, who had just finished eating their dinner. Politely declining Dee's offer to make her a plate, Joanne proceeded down the hall in the direction of Jane's room.

The door was closed, and Joanne knocked gently. She had hoped she hadn't awakened her sister from one of her long naps. Jane was in nearly a constant state of exhaustion these days, and she didn't want to disturb her. But from the other side of the door she heard a sound.

"Door's open," Jane said.

Joanne peered inside and noticed that Jane was sitting in her chair. Opposite her La-Z-Boy sat another armchair that Hubie had installed. Her television was on, and it was tuned to one of the cable channels. She could see that some sort of political panel was engaged in conversation—ranting, raving and screaming actually—about the presidential race. Joanne had always tuned these kinds of shows out.

"How's our guy doing?" Joanne asked, pointing to the TV. Just then, a live shot of Governor Foley popped up. He was holding a town hall meeting in some small Iowa town, and taking questions from the farmers in the audience. He had made something like fourteen or fifteen trips to the Hawkeye State over the past year-and-a-half and, in the process, had become popular. The Iowa farmers especially loved him. No other candidate knew—or cared—about the whole-sale price of milk.

Jane muted the sound of the television.

"Not bad," she replied. "He launched his campaign two weeks ago in Hyde Park. Took my advice and wrapped himself in Roosevelt's aura while positioning himself as the next JFK. Not a bad mix if I do say so myself."

Joanne smiled.

"Patting yourself on the back, are you?"

Jane shrugged.

"He's on top of all the polls, where I think he'll stay if he doesn't screw it up. I speak with Marcia once in awhile. There is some speculation that he's going to resign as governor so he can go at this full-time. Which is what I advised him to do a long time ago."

Joanne signaled her indifference, even boredom, with the topic. She had no use for politics but knew that it was a central part of her sister's DNA. She couldn't help herself. It was an addiction.

Jane changed the subject.

"How was your day?" she asked. Jane had always felt that Joanne could have done anything she'd wanted. That is, if she hadn't gotten mixed up with Denny as a teenager. Never mind Donna wanting to be a doctor. Joanne could have gone further.

"It was a long one, that's for sure," she replied. "I guess everybody in this town just realized that Christmas is only a few days away, and they're in panic mode. Seen it before. Of course, it's good for Darryl. Music to his ears."

"Dad says he's a nice man," Jane said. "And that he fancies you a bit, too...always has, apparently."

Joanne shook her head.

"Don't go there, sister. I'm through with men."

Jane smiled.

"You know what, Jo? I don't believe that for a minute, and I don't think you do either. In fact, you might be just getting started with your life."

"Well, some day you're gonna have to tell me about the eighty or ninety guys that came before Rob," Joanne said, flashing a half-grin. "Now that would be a story."

"Not really," Jane replied. "First, the number is nowhere near that high—I should've been so lucky? Second, until Roberto came along, they were pretty insignificant. Oh, when I was working in Rochester, there was one guy who nearly landed me. If that's the way to put it."

"Really?" Joanne asked. "There is so much of your life that I don't know…"

Her voice trailed off.

Jane nodded in agreement. The twins had been absent from each other's lives for a long time.

"Well, his name was Jack Dobie. He taught at the university and was hotter 'n hell—"

"—couldn't have been hotter 'n Alvarez!" Joanne responded.

"Well, no. No one was as smokin' hot as Rob, but Jack wasn't too bad either."

"What happened to him?"

"Well, Dobie's problem was that he was boring. A nice guy for sure, and he wanted to marry me, but I guess I just turned him away like the others."

"Like Roberto?" Joanne asked.

"In some ways, yes…"

"Why?"

Jane shrugged. "I don't know, Jo. Maybe I never trusted any of them. I don't know."

Joanne let the comment pass but felt she knew why. Maybe that night of the party twenty years ago—that Fourth of July party—provided more than a few answers.

"Jack was a physics professor and, well, he wouldn't have worked out. Hell, I wasn't like you. I barely passed physics in high school. What would we have talked about? He wanted a house in the 'burbs with a pool and a garden... and a litter. Can you imagine me with a litter? Stab me now."

Joanne disagreed.

"I think you would have done well with kids, Jane," she said. "Children have an effect on everyone, including you. I saw that when you met Makenna for the first time. I saw it loud and clear."

Jane shrugged.

"Well, guess we'll never know. So, anyway, I never really settled down." She paused again. "I always hated that word...settled."

"Yeah, I guess I'd agree with that," was all Joanne could say.

Their talk of men seemed to resonate with the both of them. But Jane's comments seemed to strike a chord with her sister; Joanne had wasted nearly two decades with Denny and now it was her turn to be now miles away in thought. Jane decided to tread softly, but tread she did.

"Dee shared some stuff with me, today, Jo," she began. She told her sister about Dee's view of their father and the life he had led with Donna. Dad had a choice too, she said. He could have left Donna. But he chose not to because that would have meant hurting them. It would have meant breaking up the family.

She was almost whispering now, continuing her monologue.

"Jo...you and Dad were both among the walking wounded," she said. "Only Denny took that abuse to such an extreme. But you both suffered. That's the only word for it."

Jane watched as her sister stared off into space. Joanne was still overwhelmed by the events of the past month and the lies that had consumed her adult life. She reminded Jane of the young women—mere girls, actually—that she covered as a reporter in Rochester. She resembled those timid and destroyed teens from the city's housing projects who cowered at the doors of their tenement apartments when she asked them where their drug-dealing, scumbag boyfriends were.

It was the worst job of her life and yet perhaps her best. They were the innocent victims of crime. But she was an idealist. If one story could save a single life, she knew her work was worthwhile. Perhaps she was simply naïve; for every life redeemed, another five or ten tragedies ensued. But she had believed she was making a difference, and it kept her going.

Now Joanne was one of those girls. Lost, terrified and hurt. She sat there in silence, grateful to Jane for dropping the subject weeks before but knowing, deep down, that she'd eventually have to open up.

To share a few details. About her life with Denny.

In an instant, Joanne made her decision. It was time.

Now was the time.

She spoke. In near whispers.

"At first, it was just a slap," she said, her voice quivering with fear. "And then he apologized over and over and said he'd never do it again. But he did...he hit me again, and it really hurt. But you know what? Denny was smart about it. Well, until the last time, maybe, when he hit me on the face and busted up my lip. But mostly, he'd hit me where it wouldn't show...on my back, on my shoulders. He always said he was sorry after, but it didn't stop..."

Joanne's tears were streaming down her face but she continued.

"But right after that he'd turn around and tell me that I was a worthless piece of shit...that no one else but him would ever want me. Let alone love me. And I believed him. I started to believe that I deserved what he was doing to me. Then, I don't know why but...he'd switch gears and say that he didn't deserve *me*."

Jane decided to speak up.

"Why—?"

"—didn't I leave?"

"Yeah."

"How could I, Jane? I only make about five hundred bucks a week, plus a few more at the café. How could I have supported Brent and myself on that kind of money? I guess I could've moved in with Dad, but Denny probably would've dragged me home...telling Dad to mind his own effing business. Once I heard about some shelter over in the next county but I was afraid he would've found me there too. Maybe even kill me. He always said he would. Or at least he would've stolen Brent away from me. When he was little. After Brent grew up and left for school, I don't know why I stayed...I have no answers."

Joanne took a deep breath. It was clear she wasn't through.

"He was such an angry man most of the time. I should've known that from high school but then I became pregnant... well, even before that, when he broke his leg and lost his football scholarship. That's why he was so jealous of Brent. Brent got the chance that he didn't. Instead, he became a septic man and started drinking heavier and heavier...every day. That's when he really started hitting me. You know, he told my friends, like Jennie, to eff off and don't come back.

And she didn't. But we'd talk once in awhile. I could hear the pity in her voice. He took my paychecks every week... saying I didn't know shit about money. I got that part-time job at the restaurant...well, to get away from him mostly but also to hide some money. You saw my Christmas Club tin... at that *friggin'* motel."

She paused for a moment. "And of course I knew about all his skanks...like that Mandy person down at the Paddle..."

Her voice stopped. She was done.

Jane just sat there in silence and shock. An overwhelming sense of sadness and guilt came over her. She had fled Morgantown in anger and recrimination while Joanne had stayed behind and suffered. If she had been a sister to Joanne—a *real* sibling for the past twenty years—Jane might have put an end to Denny's horseshit a long time ago.

But then she remembered Roberto's sage words about regret. It *was* a useless emotion. She couldn't do anything about the lost decades. Joanne had been in denial for so many years and might still be if Jane hadn't decided to come home. If she hadn't shot him dead, too. Joanne was just now acknowledging her problem. She was taking the first step to healing. She was courageous.

The sisters sat there in silence.

Both knew that they had crossed the great divide and had waded through some of the pain and humiliation.

"I should've been here for you, Jo," Jane finally said. "But at the same time I'm so proud of you. I can only imagine how hard it was for you to tell me that..."

Joanne regained her composure.

"Water under the bridge now," she said, firmly. "That part of my life is over. I just have to try and figure out where to go next, that's all."

Jane turned her head away and peered out the window. It was another winter night in the shadows of the Adirondacks. Another snowfall had begun, and out across the barren yards that separated their two houses, she could see the outline of Joanne's decaying and now abandoned home.

Her pain had worsened, and she could feel her lungs filling. Her daily cocktails of drugs were simply staving off the inevitable, she thought, and this made her even more resolute. Unwavering, almost stubborn, she was determined to complete her mission. She turned to face her sister again.

"Jo, about that Fourth of July party at the lake," she began.

"No, Jane, you don't have to go there…anymore."

"No, Jo…I do. I told Rob all about it too."

"You did?"

"Yes, he needed to know. *I* needed him to know."

Joanne exhaled loudly.

"And for Makenna's sake as well," Jane continued. "I called her in Plattsburgh today. I felt she deserved to hear the truth."

Jane paused a moment.

"And so do you."

FIFTY-SIX

Roberto reached into the back seat of his Infiniti and retrieved a couple of shopping bags, deciding to return later for his luggage. He knew that he had to leave the city and join Jane in Morgantown. In his twice daily calls, he realized that her health was not improving and that it was time to be with her. More than once, he had offered to suspend his law practice in New York to spend all of December, or what was left of it, with her. But she declined each time. Argentina, she would say, someone has to keep those Wall Street crooks from going to jail, and it may as well as be you.

The heavy rains of Manhattan had changed to light snow about half-way up the Hudson Valley, but the road crews had kept the Interstate in good shape. About two hours south of Morgantown, the skies had cleared, and Roberto decided to exit the Thruway at Herkimer before turning northeast into the foothills. He delighted in his decision. It was a winter spectacle, and the journey paid splendorous dividends. Residents here reveled in the season, and it showed. Main Streets, now packed with snow, were adorned with sparkling lights and frantic, smiling shoppers were everywhere. This was George Bailey country, he thought.

His arms weighed down with gifts, Roberto was walking towards the house when a woman he recognized as Jane's hospice worker greeted him. He had enormous respect for the former emergency room nurse. She was in the right job.

"Hi Carol," he said. "Still making house calls, even if it's Christmas Eve."

She shrugged.

"In my line of work, Mr. Alvarez, holidays are the same as every other day, I'm afraid," she replied. "And I'll be back tomorrow as well. And probably the next day, too."

He smiled grimly. Nurses performed the difficult, unheralded work at the patient level. They were the unsung heroes of the system.

"How's our patient today?"

"Not very good, I'm sorry to say, Mr. Alvarez," she replied. "Her cancer has spread, unfortunately, to just about everywhere in her body. The Albany doctors said as much a few weeks ago. That's why she's so weak and frail...and it's all I can do to keep her pain to a minimum. But she's a tough little nut. She's a fighter. I just wish she had paid more attention to her symptoms a long time ago. We might have—"

She didn't finish her sentence, and Roberto understood why. Jane had been consumed by her job in the governor's office. She had been fixated, obsessively so, on the campaign, and nothing—not even signs of looming illness—distracted her. He was about to ask the ultimate question but decided against it. Carol's warm, empathetic eyes told the story.

"Thank you, Carol, for everything you've done for Jane."

"Well, I can't say it's my pleasure...because there is certainly no pleasure in these situations, other than to make the best of a lousy situation."

He reached for her hand, kissed her on the cheek and said good-bye. Roberto looked around the driveway. Hubie's truck was gone, and Roberto suspected both he and Dee, perhaps anticipating his arrival, were still grocery shopping. He made his way up the back steps and into the house, and found Jane resting in a comfortable chair on the front porch. Hubie had kept the glass sliding doors to the living room open, but

for good measure, he brought in a portable heater. Roberto
noticed it was oscillating and the room was pleasant. Jane
loved to wheel herself to the porch to take advantage of the
southerly sunshine, and today she was basking in it.

"Happy Santa!" Roberto said, announcing his arrival.
Jane turned and smiled in his direction.

"A holly-jolly to you, too, my gorgeous man!"

Reaching for her hands, Roberto squatted to make eye
level contact with Jane. They kissed gently. Her voice was
raspy now, and she struggled with every breath. Next to
her chair he saw tubes attached to an oxygen tank. He was
saddened, momentarily, by the sight of her but remembered
the vital, beautiful woman before him. He knew that he was
looking into her soul.

"I guess I've spent too much time in the city," he replied.
"I've forgotten just how beautiful upstate New York can be at
this time of year. It was a very nice drive today."

Jane shrugged.

"I prefer Negril myself," she said. "Give me a beach and
a piña colada any day."

"How could we forget?" he asked. "That night at Grand
Lido? And remember that Bob Seger song?"

Jane laughed.

"Sunspot Baby!"

Then they both broke into song, something about *'looking
into Miami and looking at Negril but the closest they came was a
month-old bill.'* Their melodies were so bad that even a kara-
oke bartender would have been embarrassed. But no matter.
It was a warmly shared memory. One that seemed a lifetime
away yet was measured only in months.

For Jane, something had clicked after that humid afternoon at the swim-up bar overlooking the tranquil, turquoise
seas of the Caribbean. Roberto was so unlike the others before

him. But for the longest time she couldn't pinpoint why. Surprisingly, she'd had his love and respect; why, she didn't know, given her inability to commit to him, and certainly her bizarre behavior of late didn't help.

But she'd had both, and that pleased her. However, Jane needed a man whom she could like. It was one thing to love a man. But it was more important to *like* him, and Rob fit that bill nicely. His feelings, she felt, were reciprocal and unconditional. Rob liked her for who she was, and nothing could change that.

That was why she had decided to trust Alvarez with her past. She knew that he wouldn't judge her or ultimately dismiss her as tainted goods. She had trusted Rob with her emotions and he hadn't abandoned her.

"You're too good to me, Argentina," she said.

"You're not too bad yourself," Roberto replied.

"I try, Rob, I try...well, some people think I'm very trying."

"No way, babe...you're one of a kind. I realized that in Jamaica and have known that ever since."

Jane took a long affectionate look into her boyfriend's eyes.

"I love you, Rob," she said.

"I love you too, Jane."

Then he reached under her arms and lifted Jane from her chair and carried her to the couch nearby. She removed her link to her oxygen tank and dropped it to the floor. Gently, they came to rest with her in his lap. They kissed again.

"Well, in that case, you can't deny me one request, can you?" she asked, smiling. "One totally selfish, Jane-being-Jane request?"

She told him.

Roberto smiled and said he could do better than that.

He reached into his jacket pocket and retrieved a small, blue velvet box. It was the gift that he had picked out many weeks before during his shopping travels to 47th Street in Manhattan.

The next day, on a beautifully cold and clear Christmas Day, a kindly justice of the peace arrived at the house. At the request of his pal, the retired postmaster, he was making a special visit. And about fifteen minutes after his arrival, he intoned a few familiar words.

"...and, now, by the power invested in me by Morgan County and the Great State of New York, I now pronounce you husband and wife...and this is my favorite part...you may kiss your beautiful bride!"

With Dee and Hubie smiling by their sides, Joanne popped the cork on a '95 Cristal and the fine champagne bubbled over. She handed the first crystal goblets to her newly-married sister and her beaming husband.

"This ain't Johnny Walker Red, sister, but it'll have to do!" she said.

Jane smiled weakly at her sister, and pointed to the old Baldwin in the corner.

"Will you play a song for me?"

FIFTY-SEVEN

Jane died on New Year's Day.

Alone, as was probably her plan, Joanne thought. No muss, no fuss, no sentimentality whatsoever, doing what Joanne and Roberto had figured she wanted to do. Both had taken turns holding bedside vigils, especially after Jane began to fall in and out of consciousness. But late on the one day of the year when most people were vowing to make major changes to their lives, Jane had decided enough was enough. Joanne had left the room for a couple of minutes to make herself a cup of tea, only to return to find that her sister had called it quits. Through their tears, Roberto reminded Joanne that Jane always did things her way.

Right to the end.

They held her service on a windswept January day in Morgantown, but the inclement weather didn't stop Jane's friends and colleagues from around the country from attending. Joanne asked Dee if they could use the VFW hall—the biggest in town—to say good-bye to her sister. Although it was never mentioned, Joanne sensed that Jane was probably an atheist, or at least agnostic, and so a funeral at Joanne's church was out of the question. It was a good choice; twenty minutes after the memorial was to set to begin, the line outside the hall was still about sixty or seventy strong.

Marcia Bell had informed Joanne that her boss, the presidential contender, would attend and to expect a large media pool and other campaign officials as well. Plan for an onslaught, she said. But she and others would direct traffic.

As the service wound down and mourners trooped slowly from the cavernous hall and into the bar, Joanne joined Roberto, Hubie and Dee to form a greeting line. They were also joined by Roberto's parents, Ricardo and Rosaria, who had travelled from New York to mourn a woman they had met only once at a family picnic on Long Island. Two of Roberto's sisters were also there, with their husbands.

From over her shoulder, Joanne could see the governor surrounded by reporters and later, as she watched the news, saw a clip of the candidate as he told voters how much he admired and respected Jane. A heartwarming and brave gesture, she thought, and probably dangerous politically too. After all, Jane had been charged with second-degree murder. He could have sent his regards, but as Marcia told her, Foley didn't care about the possible political fallout from attending the funeral of one of his closest confidants.

Hubie was watching with mild bemusement. He had never been in the same room with such a famous person and decided to introduce himself. He walked over to the candidate and waited as Foley wrapped up yet another conversation. Finally, the governor noticed Jane's father by his side and turned to him. He held out his hand to the older man.

"Mr. Schumacher, I'm Wendell Foley," he said. "I'm honored to meet you. But I'm very sorry for your loss...well, *our* loss."

Hubie was briefly taken aback by the Democrat's warmth.

"Thank you, Governor, it's nice to meet you too," Hubie said. "I know you're a busy man but I wanted to say to you, personally, how much my family and I appreciate you coming here today."

"Well, sir, Jane was a very special person in my life and in the lives of everybody who worked with her, and so we wanted to be here. Your daughter was a wonderful woman, and we're all going to miss her...very much."

Hubie became emotional, and it obviously showed. The governor had called him 'sir'. They had shared a quiet moment of reflection. Foley, noticing the effect that he was having, tried to lighten the situation.

"Jane told me that you've never had any time for Democrats," he said with a smile.

"That's true, Governor."

"She also said that you liked to call me a socialist who wants to be king?" The Democrat was now having a bit of fun.

Hubie grimaced.

"Guilty as charged," he replied. "But don't you wanna be king?"

Foley laughed.

"Has a nice ring to it, I must admit. But any chance of me changing your mind?"

"Possibly," Hubie replied.

"Then can I count on your vote?"

"I didn't say that, Governor."

And they both broke into laughter, which wasn't lost on the rest of the mourners standing solemnly throughout the VFW hall. They shook hands, smiled once again, and Hubie resumed his place in line.

Slowly the well-wishers made their way to Joanne. Many were locals, like Darryl from the store and a number of her regulars, like Whitey, the deer butcher, who had donned a garish, copper-colored corduroy suit that looked like it came from the same Salvation Army racks where Joanne had been forced to shop. The suit was covered with hair that looked like it had originated from his golden Labrador retriever.

But Joanne didn't mind what he was wearing. Whitey was a good and gentle man.

There were many others in attendance that Joanne didn't recognize as well; reporters from Jane's time as press secretary, her old boss at *CBS Rochester* and members of the candidate's staff. Over in the hallway, Joanne noticed Boychuk in his full-dress uniform, standing by himself. She briefly scanned the room for Susan, his wife, but couldn't spot her. Maybe she couldn't make it, Joanne concluded. She glanced again at Boychuk, who looked lonely and lost and, immediately, she felt sorry for her friend of two decades. Was Jane his first and only love?

Finally, the sheriff made his way to Joanne's side.

"Jo, for the life of me, I just can't believe any of this," he said, fighting back tears. "This wasn't the way things were supposed to unfold."

Joanne smiled. She understood. After being away for so long, Jane had only just reentered both their lives, and now she was gone.

"I know, Brian...I know how you feel," she replied. "I don't think Jane could believe it either." They gave each other a long-lasting embrace. They both knew the answer to her earlier question.

Just then, Boychuk felt a tap on his shoulder. A young, elegantly-dressed woman was standing behind him. It was Makenna.

Joanne noticed her too, and a smile crept across her face. Jane had mentioned that she'd called Makenna and her parents, and they knew what had transpired. It all came into focus now, and a wave of happiness overcame Joanne. One of her prayers had been answered. Makenna had come to say good-bye to the mother she never knew.

The two women locked eyes and smiled at each other. Both suddenly felt a strong bond. For a brief moment, both were transported back to that Lake Placid ski store. No words were spoken. The warmth in Joanne's eyes said it all.

Then Makenna turned her attention to the sheriff. There was another, equally profound reason that she was here.

"Excuse me, but are you Sheriff Brian Boychuk?" the younger woman asked.

"Yes, I am."

"My name is Makenna Monteith. I met Jane Schumacher in Lake Placid in November. My parents over there—" Pausing for a moment, she pointed to an attractive couple in their early fifties who were standing by themselves in an opposite corner of the hall. They were watching the scene unfold between the police officer and their daughter.

"—thought I should introduce myself."

Witnessing the interchange, Joanne knew the rest of the story.

She spoke up.

"Brian, perhaps you and Makenna should talk…away from here," she said, pointing towards the anxious parents looking on.

"She has something very important to say to you."

A curious expression came over Boychuk. Reluctantly, he agreed and joined the young woman as they walked towards her parents.

The greeting line was thinning as mourners retreated in the direction of the VFW's bar next door. Both Joanne and Roberto knew that Jane would have insisted on buying a few rounds, and Dee had arranged for extra bartenders to handle their thirsty friends.

Suddenly, at the entrance to the corridor, Joanne saw another familiar face. It was Brent. He was with Tracy. They were wearing winter coats, and Joanne couldn't figure out whether they had just arrived or they were about to leave. Fifty feet apart, mother and son stood staring at each other. Noticing the look on both their faces, Tracy moved closer to her boyfriend and whispered a few words in his ear. He began to walk towards Joanne. Arriving at the line, they locked eyes in silence.

Finally, Brent spoke up.

"I'm sorry, Mom...I'm so sorry," he said, breaking into tears.

"I know, honey, I know," she replied, wrapping her arms around her son. She was determined not to cry again, but the sight of her son overwhelmed her. "I am too."

Brent tried to contain his emotions.

"I know now, Mom, how much you've been hurt by all of this. I know now just how *wrong* I was to blame you for any of this."

Reaching into his jacket pocket, Brent retrieved a yellow piece of paper and handed it to his mother. Immediately, Joanne recognized the note. It was the one that Jane had scribbled outside her son's Syracuse apartment on the morning after Denny's shooting.

"I just found this in our apartment—only this morning, Mom," he said. "I wasn't going to come to Aunt Jane's funeral but Tracy and I talked. We felt that we needed to be here."

She kissed him on the cheek.

"I'm so glad you came, honey," she said, as she unfolded her sister's note and began to read it.

Dear Brent,

I'm sorry I've been absent from your life for so long. There are reasons why I did what I did. But they don't matter now. What does matter is the truth. Our family secrets must end. Your mom needs you now—more than ever. She loves you so much Brent. So, please love her back....

Aunt Jane.

Joanne read the note several times before slowly refolding it and handing it back to her son. She looked into Brent's eyes and told him she loved him. He reached for his mother and wrapped his arms around her.

"What did Aunt Jane mean Mom?" he asked finally. "What are these secrets she's talking about?"

She peered into his eyes and then looked away. She took a deep breath before answering.

"Can you come home after all this is over?"

Brent nodded.

"Your Aunt Jane was right. We need to talk...later."

Brent hugged his mother again before pulling away and smiling.

"Okay. But one more question, Mom. What did you do to your hair?"

FIFTY-EIGHT

Joanne awoke with a jolt.

She'd had the dream again. And it was Denny... again. Virtually the same one over and over. But this time it was slightly different. Its ending, was...different. It had changed.

Once again, they were riding in his septic truck, and they were swerving wildly all over the gravel road, fish-tailing. As in the previous, recurring versions, few threatening words were uttered—at the beginning. She just stared into Denny's dark, menacing eyes, and they frightened her.

The enormous pumper crashed through a railing and into the fast-flowing river. As in the past similar dreams, Joanne remained unfazed, calmly rolling down her passenger window, allowing the icy waters of the Oswegatchie to rush in. Once again, she had escaped, pushing herself to the surface.

Then his vulgar demands for help began to be heard.

Why can't you save me, you bitch?

His demands grew louder, but Denny's face was nowhere to be seen—only the outline of a lone, outstretched hand bobbing above the surface of the water. This time, however, she did not plunge below in search of him. This time she watched his hand as it rose—again and again and again— above the surface, only to finally disappear.

She could not save him.

She would not save him.

She would only save herself. And as she struggled to the river's edge, a warm, comforting sensation came over her. She didn't feel wet.

Then she woke up and remembered where she was—in her old room at her father's house. Rising from the bed, she walked to the window and peered out. It was still dark. Outside, the snow that had fallen quickly and heavily in the afternoon of Jane's funeral had stopped, and a clear, full moon illuminated the skies. She looked at the digital clock on the dresser; it read four-thirty-one. She listened for sounds in the old house, but there were none. Dad must be out plowing, she surmised. Tracy and Brent were still asleep. There was total quiet.

I have to do this, she told herself.

It is time...*it is time*. To go back in.

Now. Not tomorrow or the next day or the next month.

Now!

Flicking on her lamp beside her bed, Joanne walked to the closet and found a pair of jeans and a sweatshirt, and before she knew it, she was trudging through the deep snow in the direction of her deserted house. Hubie had kept the driveway clean to allow the propane man to make his deliveries. But he didn't shovel the steps and porch, and at least sixteen inches of snow had blanketed the stoop. Pulling the screen door open and pushing back the snow, she opened the kitchen door. It wasn't locked. Why bother?

She reached for the light switch and turned it on.

The first thing that she noticed was how frigid it felt in the house. She knew that her father set the thermostat at forty-one degrees, enough to prevent the pipes from freezing, and she could see her breath. It was almost as cold inside as it was out.

Joanne took a moment to scan her kitchen. It was exactly as she had left it that night. Dishes that she'd washed after their disastrous family dinner were still in the drainer, including all the pots and pans, the turkey roaster and a few wine glasses that hadn't become victims of the rampage.

She remembered it all now. Dan and Marjory, embarrassed, had made a hasty departure. She'd just finished cleaning her kitchen, with some help from Dee before the elderly woman bid her good-bye, when Denny launched his tirade. Over the past weeks, this had been a blur; she considered herself a good wife and a decent housekeeper, and she had wondered what everyone—Boychuk and his deputies, his CSIs, the coroner maybe—had thought of her.

Without removing her boots, Joanne walked slowly from the kitchen to the hallway. As she predicted, the police had removed the old family photo from the hall, and in its place was a faded outline where the frame had once been. She walked to another light switch and turned it on.

Suddenly she heard that voice again.

Denny's voice.

Your house too? That's a goddamn joke, and you know it, Jo. You're nothin' but a clerk in a two-bit hardware store!

Joanne stopped in her tracks, trembling.

The house felt even colder, and despite her thick, woolen winter coat, she was freezing. But she soldiered on toward the entrance to the dining room. She was about to make the turn when Denny returned.

This is my house, and you better not forget it…the house that shit built.

My shit!

Then she felt the pain again. It was returning.

It was the feeling of her ponytail yanked violently back, followed by the sound of a scream. Her scream. Maybe this wasn't a good idea, she thought. Maybe I should get out of here?

No! I have to do this.

Then she felt the blow, the swift backhand delivered by her monstrous husband, a fierce slap across her face. Once again, she was flying across the room amid memories of dishes crashing and glasses breaking. She remembered her mother's church plate teetering. Once again, she could taste the blood trickling from a swollen lip.

Another voice!

This time it was Jane's.

Hit her again asshole, and I'll blow your sorry-ass brains all the way to Buffalo!

Joanne felt weak and propped herself up against the wall for a moment. She felt almost faint, but she continued on around the corner. Strange, there's no broken glass. Well, what I thinking? Boychuk's people cleaned it up. Of course they did.

Jane again.

You heard me asswipe! Get away from her, or I swear I'll blow your fucking head off!

Joanne recovered some of her strength and stood there.

Staring at the wall, she could still see the stains of Denny's blood. It looked as though Boychuk's investigators had tried to wipe the walls and the floors clean. But their efforts proved fruitless. What once had been red had turned to black. This house could use a good paint job, she thought.

No, it should be bulldozed over.

Denny's voice continued to haunt her. His venom toward Jane returned.

You shouldn't be stickin' your nose in other people's affairs, city bitch!

It was all coming back, and Joanne was nearly in tears. Tears of shock and pain.

Jane again.

...what did you call me?

The shots...the force blasted Denny against the wall.

His eyes bulging.

The look of stunned disbelief on his face.

Her last memory. There he was, sitting up, his head slumped, his eyes open.

It all came back.

Joanne took a deep breath and told herself that she could do this. That she would survive. Still weak, she pulled a chair out from under the dining room table and sat down. And for a few moments she continued to gaze, mesmerized and unblinking, at the scene before her.

Then, in a barely audible whimper, she spoke.

"You know, Denny, I could sit here and call you every name in the book. And tell you that I hope you *rot* in hell... for what you did to me, for so long. And for what you did to our son...and to Jane, *especially* Jane. But I'm not gonna do that. I want to be better than that...and be better than you. No! I *know* I'm better!"

She paused for a moment to reflect on what she was saying.

"You know, Denny, for so long...so, so long, you had me believing that I was nothing. Less than nothing, even. Well, Denny, I'm *not* nothing. Not anymore!"

She rose from the chair, took one final look at the wall and marched out of the house.

FIFTY-NINE

Brent and Tracy finished lighting the last of the forty candles and carried the tacky, turquoise-frosted cake into the kitchen. Simultaneously they broke into the birthday song, and Dee and Hubie happily joined in. Finishing the tune with a hoot and a howl, Brent placed the cake on the table, reached over to his mother and planted a big kiss on her cheek.

Joanne burst out laughing.

"I've never heard so many people sing so badly," she said, reaching for cutlery and plates. "So, so bad!"

Brent grinned widely.

"Happy birthday, Mom," he said, turning to everyone. "But I can't believe my mother is so old!"

Joanne looked up and waved a cake knife at him.

"Watch it, kid," she warned. "You know what they say? Forty is the new twenty-five!"

"Which makes you about five, Brent!" Tracy piped in.

Joanne was about to start cutting the cake, when Brent continued.

"Wait a minute! Aren't you supposed to make a wish?"

Joanne smiled at her son and scanned the room to acknowledge the rest of her family.

"I already did, baby, and it's already come true," she said, pausing briefly to take in the special moment. "But enough of this! Who wants a piece of blue sugar?"

Moments earlier, Dee had gone to the refrigerator and retrieved the last bottle of the '95 Cristal left over from Jane and Roberto's wedding night. Joanne had wanted to save it for an extraordinary occasion, and to Dee, what better time than a fortieth birthday? Hubie, of course, preferred his own version of imported bubbly, a Labatt's Blue.

She had poured each a glass of the fine wine and offered a toast.

"To Joanne," she said, affectionately and simply, their wine glasses clinking together.

Dee watched as Brent became engaged in conversation with his grandfather, and overheard predictions by the young man that Buffalo might finally figure out a way to win the Stanley Cup. Dream on, young man, Hubie replied. The Sabres are in the same leaky boat as the Bills, and you know how they loved losing Super Bowls. Brent was about to protest when Hubie advised him to follow a real sport.

"You mean basketball? You call that a sport? Why don't they just give both teams a hundred points and play for two minutes?"

Hubie feigned surprise.

"And you call yourself an *Orangeman?*" he said. "I'm calling SU and have you expelled—for treachery!"

And they laughed.

Finally, Dee pulled Joanne aside.

"Joanne, I, uh, have something for you," she said.

"What? What do you mean?"

"From Jane."

"Jane?"

"Yes, come with me."

Dee led Joanne down the hall into the living room. A large gift bag with colorful tissue spilling from its top rested on the coffee table. Joanne looked at the gift and turned quizzically towards her friend.

"Jane asked me to give you this…today," Dee said. "It's her birthday too."

"Yes…it is," Joanne replied.

Dee knew it was an emotional moment for Joanne. Both she and Hubie had hoped that Jane would live long enough for her and Joanne to celebrate this once-in-a-lifetime day together, especially after everything they had been through. But it was for not. Fate, which had played such a central role in Jane's early life, had prevented it.

"You know, I think I'll leave this to you," the older woman said. "There's probably one last glass of bubbly back there with my name on it."

Joanne slowly sat down on the couch.

Removing the tissue from the bag, she found an envelope with her name on it. She placed it beside her. She then pulled the first gift from the bag. It was a small bottle of hair dye. A small, Post-It note was attached.

Joanne read it.

Take it from me! You'll look better as a brunette!

Joanne cracked up.

"City —"

She checked herself. Nope, not going there.

"Friggin' city girl!"

She pulled a second gift from the bag. Wrapped in a simple bow was a three-pack of Nicorettes. Another note.

These should help!

"You're too late, sister!" Joanne said, casting the gum on the couch. But after a pause, she changed her mind and retrieved them.

"Well, maybe not—"

At last Joanne came to the last present and pulled it from the bag. It was beautifully festooned with colorful clowns and balloons and topped with a silver bow. It too sported a short note that read bluntly:

Read my card first!

"Lord, she's still ordering me around!" Joanne muttered.

She opened the envelope and removed the card.

In elegant script, its cover read simply, *Thinking of you...* It made Joanne's heart skip a beat. She opened the card and she heard magically her sister's voice once again.

Jo, if you're reading this, it means you've turned forty and I haven't!

Joanne smiled to herself. Only Jane...

Her sister's voice continued.

Seriously, Jo, I wish I could be with you today... on our day. You and I have missed too many of these special times because...well, because maybe it was just easier for me to stay away. But my sister, my friend, I have cherished our last few weeks together. I got to know you again and to love you for who you are...I hope you will remember the wild times we had and that they might just put a smile on your face from time to time. You're free now, Jo, to be yourself and to be happy. That's an order!

Jane.

P.S. Never say never!

Fighting what she hoped were the last of her tears, Joanne closed the card and turned her attention to the exquisitely wrapped gift. She tore away the tissue. Her heart fluttered once again.

Inside was a miniature carousel, a colorfully hand-painted merry-go-round, complete with decorative horses and a wind-up track. She cranked the key and placed it on the coffee table in front of her. Instantly its horses began bobbing up and down, its unmistakable and familiar melodies reverberating throughout the room.

Joanne's tears slowly turned to smiles.

SIXTY

The next day, Dee steered her Honda Civic through the parking lot of Turnbull's and pulled up in front of the store. Joanne, now sporting stylishly-spiked brown hair, lipstick and mascara, was engrossed in a *New York Times* crossword.

"Here's one for you, Dee," Joanne said, her eyes glued to the newspaper. "Only 20th-century president without a college degree." She looked over a Dee at the wheel.

"That would have been a better question put to your sister," the older woman said. "But I think it's 'Truman.' I don't think he went to college."

Joanne scanned the crossword again.

"Doesn't fit. Three letters."

"Then try H.S.T.," Dee replied.

Joanne smiled. "That works."

She looked up and had noticed they had arrived at her hardware store.

"Thanks again, Dee," she said as she began to exit the car, her voice heavy with resignation. "One of these days, I'll figure out the answer to my transportation problems."

Dee returned her affection.

"Happy to do it," she said. "You know, though, you can always take Jane's nice car out of Hubert's garage and drive it. She left it to you, after all."

Joanne shook her head.

"That car, like my house, holds too many sad memories for me, Dee," Joanne replied. "Probably too fancy for me, anyway. You know me. I'm like my dad. I like trucks and SUVs. But…that car of hers, I must admit, is pretty sweet. Maybe in the spring I'll take it out for a whirl."

"Suit yourself, Jo," Dee replied.

As Joanne opened the door and head to work, Dee paused for a moment before speaking. She couldn't believe the transformation that had taken place in Joanne since they had met—and especially since the events of late November.

"By the way, I really like your hair."

Joanne beamed.

"Thanks Dee!" she replied.

Joanne felt a brief moment of exhilaration. Not many people had paid her compliments over the years, and it lifted her spirits. It was the second one today. To her enormous satisfaction, Brent announced that he and Tracy would be returning to Syracuse this morning to finish their degrees in business, and there was talk of graduate school at Cornell in the fall—for both. But before they left, Brent gave his mother a huge bear hug and told her she looked beautiful.

She said good-bye to Dee, walked into the store and was about to hang up her coat in a small closet behind her register when she heard Darryl's voice call out.

"Joanne, there's a phone call for you," he said.

"Me?"

"Yes, you. Is that so hard to believe?"

"Well, maybe."

He loved to tease her.

"In your office?"

Darryl nodded and pointed towards the corner of the store. She turned and walked into his office. Amid the paper and clutter on his desk, she noticed the receiver off the hook. She picked it up.

"Hello, this is Joanne Schumacher."

"Hello, sister-in-law. A happy belated, birthday to you!" It was Roberto on the phone from New York. He was sitting at his desk in lower Manhattan and was absorbed in yet another corporate merger.

"Thank you, Rob. We had a nice little celebration last night...if turning forty is a reason to celebrate, that is. But we also made a toast to Jane, too."

"Really, Jo, that was nice."

"I miss her so much, Rob, I really do."

"So do I Joanne. So do I."

There was a long pause between them. Both had come to the painful realization just how much Jane had meant to them. But both also knew that Jane would unleash a torrent of expletives if they continued to mourn.

"Anyway, I was calling to tell you that my colleague here at the firm just left my office. Evidently, he had a good conversation with the Morgan County DA this morning."

"When do I go to jail, Rob?"

"Not gonna happen, Joanne."

"What? What do you mean?"

"Good news. The DA's decided to reduce the charges. In fact, you won't even have to go to trial if you plead no contest out of court. She's recommending to the court that you get a six-month suspended sentence with some community service—with no criminal record either. And all your charity work for cancer certainly qualifies. Sound okay to you?"

Joanne was almost speechless. Her experience in that Saranac Lake dungeon was one she didn't want to repeat.

"Rob, I'm...shocked. That's all I can say. What happened?"

Roberto chuckled.

"Well, it seems that more than a few good people in town, including your sheriff friend, made their views known to the district attorney. To tell her that you might've been through enough? Hello? No kidding. If you had any sins, and I'm not saying you have, you've said enough *Hail Marys* and *Our Fathers*."

It was Joanne's turn to laugh. She couldn't believe what Roberto was saying.

He continued.

"Apparently, she learned a lot more about Denny than she cared to know...and wisely figured that no jury would ever convict you on those charges laid by that little turd back in Saranac."

Joanne listened but remained in shock.

"I don't know what to say, Rob," she said.

"Well, we can all start by going over to the nearest mountain top and scream halle-freakin'-lu-jah, Jo!"

"Wow, to say I'm...I'm—"

"—relieved? Big time! Yes, I know, Joanne. But it's all true. Now there's some amusement park owner in Lake Placid who's still a little perturbed. But our guy here talked to him too and said you'd replace the locks. Seems this park owner is the son of a local newspaper publisher who hired Jane way back when. Did you know Jane worked at the *Tribune* there?"

"No I didn't, Rob," she said. "Unfortunately, I didn't get to know a lot about my sister before she left us."

Roberto knew what Joanne was saying. He wished he'd had more time with Jane too.

"Well, she knew everybody. Anyway, this guy calmed down and agreed not to press charges if you fix his locks."

Roberto could hear the emotion in her voice. The poor woman has been through so much, he thought, and it was high time she got some good news.

"I will, Rob, and thanks so much. You've been so good to me. And I'm so relieved!"

"You're welcome, Jo," he said. "And, once again, happy birthday!"

Joanne hung up the phone and, with both her elbows resting heavily on Darryl's messy desktop, sat there motionless, her head heavy in her hands. She knew the accessory charges against her were serious, despite what Roberto had said. But what a relief!

It was Jane again, she thought. She's helping me.

She hadn't put a gun to my head. She didn't force me to go on that escapade through the mountains after the shooting. No, I went voluntarily, even forced myself on her, Joanne thought, and that meant she was just as guilty as Jane.

But Jane died. And her death meant minimal penance would have to be paid. She never loved her sister more than she did right now. However, she would have gladly done her time if Jane could be alive today.

She rose up from the chair and was about to reenter the store when she felt something in the back pocket of her jeans. It felt like a piece of paper or cardboard, and she pulled it out. What the heck? It was a lottery ticket, one of those scratch-and-wins, and she remembered where she bought it. It was months ago at the Valero station where Jane got cash at the ATM and phoned Boychuk. The plasticized ticket had gone through at least one wash cycle but was still intact.

Curious, she found a quarter on Darryl's desk and scratched the card. Did I win anything, she asked herself? She looked at the card in hopes of a payday—even a modest one.

Nope, no such luck. Not a dime. Oh, well.

Some you win. Some you lose. And some are rained out.

Joanne began walking back to the employees' lounge. She donned the same vest jacket that she'd worn for the past fifteen years, the one with the Turnbull's insignia sewn on her lapel.

She reentered the store and immediately hoped that it would be an easy work day. To Darryl's chagrin, there were few customers; it was January after all and people were still broke from Christmas.

She was about to reach her register when, off to the side and out of the corner of her eye, she recognized a familiar face. The man, his arms crossed as if he was waiting for the next Amtrak to come along, was standing in front of a ten-foot-high display of road salt. Soon that display would be transformed into bags of lawn fertilizer. Such was the cycle of life in a hardware store.

It was Matt Booker.

He was wearing a crazy horse cowboy hat and was dangling a set of truck keys.

Joanne stopped and their eyes became frozen.

"I promised I'd take care of your truck," he said finally, shooting her a wide grin. Jane was right; he did look like the Marlboro Man.

"About time you brought it back," she responded. "I've had to bum rides around here for weeks."

"You should talk. My half-ton is stuck at my cabin in the woods and it's under about two feet of snow. And my snowmobile is in some police compound up there too. Missing a few rivets, I'm told."

She smiled, a bit embarrassed.

"Touché."

He continued to look amused.

"Like your new hairstyle, little lady," he said.

Joanne returned his smile.

"Thanks, mountain man. You don't look so bad yourself. But speaking of vehicles, did you get into any trouble?"

"Oh, yeah, the cops paid me a visit. I was booked on accessory."

"What happened?"

"Well, the DA dropped the charges to a misdemeanor, and gave me community service. Not sure yet what that means. Might have to go out with a crew a few times to clean the highways—if they even *do* that here in New York. I know if I was still in California, I'd be bustin' rocks. Or maybe I'll just get away with fillin' water bottles for the high school football team."

His grin reappeared.

Joanne smiled again.

"What about you?"

"Me too," she replied.

Matt turned his head, his eyes scanning the store. He returned his attention to Joanne.

"Good to see you again, Joanne."

"Same here, Matt."

"You like it here?" he asked.

"Pays the rent. Why?"

"Well, I had an idea," he began. "I was thinkin', you know, about this little band I want to put together. Now, I can spit out a few chords once in a while, and I don't exactly suck at singin' harmonies. And I have this drummer in mind who's pretty good even if he misses a few beats from time to time...but that's not against the law for drummers. And... and, I know this bass player who looks just like Ben Franklin and might be old enough to be his grandson."

Joanne listened, impatiently.

"Uh, huh. But what's your point, Booker? You always seem to beat around the friggin' bush."

Matt continued.

"Well, okay, I'll get to the point. And that is, me and my guys are missing somethin'."

"Yeah, and what's that?"

"Well, what we need is a piano player who can sing…or a foxy lead singer who can play the piano," he replied. "Take your pick."

"Oh, yeah?"

"Yeah. Know of anyone like that?"

She smiled coyly.

"Maybe."

Joanne looked over in Darryl's direction. Not unintentionally, he had been standing nearby, fussing over another display but eavesdropping on their conversation. She walked over to her boss and whispered a few words in his ear. A broad smile spread across his face before he tilted his head in the direction of the door.

Then he shot her a look as if to say, *'get the hell outta here.'*

She kissed him on the cheek and returned to the closet.

She grabbed her coat from the hook.

They were out the door.

ACKNOWLEDGMENTS

I am indebted to my family and friends for their encouragement and support throughout the writing of this book.

I would especially like to extend my appreciation to my long-time friend and copy editor, Corien Kershey, who spent countless hours on the manuscript in an effort to make it better.

To Marsha Casper Cook for her guidance and counsel, and who told me to 'get busy' when I told her I was considering such a project.

To my colleague and friend of more than three decades, Les Whittington, I owe enormous gratitude for helping me make this story what it is today. His experience as author, reporter and editor, his timely analysis and inspiration, were greatly appreciated.

Last, I want to thank my wife Shelley for whom this book is dedicated. As my story editor, plot developer, 'voice' coach and co-creator, she has read and re-read every line in this manuscript at least a hundred times. This book could not have been written without her. Thank you, Shelley. I love you.

ABOUT THE AUTHOR

R.M. Doyon has been a journalist, writer, public relations executive and entrepreneur for more than three decades.

Educated at the University of Western Ontario and Carleton University's School of Journalism, he began his career with the *Ottawa Citizen* before becoming a political reporter and Parliamentary Bureau Chief for *United Press International*, where he crossed paths with six Canadian prime ministers and one U.S president. After his stint with UPI, Doyon wrote for *The Vancouver Province*, *Maclean's*, and *The Financial Post* before serving as a speechwriter and senior communications advisor in two Canadian government departments. An avid observer of the American presidency, he boasts to family and friends alike that he has set foot in the Oval Office.

Though successful in business, during which he co-founded one of North America's most-admired public relations firms, he never lost his love for fiction and screenwriting. In addition to *Upcountry*, he is the author of *Pirouette*, a stage-play on the life and times of Pierre Elliott Trudeau, and has co-written two screenplays—*Shoulda, Coulda, Woulda* and *The Last Carousel* with his wife Shelley.

Inspired by true events, *Upcountry* is his first novel.

He is currently working on a sequel.

6526468R0

Made in the USA
Charleston, SC
04 November 2010